Tales of the Heart

Tales of the Heart

3-in-1 Collection

Bridget's Bargain • Kate Ties the Knot • Follow the Leader

Loree Lough

WHITAKER HOUSE

Publisher's Note:
Each novel in this collection is a work of fiction. References to real events, organizations, or places are used in a fictional context. Any resemblances to actual persons, living or dead, are entirely coincidental.
All Scripture quotations are taken from the King James Version of the Holy Bible.

TALES OF THE HEART

A 3-in-1 Collection Featuring:
Bridget's Bargain (© 1997 by Loree Lough)
Kate Ties the Knot (© 1997 by Loree Lough)
Follow the Leader (© 1995 by Loree Lough)

Loree Lough
www.loreelough.com

ISBN: 978-1-60374-167-5
Printed in the United States of America

Whitaker House
1030 Hunt Valley Circle
New Kensington, PA 15068
www.whitakerhouse.com

Library of Congress Cataloging-in-Publication Data

Lough, Loree.
Tales of the heart / by Loree Lough.
p. cm.
Summary: "Christian and romantic themes predominate in this collection of three historical, inspirational novellas—*Bridget's Bargain, Kate Ties the Knot*, and *Follow the Leader*"—Provided by publisher.
ISBN 978-1-60374-167-5 (trade pbk.)
1. Christian fiction, American. 2. Love stories, American. I. Title.
PS3562.O8147T36 2010
813'.54—dc22

2009038726

---

1 2 3 4 5 6 7 8 9 10 ꟺ 16 15 14 13 12 11 10

Dedication

First, to my faithful readers, whose support and faith keep me writing.

Second, to Larry, light of my life and stirrer of my soul, for whom I'm happy to obey 1 Corinthians 7:10: "Let not the wife depart from her husband."

Special mention to my wonderful editor, Courtney, and the ever-capable Lois.

Finally, to my once abused, now spoiled dog, who put aside his Frisbee addiction long enough for me to write these stories!

Bridget's Bargain

Chapter One

1866
Magnolia Grange, south of Richmond, Virginia

It's hard to believe you've been with us four years, Bridget."

Winking one thick-lashed blue eye, the maid grinned. "Aye, Mr. Auburn." She blew a tendril of flaming red hair away from her eye and secured a gigantic white satin bow to the railing. "Time has passed like a runaway engine."

Fumbling with his collar, Chase chuckled. "You've always been a joy to have in the house, and your way with words is but one of the reasons."

Bridget slid the ribbon up and down until it exactly matched the height of the decoration on the other side of the porch. In response to the great gulp of air he took in, she straightened from her work. "Were you this nervous the first time you were a bridegroom, sir?"

He leaned a shoulder against the pillar nearest him. "To tell the truth, I don't recall." And, raising both brows imploringly, he pointed at the lopsided knot at his throat. "Would you mind...?"

She stepped up to the man who'd been more of a big brother than an employer to her these past years. "Wouldn't mind a bit." And to think that during her long sea voyage from Ireland to Virginia, she'd envisioned him a brute and a monster!

Standing on tiptoe, Bridget repaired the damage he'd done to his black string tie. "There, now," she said, brushing imaginary lint from his broad shoulders, "that's got it."

His hand trembling, he dug a gold watch from his pocket. "The guests will begin arriving soon. Is everything—?"

"All's well, Mr. Auburn, so I pray ye'll relax. Else ye'll need another bath!" Gathering her bow-making materials, Bridget hustled through the front door. From the other side of the screen, she said, "I've a few things to see to in the kitchen, and then I'll be lookin' in on yer bride-to-be." She started toward the parlor, then stopped and faced him again. "Mr. Auburn, sir?"

He stopped rubbing his temples to say, "Yes?"

"I set aside a pitcher of lemonade. Might be just the thing to calm your nerves. Now, why don't you settle down there while I fetch you a nice tall glass?"

As she made her way toward the kitchen, she heard the unmistakable squeak of the porch swing. "Hard to believe you ever thought that dear, sweet man capable of beating his servants bloody."

"What's that?"

Scissors, ribbons, needles, and thread flew into the air, then rained down upon her at the sound of the rich, masculine voice. "Goodness gracious, sakes alive!" she gasped, hands flattened to her chest. "You just shaved ten years off m'life!"

"Sorry," said the tall intruder. "Didn't mean to frighten you."

Rolling her eyes, Bridget stooped to retrieve the fallen articles. "No harm done, I suppose." Then, narrowing one eye, she sent him a half smile. "Provided you help me clean up the mess ye're responsible for."

Immediately, he was on his hands and knees, and once they'd untangled the ribbon, she put it all in the linen cupboard. "Don't recall seein' you around here before."

"Just arrived last evening." He nodded toward the barn. "I'm bunking in the loft. Chase...uh, Mr. Auburn is hoping I can improve the lineage of his quarter horses."

"Ah," she said, returning the sewing supplies to their proper shelf, "so you're the new stable hand we've all been hearing about." Dusting off her hands, she started up the stairs, stopping on the bottom step to give him a quick once-over. "Don't know why, but I thought you'd be older."

Leaning both burly arms on the newel post, he frowned slightly. "The proper title is 'stable *master*'."

"Is that a fact, Mr. Big-for-His-Britches?" Grinning good-naturedly, she added, "Tack whatever fancy name ye choose to the work. You're still the hired help, same as me, 'cept you're likely more at home with a muck shovel in your hand than a mop or broom."

For a moment, a look of embarrassment darkened his handsome face, but, to his credit, he shook it off. "It's honest work, and the horses are my full responsibility, so they might as well be my very own."

She scrutinized him carefully. "All right, then, so you've got the master's horses, but have ye the horse sense to go with 'em?" Halfway up the curving staircase, she leaned over the landing banister. "And what might your name be, Mr. I'm-So-Sure-of-Myself...just so I'm sure to address you properly next time we meet?"

"Lance," he said. "Lance York."

Bridget's smile disappeared. "You're—you're *English*?"

Another nod. "But only half." The frown above his gray eyes deepened. "Why do you look as though you've just smelled something unpleasant? Is there something wrong with being English?"

Only if you're a poor tenant farmer in County Donegal, Ireland, she thought, continuing up the stairs. Since they both worked for Mr. Auburn, she'd likely run into this fellow often, and she had no intention of behaving like one of those uppity town girls who were so difficult to get along with. "Well," she said coolly, "I suppose we all have to be something, now, don't we?"

Her peripheral vision told her he hadn't budged as she reached the next landing. Bridget would not allow herself to look at him. *What, and give him the satisfaction of knowing an Englishman had humiliated yet another Irishman? Not in a million Sundays!*

Bridget hurried up the remaining stairs and set her mind on seeing what, if anything, Drewry might need, because in no time at all, she'd become Mrs. Chase Auburn. No doubt she'd be at least as fidgety as her bridegroom.

Funny, she thought, *how folks tend to pair off at weddings.* Most of the servants had spouses to accompany them to the shindig. All but Bridget and the hired hands' children. *More's the pity the stableman has the blood of those thievin' English flowin' in his veins,* she thought, *'cause he'd make a right handsome companion....*

Bridget watched as the servants and hired hands of Magnolia Grange raced around, putting the finishing touches on the wedding preparations. How handsome they all looked dressed in their regal best, thanks to Chase Auburn's generosity.

She remembered the day, not so long ago, when he'd stood beside the big buckboard, ushering every member of his staff into the back of the vehicle, oblivious to their slack-jawed, wide-eyed protests. "Magnolia Grange has survived locusts and storms and the Civil War, so I hardly think our little trip into town will cause its ruination." Grabbing the reins, he'd added, "When we get to Richmond, every last one of you will choose a proper wedding outfit. And remember, money is no object."

The wagon wheels had ground along the gritty road, drowning out the shocked whispers of his hired help. "Been with that boy since he was born," Matilda had said behind a wrinkled black hand, "an' I ain't never seen him smile so bright."

"I do believe he done lost his mind, Matty," Simon had said. "This is gonna cost a fortune."

"You just worry 'bout tending the fields," she'd shot back, "an' let Mistah Chase worry 'bout what he can afford."

In town, the maid, the housekeeper, the foreman, and the field hands had quickly discovered that every Richmond shopkeeper had been instructed to put the suits, gowns, shoes, and baubles chosen by Auburn employees on Chase's personal account. At first, they'd shied away from quality materials, picking through the bins for dresses of cotton and shirts of muslin. Until Chase had gotten wind of their frugality, that is.

"You'll not attend my wedding dressed like that!" he'd gently admonished them, snatching a pair of dungarees from Claib's hands. Holding some gabardine trousers in front of the tall, thin man, he'd said, "You've earned this." Then, looking at each employee in turn, he had said, "You've *all* earned this. Why, Magnolia Grange wouldn't be what it is without you!" With that, he'd disappeared into the bustling Richmond street.

Now, Bridget stepped into the full-skirted gown she'd chosen that day at Miss Dalia's Dress Shop. *Ma's cameo would have looked lovely at the throat*, she thought, buttoning its high, lace-trimmed collar. But the pin had long ago been handed over to the ruthless landlord Conyngham when he'd raised the rent yet again.

Slipping into slippers made from fabric the same shade of pink as the dress, Bridget recalled that in one of her mother's leather-bound volumes—before Conyngham had demanded those, too—she'd seen a pen-and-ink sketch of a ballerina. According to the book, ballet originated in Renaissance Italy, where, as the nobility began to see themselves as superior to the peasantry, they rejected the robust and earthy steps of traditional dance. Emulating the slower, statelier movements of the ballerinas, they believed, accentuated their own elegance. Her arms forming a graceful circle over her head, the beautiful lady's torso had curved gently to the right. Her dark hair had been pulled back tightly from her face, and on her head had been a tiny, sparkling crown. Long, shapely legs had peeked out from beneath a gauzy, knee-length gown, and on her feet had been satin slippers.

Smiling at the memory, Bridget stood at the mirror. Gathering her cinnamony hair atop her head, she secured it with a wide ribbon that matched her shoes. Lifting her skirt, she stuck out her right foot and, looking about to see if she were truly alone, grinned as mischief danced in her eyes. How long had it been since she'd struck this particular ballerina pose? Five years? Six? Then, feeling both giddy and girlish, Bridget covered her face with both hands and giggled. *Ye'd better count yer blessin's that nobody can see you, Bridget McKenna, for they'd cart y'off to the loony bin, to be sure!*

The big grandfather clock in the hall began counting out the hour. *Goodness gracious me*, she thought, hurrying to the door, *how can it be midday already? And with only an hour till the weddin'!*

When Bridget entered Drewry's room, she found the bride standing in front of a big, oval mirror like the one in her own room, smiling as Matilda pinned a white poinsettia in her long, dark hair. "You do make a lovely bride," said the housekeeper. "Mistah Chase be one lucky fella, gettin' a wife as fetchin' as you."

Blushing, Drewry hugged the woman. "Thank you, Matilda. But I'm the lucky one."

"Not lucky," Bridget said, closing the door behind her. "Blessed."

The curious glances exchanged by the bride and housekeeper told Bridget that her interruption had stunned them. True, she'd never been overly chatty, but lately....

Several months ago, Mr. Auburn had walked into the kitchen as she'd been ciphering. When she'd admitted that she'd saved almost enough to send for her family, he'd promised to find work for her father and four siblings. And just this morning, a little more ciphering told Bridget that in six months, maybe eight, she'd finally have what she needed to bring them here from Ireland. If that didn't put her in a chatty mood, a wedding was sure to do it!

"You're so right," Drewry said, grasping Bridget's hand. "Luck had nothing to do with it. It was the good Lord who brought Chase and me together."

"And He'll *keep* you together, too."

"Seems our gal here know as much about the Good Book as anyone," Matilda said.

Bridget remembered another day, not long after her arrival at Magnolia Grange, when Mr. Auburn had invited her to join the family in prayer. "How many times must I tell you, Bridget McKenna," he'd thundered, "that it's not a sin to read the Scriptures!" He'd picked up the large, leather-bound Bible and opened it for the household's morning devotions. On the other side of the big, wooden table, Bridget had begun to weep. It had been Drewry, the children's nanny, who had passed her a lace-edged hanky.

"But Mr. Auburn, sir," she'd cried, "my ma taught us that readin' the Holy Scriptures is a sin and a crime. Learnin' like that...it's only for the clergy, who are blessed by God to understand what they read." Trembling, she'd hidden her face in Drewry's hanky. "Oh, please, sir...I don't want to go to hell!"

Softening his tone, Chase had said, "I hate to disagree with your sweet mother, but I'm afraid she was mistaken."

His comment had only served to cause a fresh torrent of tears, inspiring Drewry to scoot along the bench and drape an arm around Bridget. "Mr. Auburn is right, Bridget," she'd said, her dark eyes shining and sweet voice soothing. "Our reading the Scriptures pleases God. Why else would He have given them to us?"

Bridget stopped crying and studied Drewry's face. "But...how d'ye know for sure that it's true, ma'am?"

"Because the Lord Jesus Himself said, '*Man shall not live by bread alone, but by every word that proceedeth out of the mouth of God.*' You see, going to church on Sunday and hearing about Jesus is but one way of growing closer to the Lord. Reading His Word for ourselves, why, there's no better way!" And from that moment on, life at Magnolia Grange had changed for Bridget. Having access to the comfort of God's Word was a key that unlocked a world of hope.

"So, what you think, li'l Miss Bridget?" Matilda said. "You knows the Bible as good as anybody?"

"Hardly!" she said, laughing. "The more I learn," she admitted, "the more I realize how little I know." Then she wagged a finger at the bride. "Now, you'd best be gettin' yourself downstairs, Miss Drew. Pastor Tillman has arrived, and the guests are gatherin' in the chapel. It's a mighty pretty day for a wedding, 'specially for December!"

"I have God to thank for that, too," Drewry admitted, tugging at the long snug sleeves of her white velvet gown. With arms extended, she took a deep breath as Matilda fastened the tiny pearl buttons on each cuff. After fastening her mother's cameo at the high, stand-up collar, Drewry picked up the bouquet fashioned of red roses, white poinsettias, and greenery from Chase's hothouse, which he had delivered at dawn.

"You gonna carry that to the altar, Miss Drew?"

"I most certainly am, Matilda. Perhaps Chase and I will start a trend...bridegrooms delivering flowers to their brides, and brides carrying the bouquets to the altar." She punctuated her statement with a merry giggle.

"Well, I'm as ready as I'm ever going to be, so I suppose we should get this wedding started!"

With Matilda leading the way, the women walked down the wide, curving staircase and onto the porch. Bridget saw that Claib had parked the carriage out front. He'd polished its chassis until the enamel gleamed like a black mirror. The farmhand cut quite a dashing figure in his long-tailed morning suit, and Bridget planned to tell him so the minute they returned to the kitchen to serve the guests at the reception. Bending low at the waist, Claib swept a gloved hand in front of him. "Your carriage awaits, m'lady," he said, mimicking Pastor Tillman's English butler.

The sounds of laughter and chatter grew louder as the buggy neared the chapel. "They're here!" a woman shouted.

"Start the music!" hollered a man.

As the four-piece string ensemble began to play Beethoven's Ninth, Drewry stood beside her Uncle James at the back of the chapel. *Such a lovely bride*, Bridget thought. *And this little church in the woods is lovely, too.* The red holly berries trimming the roof winked merrily, and a soft garland filled the air with the fresh, clean scent of pine. Massive arrangements of red and white poinsettias, along with evergreen boughs, flanked the altar, where Mr. Auburn waited alone.

But not for long.

Bridget and Matilda, in their new store-bought frocks, stepped importantly down the aisle in time to the music and took their places in the Auburn family pew. Chase's daughter, Sally, stepped up in front of Drewry, one hand in her basket, prepared to sprinkle rose petals along the path that her new mother's high-topped white boots would take. Behind Sally, her brother, Sam, held the white satin pillow that cushioned the wedding band. Bridget smiled as he tugged at the collar of his shirt and smiled adoringly up at Drewry.

The children love her so, and so does Mr. Auburn, Bridget thought. *And it's plain to see she loves them, too.*

Just then, the throbbing strains of the "Wedding March" poured from the organ's pipes, filling the chapel as Pastor Tillman took his place at the altar. Bridget watched Chase, resplendent in his black suit, as he focused on Drewry, the object of his hopes and dreams and promises soon to be fulfilled. "I love you," he mouthed to her.

Bridget turned in her seat just in time to see the bride answer with a wink and a smile. *Will I ever know love like that?* she wondered, facing front again. Sighing, she felt her shoulders sag. *Not likely, since all I do is work, work, work and save, save, save....* A feeling of guilt washed over Bridget, and she chastised herself for allowing such self-centered thoughts to enter her head. She had much to be grateful for, and this was Drewry and Chase's day, after all!

Still, the bride and groom's for-our-eyes-only communication made her yearn for a love like theirs—a love that reached beyond the bounds of family, binding man to woman and woman to man, cloaking them in trust, friendship, and companionship forever.

A chilly wind blew through the chapel, making Bridget shiver. Hugging herself, she focused on the rough-hewn cross that hung above the altar and, closing her eyes, prayed silently. *Dear Lord, if it's in Your plan, I wouldn't mind havin' a bit of love like that, for I'm weary of being cold and alone.*

Drewry's Uncle James and his lady friend, Joy, had arrived two days earlier. In many ways, the handsome couple reminded Bridget of Chase and Drewry.

Bridget and Joy had chatted while decorating the mansion. Joy, Bridget discovered, had been raised up north, near Baltimore. "Why, there's a Baltimore,

Ireland, too!" she'd said, excited at all she had in common with her new friend.

Bridget hadn't had as many opportunities to talk with Drewry's uncle, so when she saw him during the reception, standing alone under the willow tree, she didn't know quite how to approach him. His grief was raw and real, that much was plain to see. And she knew precisely what had destroyed his previous high-spirited mood. For as she'd been gathering plates and cups nearby, she'd overheard the conversation....

James had dropped to one knee and taken Joy's hand in his, then looked deep into her eyes and whispered hoarsely, "Miss Naomi Joy McGuire, will you do me the honor of becoming my bride?"

So romantic! Bridget had thought. She'd been taught better than to eavesdrop, but if she'd made any attempt to move just then, she would have alerted them to her presence, and what if that destroyed the whole mood? Then Joy had blinked, swallowed hard, and stiffened her back. "I can't, James," she'd said. Then, snatching back her hand, she'd lifted the billowing blue satin of her skirt and raced across the lawn to the house.

Hours passed before Bridget returned to collect the last of the dishes and glasses scattered about by the guests. Yet he still stood alone where she'd last seen him. "Is there anything I can do for you, sir?"

Without looking up, James shook his head.

"Won't you come inside and let me brew you a cup of tea?"

But he only shook his head again.

"But sir, ye're pale as a ghost, and I can't in good conscience leave you here alone. I'll make a pest of myself, if I must, to get you inside, where it's warm." She gestured toward the yard. "Ye'll catch yer death if you stay out here."

When he gave no response, she linked her arm with his and led him to the house, chattering nonstop the whole way about the way Pastor Tillman had nearly choked on a wad of tobacco before pronouncing Drewry and Chase husband and wife; about the perfect weather, the delicious food, the pretty decorations...anything but the ceremony itself. "My name is Bridget, sir," she said as they approached the front porch. "Bridget McKenna."

The way he climbed the steps, Bridget couldn't help but picture the tin soldiers lined up on the shelf at McDoogle's Store back home. The poor man had found the woman he wanted to spend the rest of his days with, and her refusal had broken his spirit. Surely, Joy had a good reason for saying no, but that didn't stop Bridget from feeling sorry for him.

Once inside, she stopped at the parlor door. "Why not have a seat there by the fire? I'll fetch you a nice hot cup of tea."

"I think I'd rather just go to bed."

As she opened the door to his room, she said, "If you need anything, anything at all, just ring for me."

Though he nodded as he stepped into the room, Bridget had a feeling he wouldn't ring. In fact, something told her she might not see him at all before he returned to Baltimore. "Well," she muttered as he closed the door, "I don't suppose *all* matches are made in heaven...."

"Like Drewry and Chase, you mean?"

A tiny shriek escaped her lungs. "Land sakes, man," she said, recognizing Lance. "Ye'll be the death of me, sure!" Bridget regarded him with a wary eye. "Ye've got cat's paws for feet. How else can I explain how you slink around without making a sound?"

Chuckling, Lance pocketed both hands. "I wasn't slinking. You were so deep in thought, a herd of cattle could have thundered through here, and you wouldn't have noticed until the dust cleared."

Bridget raised an eyebrow. "Oh, I might've noticed a wee bit before then." Pointing at his feet, she said, "There'd have been the stink of the stuff you've tracked across my clean floor to bring me around." Planting both fists on her hips, she met his eyes. "Perhaps you have been raised as fine as those fancy airs you put on, Mr. York, for no self-respecting stable hand would enter the master's house without first puttin' his soles to the boot scrape by the servants' entrance!"

Lance glanced down at his boots and the telltale clumps of mud and horse manure that showed the path he'd taken since entering the foyer. Feeling strangely like an errant child caught sneaking cookies before dinner, he was about to inform her that although this was indeed a grand mansion, it sat upon fertile pastureland. Did she really expect everyone who entered to wipe his boots? And who did she think she was, anyway, scolding him as if he were an ordinary—

Yet the moment he looked into her eyes to deliver his rebuttal, Lance's ire abated. She was perhaps the loveliest creature he'd ever seen, tiny and feminine and just scrappy enough to be reckoned with. A mass of shining brick-red waves framed her heart-shaped face, and even after a long day of tending to and tidying up after wedding guests, her milky skin glowed with healthy radiance, making the pale freckles sprinkling her nose even more noticeable.

And those eyes! He'd seen her before, both up close and from a distance. Why hadn't he noticed how large and thickly lashed they were?

"So, there's another lesson yer ma obviously didn't teach you. First, you thoughtlessly mess up the floors, and then, you stare like a simpleton."

Lance blinked, then frowned in response to her anger. "What? I—I wasn't—"

"You were, and you still are," she interrupted him, crossing her arms over her chest as she lifted her chin.

If he didn't know better, he'd say she was daring him to disagree!

Lance had no earthly idea where the thought came from, but, suddenly, he wanted nothing more than to grasp the narrow shoulders she'd thrown back in defiance and kiss her square on those full, pink lips. *Sweet Jesus,* he prayed, *keep me true to my vow....*

Newly resolved and strengthened, he straightened to his full five-foot eleven-inch height. "I didn't mean to track dirt into the house," he said at last. "If you like, I'll help you clean it up. And you have my word, it won't happen again."

Grinning, she wiggled her perfectly arched brows. "Oh, that won't be necessary." Then, "I suppose I could have been a mite gentler with you, now, couldn't I?" On the heels of a deep breath, Bridget added, "It's been a long, hard day, not that that's a good excuse for my harshness." With one hand up to silence his denial, she continued, "I set aside a bit of cake and lemonade. Will you let me get it for you, as a peace offerin'?"

Truth was, he'd stuffed himself at the reception and had no idea where he'd put another bite of food, so his answer surprised him. "Only if you'll share it with me."

She turned on her heel and, wiggling a finger over her shoulder, said, "Then follow me, English."

He did, too, like a pup on his boy's heels. As they made their way down the stairs, she said, "What you said earlier...."

Lance fell into step beside her. "In response to your 'not all matches are made in heaven' comment?"

Rounding the corner into the kitchen, she nodded. "How'd you know that's what I meant?"

He straddled a stool and leaned both elbows on the table. No woman had ever willingly served him before, unless he counted roadside tavern maids. Lance rather enjoyed watching Bridget bustling about, preparing the snack that had been *her* idea. "I overheard what went on between Drewry's uncle and his lady friend, too," he said. His smile became a frown. "Sad, the way she treated the bloke."

Bridget laid a neatly folded napkin near his left elbow and unceremoniously plopped a silver fork atop it. "Now, let's not be too quick to judge, English. We have no way of knowing why she said what she did."

By the time she set the tall goblet of lemonade near the tines of his fork, he was all but scowling. "It's been my experience," he began, "that women don't need a reason to be cruel." He sat up straighter and feigned a dainty pose. "You're such a *darling* man," he sighed in a high-pitched falsetto. "Is that your heart?" he asked, pointing a dainty finger at his imaginary tablemate's chest. Then, his hand formed an ugly claw as he pretended to tear into the invisible man's rib cage. "I've *got* it!" he all but shouted, pretending to stuff it into his mouth.

Bridget stood gawking with one hand on her hip and then wrinkled her nose. "After ye've learned to wipe yer feet," she said, sliding the cake plate in front of him, "we'll have a go at teachin' you how to make interesting table conversation." After taking a sip of her own lemonade, she sat down across from him. "A body could only guess from that sorry demonstration that you've been wounded a time or two by love."

"Not really," he said around a bite of frosting. "And I'm sorry for the outburst."

Smiling, she pressed a hand to his forearm. "You can apologize for scarin' the soul from m'body, for dirtyin' my floor." Leaning closer, Bridget narrowed her eyes. "But don't ever let me hear you say you're sorry for what you *feel*, English."

Resting his elbow on the table, Lance let the empty fork dangle from his hand. "What have you got against the English, if you don't mind my asking?" Slicing off another hunk of cake, he added, "Keep in mind, I'm English only on my father's side...."

Sighing, Bridget sat back. "Have you ever been to Ireland?"

Lance shook his head.

"And what do you know about the way your people dealt with the Irish during the famine?"

In place of an answer, Lance only shrugged.

She folded her hands on the tabletop. "Now, I'll warn ye, 'tisn't a pretty story." Winking, she looked from side to side, as if in search of a spy. "And there's a good chance you'll dislike your folks as much as I do when I've finished." Pausing, she said, "You sure you want me to go on?"

"I'm sure," he said with a grin.

And for the next hour, she held him spellbound with her tale.

Chapter Two

Bridget's eyes and voice reflected her mood as she tried to teach Lance what had happened in the Old Country.

It seemed the only landowners of note were either Anglo-Irish or full-blooded English citizens who rented three- to five-acre parcels to the locals. It had never been an easy life for the tenants, yet somehow they'd managed to get by.

That is, until the potato blight wiped out the entire crop in 1845, she explained. The potato, being the main staple, made it a "two steps forward, three steps back" proposition for the farmers, who, by and large, ate the potatoes they grew and sold their barley, oats, and wheat to earn funds for next year's seeds.

"Wasn't there something they could do to kill the blight? Soak them in lime, maybe?"

Bridget smiled sadly. "They tried that, along with every remedy known to man and modern science. Like storin' the potatoes in pits lined with yer precious lime, but that didn't work. Then the farmers were told if they baked the potatoes at one hundred and eighty degrees, the potatoes would turn white. But that didn't work, either. Next, they were told to grate the potatoes and mix 'em with oatmeal to make pancakes. Not only did that not kill the fungus, it also made anybody who ate the pancakes sick.

"By now, they were so desperate, they gave magic a try. Some thought maybe the blight had been created by static electricity in the clouds, caused by the smoke of those newfangled locomotive trains going to and fro. Others believed seagull droppings were to blame. Still others blamed the faeries and the wee people, and set about blessin' the fields with rabbits' feet and other such nonsense.

"But the English," she said, folding her hands in sarcastic reverence, "ah, the *English* believed the blight was God's punishment on the Irish."

"Punishment? Punishment for what?"

"For bein' poor, that's what," she all but snarled. She gave him a narrow-eyed look. "For not bein' English, if y'want the real truth."

Lance tried to ignore her spiteful tone. "Well, I spent four years in seminary," he said cautiously, "and learned that superstition is a dangerous thing. It riles the Almighty."

"Easy for you to say from where you sit, with your belly full of healthy food and your back warmed by a roarin' fire. Don't you think me Da's people tried prayer? They were a God-fearin' folk, almost from the time the world began."

She narrowed her eyes again. "You try watchin' your loved ones starve to death, fadin' away, day by day. It was only when decades of prayer did 'em no good that they tried other methods."

"I've never heard any of this before," he said, confused. "How'd a girl like you learn all about—"

"A poor, uneducated scullery maid, y'mean?"

Lance blanched. "No. Of course that's not what I meant." He hadn't intended to sound smug or superior, but that's exactly how she'd read his question. He felt like a heel for entertaining those thoughts. Felt more so for allowing her to read them. "It's just—it's just that you seem so genteel and refined, and this information...well, it's anything *but.* It makes me wonder how you came by it all."

"I know what I know," she steamed, "partly 'cause I lived it, and partly thanks to a conversation I overheard when me Da came in late one night. He'd had a serious row with Conyngham, our landlord, and it had put him in a foul, self-pitying mood. Ma had died not six months earlier, y'see, and aside from missin' her bad, there was all her work to do, as well as his.

"I tried to fill her shoes, but bein' barely ten at the time, I'm afraid I didn't do a very good job. There were six young'uns, after all, from an infant to age eight, to care for, and much as I hate to admit it, I'd been feelin' powerful sorry for me own self when he dragged himself in that night, wailin' and cryin' about our plight. His cousin Cullen had come in with him, and there the two of 'em sat, bemoanin' the condition of County Donegal and all of Ireland.

"''Tain't right,' cousin Cullen said, 'how Conyngham takes advantage of his power to evict.' And Da agreed. ''T'ain't moral, either, but the man can do as he pleases with what's his own.'"

Lance sat, mystified, as she explained how Conyngham got control of her relatives' land, then threatened to throw them off of it every chance he got. Lance tamped down an overwhelming desire to comfort her, to ease the pain etched on her pretty face, to erase the hard memories that dulled the gleam in her bright eyes.

"When me Da was a boy," she said, "there was a system in place known as the Rundale, where landowners would sublet farms in five-acre tracts that might be scattered in twenty different places, miles and miles apart, in wee quarter-acre parcels."

"Like a patchwork quilt," Lance interjected. "That must have made it hard to earn a living."

"Indeed, but somehow, they survived that wicked scheme of the English to drive them from land that was rightly theirs." On the heels of a sigh, she said, "Sadly, they survived that, only to meet another." Bridget then described the way that landlords forced tenants from their land, rendering them homeless. In the days and weeks that passed, the landlords rearranged property lines, segmenting the farms into connected five-acre parcels. "Only then were the farmers allowed to return to their own land...but at double the rent."

"Double? But they were getting the exact same amount of land back!"

"Aye," she said quietly. "But now, at least it was all in one place. The price hike, said the landlords, was on account of how easy the farmers would have it, now that they didn't have to traipse all across the countryside to do their work."

As they had several times during her story, Bridget's beautiful blue eyes filled with tears, and her lovely lips quivered as she struggled to compose herself. Her cheeks glowed bright and rosy as the heat of her rage inflamed her. "So, anyway, after that, the landlords took to sendin' bailiffs out to the islands and into the peat bogs to collect up all the livestock and anything else the farmers might've grown or owned."

"But—it was the farmers' property. Why didn't they *fight* for it?"

"Because, by then, landlords like Conyngham had taken all the fight out of them," was her quiet reply. "It's hard to believe, I know, but they handed over what little they had, and did it willingly, because eviction was the threat if they didn't...and eviction would've been the same as a death sentence."

"Sad," Lance said, nodding, "because, either way, they were doomed."

Bridget tucked a wayward curl behind her ear. "True enough, and it's because the Irish remained a proud lot that they went along with the Rundale. Better to wither away within the privacy of their own cottage walls than die of starvation on the open roads."

He rubbed his face with both hands in frustration. "And no one in England stepped in to help? No one saw the injustice in it all?"

"Oh, there were a few kind saviors. Like the fancy official who devised a plan to pay the menfolk eight pence a day to repair roads and build walls. Trouble was, those roads never got fixed, and the walls never got built. No one knows what became of the money set aside to get it all done." She shrugged. "By the time the Quakers and the Belfast Ladies' Association stepped in, the famine had so weakened the people that disease had begun to—"

"Typhus!" Lance said, slamming a fist onto the tabletop. "I read about that in the *London Times*. 'So slow, yet so certain....' That's how one reporter quoted Francis Forster. Why, that sickness killed thousands!"

"Millions is more like it," she corrected him, her voice thick with misery.

"Wasn't there something else they could eat—besides potatoes, I mean? Like fish or game animals or birds?"

Bridget's bitter laugh hung like a spider web in the air between them. "Most of 'em were just dirt-poor farmers, some who lived high in the mountains. Too few had the money to buy boats and nets and bait, and even if they could've scraped enough together, who was gonna teach 'em to use the stuff?

"They took to trappin' rabbits, so many that the poor critters nearly became extinct." She met his gaze. "Oh, I can promise you, they *tried* to survive. Need I remind you that the Irish are a warrior race?"

During the next moments, the only sounds in the room were the steady *ticktock*, *ticktock* of the mantle clock, the hiss and pop of the fire, and the dull drumming of Bridget's fingers on the table.

Her soft voice broke the silence. "They'd never have admitted a word of it if they'd been sober, m'Da and Cullen, but shame and fear do funny things to a man."

Lance placed a hand firmly over her hand and fused his gaze to hers. "If I could go back in time and change history, I'd do it. I swear I would. I hope I never discover that any of my own blood kin were involved in what happened to your people, to Ireland." Gently, he squeezed her fingers. "I've said it many times since we met, Bridget, but I've never meant it more...I'm sorry. Truly, I am."

For the longest time, she merely sat, blinking those huge eyes at him. After a while, he got up and stood beside her. Still holding her hand, he brought her to her feet. "So you're here in the States to earn money to send back home, aren't you?"

She bowed her head and whispered, "Yes."

Lance lifted her chin with the tip of his forefinger. "It's nothing to be ashamed of, Bridget. Your family couldn't help what happened to them."

She exhaled a shaky breath. "I know...."

When she'd begun her story, she'd said that he might dislike the English as much as she did when it concluded. *She* had nothing to be ashamed of, but *he* did. Because of what his people had done, this beautiful young woman had been forced to flee her homeland to do the backbreaking work of a scullery maid in the hope that her pittance of a salary might ease the lives of her loved ones, still trapped in Ireland. "How long till you've saved up enough to bring them here?"

A tiny spark of humor glinted in her eyes when she said, "What makes you think I'm savin' to bring 'em here? Maybe I'm savin' to go home again."

Smiling, he traced the contour of her jaw with his finger. "No, because in America, you can introduce them to a whole new life of plenty. Rice pudding, wedding cakes, polished carriages...."

The spark in her eyes flashed brighter, and her entire face lit up with a playful smile. "We have carriages in Ireland, y'know."

He could see by her expression that Bridget expected him to issue a challenge. Instead, he gathered her close.

A quiet voice deep inside warned Bridget to step back, to pull away, but she paid it no heed. His muscular arms felt good wrapped around her; the steady thrumming of his heart was reassuring. Blaming the romantic mood set by the wedding and the loving looks exchanged by Drewry and Chase, she rested her head on his chest and slid her arms around his waist. For a reason she couldn't explain, being held this way felt old-shoe comfortable.

It seemed so natural to let him tilt her face and to receive his sweet kiss that Bridget decided she wouldn't dwell on the fact that Lance was English. For if she gave it even a moment's thought, she'd have no choice but to break free from his embrace and dash from the room like a rabbit being pursued by a starving Irishman.

It was just a kiss, after all. Just one kiss....

But as she felt his fingers comb through her soft, blonde locks curling over his shirt collar, she knew it felt too good, too right, to be "just" anything.

With Drewry and Chase in Richmond on their honeymoon, Bridget had been charged with the care of Sally and Sam. Before the wedding, Drewry had been the children's nanny, but as Mrs. Chase Auburn, the lady of the manor would have much to do. They'd offered the job to Bridget and gave her the week to think about it.

Sitting in the garden now, watching Sally slip a new dress onto her doll and Sam push a wooden cart across the lush, green lawn, Bridget remembered what Chase had said when she and the children said their final good-byes to him and his bride. From inside the carriage, he'd fired a volley of reasons he hoped she'd accept the position, such as the arithmetic problems she'd helped Sally solve or the times when she'd read to Sam in her free time. "I like the gentle way you have with them, Bridget."

She'd responded with good-natured irreverence. "Oh, Mr. Auburn, ye're just so shocked that I even know m' three Rs that you've sweetened your opinion of my teachin' methods, poor though they be."

"And it's that sense of humor of yours that'll teach them the most about life," he'd countered.

Many times, her father had told her what a talent she had with the young ones. "Ye're as warm and sweet as their very own ma," Liam would say about how she cared for her siblings. "Wi'out you, Lord only knows what might've become of 'em."

Bridget smiled at Sally and Sam. Being their nanny would mean moving from her cozy fourth-floor quarters to the room connecting Sam's and Sally's on the second story of the mansion. Oh, the changes she'd encountered in a few short years...first, leaving the dim, two-room thatched cottage in Malinmore for the cramped and crowded bowels of a ship that reeked of body odor and vomit, then moving to the tiny attic room overlooking the rose garden, and finally occupying a space with French doors that opened onto a balcony with a south-looking view of Magnolia Grange.

Gone was the straw pallet shared with two sisters. And she'd never again be required to take turns catching a few winks on a rock-hard cot in the belly of a lurching boat. There would not be another narrow bed in a room with three more just like it, where Matilda snored and the others tossed and turned all through the night. Instead, she'd soon sleep upon a fat feather mattress shrouded by a canopy of Spanish lace.

How many changes can a body stand in a lifetime? she wondered. Then, feeling instantly petty and small for complaining about change when her family struggled just to fill their bellies, Bridget quickly dismissed the question. Better, she thought, to focus on her father's good advice: "If ye're goin' to do a thing, give it yer all or don't waste time nor energy on it."

Hard work was in her blood, just as surely as strength and bravado, so she had never minded the chores that went hand in hand with the title of scullery maid. She'd been raised to live within her means—and on less than that, whenever possible—and had been taught that reaching too far beyond one's station would bring only shame and bitter regret.

It was a lesson hammered home time and again by Pastor O'Toole, whose favorite Bible passage could be found in the book of Luke. Somehow, the cleric found reason to read Luke 14:8–11 at nearly every gathering of his flock: "*When thou art bidden of any man to a wedding, sit not down in the highest room; lest a more honourable man than thou be bidden of him; and he that bade thee and him come and say to thee, Give this man place; and thou begin with shame to take the lowest room. But when thou art bidden, go and sit down in the lowest room; that when he that bade thee cometh, he may say unto thee, Friend, go up higher: then shalt thou have worship in the presence of them that sit at meat with thee. For whoever exhaltest himself shall be abased; and he that humbleth himself shall be exalted.*"

Once, when Bridget was barely nine years old, the pastor had asked what she thought it meant. "Far better to ask for less and be invited to take more," she'd said, "than to grab what isn't yours and have your hand slapped!"

Though she'd since figured out that her childish definition came very close to what Pastor O'Toole believed, she still didn't understand why her answer had provoked rousing laughter from the congregation. But the mindset had long since kept her focused on whatever task she'd been assigned, and she saw no reason to view her work at Magnolia Grange differently. She'd never set her sights on higher stations at the plantation, and, in her opinion, that attitude—along with divine providence—was responsible for her promotion from maid to nanny, a job that would allow her even less time for a love of her own. So why, she wondered, had she voluntarily shared so much of her past with the likes of Lance York?

Admittedly, he was a nice fellow. Or so it seemed, given the way he'd listened intently to her story. And his apology for the suffering of her family had sounded quite genuine. Still, she couldn't get another of her father's witticisms out of her head: "It is what it is," Liam would say when folks refused to accept things—and people—for what they were.

Lance was English, and that alone was reason enough to stop thinking silly romantic thoughts about him. So why, then, couldn't she get his kiss out of her mind? If she closed her eyes and sat very still, she could still smell the scents of fresh hay and saddle soap that clung to his shirt. Could almost see lamplight glinting from his shining, golden hair. So real was the memory that if she held her breath, she could even hear the gentle grating of his voice as it whispered in her ear and taste the sweetness of cake icing as his lips touched hers.

She'd left Ireland mere days after her fourteenth birthday. Until then, the only male lips to touch her own had been her father's and brothers'. And since coming to America, the only boy she'd kissed had been Sam.

Until last night.

Bridget sighed. Would her father consider her a traitor to her people if she gave her heart to an Englishman? Even one who was only half-English? "He is what he is," she said to herself.

"Who?" Sally wanted to know. "And what *is* he?"

Giggling, Bridget waved the question away. "Sally, darlin', did Miss Drew ever talk to herself?"

The eight-year-old twirled a sunny blonde curl. "Why would she talk to herself," her dark-haired brother asked, "when she had us?"

"I take it the answer is no," Bridget said. "Well, I'm afraid you'll have to get used to hearin' me converse with myself, darlin's." Clapping her hands together, she added, "As me da always says, 'Talkin' to yerself is one surefire way to make sure somebody's listenin'!'"

The children's merry laughter echoed through the garden as they flanked Bridget on the stone bench. Setting her book aside, she gathered them close.

"Why do you talk so funny?" Sam asked, climbing onto her lap.

She kissed the top of his head. "If we were in Ireland, where I come from, *you'd* be the one talking funny!"

"Father showed me where it is on the big map in his library." Sally's brow crinkled above pale-blue eyes. "It's very, very far away, isn't it?"

Bridget pictured Bunglass Point, Malin Bay, and Sleive League, and her heart skipped a beat. "Aye," she said softly, "that it is."

"Do you miss it?"

She met the girl's intense gaze. Recognizing the child's need for assurance that she wouldn't leave her, Bridget placed a hand gently on her cheek. "Sometimes, when the wind blows the chimney smoke about, I'm reminded of the scent of burnin' turf, and I miss that." She smiled. "In Ireland, they burn peat, not wood, y'see."

"Why do they call Ireland the Emerald Isle?"

"Well, Sally, m'darlin', some folks say the grass is greener there than anywhere else on earth. Ireland does get about ten times the rainfall that we get here in the States. But the fact of the matter is, I've seen both, and it's no greener there than it is here in Virginia."

"So, I guess you're over missing Ireland," Sam said, his dark eyes glittering with boyish confidence.

Bridget chuckled. "Is that so, little man? And how would you know that?"

"Because you say 'they' and 'there.' You might have been born in Ireland, Bridget, but in your heart, you're an American now!"

He seemed so proud of his assessment that she couldn't help but laugh, despite the disturbing thoughts flitting through her head. "Sam, m'boy," she said, ruffling his hair, "are you sure you're only six?"

"Six and a half!"

"Ye're a bunch of stuff and nonsense, that's what you are! Now, let's get inside, where it's warm and toasty. I'm catchin' a bit of a chill out here in this evening air."

"When you tuck us in tonight, will you tell us all about Ireland, Bridget?"

She walked between them, her hands on two small shoulders, and forced a smile. What Sam had said was still ringing in her ears, because twice in less than twenty-four hours, she'd betrayed her homeland—first, by speaking of it with a stranger; second, by considering handing over her heart to the Englishman. In her opinion, the latter was the greater sin. For generations, her family had handed over what was theirs to the English. It may well be that her Irish references had sounded more past tense than present, but she wouldn't turn her back on Ireland by consorting with the enemy!

"Oh, yes," Sally echoed, "tell us all about Ireland!"

"We'll see how much time is left after your supper and baths."

Bridget knew she couldn't stall these intelligent, inquisitive children for long. Sooner or later, they'd press her for details about the place where she had been born. And what would she tell them? That millions of her countrymen had succumbed to disease? That the greed of

English land barons was still forcing families from plots of land they'd farmed for thousands of years, all because they'd allowed the fight to be beaten out of them?

An ugly thought stirred in her mind, and it tortured her soul. Deep inside, she realized she had always resented her people for giving in to the English. Her great-great-grandfather, her great-grandfather, and her grandfather alike had turned tail and run.

The reasons didn't matter. What mattered were their actions—or, more correctly, their *in*action—which sentenced their offspring to a lifetime of similar subservience. *Well, the chain is hereby broken!* she affirmed to herself.

Bridget would be the best nanny any plantation owner ever saw, and with her additional income, she'd someday bring her da, her brothers, and her sisters to Virginia, where no one could take what was theirs.

For the first time in her life, she understood why her ancestors hadn't talked about the horrible events of the past. Finally, she knew what had driven her father out on so many cold, dark nights to drink the pub porter that soothed his soul...and loosed his tongue.

One word described it all—a word that, if one heard it without knowing the meaning, sounded soft and soothing as a summer breeze; a word that, when clearly defined and understood, gripped one's throat like a wintry chill...

Shame.

Lance knew by the way she talked to him that Bridget had no idea who he really was. She believed him to be Chase's latest hired hand, and Lance hadn't corrected her, in part because he'd come to Magnolia Grange to slay the ghosts of his past, in part because he'd seen the way she treated Chase—with the deference and respect reserved for the wealthy—and he had no desire to have her treat him that way.

He'd been at the plantation just over a month now. Work had helped him forget some of the more painful episodes of his life...at least while he was hard at it. Try as he might to wear himself out during the day in the hope of earning a restful night's sleep, the echoes of what had been haunted his dreams.

The first of many disappointments had come with the realization that his once-devout Christian mother had become an opium addict, turning to the narcotic rather than facing his railroad-rich father's corrupt business practices and the political cartwheels his brother performed to make it all possible.

Lance had hidden from the humiliation in his own way by entering the seminary. He had hoped that once he became a full-fledged pastor, he could save his mother—and, perhaps, his father and brother, too—from the world of temptation that had put them at odds with God.

When Lance was serving his apprenticeship in a small New York church, temptation had waltzed into his own life, disguised as a purebred lady. The chubby little blonde who'd set her cap for him could see, even at the tender age of seventeen, that the meek and mild preacher-to-be would someday inherit, if not the earth, at least the York family business. Midway through the first year of their courtship, Lance had found himself on bended knee, proposing marriage. Later, when he'd realized he had committed himself to a woman he did not love, Lance had suggested that perhaps he and Kay should spend less time together.

And so the would-be minister had his first experience with the power of feminine wiles. Kay had cried bitterly, and despite the fact that he'd given her only the chastest of kisses, she'd accused him of using her, of abusing her innocence. To put an end to the torrent of tears, he had disavowed all he'd said about youth and freedom...and had gone along with the wedding plans.

Shortly thereafter, Kay's mother had confided in him that her second husband—Kay's father—had left her with four hungry children to feed. Pity had made him offer his condolences and his prayers to Kay once she informed him, amid a flurry of fists and angry words, that she'd been told that her father had died. Less than an hour later, as he'd offered assurances of his fidelity and love, the guilt-ridden young seminary student had sunk deeper into the hole where, it appeared, he'd spend his future.

He'd always entered Alicia's house by way of the back porch, and one spring afternoon, days after the truth about Kay's father had slipped out, he'd climbed the steps as usual. The inner door stood ajar, preventing mother and daughter from seeing his approach. For surely, if they had seen him, his presence would have silenced the gales of laughter inspired by how well their sad tale of woe had trapped the trusting young seminarian into marriage with Kay...and the care of her entire family.

He'd been a young man, but Lance was, after all, a man. As such, he took his responsibilities seriously, a fact that the mother and daughter understood even better than he did. If he hadn't turned around and walked away right that minute, he'd have been yoked to the round-faced little liar—for life!

As he'd headed home that night, Lance had sent a bitter prayer heavenward. Alicia and Kay had taught him two valuable life lessons: There was no room in his life for a woman, and no room for God's work, either; if he could so easily be deceived by two conniving females, how could he expect to shepherd a flock?

As he'd seen it, Lance had a very long way to go before reaching emotional and spiritual maturity. Muttering John 8:32, "'*The truth shall make you free,*'" Lance had locked himself in his room and stayed there for three days straight. When at last he'd reappeared among the living, he'd announced his decision to leave the seminary...and earn back God's approval.

Several years had passed as he'd sought redemption and forgiveness, for he'd made the decision to marry Kay without consulting the Lord. Much to his bitter regret, new sins had begun piling atop that one. And as his time away from the seminary had increased, he'd grown farther and farther from the Almighty.

When Lance had received Chase's letter, he'd decided to devote his time and talents to helping his cousin develop a line of prizewinning quarter horses. Besides, the way Chase had described Virginia's rolling hills and grassy pasturelands, it sounded like the perfect place to repent...and heal.

But he hadn't counted on meeting one Bridget McKenna at Magnolia Grange!

He'd never met anyone like her. The petite redhead's spunk had no match. She'd survived near starvation in Ireland and a voyage on her own across the stormy Atlantic at the tender age of fourteen. She'd spent years away from her home and loved ones, slaving away to earn the passage that would reunite the family, yet she managed to hold fast to her convictions.

She had more hair on her head than any three humans combined, and its fiery color reflected her sparkling personality. The lilt of her oh-so-Irish voice caressed his ears like an angel's song. At times, she moved with the grace of a doe, while at others, she skittered about like a nervous squirrel. Her eyes sparkled like cobalt when something excited her, glittered like ice when she grew angry. And her whole face moved with every word that exited that beautiful, kissable mouth.

Peering out the loft window beside his cot, Lance focused on the room where Bridget was no doubt sleeping.

Too bad she needs sleep, he thought ruefully. *Seems a shame to shut the world away from those mesmerizing eyes.*

Lance lay back and clasped his hands behind his head. Closing his eyes, he took a deep breath and tried to imagine what she might look like asleep...long lashes dusting lightly freckled cheeks, pink lips slightly parted, strong yet delicate hands rising and falling where they rested on her waist, hair spread across her pillow like a red silk fan.

He wondered how old she might be, then remembered that she'd come to America at the age of fourteen. And hadn't she said she'd been with Chase for four years? Lance sat up on the edge of his cot. How could she be eighteen when she didn't look a day over fourteen? *Why hasn't some young maverick snapped her up and made her his wife?* he wondered.

The thought of another man courting her, wooing her, holding her as he had that night in the kitchen sent sizzling waves of envy through him. The image of another man kissing her as he'd kissed her put Lance on his feet, slamming a fist into an open palm. He didn't understand his pounding heart or perspiring brow, and he tucked his hands into his trouser pockets to still their trembling.

You have no right to feel this way, he told himself. *You have no claim on her.*

Bridget was everything Kay hadn't been...and never could be. The girl met life head-on, with practicality and straightforwardness, speaking words rooted in honesty. He hadn't known her long, but something told him Bridget had too much self-respect to use feminine wiles to get what she hadn't earned. Pride motivated her to work hard, to do her best at every task, and to treat others with kindness and respect—even when she believed them to be lowly, English stable hands.

Lance remembered what she'd said in the foyer after he'd almost upbraided her for pointing out that he'd tracked mud and dung on her clean floor. She'd admitted, in her matter-of-fact way, that she hadn't needed to speak so harshly. *Hard words*, she'd called her little scolding. Chuckling, Lance lay back down and shook his head. *Hard words, my big foot!* he thought, thinking of the last tongue-lashing Kay had given him.

He'd walked away from Kay without a single regret. In the months that had passed since their parting, he'd courted a few girls, mostly choosing the homely or overweight ones who sat alone at every social function. His attentions brought them much-needed cheer, and he got to hold fast to his bachelorhood.

And then Bridget McKenna came along and made him question every self-written rule. He had determined to remain single as punishment for not seeking God's will regarding marriage to Kay, and he'd decided not to return to the seminary until he'd performed enough good deeds to balance the wrongs he'd committed since being duped by those two wily women. Maybe by then he would have developed the backbone to lead a flock.

He couldn't help wondering if his quickly growing feelings for the beautiful Irish lass were a sign that God had heard his prayers and had forgiven him. Was he free to marry this lovely, loving young woman? If yes, perhaps God would show him a sign by blessing his dreams with images of her tonight.

With that thought secure in his mind, Lance drifted into the first deep and peaceful slumber he'd enjoyed in months.

Chapter Three

The moment the hired hand returned from town, Bridget ran down the back steps to greet him while he was still sitting on the carriage seat. "Claib," she said, placing a hand on his forearm, "did y'go to the post office? Was there mail waiting there? A letter for me, perhaps?"

Chuckling, the elderly black man shook his head. "Now, now, Miss Bridget, how you 'spect me to dig the envelope what's addressed to you from my bag 'less you turn loose o' my sleeve?"

Blushing, Bridget let go of him. "Sorry, Claib. Didn't mean to assault you." She giggled. "It's just—"

He held up a withered hand, stripped of most of its function years ago when it got caught in a cotton gin. "No need to 'splain, missy. I knows how hard it must be for you, havin' no kinfolk hereabouts. An' since the mail runs jus' once a month, news from home don't come near often enough."

Bridget smiled patiently, relieved to know Claib understood how she felt. But gratitude couldn't quell her desire to hold that letter in her hands, to read what her family had written.

"Enough suspense," he said. Reaching into the satchel on the seat beside him, he withdrew a rectangular, cream-colored envelope. "There y'go, Miss Bridget. Y'all run along, now, see what yo' li'l sister have to say this time."

She gave his hand an affectionate squeeze. "There's a sandwich and some lemonade waiting for you in the kitchen," she said, then dashed off.

Bridget didn't want to be cooped up in her room to read Suisan's letter. The words needed to be read out of doors, where the sunshine could warm her skin and the breeze could carry away the heat of missing her family. Lifting her skirts, she raced around to the side of the house and perched on the low stone wall surrounding the terrace. With fluttering heart and trembling fingers, Bridget forcefully broke the seal and, after removing the neatly folded pages, tucked the envelope into her apron pocket.

Dearest Bridget,

We received your letter only yesterday. As usual, the family sat around the table as I read it to them. We're all praising God, for it's good to hear you are doing well. I needn't tell you how often we think of you, all alone on the other side of the Atlantic.

It sounds like your Mr. Auburn's wedding was the social event of the decade! Aileen asked if he has a son, and if he plans to put on a show like that for his boy, for if that's the case, she'd pack up to move to America, too...to be the bride!

Speaking of Aileen, you know how often we joked that her slow progress in school might have been because the midwife dropped her on her noggin? Well, you'll be happy to know, that sister of ours isn't just reading from the book you sent, but she's writing her name all over the place, as well. She says to tell you she'll be writing her own letter to you one day soon.

Caitlin goes to town three days a week to work for Conyngham. He and Da struck a deal last time the old buzzard raised the rent. Without warning, as usual. Seems his wife isn't well and can't handle even the simplest of household tasks. So, instead of paying more rent, our girl will cook and clean for his old crone. Da may not have gone to university, like Conyngham, but he's a genius by comparison—he waited until after the codger named his price to separate all the tasks Caitlin would perform and charged separately for each, saying the chores Conyngham listed were a lot to expect from a ten-year-old girl. The way it ended up, the rent will stay the same...and the tightwad will pay Caitlin eight pence at the end of each week, to boot!

Caitlin and Aileen could have been twins, if three years hadn't separated their births. Their sunny red hair and warm smiles had always reminded Bridget of the two wee cherubs floating above the image of the Christ child in the stained glass window of the Malinmore Church of God. Smiling, Bridget read on:

Sean went to town on his twelfth birthday, saying he intended to find himself a man's job. Instead, he found a book while rummaging in a rubbish bin at the hotel. He must have read it twenty times already. In fact, he looks odd now when the wrinkled old thing isn't in his hands. We're proud of him, too, walking down the street with a book tucked under his arm. Makes me think how far we've come since the days of the Pena Laws and the hedgerow schoolteachers, when the English forbade the sons and daughters of the sod, under pain of death, to learn to read or write. So, to keep Conyngham from taking it away, Sean dug a little hole in the back floor of the cottage. He puts his precious book in there when he isn't reading it.

It seemed to Bridget that God had decreed the McKenna boys to be dark and the girls to be light, for her brothers had all been born with black hair and eyes as dark as coffee beans. And Sean's were darkest of all....

Cormac likely outweighs Da by now, though he's got a mite to grow before he's taller than Sean. For his thirteenth birthday, I cooked up a kettle of stew. Salted up the meat and cooked down the bones so we'd have a bit of flavor to add to the potatoes for the rest of the week, too. Got the meat by trading the linen napkins Ma got from her auntie as a wedding present. Wasn't exactly a fair trade, since they were so threadbare, but Mrs. Baedeker seemed happy. She bagged up enough pork to feed us for a week. But Cormac's surprise stew didn't turn out quite as I thought it might. Having a sample of what a decent meal can taste like only made Cormac see how horrid our regular meals have been. Now I understand that old saying, "Ignorance is bliss," because he's done little more than whine and complain ever since. He says that since he's bigger and stronger than most men in Malinmore, he'll head for the docks and hop a ride on the next boat bound for America. But I'll believe that when I see it. You and I both know how scared that boy is of water deeper than what he can collect in a bucket.

Eamon is Cormac's shadow these days. He declared that if Cormac was going to America, he'd be going, too. The discussion got Da riled up good, and he managed to talk both boys out of leaving. At least for now. Or until Cormac remembers his fear of water! Still, I fear it's a subject that will come up again soon. That look in Cormac's eyes, like he inhaled a whiff of wanderlust when he lifted that lid from the stewpot, means it's just a matter of time before he makes good on his promise to put Ireland behind him. Would you believe I heard him praying just the other night that the good Lord would rid him of his fear of deep water?

Cormac had always been broader and stronger than the rest of them, so it was no surprise to Bridget that the soles of his big feet itched to move on....

Searlass O'Connell has been hanging around a lot these days. He starts out with a good excuse for stopping by, like do I have half a potato to spare? Or might I sew a button on his cuff? At first, I thought he was just missing his ma. (Did I tell you she and her newborn died a few months back?) He might have been missing her at first, but lately, there's no doubt in my mind he has but one purpose for stopping by, and that's to see yours truly.

Last time he rapped at the door, hands deep in the pockets of his raggedy pants, he said, "Suisan, I do believe you're the prettiest colleen in all of Ireland!" It poured from his mouth like river water rushing over the rocks and surprised me so much that I said, "Now, Searlass, how would you know a thing like that when you've never set foot outside County Donegal?" Well, Bridgie, from the look on his face, you'd think I had clubbed him with my broom handle instead of telling a wee joke. I can tell you this: I won't say anything like it again.

Now, you remember Searlass, with his froggy eyes and rabbit teeth and all that carrot-red hair. To be sure, he's not the most handsome boy I've ever set eyes on, but he most assuredly is the sweetest. Why, I sometimes think his heart must be as big as his head. And oh, what a sense of humor! There isn't much to laugh about here in Malinmore these days, but God bless the boy for giving me reason to enjoy life, even if just a little bit, and for a little while.

I don't love him, Bridgie, not like we used to giggle and dream about before Da turned out the lamplight. But I think I could, in time. If I'm right, he's gearing up to pop the question, and if he does, I'm going to say yes. There are plenty of reasons to marry him. One less mouth for Da to feed, for one. And Caitlin's old enough to take over my duties, though I'd only be up the road a bit. But the best reason of all is that Searlass says his da somehow managed to buy up the O'Connell land, outright. Makes me wonder whose old donkey old Seamus had to kiss to accomplish that! Anyway, I'm sure you know that if I'm living on O'Connell land, I can always help Da and the young ones with food and such.

Married? Her little sister? *A wedding,* Bridget thought, *should be for love and no other reason.* Then the practical side of her mind took over, and she saw the good sense in Suisan's plan. Still, it seemed a shame that the poor girl would have to marry a boy she didn't love just to help keep the wolf from the door.

Bridget pictured Drewry and Chase. Before, during, and after the wedding, their eyes had glowed with love for each other. Sooner or later, Suisan would marry. So why *shouldn't* it be for love?

Da has just sat down here at the table, and he says there are things he'd like me to tell you: "My darling daughter," he's saying, "it's good to hear you are doing well. I pray every day, Bridget, that you are safe and happy there in the green fields of Americay. I pray for your Mr. Auburn, too, since he's the reason you're fed and clothed and have money enough to see to your needs after sending some over here. One day, Lord willing, I'll thank that kind and generous man in person for taking such good care of my girl. When you were but a little tyke, one peal of thunder was enough to send you flying into my lap for protection. So when storm clouds brew above your Magnolia Grove, and you shiver with fright like you did when you were small, remember that no matter where you are, Da is here, wrapping his loving arms around you in his heart and mind."

He'd skin me alive, Bridgie, if I told you this, but Da had more to say. Much more. Only he couldn't speak past the lump in his throat. He misses you so, sister dear, more than all the rest of us put together. I've thought on it a great deal, and I think that's because he feels it's his fault you had to leave us. And I've saved the worst for last.

Dread drummed in Bridget's heart. She licked her lips and held her breath, hoping the worst wouldn't be too bad....

Da has a terrible cough.

Bridget clutched the letter to her chest and closed her eyes. "Dear God," she whispered, "let the next line say he's better now, or, at the very least, that he's on the road to recovery...."

There's a bit of blood in the spittle, so we're hoping it isn't consumption. No matter what I do for him, he can't seem to get a minute's peace from it. I say he got it digging peat two weeks ago, since in place of the gentle rains his body is used to, the skies turned angry and black and opened up like a bursting dam, and Da was drenched by the time he got home from the bogs that night. I brewed him weak tea and got a bit of potato broth into him. I nag him endlessly to see that he rubs camphor on his chest before turning in for the night, and Caitlin and I have taken to sharing a blanket so Da can have his on top of him. And still the cough hangs on. It's times like these I wish you were here, Bridgie. You always knew exactly what to do. I'm a pitiful replacement for you, I'm afraid.

Well, Bridgie dear, I hate to leave you on that sour note, but I've got mending to do before I blow out the candle. I set aside the coins you sent to post this letter. I know it isn't near as good as talking face-to-face, the way we did all those nights in the corner of the cottage, but it's as good as we've got for now.

Take care of yourself, sister dear, and write to me soon, for your letters always lift my spirits.

Your favorite sibling (ha ha!),

Suisan

PS: Da has me teaching him to read and write! He says he wants to learn because, if he's ever able to come to America, he doesn't want to look like an illiterate dolt. But the real reason, I think, is that he wants to read your letters with his own eyes and write a response with his own hand. Now, don't you let on that I've told his secret, or I'll be minus a head next time you see me!

Bridget refolded Suisan's letter in the envelope, which she tucked back in her apron pocket, and stared silently across the yard. The stream running along the edge of the property bubbled around gnarled tree roots and gurgled over mossy rocks. Above her, a raspberry-red cardinal peeped from his perch in the sugar maple, and his bride chirped her merry response. The early June breeze hustled up the drive, sighing through the magnolia leaves and rustling the velvety roses in the garden. A honeybee lit in the center of one lily-white bloom, tapped its fuzzy feet across the petals and sipped sweet nectar, then buzzed off in search of more. *Dear Lord in heaven, I pray for full bellies and warm hearts for them all, and...and oh, God eternal, keep the dark faeries from Da's door....*

Though the afternoon sun beat down hard, cloaking her shoulders with yellow light, Bridget felt none of its warmth, and she paid little attention to God's beauty all around her. Her focus was on the letter. Suisan's fanciful script could not disguise the suffering of her family. Oh, how she wanted to see them, to throw her arms around each of them and hug them tight! If only she could have them here with her, right this minute, so she could rest easy, knowing they were warm and dry and well fed...and that Da was getting the proper treatment for his cough.

Overwhelmed by her own powerlessness, she lowered her head, closed her eyes, and covered her face with both hands as she wept.

Lance had climbed up to the loft to change the shirt he'd torn on a nail in the barn. As he stood beside his cot and fastened the buttons, he peered down into the yard through his tiny, four-paned window and spied Bridget in the garden.

He couldn't remember the last time he'd seen her without the children at her side. Leaning forward slightly to glance left and right in search of them, Lance frowned, wondering where they might be. But thoughts of their whereabouts ended the moment his gaze returned to her.

Resting his palms on the windowsill, Lance smiled tenderly as a gentle wind riffled the long, thick hair curling and curving down her slender back. She wore a white pinafore over a blue housedress, its ruffles angling up from her shoulders like butterfly wings. Now and again, as she inclined her head, he caught a peek of creamy cheek, and he found himself longing to trace its contour with the tip of his finger, as he had the night of Chase's wedding in December.

Had it really been six months since that glorious kiss? It surely didn't seem so. If he let himself—and he'd let himself scores of times since—Lance could almost feel that same cheek pressed against his chest. He remembered, too, how, when his arms wrapped around her, he'd felt a bit like the giant at the top of Jack's beanstalk. But the best memory, he believed, had been the moment he'd cradled her pretty face in his hands, tilting it up so he could gaze deep into her eyes....

Every time he relived the scene, Lance considered the possibility that it had been a dream. During that sliver in time, it had felt as though he'd fallen into a whirlpool, for the clear blue of her love-lit eyes had pulled him deeper, deeper, until he'd surrendered and pressed his lips to hers. If it hadn't been for the dulcet tones of that lilting voice, reminding him of the late hour, he might still be spinning breathlessly in the powerful current.

Several times since then, he'd looked for opportunities to duplicate the moment. Once, he'd called her to the rear of the buckboard, saying he wanted to show her something. He'd taken care to park it in the shade of the willow beyond the drive so that its drooping branches would provide shelter...and privacy. But Bridget had misread his cue and waited beside the wagon instead, chattering like a chipmunk while he pretended to search for the imaginary thing he'd told her to come see. If she'd thought him a mindless fool when he'd finally displayed a box of horseshoes, her eyes hadn't betrayed her. "Why, they're bright and shiny as new pennies," she'd cooed in her heavenly Irish brogue.

Weeks later, he'd sidled into the kitchen, where Bridget had stood tapping her chin as Sally and Sam recited from their McGuffey readers. "My left hand's too clumsy to cut out this splinter," Lance had announced, hoping she'd be so engrossed in nursing his injury that she'd scarcely notice his arms wrapping around her. But he hadn't counted on Matilda bursting from the pantry when he made his plea for medical attention. "You keep on with them young'uns' lessons," the older woman said, "whilst I see to this here clumsy man." The sting of the sliver as she jerked it from his palm hadn't hurt nearly as much as the slap to his ego when Bridget had winked and said, "Ye're mighty brave and strong...for an Englishman."

The memory made him smile. Never before had the sound of a female voice turned his throat dry and his palms damp. But the mere sight of Bridget, even from the distance between his window and her seat on the garden wall, was enough to make his heart pound like a parade drum.

Exhaling a long sigh, Lance stepped away from the window and tucked in his shirt. As he'd lain on his back and tried to summon sleep on the night of their kiss, he'd known without a doubt that he could fall in love with this girl. *But put on the brakes, man,* he'd warned himself. *She's pure and innocent, and you're anything but. She deserves far better than the likes of you, and if you don't stamp out these feelings right quick, you're headed for a good heart-kicking when she realizes it, too!*

A glance at his pocket watch told him he'd better get back to work. But first, one last look into the garden....

He saw Bridget bow her head, then cover her face with both hands. As he watched her shoulders rise and fall, he realized she was weeping. In a heartbeat, he was scrambling down the ladder. Whatever, *whoever* had made her cry had better have a good explanation!

He'd always been a strong, speedy runner, so why did it seem like his booted feet clumped across the mossy lawn more slowly than each stroke of a clock in need of a good winding?

As he moved closer, a portentous thought flitted through his mind, and as he leapt over the garden wall to sit down beside her, he hoped that it wasn't foolish to ignore it.

Take care, his heart cautioned him as he gathered her close. And as he said, "There, there, hush now," it warned him again, *Take care....*

She slid into his arms like the warm breezes that slipped through his window. Her sobs shook him to the marrow of his bones. Lance sensed that words were not what she needed at the moment. And he was grateful, for what could he have said to comfort her when he had no idea what had caused such raw, deep grief? She'd always seemed so strong, so sure of herself, so the tears soaking through the coarse material of his shirt unnerved him.

And then, just as dark skies clear after a heavy rain, her misery abated.

"I'm sorry," she whispered when it was over. "I didn't mean to get yer shirt all wet. I'm happy to launder it, if y'like."

Smiling, he said, "The dampness actually feels good in this heat. Besides, I should be thanking you, because you did me a favor," he added, stroking her chin with his forefinger. "I'd been walking around all morning, down in the mouth and in need of a hug, and here you sat, willing to give one."

Sniffing daintily, Bridget mopped her face with the hem of her pinafore. "Well," she said, forcing a grin, "ye're welcome, English." Then, "Now I'd best get back to the children. I told Drewry and Matilda I'd be only a minute, and it's been ten, at least. Soon, they'll gather up a search party to find me."

Lance sandwiched her hands between his own. "All right, but first, may I ask you a question, Bridget?"

She took a shuddering breath and let it out slowly. "Y'can ask, I suppose," she said, "but I'll not guarantee an answer."

He made note of the fact that her smile never quite reached her eyes. "Fair enough," he said. "Will you tell me what made you so sad?"

After a sigh, she said, "Oh, 'tis nothing, really. Got a letter from home, is all. Sometimes I get to missin' Ireland and the family so much I think my heart just might break." Shrugging, she held out both hands, as if to catch her heart should that happen. "I know it's got to be this way," she said, straightening her back. "They'd starve, sure, if I weren't over here sendin' money. I only wish there were something I could do about Da's cough...."

"I've never known anyone quite like you, Bridget McKenna."

A little giggle popped from her mouth. "Never known a bigger crybaby, y'mean."

Placing both hands on her shoulders, he turned her to face him. "Quite the contrary. You're the strongest woman I know. Why, there are men who could take lessons in bravery from you. I'm sure you're a hero to those folks back home."

"That's what Da said the day I left." But she wasn't smiling when she said, "Only heroic thing I did, really, was agree to go, to give him one less mouth to feed." Shaking her head, Bridget pursed her lips. "'Twasn't a hero that day, and I'm no hero now." She met his eyes, blinked, and added, "Sometimes, I feel like a big jellyfish, just tryin' to float by, one day at a time." She focused on something beyond his right shoulder as her face took on a faraway expression. "One day at a time, here in Americay, prayin' that someday soon, I can send for them."

"Could you bring them over one at a time, maybe, to speed things up?"

She shook her head. "Suggested that in every letter I wrote home that first year, but Da wouldn't hear of it. 'We'll come together,' he made Suisan write, 'or die together.'" Bridget cringed and glanced heavenward. "So I gave up arguin' and put my energies into workin' all the harder to bring all of them here sooner."

Amazed, Lance watched her transformation from teary-eyed girl to resolute young woman.

Bridget squared her shoulders and lifted her chin. "Self-pity's the ruination of more than a gal's rouge, I always say."

The big clock in the front hall gonged, its chiming notes floating to them on the summery breeze. "Goodness gracious, sakes alive," she announced, "it's goin' on noon. Time to feed the children!" Grinning mischievously, she held out her hand to him. "Come with me to the kitchen, and I'll fix you a bite of lunch, too."

And like a schoolboy in the throes of his first crush, he followed. Again.

"What have ye a hankering for today, English? A slab of ham? A chunk of cheese? A turkey leg, or maybe a bowl of bubblin' stew?"

The steaming rabbit stew she'd fed him the day before was still clinging to his ribs when Lance had sat down for supper: a mountainous plate of boiled ham and cabbage, topped off by a wedge of apple pie. Licking his lips, he marveled at the boundless energy that allowed Bridget to care for the Auburn children and help the aging Matilda in the kitchen, as well.

❀

In bed that night, Lance linked his fingers behind his head, crossed his ankles, and stared up at the ceiling. "Dear Lord," he prayed, "give me the strength to keep a careful distance from her...or send me a sign that You want me close, so I can watch over her."

That was the extent of his devotions that night. Rolling on his side, Lance punched his pillow and closed his eyes. Thoughts of his brother, his father, and his mother pulsed in his memory, and, gritting his teeth, he forced them back into the deep, dark recesses of his brain. He hated them. Hated them all. Hated even their memory, because they'd left him alone by choice to pursue their assorted sinful lives.

But despite his best efforts, they hovered like wisps of smoke at the edges of his mind, reaching out, calling to his consciousness, even as he willed himself to fall sleep.

Lance's dreaming mind tugged him back in time to the days when his family owned a large, elegant house near New York's newly opened Central Park. It was a sunny autumn day as he shuffled home from school, books slung haphazardly over one shoulder, and sent his "kicking stone" sailing over the iron-barred wall surrounding York Manor. Shoving through the ornate gates, he frowned, for his mother had left the front door open. Again.

The last time Diana York had gone off this way, a pair of rambunctious squirrels had scampered inside the house. It hadn't been until books started falling from the library shelves and china began crashing to the dining room floor that the maid had realized intruders were afoot. The fuzzy-tailed rodents had left a trail of broken glass and stoneware in their wake before she'd managed to shoo them back into the great outdoors with the business end of her broom.

What manner of destruction awaits me today? Lance wondered, peering cautiously into the semidark foyer. Relieved when careful inspection proved the four-footed visitors had not paid a return call, Lance went into the backyard to romp with the dogs. His favorite, Target, was chasing a leather ball, and the pair might have played until dark...if a somber-faced constable hadn't stepped onto the back porch....

"I've brought your mother home," the man said, one hand on his billy club. "The maid said your father isn't home, and she told me to speak with you."

No surprise there. Whenever Lance's father made himself scarce—which was more often than not—his mother reacted with a disappearing act. And since his older brother was no more dependable than his parents, the staff had little choice but to turn to fourteen-year-old Lance for direction.

Seeing the distress on the constable's face, Lance felt his heart thunder. "What trouble is she in this time?"

"She's been robbed, down on the Bowery."

Frowning, Lance started to ask why his mother had gone there alone in the first place. But it was pointless asking this total stranger to explain her erratic behavior when he didn't understand it himself.

"Her furs and jewels were stolen when the thief dragged her into an alley," said the constable. Flipping through his notebook, he read off a list, then shook his head. "He got away, I'm afraid, so we weren't able to recover any of it."

But she hadn't been mugged. Lance knew it as well as the constable did. His mother had traded her goods for opium. Again. Molars grinding, Lance asked, "Where is she?"

"Out front, safe in my paddy wagon. Shall I bring her around?"

Disgusted, Lance shook his head. "No need. I'll meet you out there." The neighbor ladies were already having a field day yammering about his mother's antics. If the constable tried to get her inside all by himself, they'd have months' worth of fodder for their gossip mill.

It took some doing, but once they'd secured her in her room, Lance walked the officer to the door, where the man hesitated. It hadn't been the first time the fellow had showed up with a kicking, screaming Diana in tow, and from the look on his face, it was clear he didn't think it would be his last visit to York Manor. "Can you get word to your pa?"

"Of course." If the man knew it was a lie, he gave no sign of it. "Thank you," Lance said, wincing at the caterwauling coming from his mother's room. "For bringing her home, I mean."

"All in the line of duty, son," he said. And, touching a fingertip to the bill of his cap, he left Lance to deal with his mother by himself.

Two short weeks later, she went missing yet again, and Lance made up his mind to find her himself. A few coins pressed into grimy palms helped him follow her trail. After an hour of traipsing the gritty streets, he made his way to Chang's Emporium, where he stood face-to-face with the shirtless giant who guarded the door. Somehow, he managed to dart around the man and enter a doorway of strands of beads, then found himself in a room where strange music and peculiar voices blended in eerie harmony.

And there, amid a gaggle of bleary-eyed men, sat his mother.

Her once-shining blonde hair frizzed around her face like a mound of straw, and her eyes, which not so long ago had glowed like blue moonlight, glared with glassy indifference as they settled on this intruder—her youngest son.

A gray-white cloud hovered like a ghostly apparition above those sprawled atop the short-legged round table. After sipping from the stem of a rough-hewn wood pipe, they passed it from hand to hand. When it was Diana's turn, she eyed it hungrily, then grabbed it and, cradling its bowl lovingly, greedily licked her lips and inhaled deeply.

Her eyelids fluttered, then squeezed shut, and her head lolled back when she exhaled. Lance watched, shocked into silence, his feet frozen to the floor. Dark lashes pulsed against her cheekbones, and she opened her eyes, seemingly oblivious to the world around her, thanks to her chemically induced euphoria.

"What are *you* doing here?" she demanded in a voice he didn't recognize.

"I—I've come to take you home."

"I *am* home," was her raspy response.

"Sweet Jesus," he prayed quietly, "how do I help her?"

He'd used every bit of his money just to find her. The only thing of worth left on his person was his pocket watch, a gift from his maternal grandfather. He showed it to the giant who'd been guarding the door. "If you help me get her home," he whispered, "it's yours."

Greed glinted in the big man's eyes as he turned the watch over and over in his meaty palm. "Gold?"

Nodding, Lance said, "Yessir, it's solid gold. Worth lots of money."

Smirking, the guard tossed Diana over one shoulder. "I follow," he said, pointing to the street as she kicked and shrieked. "You lead."

All the way home, she'd fought like a tiger, yet he had held tight as Lance led him through back alleys and streets toward York Manor, pretending he didn't notice the disgusted glances of the people they passed along the way.

"I hate you," his mother snarled at Lance as the giant heaved her onto her bed. "I never wanted children in the first place, if you want the truth, so why did I get stuck with the likes of *you*, the sorriest excuse for a son a mother ever had?"

No one was more surprised than Lance when his father, William York, met them at the door. The only words he spoke were to instruct the housekeeper's husband to nail boards across the French doors leading to Diana's balcony, and to do the same across the main entrance to her bedroom. And though Lance covered his ears, he couldn't block out the sound of her shouting, "I'll never forgive you for this, Lance. *Never!*"

The next morning, revulsion glowed hot on his father's face as he looked at his wife of twenty-two years. "You've left me no choice," he said, his voice as cold as the steel-blue of his eyes. "I've arranged for you to be hospitalized."

She argued, cried, pleaded, and even promised to give up the opium. But it was no use. Lance's father had made up his mind. "It's for your own good," he said, coolly and calmly. "The attendants will be here any minute now to take you to the asylum." It was the best hospital of its type on the East Coast, he said. They'd take excellent care of her, and she'd be home in no time, he added.

Diana had been gone nearly a week when Lance screwed up the courage to ask his father when she might be well enough to come home.

"She's in good hands," he said without glancing up from his ledger book. "That's all you need to know."

That's all you need to know....

Dawn was breaking when Lance awoke, drenched with sweat and trembling from head to toe. Perched on the edge of his cot, he listened to the sounds of his own ragged breaths. His greatest fear had always been that perhaps he'd inherited the same self-centered weakness that had made his mother crave the drug that had nearly killed her.

He'd prayed for a sign, and in place of the answers he'd hoped for, God had given him back the nightmare he hadn't had in years.

Lance saw it as proof that the Almighty wanted him to call an immediate halt to his dreams of a life with Bridget.

Dear, sweet, beautiful Bridget....

Chapter Four

If her father or siblings were to suspect how much pain she was in, they'd worry endlessly. *And how good would that be for Da's health?* Before she responded to Suisan's letter, Bridget would get control of her roiling emotions—not an easy task when one line kept leaping from the pages of that letter: *"Da has a terrible cough...."*

She pictured Liam as he'd looked when last she'd seen him, the dark-blue collar of his coat turned up to block the Atlantic's blustery winds, his shoulders hunched against the biting cold of that bleak autumn day. His dark hair had gone silver at the temples; his once-thick black beard had grown gray.

Life to that point had taught her that the past mattered little and the future mattered much, so Bridget had looked at him long and hard, there on the dock, willing his image to fuse itself to her brain so that whenever she missed him—and, no doubt, it would be often—she could call the vision to mind and feast her lonely eyes on the pictures in her head.

She remembered, too, the touch of his calloused hands as he'd tenderly wrapped a scarf of hand-spun wool around her neck; the way his lips had slanted, tilting the dark mustache above his mouth. Inhaling the scents of peat and smoke that clung to his dark blue coat, she had watched as his eyes had misted with sadness.

Liam had never been a very tall man, measuring no more than five feet seven inches by the Americans' rule, but as for sinew and bone, he could likely outperform his stateside counterparts in a peat-digging match with one hand tied behind his back. But his strength had belied him that day, for Liam had lost the contest for the control of his emotions to a sob and a tear.

Even wet with worry, his eyes were as soft and gray as a snowy sky, and his ruddy cheeks reminded her of the story he liked to tell, the one handed down through the generations about the great hero, King Niall. According to the tale, Niall had lashes and brows as black as the pupils of his eyes, teeth of the purest white, and red lips that never reproved in anger. Bridget had always loved listening as Liam had spun his fables exactly as the *seanachies* had woven their tales so long ago.

He had called her a hero that day on the dock, though, in her eyes, he'd earned the title a thousand times over. Keeping her close by would have been easier on him—on all of them—but only in the short run. Sooner or later, the food would have run out, or the peat, or the land. And, one by one, the McKennas would have been snuffed out like the faltering flames of candles in the wind. Liam's love had proved true in the long run, for as hard as it had been, he'd sent his eldest child away.

And she'd been gone nearly five years now.

It had been five years since she'd last seen him, felt his caring touch, heard his melodious voice.

Five long years....

Bridget retreated to the privacy of her room to seek divine guidance. On her knees beside the high four-poster bed, she rested her forehead on folded hands. "Dear heavenly Father," she began in a wavering whisper, "calm m'soul with Yer blessed love, and put the words in my heart and head that'll bring Yer peace to my loved ones."

Often, as she had walked the coastal road with her father, he'd sing an ancient Irish hymn. She closed her eyes now and softly sang in harmony with the voice in her memory, "To Christ the seed, to Christ the harvest, to the barn of Christ may we be brought. To Christ the sea, to Christ the fish, in nets of Christ may we be caught. From birth to age, from age to death, Your two arms, Christ, about us safe. From death to ending, not ended but regrown, in the paradise of grace may we be transplanted."

As she paused in her prayers, Bridget thought of her mother, too, who had passed on to the heavenly kingdom almost ten years earlier. Maire McKenna had always been a devout Christian. She'd memorized the verses that had been read to her by the pastor during Sunday services and would often recite what she'd heard, calling to mind a reading that matched each situation precisely and solved almost any problem life could throw at them.

Once, when Liam didn't return from the bogs at the anticipated time, Maire sat her children down and told them to fold their hands and join her as she prayed for his safe return. Her mother's favorite prayer surfaced in Bridget's mind now, and as she repeated it, her mother's angelic voice echoed in her ears:

"Grant, O God, thy protection, and in protection, strength, and in strength, understanding, and in understanding, perception of justice, and in perception of justice, the love of it, and in the love of it, the love of all life, and in all life, to love God, God and all goodness. Amen."

Renewed in spirit, Bridget sat down at her desk and slipped a sheet of rose-scented paper from a brass-knobbed drawer. Taking a deep breath, she dipped her pen into the inkwell and began:

My dearest family,

I so enjoyed Suisan's letter. It's a wonder I haven't turned the pages into shreds, I've read it so many times!

I'm glad to hear you're reading and writing on your own, Aileen. Having an education will come in handy someday, though I'm sure you don't believe it now, while the hard studying is required of you. When I first arrived in America, the books in Mr. Auburn's study were the only friends I had. I truly don't know how I'd have gotten by if Ma hadn't taught me all she did about reading and writing.

Cormac and Eamon, Suisan writes that you're both as tall as trees and as strong as oxen. I'm happy to hear it, my big little brothers, for you'll have no trouble finding work when you join me in America.

I've talked with Mr. Auburn, and he assures me there's plenty to do right here on Magnolia Grange for each and every one of the McKennas. In the valley behind his house, he built a whole row of little houses for his hired hands. They're not large or fancy, but the roofs don't leak, and every kitchen has a cookstove and a fireplace. Behind each house, there's space for a garden. Most of the families here start the season with leaf lettuce and spring onions and radishes, too. Later, they plant tomatoes and green peppers, peas and green beans. And every worker gets his or her own bed! So be patient, boys, for in no time, I'll have saved up enough to bring all of you here together!

Sean, Suisan tells me you've found a book that you're enjoying. Mr. Auburn cleared off one of his library shelves a few months ago and told the staff to help themselves to the books. I will send a few along to you, in case you're tired of reading that same old story over and over again. Perhaps you'll write and let me know if you enjoyed the antics of the family in Pride and Prejudice *as much as I did.*

Caitlin, don't forget the camphor when you've finished your day's work at the Conyingham place. It'll protect your skin from the lye in the soap and the raw, red bite that comes when the water in your cleaning bucket meets with the wind on the backs of your hands.

And Da...dear, dear Da...what can I say, except that I miss and love you more than there are words in the universe? Don't ever stop praying for me, Da, for I need the reassurance of knowing your words are reaching God's ear. I think you know without my telling you that I say a prayer for you every morning and every night of my life, but I'll say so anyway, so you'll feel guilty not to do the same for me!

Suisan, now that you've read the rest of the family a personal word or two from me, the rest of this letter is for your eyes only. I'm so glad to hear that Searlass is putting moments of joy into your life. If he makes you happy, Suisie, then by all means take him for a husband. But don't let yourself settle for less than you deserve. Do you remember the blessing Da always gave at weddings? "Length of life and sunny days, and may your souls not go homewards till your child falls in love!" To walk together to the end of your lives—that's what you'll vow at the altar, a terribly long time if love doesn't bind you, one to the other. Love will keep you warm when you're cold, and it'll give you hope when life grows bleak. So, don't make a choice today that will set hard with you when you're old.

I'm your sister, not your mother, so I'll not nag you beyond this: Listen closely to your heart, Suisan, for God dwells there. Ask Him if Searlass is the man you ought to marry. He would never steer you wrong.

It's time now for me to round up the Auburn children for their afternoon lessons, so I'll leave you with my love and best wishes, as well as my promise to keep praying for your happiness. I love you dearly and miss you terribly. And as the Irish have been saying to one another since there has been an Ireland: "May the road rise to meet you, may the wind always be at your back; may the sun shine warm upon your face, the rains fall soft upon your fields. And until we meet again, may God hold you in the palm of His hand."

Your sister,

Bridget

She folded the letter in half, then in half again, and slid it into a matching envelope. Then, lighting the candle on her desk, Bridget let a bit of wax fall onto the seal and pressed it flat with the heavy brass A, the symbol of Chase Auburn's grand plantation.

Claib had been going to town every Thursday for as long as she'd been at Magnolia Grange, and tomorrow was Thursday. He wouldn't be the least bit surprised when she handed him the envelope. As always, he'd promise to mail it the minute he arrived in Richmond. And, as always, she'd hug him and whisper a heartfelt thanks in his ear.

Late that night, Bridget stretched out beneath her smooth, cottony sheets and sighed deeply. She loved everything about her new room, from the downy mattress on her big bed to the pair of crystalline lanterns that stood on the round mahogany tables flanking it. When lit, the lamps flashed thousands of tiny rainbows on the walls and ceilings.

Rainbows...she'd seen one or two since arriving at Magnolia Grange, but none that could match the width and height and colors of an Irish rainbow!

She'd never set eyes on a window seat before, but now she had one of her very own. Often, when sleep eluded her, Bridget would settle on its thick cushion and snuggle among the dozens of puffy pillows lining the wall beneath the window. Beside it, French doors opened onto a wide, covered balcony. If she stood at one end of it, she could see the plantation's northern boundary. From the other end, the gardens around the terrace came into view.

The thick, blood-red Persian carpet that covered most of the pine-planked floor protected her feet from the cold when she slipped from bed on chilly mornings. And the maple chiffonier was large enough to accommodate every article of clothing she'd ever owned. She had a bedroom with furniture the likes of which they'd never seen at home.

Home....

What would her father and siblings be doing now as she lay luxuriating in this magnificent bed? The younger ones would likely be shuffling from their beds and rubbing sleep from their eyes as Caitlin stirred up a pot of porridge...if she'd been lucky enough the day before to get her hands on some meal and milk to boil up. And Da would be in the fields already, shaping bricks of peat from the earth and stacking them near the roadside, or digging platter-sized rocks from the dirt to add to the knee-high walls surrounding each miniscule parcel he tended for Conyngham.

Bridget had often wondered what those walls must look like from a bird's-eye view. There were so many of them crisscrossing the countryside that she imagined the land must look like a patchwork quilt, just as Lance had said.

Lance....

Bridget sighed heavily and rolled onto her side to stare out through the French doors. The moon hung high in the black-velvet sky, glowing round and white like a silver dollar. Its light shimmered down upon the earth like a sparkling beacon, illuminating the cream-colored envelope on her bedside table. Bridget turned her back on it. *Just one night without dreams of them*, she pleaded silently, chewing the tip of her thumbnail. *Just one night without seein' their faces and hearin' their voices....*

She sighed and sat up to light one of the twin lanterns. This would be one of those nights, she could tell, when sleep eluded her. Resignedly, she slipped out of bed and padded across the carpeted floor. Settled amid the cushions on the window seat, she lifted the copy of *The Vicar of Wakefield* that Drewry had recommended.

Unable to concentrate on the words printed on its pages, however, she put it down and picked up Charlotte Yonge's *Amy Herbert*, instead. This novel did no more to calm her jangled nerves than the other, so Bridget began a circular tour of her room, her elbows cupped in her palms, her head down as she frowned at the delicate floral patterns in the rug beneath her feet. The brilliant iridescence of the lantern's flickering glow could almost always lift her spirits. But not this night.

Grabbing her Bible from the nightstand, she hugged it to her and bit her lower lip. But even this was no use. She missed them all terribly, and the Lord knew that better than anyone, for she'd told Him so in nearly every heartfelt prayer!

Bridget put the Holy Book back where she'd found it, threw herself on the bed, and let the tears come.

Chapter Five

Lance couldn't have been more than six years old the last time he'd deliberately eavesdropped on a private conversation. If his father caught him with his ear to a bedroom door, he would always be soundly lashed. But the harsh, angry words spoken between his mother and father had burned hotter than the strap ever could have—and stung in his mind still.

Lance followed his nose toward the delectable scents of cinnamon and sugar, and it led him straight to the kitchen. Rubbing his palms together as he made his way down the long, narrow hallway, he grinned. No doubt Matilda was baking pie or cobbler, or some of her famous apple dumplings. Maybe she'd give him a taste, straight out of the oven, and let him have the peels to feed the horses. The sound of Bridget's voice stopped him just outside the door.

"It's true," he heard her say, "I do like him. Quite a lot. But Matilda, he's—he's *English*!"

"Honey chil', folks been judgin' me 'cause of the color of my skin since I was borned. You think that's fair?"

"Of course, it isn't!" she said emphatically. "The Bible tells us that God loves all His children. It doesn't say He loves some more and others less because of the color of their skin."

"Well, then, darlin', I gots to ask you...which is it?"

"Which is what?"

"Do you believe it's wrong to judge folks on account of the color of their skin?"

"I do...."

"Then it's just as wrong to judge that fine young fella on account o' him bein' born of English stock."

The stillness in the room seemed deafening to Lance. Half of him hoped Bridget wouldn't change her mind, because if she kept her distance on account of his heritage, it would spare him having to avoid *her*.

After what seemed an eternity, he heard Bridget say, "The English did many dreadful things to the Irish. Why, they're *still* doin' dreadful things!"

"That may be true enough, Miss Bridget, but what does any of that got to do with Mr. Lance?"

The question put a smile on his face, because while Bridget's attitude might have made it easier to stick to his decision, he didn't much like knowing she viewed him as just one more despicable Englishman.

"I haven't met one yet that I liked. Give 'em an inch and they'll take—"

"A mile?"

"The whole country!"

Matilda's laughter echoed through the kitchen and spilled into the hall. "He's jus' a poor stable boy, honey chil'. What harm he gonna do you or your people?"

Lance heard Bridget take a deep breath and then let it out again. "I suppose you're right. It's the ones with money who do all the damage. The more they have, the more they want. And they'll take it from anybody, any way they can."

Her usually sweet voice was laced with years of venomous rage, and the sound of it wiped the smile from Lance's face.

"He's taken a shine to you," Matilda said.

Bridget giggled, then said, "Oh, and how would you know a thing like that? Surely, he didn't tell you—"

"Didn't have to. It's wrote all over his face. Why, ever' time that lad looks at you, them eyes of his glow like a beacon!"

The sound of her merry laughter was certainly easier to hear than the grating words she'd spoken earlier, even if he was left feeling more conflicted than ever.

"What you think of him?" Matilda pressed. "'Sides hatin' him for bein' English, that is."

He heard Bridget's sharp intake of air. "I never said I hated him. I could never say that!"

"Why not?"

"Because...because I *don't* hate him, that's why. What possible reason could I have to hate him?"

"You said yo'self, 'cause he's *English*!"

A pause, and then, "Yes, but—but—he can't help that, now, can he? I can't very well hate him for something he has no control over."

Lance heard the oven door squeak open and Matilda slide a metal pie pan onto its shelf. "Wouldn't be Christian to hate him fo' a thing like that."

"I know where you're going with this, Matilda, and I'll admit, I admire you greatly."

"Whatever for?"

"Just look what some of them have done to your own people, making them scrape and bow to the master...."

Matilda's voice dropped in volume and timbre when she said, "Ain't no man my master, Bridget McKenna. Only Master I answer to is Jesus the Lord, and you best be rememberin' that, yo'self!"

The comment hung in the air for several moments before Bridget spoke again. "Actually," she said, "I rather like Lance. He's quite smart...for a stable hand...."

"Mmm-hmm. Fo' a stable hand."

"And he can be very sweet and thoughtful, too, 'specially for a man who works with horses all day."

"Mmm-hmm, horses...."

Lance heard the smile in Matilda's voice, and he smiled with her.

"He's handsome, too, but if you ever tell him I said so, I'll deny it!"

Matilda snickered. "Yo' secret's safe with me, missy."

"All right, then, I guess I have to admit, I like him. A little. I like him just fine."

"So, you has taken a shine to him, too, has you?"

Lance's jaw ached from clenching his teeth. How on earth did he hope to cut her from his life if she said yes?

"We have a good bit in common, I suppose, English and me. He's from poor, workin' folks, and far from his family, and I believe he loves the Lord...."

"So what you gonna do about it?"

"Do?"

"You gonna pursue this, uh, this romance?"

Now Lance's fingers ached from nervously clenching them into fists. If he had any courage, any courage at all, he'd pray that the good Lord would make Bridget say no, loud and clear. But he couldn't, for fear God might just answer his prayer.

"Matilda, has anyone ever told you that you're a woman of many talents?"

"Not that I recollect."

"Well, you're a marvel in the kitchen, and I don't believe I've ever seen anyone work as many miracles with laundry stains. You keep this house as clean as a tin whistle...and you're a natural born matchmaker, too."

"I knowed it! Praise the Lord!"

"What?"

"That you is gonna open the door to love with Mr. Lance, that's what! Hallelujah!"

"I'll pray on it, and if the Lord shows me a sign that English is the one for me, well, maybe I'll entertain thoughts of a romance with him...if that's what he has in mind, too."

"Don't you worry none about that, missy. He got romance on his mind, all right...."

Lance realized he'd been holding his breath, hoping for his sake that Bridget would answer exactly as she had....

And, for her sake, hoping that she wouldn't.

"I'm only too happy to help, cousin," Chase said, "but not if it means I have to lie."

Lance stared at the toes of his dusty boots. "I'm not asking you to lie. Just...just don't volunteer any of the truth."

Chase tucked in one corner of his mouth and, shaking his head, said, "The truth will come out sooner or later, anyway. So—"

"The truth about what?" Drewry asked, settling upon the arm of her husband's chair.

With a move that seemed as natural as breathing, his cousin slipped an arm around his wife's waist, and she looked lovingly into his eyes. *If only Bridget could look at me that way someday,* he thought, *I'd consider myself right blessed, indeed.*

"Lance here," Chase explained, "doesn't want Bridget to know about his background."

Her big, dark eyes widened. "Why ever not?"

"Surely, he's told you about my family," Lance said.

"He has. And it doesn't matter any more to me than it does to Chase. Nor will it matter to anyone worth her salt."

"My mother is insane," Lance said, his voice barely a whisper. "And it caused Father to do all sorts of things to—"

"That hasn't anything to do with you, Lance," Drewry said.

He couldn't love her more if she was his own sister, but he couldn't look into those imploring eyes of hers, either. "The English have put Bridget's people through a world of suffering. It's only natural that she harbors resentment against them."

"She's no fool," Chase interjected. "The girl is smart enough to know you had nothing to do with what happened in Ireland."

Shrugging, Lance shook his head, remembering the conversation he'd overheard that very morning. "I have a chance with her," he began, "but not if she knows where I come from."

"But Lance...."

He held up a hand to silence Drewry's rebuttal. "I happen to know the only thing she hates more than an Englishman is a *rich* Englishman."

Chuckling, Chase said, "Then it looks to me like you're doomed, man. Doomed!"

"Chase," Drewry scolded gently, "this is no time to tease him. Can't you see he's hurting?"

"I'm not asking either of you to lie for me," Lance said as if neither of them had spoken. "Only that you refrain from offering information."

Drewry and Chase exchanged a long, penetrating look that had meaning for only the two of them, and again, Lance found himself envying their deep, abiding love.

Drewry's skirts whispered as she crossed the small expanse of carpet separating them. Kneeling beside him, she laid a hand on his sleeve. "I know a little something about deception, Lance." She cut a quick glance to Chase and smiled forlornly. "The whole beginning of our relationship," she said, "was a lie."

A disbelieving chuckle popped from his lips. "You? Deceptive? I don't believe it."

She ignored his noble compliment and continued. "I came to Magnolia Grange posing as the woman Chase had hired as the children's nanny. I was running from an unpleasant past, just as you are. I'd sat beside the *real* nanny on the train from Baltimore. She got off at a whistle stop just south of Washington, supposedly to marry a soldier who'd captured her fancy, and I saw my chance."

In the next few minutes that ticked by, Drewry held Lance spellbound with her story. She explained how she had used the information shared by her seatmate to bluff her way into the job as Sally and Sam's nanny, and how, throughout those first months, the agony of her secret had eaten away at any sense of peace and contentment she might have enjoyed if only she'd been honest at the outset. "Our situations aren't so very different, Lance," she stated. "My lies nearly cost me the best thing that ever happened in my life. It's just lucky for me that your cousin has a big, forgiving Christian heart!" She stared into Lance's eyes, then asked, "Do you love Bridget?"

Love? He didn't know if he'd call it *love*. At least not yet. But he couldn't say it *wasn't* love, either. "I care for her a great deal," was all he could bring himself to say.

"Enough that you've been thinking about a future with her?"

In all honesty, the idea of spending a lifetime with a woman like Bridget seemed like the promise of heaven on earth. "I can't let her find out about my father's illegal activities, my mother's drug addiction, my brother's compliance in both...or, for that matter, the fact that I'm one of the so-called wealthy Englishmen she's come to mistrust."

"But don't you see that by not telling her the truth, you *are* a dishonest Englishman? Think about how hurt and disappointed she'll be if she learns about your background from anyone but you."

He'd thought of all that, too many times to count.

Drewry grabbed his hands and squeezed them tight. "If she would refuse your love because of things your family did, or because of your heritage, then she isn't the woman I think she is...and she doesn't deserve you."

In all likelihood, Drewry was right. But he couldn't take that chance.

She placed a sisterly hand on his cheek. "Chase is right, you know. Someday, she will learn the truth.

Have you considered what she'll think of you when that happens?"

Lance swallowed. Hard. She'd hate him more than the English who'd hurt her people.

"Not everyone is as loving and forgiving as your cousin, here."

"You can't build a life on a foundation of lies," Chase said. "Drewry confessed the truth, but I have a confession of my own. I had fallen in love with her months before she fessed up, and it's only because I'd had ample opportunity to witness her goodness that I could listen when she finally told me the whole story. I'd watched her with the children and knew she was the most gentle soul I'd likely ever meet. And when I learned *why* she'd kept the truth from me—that she'd been hiding from a ruthless uncle who planned to trade her like some farm animal to pay a gambling debt...well, it was an easy lie to understand—and forgive."

He leaned forward and balanced his elbows on his knees, adding, "Frankly, Lance, your reasons are hardly life-threatening."

The memory of his mother screaming like a banshee as the orderlies carted her off to the mental institution flashed in his mind. And the image of his father laying paper money on the palm of the largest man as though he were dealing cards flashed behind it. Money had caused his mother's problems, and his father's and brother's, too. And money, in Bridget's eyes, was the root of the evil that plagued her homeland.

Drewry and Chase meant well, he knew, but they didn't understand. And Lance knew they'd never understand why he must keep his past a secret if he hoped to share anything with Bridget.

"I appreciate your good advice," he said, standing up, "and I'm grateful that you won't tell her about me... unless she asks." He stressed those last three words, needing to be sure they understood *that*, at least.

"I'll be in the barn if you need me," he added.

He'd barely wrapped his hand around the front doorknob when he heard Drewry say, "If only we could *pray* him to his senses!" to which Chase responded, "If he loves her, he'll come around. *You* did, thank God."

The rustle of fabric, followed by silence, told him Chase and Drewry had sealed their hope with a kiss. He stepped onto the porch and thanked them silently for the prayers they'd already prayed on his behalf—and for those he knew they'd pray in the days and weeks to come.

Because Lance had a feeling he was going to need all the prayers he could get.

Two times in as many days, he found himself eavesdropping on her. *If you're not careful,* he told himself, *this is going to become a nasty habit.*

"Don't wander too far from the house, now," Bridget called to the children. "It's just a few minutes till suppertime."

"We'll stay close," Sam hollered over his shoulder as he ran toward the stream that bubbled and gurgled along the far north boundary of Magnolia Grange.

"We promise," Sally added, skipping along beside him.

Bridget stood watching them and smiled fondly. From the look on her face, Lance knew she couldn't love them more if she'd given birth to them herself. "You spoil them," he said.

She whirled around and faced him, wide-eyed and open-mouthed. "I have a bit of advice for you, English," she said once she'd caught her breath.

He grinned. "And what might that be?"

She marched right up to him and stood before him, her hands on her hips, looking up at his face. "Set aside a bit of your pay each week so that when one of your surprise visits scares the life clean out of me, you can buy me a dandy coffin."

"Sorry," he said. "I do seem to forever be startling you, don't I?"

"You might at least try to sound sincere." She narrowed one eye to add, "Because a body who meant what he said wouldn't keep making the same mistake over and over again."

Resting his hands on her shoulders, Lance gazed into her eyes. Oh, how he longed to pull her close and press his lips against hers. How he yearned to tangle his fingers in her luxurious, fiery locks. He might have stood there staring into her face forever if voices from above hadn't interrupted them.

"What are you doing?"

"Hugging you, that's what."

It was Chase and Drewry. But what were they doing in the children's tree house?

Her eyes alight with playfulness, Bridget pressed a finger to her lips, indicating that Lance should remain silent. "Don't disturb them," she mouthed.

But if they weren't to disturb them, they'd have to stay exactly where they were—pressed tightly against the stucco in the shade of the willow—until his crazy cousin and his wife decided to descend the ladder leading into the tree house. Wincing, Lance held out his palms. "We can't stay here," he mouthed back.

Her response? A mad flapping of her hands and a violent shaking of her head. Under other circumstances, she might have stamped one tiny foot, as well. However, she had no choice but to grin and shake a warning fist under his nose. "They're newlyweds," her perky pink lips said. "They need privacy!"

"Privacy?" he nearly shouted. With the two of them standing beneath the tree house, Chase and Drewry might as well have positioned themselves on a curtained stage and charged admission for their performance!

After a moment's thought, Lance had to admit that he didn't really mind being this close to Bridget. Smiling, he sent a silent message upward. *Take your time, cousin. Take your time!*

As though she'd been doing it for a lifetime, Bridget leaned her cheek against his chest, then slid one arm around his waist as she curled the other over his shoulder. *Take your time*, he repeated, meaning it even more than before.

"All right, Mrs. Auburn," they heard Chase say, "out with it. Why did you insist that I follow you up here?"

"Do you love me, Chase?"

Gruff laughter answered her question. "Oh, I have my moments."

Instinct drew Lance and Bridget's gazes upward, and through the leafy branches, they saw Drewry comb her fingers through Chase's dark waves. "Good, because I love you, too," she said, nodding. "It's a very important thing, you know...."

"What's important?" he asked, kissing the tip of her nose.

"Why, for parents to love each other, of course."

A pause, and then, "What?"

Bridget and Lance watched as Chase dotted Drewry's face with kisses. "You're—we're—are you sure?"

"Absolutely."

Lance grinned as Bridget jumped up and down in his arms, trying her best to hold back her squeals of glee.

"We're going to have a baby?"

"Absolutely," Drewry repeated.

"How long have you known?"

"Only a few days. I wanted to be certain before I got your hopes up...."

Now, Bridget pummeled Lance's chest with gentle punches as Chase's laughter filled the yard.

"Ah, Drewry," Chase said, "what a wonderful surprise." Then, "Have you told Sally and Sam?"

"Of course not! I wanted you to be the first to know."

Bridget pointed at Lance and then at herself, then held up one finger, indicating that while Chase was the first to know, they'd heard the news at the same moment.

"Let's get down from here," Chase said. "We'll find the children and tell them together."

Lance didn't know what to, and he looked to Bridget for guidance. "Run for cover?" was his silent question.

"No-o-o!" came her hoarse whisper. She clamped a hand over her mouth, then hung her head. "Uh-oh," she mouthed.

"What was that?" Drewry asked.

"Who cares?" Chase said, silencing her with a long kiss.

Will Bridget suggest we take advantage of the moment to skedaddle? Lance wondered, searching her face. Nothing could have surprised him more than the tears sparkling in her big, blue eyes. And, as though ashamed that he'd witnessed her emotional display, she covered her face with both hands, broke free from his embrace, and dashed toward the house.

Did it mean she wasn't looking forward to children of her own someday? Or was it *his* children she didn't want? The mere possibility of that being the reason she'd run off caused an ache inside him like none he'd ever experienced, because he'd have liked nothing more than to make her his wife, to share her life, and to watch as she mothered their children.

The thought struck him dumb for a moment. When his senses returned, Lance remembered that when Drewry had asked him if he loved Bridget, he'd stupidly said, "I care about her."

He had a powerful lot of thinking to do—because, like it or not, he loved the fiery-tempered Irish lass.

Chapter Six

If a day had passed since her mother's death when she hadn't thought of marriage and family, Bridget couldn't remember it. That wasn't so strange, really, considering that caring for home and hearth had become her duty at the tender age of eleven. Bridget had never minded the sometimes arduous tasks that were part and parcel of a mother's obligations, for they were balanced by the satisfied feeling that came with knowing her hard work made her father and siblings' lives a bit more bearable, a mite easier, a little happier.

If they'd noticed the chapped hands and brittle fingernails that were the result of many hours of scrubbing on their behalf, they'd never spoken of it. And if they'd realized the anxiety she'd sometimes suffered while trying to figure out how to make a meal for seven from two or three potatoes, they hadn't said so. If they'd seen how much time went into each reading and arithmetic lesson, it hadn't shown on the surface.

But Bridget knew in her heart, even at a young age, that they understood, each in his or her own unique way—not by speaking aloud their appreciation of her willingness to cook and clean, launder and mend, counsel and teach, but by showering her with sweet kisses, frequent hugs, and—despite their difficult living conditions—contented smiles.

Not long before she died, Maire had gotten up in the middle of the night to feed Aileen, and Bridget had tiptoed to the hearth to sit on the floor at her feet. "Don't ye get sick to death of always doin' for the lot of us?" she'd whispered. Blinking a tear from her eye, Maire had pressed her palm to Bridget's cheek. "Oh, darlin' girl," she'd sighed, "I don't mind a bit." And, wrapping a tendril of her daughter's coppery hair around her finger, she'd leaned back in the rocker and closed her eyes.

Maire had sat that way for so long, Bridget had thought she'd fallen asleep. She'd been about to head back to bed when her mother's dark eyes had opened, and she'd said, "Since the dawn of man, the good Lord has given great power and many riches to the kings of the world." Winking, she'd held a forefinger in the air. "But He's saved a special place in His heart for mothers, and the proof is, He gave them *more*."

Laughing softly, she'd added, "Mothers have the power to make the world a mite better for their children. The more we're willin' to do, the better a place it is." She'd lovingly stroked the baby's head, then caressed Bridget's cheek. "And seein' yer babes sleepin' sound and deep and unafraid, simply because they know you're near? Well, y'just can't get any richer than that."

Many times, as she'd been drifting into an exhausted slumber, Bridget had acknowledged that performing her mother's duties gave her a sip of the power and richness Maire had spoken of that dark, quiet night. Yet she'd sensed what she was feeling only hinted at the warmth that might be hers when caring for a husband and children of her very own. To have the affection her siblings gave in return for her efforts *and* love such as her da showered on her mother would be the answer to heartfelt prayers!

While crossing the Atlantic all those years ago, Bridget had asked God to send her a husband like her father who'd give her a dozen young'uns. Life in the New World wouldn't be nearly so frightening, and the work wouldn't seem nearly as hard, if she had a good, God-fearing man to share her most private thoughts with....

Whether the Almighty hadn't heard her constant pleas or had chosen to ignore them, Bridget couldn't say. The Bible made it perfectly clear that a woman's desire for home and her family were precisely what He wanted of her. So, she could assume only one of two things: In God's eyes, she had not yet earned the right to that kind of joy; or, He hadn't yet revealed to her the man with whom she'd share it.

She had chosen to believe the latter. Better that than to grow bitter, to question the Lord for not instantly giving her what she'd asked for. And so Bridget had made a conscious decision to lay her dreams at the foot of the cross and wait patiently while the Lord searched the earth for her perfect mate. Putting it out of her mind had made it easier to live without her dream, but hearing what should have been a private conversation between Drewry and Chase had reopened the wound.

And what a wound it was! All her life, she'd started and ended every day with prayer. Ever since she could remember, she'd silently shared what little she had with those less fortunate. She did not curse or partake of alcohol, like her da and his cronies at the pub, nor did she use tobacco products, like the Widow Keane. Pastor O'Toole had often said, "Yer body is God's temple, and y'have a duty to treat it well."

She avoided temptation as best she could, and she believed in God's Word. She might not be the most perfect human on earth, but she wasn't the worst, either. So why, then, was He asking her to be content with raising *another woman's* children?

It came to her in a flash as bright as any lightning bolt: Perhaps she wasn't the worst sinner He'd seen, but she was a sinner, nonetheless. Her sin? Envy! And Bridget did envy what Drewry had—a loving spouse, children who adored her, a baby on the way, and more than enough to feed them all in their beautiful, safe haven of a home....

It was a lot to consider, so Bridget slipped off to the spot where she always went to think. She'd found it during her first weeks at Magnolia Grange. Chase had suggested she walk the grounds to familiarize herself with the place, and she'd discovered the stream on the property's north border. The rough rustle of water, rushing over the black rock dam, had calmed her hungry heart and soothed her lonesome soul, for there, beneath a canopy of pine boughs, it looked like Ireland.

She'd had a spot in Donegal, too, where she would go when life weighed heavily on her young shoulders. She called it Beyond the Glade. Amid water that cascaded over gnarled tree roots, where ferns and moss grew thick, deep shadows led to a quaint little bridge. And there, Bridget could search her soul.

Oh, how she missed her homeland! To Bridget, Ireland was a land of endless fascination, filled with nooks and crannies where abundant rains created a lushness and seclusion shrouding every glen and bog and hillside that hid from the larger world. Bridget had long believed one must visit each spot to discover Ireland's sweetest secrets. *Those willing to step off the road to discover, to learn,* she'd often thought, *will realize the awakening of all five senses.* Yes, only the curious would see and hear, smell and touch, and, with every step and glance, be rewarded for their willingness to investigate...beyond the glade.

Here in this place that was so much like her home, Bridget thought of Suisan being courted by the froggy-eyed Searlass, and she smiled wanly. He wasn't the most beautiful boy in the country, but at least he was Irish!

That thought led to another: Lance.

Matilda's wise words echoed in her mind: "*It's just as wrong to judge that fine young fella on account o' him bein' born of English stock.*"

Bridget squirmed uneasily on her seat of gray boulder and nervously adjusted the folds of her dress. She hadn't appreciated being judged by the Brits in her homeland. Was she any better than the Conynghams of the world for doing the same to Lance?

Still an' all, it's a mite different wi' him, since he's of the same stock that....

Guilt tugged at her heart, making it impossible to enjoy the breeze or the sunshine. A nail keg floating in the foam caught her eye. In no time, she was mesmerized by the way it rolled and tumbled, tumbled and rolled in the churning waters at the foot of the dam.

She felt a bit like that small barrel of shiny, wet wood, whirling round and round through life, wishing for the safety of the shore yet helpless to reach it because of the water's powerful pull.

Bridget didn't know how long the vulnerable bit of wood somersaulted in the suds before surrendering, but she watched with amazement as it gave one last struggle to stay topside, then slipped out of sight forever.

Leaning against the bark of the giant oak behind her, she closed her eyes and took a deep breath of sultry summer air. The first picture to dance in her memory was Lance, and in spite of herself, Bridget smiled.

Sometime during his youth, he'd developed the habit of running one hand or the other through his mop of sandy-blond hair. His thick, manly fingers looked nothing like the teeth of a comb, and perhaps, she mused, that was why the shining waves never seemed to cooperate.

There was nothing delicate about Lance York! His face was all sharp angles and hard planes, from his well-defined brow to his patrician nose. She guessed his height to be nearly six feet, and he'd likely tip the scales at close to two hundred American pounds of solid muscle.

Several times, while pretending to watch Sally and Sam practice their letters and numbers at the terrace table, she'd instead watched Lance flexing his muscles as he balanced bulging sacks of feed on his broad shoulders. Once, when the rough-hewn wagon accidentally lurched forward and rolled onto Simon's boot, she saw Lance lift it—sacks of wheat and oats and all—to free the foot trapped by the giant wooden wheel.

In the months she'd known Lance, Bridget had learned to judge his moods by reading his face. If that well-arched left eyebrow was high on his forehead, it was safe to tease and joke. But if the muscles in that broad jaw were working....

Bridget had seen him angry on only one occasion, but it had been a momentous one, indeed. She'd gone to the barn to fetch a few handfuls of hay to soak up the drops of oil she'd spilled while filling lanterns on the mud porch. There, she'd found Lance on his hands and knees, sleeves rolled to the elbows, helping a frightened, squealing mare birth her foal. So engrossed in the job was he that Lance had never noticed her standing there, her chin in her arms atop the stall gate. If a gaggle of field hands' children hadn't raced through, yelling as they chased a runaway piglet, he might never have seen her at all.

The noisy disturbance had terrified the mare such that she'd nearly kicked down the stall wall. "She's gone breech, and that's bad enough!" Lance had bellowed, silencing the giggling girls and boys. "She doesn't need to contend with the lot of you, roughhousing where you don't belong in the first place!"

"But—," one boy had started, "we were just—"

He'd pointed blood-slicked fingers toward the double barn doors. "She needs peace and quiet, not your excuses, son. Now out of here, all of you, before I take a strap and blister your behinds but good!"

The two youngest girls had fled, sobbing, as the older ones were blinking back tears. But they obeyed. "What about the piggy?" one dark-haired boy had asked Bridget as he'd slunk past her toward safety.

Placing one hand on his shoulder, she'd ushered him out the door. "It's likely already asleep in the hay," she'd whispered. "When it wakes, it'll find its way back to its ma, so don't you worry." Then she'd closed the door, effectively shutting Lance away from the rambunctious youngsters.

Outside, she'd hidden her anger while consoling the blubbering girls. They hadn't intended to frighten the mare, hadn't meant to rile the stableman, either. Hadn't he understood that? Why had he been so impatient?

In Bridget's mind, there was but one answer: *That English, he doesn't like children.*

Two nights before, she'd awakened from a delightful dream and, smiling like a giddy schoolgirl, remembered that in it, she'd been married to the handsome Englishman. How pleased and proud he'd been as she'd nursed their babe! How happy and content he'd seemed, calling her his wife! *Well,* she thought now, *that's why the wise ones call dreams the 'will-o'-the-wisp.' They're deceiving and misleading.*

It had been a major disappointment to see him as he really was that day in the barn, and as she watched the leathery liquid slosh by, Bridget stared hard, searching for the keg, hoping that, perhaps, it had found one last surge of strength—just enough to bring it back to the surface.

But it hadn't, and she sighed. She had no business thinking romantic thoughts about the man. She had Sally and Sam to watch over and no time for such silliness, anyway. The keg was gone, and she had to stop hoping it would reappear.

Just as she had to stop hoping for a future with Lance.

❀

Sequestered in the privacy of his room above the barn, Lance sat on the edge of his cot, staring through the small window that overlooked the yard, and went over and over it in his mind: Drewry telling Chase they'd soon add another child to the Auburn family...Chase erupting with joy and delight...Bridget pressing close to his chest as she listened, then darting away tearfully without as much as a backward glance or any apparent rhyme or reason.

Soon after meeting her, Lance had determined that keeping his distance from the pretty Irish lass would be the smartest course of action for both their sakes. He'd been right. And something told him that, having witnessed that private moment between Chase and Drewry, she knew it, too.

So all this talk of keeping his past a secret had been unnecessary. The first chance he got, Lance would apologize to his cousin, and to Drewry, too, for asking them to take part in his deceptive plot.

He stretched out on the bed, crossing his booted feet at the ankles, and linked his fingers atop his chest. *You've been living the lies for so long, you're beginning to believe them yourself*, was his dismal thought. Perhaps he was insane, like his mother, and lying was but one of the symptoms....

Ever since he'd first witnessed his mother's dementia, Lance had fretted that, sooner or later, the signs of mental illness would show up in his own behavior. If he had a penny for every time he'd awakened with a start with that very fear beating hard in his heart, or had drifted off to sleep with it nagging at his brain...well, he'd have a pocketful of coins, to be sure.

Sadly, work did little to distract him from the troubling thoughts. And prayer hadn't worked, either. He had but two diversions from his greatest concern: time spent with Bridget and moments with little Sam.

Lance laced his fingers behind his head and stared at the knotholes in the pine board ceiling. A smile flickered across his face as he remembered the first time the boy had visited him in the barn.

"Why do you have to put shoes on the horses?" Sam had asked.

And Lance, holding a stallion's foreleg between his knees, had gently massaged hoof salve into the coronet rim. "Horseshoes protect the hooves from grit and stones."

"But their feet seem hard as stones!"

Chuckling, Lance had continued rubbing in the bay leaf oil. "Looks can be deceiving, Sam. The hooves seem hard as rocks, but they're surprisingly delicate. If we don't take care to protect them, and keep the hooves clean and moist, the horses can get laminitis."

"Lami—la...what's that?" the boy had asked, frowning.

"It's a disease," he'd begun, pointing to the tip of the horse's pedal bone. "If laminitis sets in, this will collapse, forcing the animal to walk on the back part of the hoof, here, which will make him bleed. Then, infection sets in, and, in no time, a horse can die of it."

Sam's young face had wrinkled with deep thought. Nodding, he'd said, "You know a lot about horses, don't you, Cousin Lance?"

"Oh, I know enough to get by, I suppose."

"That's not what Papa says. He says you're an expert, and that, thanks to you, we're going to raise a whole passel of the best quarter horses Virginia ever saw!"

Chuckling, Lance had said, "We'll do our best to make that happen."

"We?" echoed Sam. "You mean I can help? I love horses. Been riding since I was three!"

"Is that so?"

"Yep. And I can almost get a saddle up on my own...if I stand on the gate." Frowning, he'd added, "Not quite strong enough yet, but I'm workin' on it." Puffing out his chest, Sam had added, "Every morning, I fill two buckets with water, and I lift 'em up and down twenty-five times!"

"That'll build solid muscle," Lance had assured him.

"So I can help?

"I don't see why not...provided you get permission from your pa, first."

"Oh, he'll say yes. I just know he will." Then, "You think I'll get paid for helping, like Claib and Simon and Bridget and...?"

Lance hadn't heard a word after *Bridget*. And even now, the mere thought of her was enough to start his heart beating twice as fast as normal. Shaking his head, he forced his mind back to that day with Sam, when he'd told the boy that not every man was cut out to work with horses.

"They're smarter than most folks give them credit for, and they can tell if a person has their best interests at heart...or not. And there are lots of dirty, thankless jobs to be done if a horse is to stay healthy. It's a hard job, Sam...."

And Sam had smiled up at him to say, "Papa says hard work will make a good man of me." His eyes had widened. "Maybe if I work hard *and* get good and dirty, it'll make a *great* man of me!"

Even now, Lance was tempted to laugh out loud at the boy's comment, just as he'd laughed that day. "Or a smelly man," he'd said. "Work smart and hard, though, or you'll end up with muscles in your head, as well as in your arms."

"A muscle-head. Ha! You'll see, I'll work hard!"

True to his word, the boy had roused himself with the chickens the next morning and had ambled into the barn munching a cheese sandwich—one he'd proudly announced he'd made all by himself. In the months since,

Lance had grown quite fond of Sam as they'd worked side by side in the stables, in the barn, at the corral. If he could have a son of his own, he'd want him to be just like Sam.

Frowning into the growing darkness, Lance shook his head, for he'd never have a son of his own, thanks to his mother. What if her defective nature could be passed down through the family bloodline, like hair color or body structure? Surely, her addictive personality was a hereditary trait. How else was he to explain his own weakness for gambling?

He'd left home years ago, determined to make a go of it on his own, determined to prove to himself that a simple life was healthier, both physically and mentally. And so, Lance had taken nothing with him but a change of clothes and the saddle for his horse. Working odd jobs had provided him with food and lodging and lessons that had helped him find more work on the road. In Nashville, he'd learned carpentry. In Philadelphia, a sampling of the millwright's trade. But it was in Denver that he'd discovered he had a way with horses. If he couldn't be a preacher, why pretend to be holy at all? He'd spent every coin pressed into his hands by employers from New York to Montana on one of two things: drinking beer or playing cards in the local saloons. And, more often than not, on both.

The beer he could live without. But the cards? Ah, how he loved the feel of a deck in his hands, the aroma of a new pack wafting into his nostrils. It hadn't taken long to discover he had a knack for poker, too. At least, some of the time. If God had decided not to smile upon him, Lance thought, maybe Lady Luck would.

Then, on a train bound for Chicago, he'd run into a sad-eyed ex-soldier who had admitted that gambling had made him do things that had nearly destroyed him—and those he loved. Something deep in Lance's soul had listened closely to the man, and, before stepping from that car, he'd vowed never to allow his love of gambling to take hold of him the way cards and whiskey had gotten ahold of him.

He'd planned only a short visit to his cousin's plantation—a place where he could hide out from the outlaws he'd double-crossed in Chicago. But when Chase had engaged him in a conversation about horses and found out how much Lance knew about them, he'd asked his cousin to stay and help him build his stables.

Lance hadn't expected to stay long—just long enough to get Chase started. But then he'd met Sam. Right from the start, his three-foot shadow had gone everywhere with him—copying his every move, repeating his every word—and he'd found himself feeling responsible for the vulnerable boy. He'd determined to set a good example, and in the process, Lance had begun to respect himself again.

He couldn't love the boy more if he had been his own. And that would have to be enough. He had no right to enjoy the things other men took for granted. The most he could hope for was that Lady Luck would convince God to forgive him for his many sins. And until he'd earned that forgiveness, Lance would work hard. He owed that much to Chase for providing a sanctuary, for sharing his home...and his son.

He'd never forget the man he'd been, of course, but someday, hopefully, he'd forgive himself for the things he'd done. Until then, his heart would ache, because he loved Bridget...and couldn't have her.

"Samuel George Auburn, you get back here right this instant!" Sally scolded her younger brother.

As if she hadn't spoken at all, the boy continued crawling farther out on the stone wall leading to the dam. His big sister stamped one black-booted foot on the loamy stream bank and wagged a finger at him. "Bridget is going to be very angry when she finds out you're up here again. How many times has she told us, 'Never, *never* go near the dam!'?"

A hot breeze blew a lock of sandy brown hair over Sam's hazel eyes. On his hands and knees, he shook his head to move it and stared at his sister. "She said it ten thousand million times," he hollered. Grinning mischievously, he added, "But she won't find out if you don't tell her."

With her hands on her hips, Sally scowled. "If you aren't standing here beside me by the time I count to ten," she warned him, "I'm going to the house to find her."

"But Sally, I'm almost there. I've never made it this far before." He used his chin as a pointer. "There's a box turtle over there...."

"Boys," Sally muttered, looking up at the bright blue sky. "You already have more turtles than you can count," she said. "Now get back here, or I'm telling Bridget. I mean it, you silly goose!"

"I'm *not* a silly goose," he countered, rising to his knees, "and I can count my turtles. I have seven of them." Standing up, he punched the air with one small fist. "So *there*!" he bellowed, nearly losing his balance.

As his arms windmilled, Sally covered her face with her hands. Peeking between her fingers, she said, "Sam, I'm counting...."

Steady on his feet for a moment, Sam pursed his lips in a thin line. "Go ahead and count, smarty-pants. And stop treating me like a baby. I'm eight years old, and—"

"You're seven," she corrected him, her chin high as she crossed her arms over her chest. "And I'm treating you like a baby because you're acting like one. Here I go: one, two, three—"

"I'll be eight in just three months," Sam sneered, bending at the waist. "And anyway, you can't tell me what to do. You're my sister, not my mother. So go ahead. Count. Tattle if you want to, because before you get back here with Bridget, I'll be halfway to the house with another turtle for my collection!"

"You're a spoiled, bratty little boy," Sally fumed. "Just see if I sneak you any dessert when *this* gets you sent to your room!"

The scolding strains of Sally's voice were joined by the sound of water rushing and wind whispering in the trees. An eagle screeched overhead as a robin chirped in the branches of a scrub pine, and the distant sounds of the plantation's cattle lowing completed nature's harmonious song.

"Just see if I'll sneak you any dessert," Sam echoed her in a mocking tone. Then, thrusting his thumbs in his ears, he wiggled his fingers on either side of his head.

Maybe if he hadn't stuck out his tongue, maybe if he hadn't wiggled the top half of his body, maybe if he hadn't thrust out his chin in stubborn defiance...he'd have maintained his precarious balance on the slick stones.

Chapter Seven

In less than a week, Matilda would celebrate her sixty-seventh birthday, and Bridget was determined to make it a day she would never forget. One by one, she'd invited every household servant and field hand for miles around to the grand celebration that would take place in Chase's apple orchard the following Saturday. There was but one employee left to inform....

Weeks earlier, she'd heard Sam ask Lance why every one of his shirts was blue. "Never really gave it much thought," he'd said, tousling the boy's hair. "Guess I buy 'em blue 'cause that's my favorite color." And so, knowing she'd be speaking to him about the party at some point during the day, Bridget had put on a blue gingham housedress that morning. She'd polished her boots, too—telling herself it was only because they needed it—and woven a blue satin ribbon through the thick braid that hung halfway down her back.

The tall clock in the hall gonged twelve times, announcing the noon hour. The children had already completed their morning lesson, and she'd given them permission to take a brief walk before lunch and their afternoon session. So, for the moment, with nothing better to do, she decided to let Lance know it was nearly time for the midday meal.

She'd done her best to put thoughts of a life with him out of her mind, but that didn't mean they couldn't enjoy cordial conversations from time to time. Despite her stay-a-distance mind-set, she was looking forward to seeing him. Humming as she stepped lightly down the flagstone path from the house to the barn, Bridget unconsciously patted her hair, smoothed her apron, and tidied the bow at the back of her waist. "Say, English," she called, one hand on the open door, "you in there?"

"Depends who wants to know," came the rich-timbred voice.

"As if ye didn't recognize the brogue the moment I opened my mouth," she teased from the threshold. In the millisecond that ticked by after she'd said it, Bridget realized that the hardy summer breeze had loosened her braid, for her hair now poured over her shoulders. She blinked in stunned silence at her silhouette on the hay-strewn floorboards. Sunshine shimmering through her thick tresses gave the illusion that she wore a gauzy veil, and its light cast a shadow figure. Her flat, black twin was a bride!

Lance, who'd been squatting to inspect an old filly's shoe, stood up. "What on earth is so fascinating about that floor?" he asked around the piece of straw between his teeth.

Her hands over her thundering heart, Bridget licked her lips and forced herself to take a faltering step forward. She couldn't very well tell him what had struck her temporarily dumb, but she wouldn't lie, either. "I've come to invite you to a party," she said, avoiding his question altogether, "and to tell you that lunch is nearly ready."

He sauntered out from the stall, then latched its gate and, leaning an elbow atop it, moved the hay stick to the other side of his mouth. His stance was elegantly masculine, angled with one booted foot crossed over the other. If he was aware he'd stirred something in her, Lance didn't show it.

"A party, eh? What's the occasion?"

Above them, the wide door of the loft stood open. Warm, golden light poured in through the opening, spilling down the ladder and puddling at his feet, bringing with it a gentle breeze that riffled his hair. Lance put it back in place by driving a leather-gloved hand through the sandy-blond waves.

She'd never understood why the word *beautiful* seemed reserved for women alone, for there were many men whose physical appearances earned them the right to be described by the word. *Lance is such a man*, she thought, smiling.

Fondness beamed from eyes as gray as a rainy sky. From his smile, too. He straightened, distributing his weight equally on both feet, and regarded her for a moment. Then, with the same gloved hand that had tidied his hair, he gripped the tip of the hay he'd been chewing. One well-arched eyebrow rose as he said, "Cat got your tongue?"

Ye're actin' a fool, Bridget McKenna. Get ahold of yourself, afore he thinks ye're daft! "Must be the heat," she said, fanning herself with her hand. "It's unbearable out there in the yard...."

"So come inside, then."

She moved slowly closer. "Ye may have heard that our Matilda will have a birthday soon."

He nodded. "Three score and seven years ago," he said, grinning. "I can only hope to be half as spry when I'm her age. If I live that long."

"She's been talkin' about retiring, packing up her things and moving to North Carolina to live with her sister. I thought perhaps, if we show her how much we love her, how much we appreciate her, she might change her mind." Bridget was rambling and knew it, but she felt powerless to stanch the steady flow of words. "Because if she is...going to retire, that is...we may never get another chance to tell her how we feel. So it's now or never, the way I see it."

Stop runnin' yer yap! she scolded herself. *Ye sound like one of the chickens in the henhouse, cluckin' nonstop about nothin' in particular.*

The light in his eyes softened, and so did his smile. He stood looking at her for a silent moment, then said, "You have a heart as big as your head, Bridget McKenna."

Thoughtlessly, she ran a hand through her hair, as if checking the size of her head, and snagged her fingers on an earbob. It clattered to the floor, rolled, and disappeared under a mound of hay. "Goodness gracious, sakes alive," she complained, getting down on her knees. "Drewry gave me these for helpin' out on her weddin' day. She'll think me an ungrateful clod if I've gone and lost one already!"

Lance joined her on the floor, and together, they crawled around, picking through the straw and squinting with concentration. A moment later, oblivious to the whereabouts of each other, they bumped heads. Lance sat back on his heels, rubbing his forehead.

"Sorry," Bridget said. "Did that hurt you as much as it hurt me?"

"That's some hard skull you've got there."

Mirroring his kneeling posture, she fingered the already-swelling bump on her own forehead. "Listen to the beach, pointing out a grain of sand!" Giggling, she added, "Feels like I've taken a hammer to me skull!"

"Better a hard head than a hard heart, I suppose," he countered, grabbing the earring. Walking on his knees, he approached her and attempted to thread it through the tiny hole in her earlobe. After a few clumsy tries, he laughed. "Maybe you should just stick it in your pocket for now."

He held out his hand, and when she reached out to retrieve the earring, their eyes fused in an invisible thread of longing. Lance dropped the earring into her upturned palm, touching her fingers. Eddies of breathtaking surprise pulsed from her fingertips to her heart to her brain. Still nose to nose with Bridget, he wrapped his hand around hers, the supple brown leather of his glove smooth as butter against her skin. She didn't know what possessed her to do it, but she reached up to stroke his cheek.

"Don't," he rasped, grabbing her wrist.

She inclined her head in honest confusion as he opened his mouth—probably to explain, she figured. But no sound escaped. She watched him intently, her gaze traveling from the glint of his snow-white teeth to the glitter of his gray eyes. She'd noticed their color before, but until now, she hadn't realized how much Lance's eyes resembled her father's—not just in hue, but in other ways, as well.

Ah, but you're beautiful inside and out, and it shows there in your eyes, she thought as she reached up, anyway, and grazed his cheek with her knuckles. She heard his sharp intake of air, saw the pupils in his pale eyes constrict, and felt the warmth as he squeezed her hand a bit more tightly. *Lord in heaven,* she prayed silently, *he may well be an Englishman, but I love him all the same. Show me a sign if You're in agreement that he's the one You've chosen for me.*

While waiting for God's response, Bridget counted her heartbeats. *One, two, three....* Surely, Lance could have counted them, too, considering how loud they sounded. *Four, five, six*, she continued, noticing the russet streaks in his hair, the blue flecks in his eyes. *Seven, eight, nine* went her heart as her gaze followed the contours of his lips.

A picture of him teaching Sam to cinch a saddle flashed in her mind. Then, she remembered the time he'd climbed to the top of the big oak to rescue Sally's kitten. She'd seen him place a box of creamy chocolates he'd bought in town on the porch, then listened to him pretend he had no idea who'd put it there when Matilda had tittered, "Who done brung my favorite candies?" He'd looked truly pained the night she'd told him what the English had done to her people, making her admit he'd been justified in losing his temper when the field hands' children had frightened the foaling mare. *Ten*, she counted, then pressed her lips to his.

His powerful arms had wrapped around her by the time she'd reached *eleven*, and before she could even think *twelve*, Bridget knew that God had, at long last, given His answer. *Thank You, Lord,* she prayed happily. *Thank You!* How could she have expected every ounce of joy in her heart to register in that kiss?

When Lance pulled away, her disappointment was quelled when he cupped her face in one hand and looked deep into her eyes. His voice was thick and hoarse with emotion when he said, "You deserve better, much better than the likes of me."

"How 'bout you let me be the judge of that?" she said softly. "Besides, there *is* no better than the likes of you."

"What am I to do with a woman as stubborn and single-minded as you?"

She'd put her faith in God, and He'd rewarded her. Blessed delight filled her heart, for her world—a world so long upside-down—had finally righted itself. With the Lord on her side, what could go wrong? Bridget tilted her head and said, "You can do that again, for starters."

The corners of Lance's eyes crinkled with amusement. "Do what again?"

Slowly, deliberately, she bracketed his face with her hands and pulled him nearer. "I'll give you three guesses, English, an' the first two won't count."

A deep chuckle rumbled in his chest. "God help me," he said huskily. "You're irresistible."

But if he felt that way, why had the light in his eyes dimmed? Why had his smile faded?

"God help *you*," he said, holding her at arm's length.

She pressed a finger to his lips. "You talk too much, English." And before he had a chance to verbalize whatever had caused his sudden shift in mood, she kissed him again. For now, at least, she'd bask in the warmth of his embrace, trusting that God would take care of the rest.

Their fervor died at the sound of a quick, urgent cry. "Bridget!" Sally wailed. "Bridget, come quick!"

Though Lance and Bridget had already scrambled to their feet, Lance refused to turn her loose. Hand in hand, they ran into the yard, where the teary-eyed girl was jumping up and down, flapping her hands as she sobbed uncontrollably.

Bridget wriggled free of his grasp and pulled the child into a hug. "Sally, m'darlin', what's wrong?"

"It's Sam," she wailed. "He fell...."

Lance slapped both palms against his skull. "No," he whispered, "not Sam. Please, God, not Sam...." He grasped the girl's shoulders, gave a gentle shake, and forced her to make eye contact. "Where is he, Sally? Where did Sam fall?"

She pointed north, toward the stream. "He wanted a turtle," she hiccupped, "on the other side of the water."

Panic seized Bridget's heart, momentarily choking off her words. But she stiffened her resolve and took the child's hand. "Show us, Sally. Take us to Sam."

She turned to Lance, but he'd darted into the barn and was already heading back to them, a coil of thick rope over one shoulder.

"Did you follow the path?" he asked, lifting Sally up as he ran full steam ahead.

Nodding, she wrapped her arms around him.

"How long ago? When did he fall?"

"Just...just a minute ago."

Then he faced Bridget. "The spillway," he said. "Not a moment to lose. You get Claib and Simon. Tell 'em to harness the horses to the buckboard. We may need it to get Sam into town. Then meet me down there. The boy will no doubt want you near when I pull him out." With that, he was gone, his long legs churning, his free arm pumping to speed him along.

It seemed to take hours for Bridget to hunt up Claib—whom she'd sent in search of Simon—and finally join Lance at the stream. As she ran, all she could think of was that pitiful keg, tossing and turning in the churning water. If Sam had fallen there....

Finally, the dam came into view. Lance had already tied one end of the rope to the trunk of a sturdy tree, the other around his waist, and he was heading downstream, picking his way along the slippery bank.

It seemed like some invisible force had brought time to a halt, and the scene unfolded with excruciating slowness. There was Sam, struggling to stay above water in the bubbling, burbling foam beneath the dam. No sooner would one small hand reach up and rake through the waves than the other would splash out of sight. Coughing and sputtering, he tried to keep his chin and nose in the air; each breath threatened to be his last.

"He's a strong swimmer," Bridget said to comfort Sally. *But why can't he break free*, she wondered, *and get to the calm waters beyond the dam?*

Chest-deep in the water now, Lance tested the rope with a strong tug. "Lots of suction just under the surface!" he shouted. "It won't let him break free!"

Peering through the fingers covering her eyes, Bridget thought again of the keg. "Oh, sweet Jesus," she prayed aloud, "don't let Sam end up like that."

"Sam!" Sally shrieked. "Sam, I'm sorry!"

Bridget knelt beside her, pulling her close. "Don't fret, m'darlin'. Lance is nearly with him, see? He'll pull Sam out, bring him back safe and sound. You'll see."

No sooner had she spoken than Sam's struggle ended. He was floating, arms akimbo, and, like the keg, he began rolling in the foaming water. Instinct would have forced him to inhale and exhale—if he were conscious. If he stayed there much longer....

It was too horrible a thought to complete. Lance would save him. He *had* to save him!

Each time Sam's little face appeared, Bridget's heart lurched, for though his eyes were shut tight, the rest of him had gone as limp as a rag doll. Clutching Sally nearer still, she prayed, *Dear God in heaven, keep watch over him until English gets ahold of him.*

As if to punctuate the prayer, Lance slogged closer, closer, and now she prayed there would be enough rope. He reached out, stretching as far as he could, and clawed aimlessly at the water. Then, a miracle: his fingers closed around the dark, ballooning fabric of Sam's blue shirt. The strain was evident on his handsome face as he fought to keep the boy afloat—and to stay above the water's surface himself. With a great, guttural groan, he clamped his teeth together and yanked.

Sam, on his back now, looked for all the world like a child asleep. His slack limbs bobbled a bit, and it seemed that Lance—despite his efforts, despite the fact that he'd taken hold of the boy—would not be able to break the water's hold.

Mercifully, Sam's body slowly lifted and, buoyed by Lance's muscular arm, rode the choppy water toward safety. When at last Sam was near enough, Lance wrapped his arm around the boy and held him tight, then turned and swam to shore, paddling with only one arm.

Bridget saw him struggling and searched for a way to help. Spying a long, gnarled limb nearby, she hefted it up and ran toward the bank. Flopping onto her stomach, she wrapped her legs around a tree trunk and extended the limb. "Grab on, English!" she hollered. "I'll steady you till you can climb ashore."

In his eyes, she read fear mingled with gratitude as he attempted to take hold of the stick. They read pure relief when he snagged it. "That's the way," she said through clenched teeth, "I've got you. I've got you, English!"

Gradually, he worked his way nearer, nearer, then crawled up the bank. He laid Sam gently on his side, then got right to work pumping water from the boy's lungs.

"What's going on here?" came Chase's worried voice.

"We done park the wagon at the top of the hill," Claib announced, "jus' like Mister Lance say." Kneeling beside the stableman, he covered the child with a blanket. "Mo' blankets and pillows in the wagon," he said as Sam began coughing and sputtering.

A spray of water sprang from his mouth. He took a huge gulp of air, sat up, and emitted a frail, pathetic wail. "Sorry, Bridget," he cried. "I know I wasn't supposed to—"

At the sound of the boy's voice, Lance bowed his head. "Thank God. Praise the Lord."

"Amen to that!" Chase agreed, lifting the boy into his arms. "What were you thinking, young man?" he scolded his son gently. Hugging him fiercely, he kissed his cheeks, forehead, and chin. "Haven't we all told you dozens of times to stay away from that wall?"

"Yes, Papa," Sam said, nodding weakly. "Sorry...."

"Well, never mind that now," Chase said, tightening the blanket around his boy. "Let's head into town so the doctor can have a look at you."

Sam's back straightened at the mention of the doctor, and there was renewed strength in his voice when he said, "I don't need a doctor, Papa. I'm fine." Fresh tears welled in his eyes. "I won't go onto the wall again, I promise!"

But Chase walked purposefully toward the wagon. "I'm sure you are fine, son, but we're going to have you checked out, just to be sure."

Claib and Simon followed Chase up the gentle incline, and Lance moved to join them. Bridget, however, sat where she'd been when Sam first came out of the water. *'Tis your fault*, she thought, biting a knuckle, *'cause you know he can be a rambunctious young'un. 'Twas your duty to keep a watchful eye on him, and what were you doin', instead? Smoochin' like a lovesick fool in the barn, that's what!*

She hung her head, cheeks flaming with shame, and thanked God that the boy was safe. She said a quick prayer that there would be no aftereffects, even as the memory of his helpless little body floating in the foam flashed in her mind.

"Bridget?"

She looked up at Lance, then hid her face in her hands, too humiliated to look into his eyes. What must he think of her?

He knelt beside her, sliding an arm around her back. "I know what you're thinking," he said.

"So we'll add mind reading to the long list of your talents, then."

Chuckling, he brought her to her feet. "What happened wasn't your fault. The children have been playing near that stream since they learned to walk. I heard Chase say so, just the other day."

Her head down, she hugged herself. "Maybe so, but I should have been with him. 'Twas my responsibility."

Lifting her chin with a forefinger, he said, "I've heard you tell them—dozens of times—to stay away from that bank, from that wall. Heard their mother and father, and Claib and Simon and Matilda, say it, too. I believe all those noes made it all the more appealing, and he'd have gone down there no matter what." Now, he cupped her chin in his palm. "Thank God he didn't go alone, and Sally was there to fetch us."

"They're just young'uns," she said around a sob. "They need guidance and supervision. I shirked m'duties, English. Sugarcoat it all you like, that's the truth, and you know it as well as I do."

"He'll be right as rain in no time. I've seen this before, several times, in fact. You'll see...a nice, hot bath, some dry clothes, and a bowl of Matilda's chicken soup, and he'll be his mischievous self again."

But she could not be comforted. *Would not* be comforted. "How will I ever make it up to Mr. Auburn and

Drewry? And poor Sally. Why, she'll have nightmares over this for years!"

Lance pulled her to him, resting his chin atop her head. "All right, then, have it your way. We'll put every ounce of the blame on your shoulders." Holding her at arm's length, he gave her a gentle shake. "Maybe, after supper, Claib and Simon and I will build a gallows," he teased, "and at dawn, we'll put your neck in a noose and—"

Bridget jerked free from his embrace and turned away, shivering, though the day was hot and dry. "I *should* be hanged! It's a better end than I deserve."

A moment slipped by, and as she took a deep, shuddering breath, Lance ran a hand through his wet hair. She saw a bright red splotch on his palm and, taking the hand in hers, inspected it. "Ye're bleedin', English."

"It's nothing. Just a splinter from the hemp."

"We'd best get back so we can clean and dress this. So you can get out of those wet clothes." She lifted her skirts and, still holding his hand, headed for the house. "So I can take m'medicine, and pray Mr. Auburn won't send me packin'. Stop yer lollygaggin'," she said, frowning as she tried to hurry him on. "Just 'cause it's warm out doesn't mean you can't catch a chill. Besides, I want to see if Mr. Auburn will let me ride into town with them...."

"Right after he fires you, you mean," Lance said, chuckling.

"You pick some odd times to joke, English." She slowed her pace to add, "Can I trust you to show that hand to Matilda? Let her clean and dress it, good and proper? And change into dry clothes?"

"You can trust me," he said, meaning every word.

With a nod, she ran ahead, and he watched her climb into the wagon, sit down, and cuddle Sam in her lap. Her lips moved a mile a minute, no doubt begging Chase's forgiveness—and Sam's, and Drewry's, and God's. His hands in his pockets, Lance watched the wagon disappear over the rise, then sauntered toward the house, shaking his head and smiling sadly. He'd told her straight out that he didn't deserve her, and he'd meant it, too.

But deserving or not, he wanted her—more than anything he'd ever wanted in his life.

Chapter Eight

It seemed to Bridget a lifetime since they'd nearly lost Sam to the dam's hearty appetite, and yet the picture was so clear in her mind that the near tragedy might have happened mere moments ago. She'd thought about it all through the night, pacing the carpeted floor of her room. Battling tears, she had whispered heartfelt thanks to the Almighty for sparing the boy.

As the purple sky darkened to a gritty charcoal hue, Bridget wanted nothing more than to fling herself across the wide, downy mattress like a character in one of the Regency novels she'd read and sob herself into exhausted slumber. It wouldn't have been difficult to rustle up a hefty portion of self-pity, considering all that was on her mind.

For one thing, she still hadn't saved enough to pay her family's passage to America; for another, she hadn't heard from Suisan in months and had no way of knowing whether her father had recuperated from his violent cough. The doctor had said that the boy's scrapes and bruises would heal, as would his broken arm. But the pelvic injury could very well leave him with a permanent limp, and if it did, that would be her fault, too.

Yes, there was plenty in her life to cry about—if she were the type to allow herself to cry.

Tears, her father had taught her, were a sign of weakness, something no one could afford to give in to. "If ye're feelin' sorry for yerself," he'd say, "just look around and ye'll find someone in every direction far worse off than y'*think* y'are."

Now, huddled on the window seat with her knees hugged to her chest, Bridget watched as the morning sun peeked over the hilltops. At first, the fireball's bright, opalescent outline illuminated the earth in flaxen fragments. Then, like buttery fingers, its beams touched ground, gilding each blade of grass and field flower with amber light.

Mourning doves cooed from their perch on a needle-studded pine bough within arm's reach, their beady black eyes squinting as they lovingly entwined their feathery necks. In the pasture beyond, one of Chase's four prized quarter horses whinnied in harmony with the mooing cattle. The cool, early morning breeze fluttered over the casement, ruffling her hair, and Bridget closed her eyes to inhale the sweet aroma of roses that floated up on its whisper-soft current. In every way, it seemed a perfect, peaceful, late-summer morn.

But Bridget's heart did not rejoice in that peace. Her mind was far too full of yesterday's memories—Sam struggling in the water, Lance carrying his limp body to shore, her discussion with Drewry and Chase in the library late last night....

They'd been so kind. Few parents would have forgiven a sin as serious as hers. But if they thought she'd fallen for their forgiving pretense, the Auburns were sadly mistaken. She knew full well what had affected the friendly late-night chat. To put it plainly, Bridget believed the couple had set aside their own worries and concerns on behalf of hers. *It was only one mistake*, they must have thought. *No real harm done. Besides, she's done a good job till now; let's give the girl another chance.*

Resting her chin on her knees, Bridget folded her hands. "Dear Lord in heaven, I thank Ye for putting me in a place where I'm surrounded by proof of Your everlasting love. I know I deserved to be flogged good and hard for what nearly happened on my watch, yet I've been forgiven." She shook her head in amazement. *Forgiven!*

One silvery tear tracked down the curve of her cheek, and she immediately swiped it away. "I'm countin' on You, Lord, to guide my every step, my every word, so I'll be worthy of the faith and trust they've put in me, though I haven't earned it."

Just then, she heard Matilda open the kitchen windows below her room, and she listened to the unmistakable bump and clatter of breakfast being prepared. A glance at the mantle clock told her the children would sleep for another hour. At least, Sally would. *No telling how late Sam might stay abed, thanks to me.*

With a deep sigh, Bridget stood up and walked to the chiffonier, where she absentmindedly poked through the half-dozen outfits she'd sewn for herself since arriving at Magnolia Grange, and at the dresses Chase had insisted she buy in town once he'd made her the children's nanny. In no mood for the piped borders or covered buttons trimming even her plainest housedress, she chose a white shirt and a black skirt, hand-me-downs from Drewry—another kindness from another moment in time....

If it took until Sam and Sally were grown with children of their own, Bridget would continue proving her worth to the Auburns.

The tepid water in her washbasin did nothing to refresh her, but she splashed it on her face, anyway. Dressing quickly, she tied her hair in a topknot, then made up her bed. Hiking up her skirts, Bridget hurried down the stairs and headed straight for the kitchen. If work could temporarily distract her from her problems, as her mother had taught her, perhaps helping Matilda would deliver a moment of respite from the nagging guilt that refused to lift from her heart.

It was from this big, brick-floored room that Matilda controlled the goings-on of the entire house. The woman who had raised Chase was rewarded years ago, when her duties as nanny became too taxing for her overworked body, with the title of Household Manager. And she took her duties seriously. "May not be able to run after young'uns no more," she'd say when one of the hands questioned her authority, "but I can keep this place in good runnin' order!" And to prove it, she'd wave a wooden spoon.

In a drawer near the stove, she kept a little black book that listed supplies to be bought and chores that needed to be done; beside each item appeared the name of the Auburn employee assigned to perform that particular task.

When Bridget entered the kitchen, she found Matilda standing in the middle of her domain, her hands on her broad hips, shaking her head. An expression of pity crossed her face, but she blinked it away, proof to Bridget that the woman understood the beating her heart had taken.

Pointing at a bowl on the counter, she said, "I mixed up the dough, so you roll it flat and cut me some biscuits." Turning her back on the young nanny, she poked at the bubbling contents of the big kettle on the stove. "Ain't got time for chitchat this mawnin'," she said, "so don't y'all be distractin' me now, hear?"

Grateful to have a chore to occupy her hands, Bridget got right to work. With each pass of the rolling pin over the well-floured dough, the tool emitted a high-pitched squeal that reminded her too much of Sam's frantic cries as he'd struggled to stay afloat. Peeling potatoes did little to erase the sights and sounds from her memory, but at least chopping onions provided a reasonable explanation for the tears that stung her eyes.

If only she could eat here in the kitchen with Claib and Simon and Matilda, the way she had when scrubbing was her main duty. But as the children's governess, Bridget was expected to sit at the dining room table and help Drewry and Chase teach them proper etiquette.

It seemed that the meal took place in some surreal, underwater world, for the family's voices droned, and their movements slowed, reminding her of the way things looked and sounded during those playful occasions when she'd swim deep in the pond at Magnolia Grange to surprise the children by tickling their toes.

Just as he did every morning, Chase recited the list of things he hoped to accomplish before day's end. When he finished, he stood up beside Drewry. "Choose a level of the house where you'll be comfortable," he said, bending to kiss her cheek. "You know what the doctor said about climbing the stairs...."

It seemed to Bridget that, despite Drewry's warm smile, she looked much paler than usual. Was it a consequence of the pregnancy or concern over yesterday's near tragedy?

"I think I'll stay upstairs to keep Sam company," Drewry said, patting Chase's hand.

Bridget had planned to take the children on a long hike through the woods, where they'd collect tadpoles from the stream as part of their science project. When she'd outlined the idea for them yesterday, they'd squealed with excitement and enthusiasm about watching the tadpoles develop into frogs. But there'd be no hike today, and if the boy's injury didn't improve, there'd be none tomorrow, either.

When the seemingly endless meal finally concluded, Bridget mustered up her courage and climbed the stairs, carrying a silver tray laden with all of Sam's favorite breakfast foods. She'd toasted the bread and poached the eggs herself, exactly the way he liked them. As long as she'd known him, Sam had loved coffee with plenty of cream and sugar, though he'd been allowed to partake of it only on Christmas morning. He'd get a mug of it today, though!

When she entered the room, he was sitting up in bed, supported by pillows on either side. "Look, Bridget," he said, grinning, "I've made myself a fancy decoration."

"So, tell me," she said, making room on his lap for the tray, "how are you feeling this morning?"

"My arm hurts a little, but my shiner is a beauty, don't you think?"

She forced a smile. "Aye, that's some black eye you have there."

"Doc says if it doesn't hurt to stand, I can get out of bed tomorrow." Then he whispered behind a cupped hand, "I sneaked out this morning, and it doesn't hurt." In a louder voice, he continued, "So, do you think I can be up and about today?"

Relief flooded through her as she perched on the edge of his mattress. "I'll send Claib into town to fetch the doctor to take a look at you, and if he says it's all right, then yes, you can get up."

"Aw, why do we need that old doctor to tell us what I already know?" Sam whined. "I'm fine!"

"Just to be safe, let's let him be the judge of that."

"Sounds like a good idea to me," said a deep male voice from the doorway.

Bridget leaped to her feet, clutching at the top button of her blouse.

"Wow, Bridget," Sam said around a bite of egg, "I never knew you could jump so high." Giggling behind his fork, he added, "Or so fast."

Her gaze fused to Lance's as she spoke through clenched teeth. "'Tis amazin' what a body can do, Sam, when frightened out of its wits."

Lance crossed the space between them in three long strides. "Sorry," he said, looking sheepish. "Didn't mean to scare you. Again."

And before Bridget had a chance to point out that they'd had the very same conversation several times before, he rested both hands on the footboard of Sam's bed. "Speaking of scaring folks, you win the prize, young man. Your little swim worried us half to death!"

"Sorry," Sam said, echoing Lance's apology. "I didn't mean to."

"Now, now," Bridget soothed him, blotting yolk from the corner of the boy's mouth, "none of that. Just finish up your breakfast before everything is cold as ice."

"And before Matilda starts hollering that she wants her fancy tray back," Lance put in, winking. Then, facing her, he said, "Claib went into town early this morning, brought this back, and asked me to give it to you."

She inhaled sharply. "A letter? From Ireland?"

"Says 'Malinmore, County Donegal, Ireland.'"

Their fingers touched when she took the envelope from him, and she looked into his handsome face. She couldn't describe his expression, because she'd never seen one like it before. Lance stared with eyes that glittered like gray diamonds, the brows above them drawn together, his usually generous mouth a taut line. The muscles of his jaw flexed, relaxed, then flexed again, as did the fingers of his free hand. Oh, to be back in the comforting circle of his arms, warm and safe, as she'd been yesterday.

Yesterday.

A lifetime ago.

The unidentifiable look, Bridget believed, might have been disgust. With her. He adored Sam, after all, and she'd been the doddering idiot who'd shirked her duties and—

"Are you finished, Sam?" Lance asked.

His cheeks puffed with toast, the boy nodded.

"Feeling like a nap?" he asked when Sam yawned.

"Not sleepy," Sam said. "*Bored.*" He sat up straighter and grinned. "If I take a nap, though, *then* can I get out of bed?"

"We'll see," Bridget answered, stacking plates on his tray. Laying the letter alongside his breakfast plate, she lifted the tray and headed for the door. "Nice of you to pay the boy a visit," she said to Lance, "but don't stay too long. He needs his rest."

Even before she reached the stairs, she noticed the chill that had wrapped around her. She *had* felt safe and warm in Lance's arms. Safe and warm and, for the first time in her life, womanly.

If he'd ever entertained the notion of making her his own, surely he wouldn't want that now. Not after what she'd almost allowed to happen to his little friend. She moved down the stairs as if in a trance, clenching her teeth against the chill that descended when she realized that if Lance didn't want her, she may never feel warm—truly warm—ever again.

Matilda had already finished washing the dishes when Bridget returned to the kitchen. She could hear the older woman humming hymns as she puttered around in the dining room. Claib, she knew, would be in the barn, oiling the door's hinges, and Simon had one end of the wagon up on a hoist to repair its axel. In his library, Chase was likely poring over an agriculture or animal husbandry book, while Drewry snuggled with Sam, reading fairy tales. And Sally....

She found Sally alone on the back porch swing, staring blankly into the yard. *Seein' her brother helpless in the churning water, no doubt*, Bridget thought. *Such a heavy burden for shoulders so small.*

At the screen door, she clasped both hands under her chin and prayed the Lord would help her know how to comfort the girl.

"Hey, Bridget," Sally said as the nanny sat down beside her. "I'm glad you're here." Tears pooled in her eyes as she added, "I want to tell you I'm sorry that I didn't mind you. That I goaded Sam into an argument, even though you said not to. If I'd listened...."

Her voice trailed off as Bridget slid an arm across her shoulders. "Ah, darlin' Sally, ye're blamin' the wrong girl. 'Tis my fault we nearly lost our boy."

Rubbing her eyes, Sally said, "*Your* fault? But you told him hundreds of times not to go there, not to—"

"'Twas my job to be there, to be sure he didn't."

Sniffing, Sally opened her mouth to protest when Chase said, "Sally, will you do me a favor and see if Sam needs anything?" And in reaction to her puzzled expression, he said, "I'd like a word with Bridget...."

"Yes, Papa," Sally said, and disappeared inside.

Chase leaned against the white-painted porch rail and folded both arms across his chest. "I'll not have you blaming yourself, Bridget, for what happened yesterday." He held up a hand to silence her protests. "I've been watching you ever since we got back from the doctor's, and the guilt is written all over your face. You must stop it, you hear? Stop it now."

"But, sir," she began, hands clamped in her lap, "I—"

"What happened is *no one's* fault. You know, don't you, that Sam and Sally blame themselves?"

"Aye."

"And you know, don't you, that if you keep walking around here with that hangdog look on your face, they'll keep right on believing they're responsible for...." Chase licked his lips, unable to finish his sentence. "You don't want them carrying that around with them, do you?"

"Of course not, Mr. Auburn, sir, but—"

"Then take me at my word: there *is* no 'but.' Your energies will be far better spent trying to convince the children that what happened was nothing but a freak accident, nobody's fault, and that God, in His wisdom and mercy, sent Lance at exactly the right moment to... well, to make things right."

He'd said as much last night. And so had Drewry. Still.... "I can't tell y'how sorry I am," Bridget said, echoing the very words she'd said the night before. "If I could turn back the clock, if I could relive the day, I'd—"

"Bridget, we've been over this before."

"But I need to make you understand, sir, how awful I feel. M'own ma died when I was eleven, see, leavin' me to care for three brothers and three sisters. I mothered the lot of 'em long enough to know better than to leave a young'un alone in a place as tempting as the dam. There's no excuse good enough to explain why I shirked m'duties, but you have my word, it won't happen again."

He lifted his bearded chin and said, "Are you quite through, young lady?"

So this was it, then. He'd either fire her on the spot or insist that she allow some town girl to come to Magnolia Grange to help her with Sally and Sam. Bridget sighed and said, "Aye, I'm through." How could he sit there, calm as you please, and grin? "I've said all I can say in my own defense, Mr. Auburn, sir."

Exhaling an exasperated sigh, he lifted both arms in the air. "Well, thank the good Lord for *that*! Because if you'd just let me get a word in edgewise, I'd thank you."

"Thank me?" she gasped. "I'm single-handedly responsible for nearly drownin' yer only son! If he walks through life with a limp, well, that's on me, too. The fact that he's alive at all is all Lance's doin'. It's *Lance* you should be thankin', not me! Without his quick thinking...." She blinked and swallowed, then bit her lip, unable to utter the unspeakable truth.

"Is stubbornness a trait of the Irish, or is our Bridget the exception to the rule?" Chase asked, looking to the heavens. He met her eyes to say, "Unless the Almighty has seen fit to gift you with powers no other human possesses, you have no way of predicting the future."

"Doesn't take a fortune-teller to see the obvious."

"The real reason I wanted to speak with you alone, silly girl, is to share something with you about Drewry's condition." He raced through what the doctor had said—that she wasn't to lift anything or climb stairs; that she must stay off her feet as much as possible to avoid a miscarriage. "You'll have even more to do," he continued, "and once the new baby arrives, there will be three children to care for. So I want to offer you an incentive to stay on."

Bridget couldn't believe her ears. "Incentive? To stay...?" She shook her head. "I'm afraid I don't—"

"We know how much you love Sally and Sam, Bridget," he said gently. "It shows in everything you say to them, everything you do for them. But Drewry and I realize we're asking a lot of you, now that you've met someone. It's only natural you'd want to marry, start a family of your own. And we were afraid that with Sam's misbehavior—because we all know this isn't the first time he deliberately disobeyed you—you might just decide to take that step sooner rather than later. We're only too aware how stubborn and disobedient he can be, and—"

"Stubborn? Disobedient? Why, Sam's neither of those things. He's a dear lad. Curious and intelligent, is all, and that's why he needs close supervision. Don't y'see, Mr. Auburn, that's the reason—"

"There's a raise in pay for you if you decide to stay."

A raise. More responsibility. Had yesterday's trauma rendered the man daft?

"How does a dollar a day sound to you?"

"Sounds like madness, that's what," she admitted.

"I'll take that to mean you'll stay."

"'Course I'll stay!"

"Then you have work to do—convince those children that neither of them is to blame for yesterday's events." With that, he winked and then left her alone on the porch swing.

With more money each week, she'd be able to send for her family that much sooner. *There truly is a silver linin' in every storm cloud*, she thought. And, staring into the powdery blue sky, Bridget got to her feet and took a deep breath, praising God, thanking Jesus, and feeling grateful to Chase and Drewry.

"Ain't likely you'll see the shiny innards of a storm cloud any time soon. Not as long as Mr. Chase Auburn has anything to say about it!"

Chapter Nine

I thought this was your afternoon off." Lance didn't look up as he spoke but continued brushing the mare's coppery mane. "Figured you'd be in town, shopping for pretty dresses and trying on hats."

"I have no time or money for such silliness," Bridget said matter-of-factly. "Besides, I prefer to make m'own dresses. I'm here as a favor for Matilda." She held out a napkin-covered tray. "Seems the poor woman's worried her favorite hired hand will starve to death since he skipped breakfast. Again."

"I have no time for such silliness," he teased, smirking as he patted the horse's flank. "This girl delivered twins this morning." Nodding, he invited Bridget to see for herself.

She placed the tray on a nearby hay bale and peered over the wall. "Goodness gracious, sakes alive," she whispered, smiling. "They're just beautiful, Lance, simply beautiful!"

"What have we here?" he asked, peeking under the red-and-white checked napkin.

"Fried chicken, biscuits, and a slice of apple pie," she said, standing on tiptoe to better see the twin foals. "Could...could I pet them, do you think?"

He'd just bitten into a crispy drumstick but quickly laid it aside. And with a grand sweep of his arm, he ushered her into the next stall, where she bent at the waist and gently stroked each foal's head. "Ye're a beauty," she cooed, "though ye're barely born. Imagine what a few months will do for you!" Glancing up at Lance, she asked, "Have y'named 'em yet?"

He shook his head. "Any suggestions?"

She ruffled their manes. "Guess I'd need to know if they're boys or girls before I—"

"Not 'boys and girls,'" he corrected her, wincing. "Males and females. And, as it so happens, Willard here was blessed with one of each."

Both eyebrows rose on her forehead. "Willard? But that's a—a male name!"

Chuckling, he nodded. "I guess the person who named her didn't bother to ask, 'Boy or girl?'" He dug out a sugar cube from his pocket and held it under Willard's nose. "There you go," he crooned as she nibbled from his palm, "and there's more where that came from, since you're the first."

"The first what?" Bridget asked.

Wiping his now-damp palm on the seat of his trousers, Lance said, "The first to produce offspring from Chase's breeding stock. These twins are the first in a long line of quality quarter horses."

"Where's their da?" she asked, stepping from the stall.

"In the corral." Lance broke off a bit of biscuit and popped it into his mouth. "Willard here had me worried for a while, 'cause she didn't think too highly of their daddy at first."

"Why," she said, grinning and helping herself to a biscuit, "is he English?"

"Actually," he said, smiling, "I think he's Irish. Very high-strung and stubborn."

Bridget looked through the open doors at the stallion high-stepping out in the corral. "Just look at him," she said, "nose in the air, strutting around like he owns the place. I say he's English. No wonder Willard was wary of him at first."

Lance swallowed the lemonade Matilda had poured into a canning jar and wiped his lips with the back of his hand. "I said she didn't think highly of him. Never said she was wary."

Frowning, she faced him. "Perhaps you'll be so kind as to explain, o master of horse sense, what the difference is?"

Using a drumstick as a pointer, he said, "Horses aren't like people, Bridget. They're not attracted to one another by a fetching face or an attractive form. They seem to know, instinctively, which mate will protect their lineage. Father material and husband material are two very different things. Sometimes, the more arrogant the male, the better sire he'll be."

"So, what you're saying is, male arrogance is appealing to female horses?"

Shrugging, Lance nodded. "To her, that's the proof he's confident and strong, and she knows the best of these things will appear in her offspring."

"Then it's safe to say there are fundamental differences between humans an' horses...."

"Um...."

"Because *human* females, y'see, find arrogant males anything *but* appealing." She slid his pie plate onto the hay bale and picked up the now-empty tray. "Not that I'm the last word on the subject, mind you...."

Holding the remnants of a chicken leg in one hand, half a biscuit in the other, he stared in stunned silence as she walked away. Then, laughing softly, Lance shook his head and ate the last bite of his bread. She was something else, that Bridget McKenna. She'd never been afraid to speak her mind; she never backed away from a challenge. If a job needed doing, she got it done, whether it was hers to do or not. And it didn't hurt that she was mighty easy on the eyes, either.

Speaking of eyes, the only creatures he could name with larger eyes were the deer in the fields. The last time they'd kissed, he'd noticed that she hadn't closed her eyes, but he hadn't pointed it out, because, knowing Bridget, she'd have said, "How would you know, unless yer own eyes were open, too?"

She met the world head-on, like a miniature prize-fighter, crouched and fisted for battle, eyes blazing with drive and determination. Simon had once said she could tame a wildcat if she had a mind to and have it purrin' like a kitten in no time. Of all of her traits, Lance admired her courage most of all, though lately, life had taken the starch out of her. He blamed Sam's accident for that. Maybe, in time, she'd believe what everyone kept telling her—that it hadn't been her fault.

When she'd delivered his lunch moments ago, she'd seemed more like her old self. She'd held his gaze and matched him quip for quip, even managing to get in the last word. It had done his heart good to see a glimmer of her old fire glowing in her eyes. *If bickering with me will pull her from the doldrums, I'm happy to oblige*, he thought, grinning.

"What's goin' on in that head of yours?" Simon asked, clomping into the barn with a sack of grain on one shoulder. "You look like the cat what swallowed the canary," he added, grunting as he dropped his load to the floor.

"Never much going on in here," Lance said, tapping his temple.

Laughing, Simon rested on a bale of hay. "Got it bad for her, eh?"

Lance's smile faded. "Got it bad for whom?"

"As if you didn't know." The elderly black man shook his head. "You can just wipe that innocent look off your face, boy, 'cause it ain't foolin' no one. Least of all, me."

"I can't even recall the last time anyone used the word 'innocent' to describe me," he said.

"And you can't change the subject on me that easy, either."

Lance went back to chucking hay into Willard's stall. "How I feel is beside the point, Simon. Bridget, she...well, we're not what you'd call a love match."

Simon ran a hand over his nappy head. "Well, now, don't you just beat all? I see the way you look at each other, 'specially when you think nobody's lookin'. If that ain't a love match, what is?"

Lance considered explaining how Bridget was Irish, he English, and how that made a relationship between them difficult, if not impossible.

"I seen you kissin' Bridget, son, and the way that li'l gal kissed you, right? Shoo-eeee."

The men went back and forth for a few minutes, with Simon underscoring his belief that Bridget loved Lance, and that he loved her right back...with Lance pointing out the futility of it all, considering how she felt about the English. After a while, Lance tired of the debate and said, "All right, Simon, you asked for it...but don't say I didn't warn you."

The words tumbled from him as river waters rush over the falls: his mother's mental condition, the illegal activities of his father and brother, his own past of gambling and drinking, and why he'd walked away from his studies at the seminary. He concluded with, "Surely, now you can see that she deserves better than me."

"All I see is a hardheaded young'un who's about to throw away the best thing ever walked into his life."

"But Simon—"

"But nothin'! Had me the same conversation with Bridget not two days ago. I do declare," he said, shaking his head, "you young folks sure can try an old man's patience. There she be, yonder in the house, thinkin' she ain't good enough for the likes of you, and here you is in the barn, thinkin' the selfsame thing." He sighed. "Leaves a body to wonder if y'all is both dumb as fence posts, or stubborn as mules, or both." On his feet, Simon aimed a bony finger at Lance. "Open your eyes, boy, and see that the good Lawd put a blessed gift right under your nose!"

"What do you mean, she thinks she isn't good enough for me?"

"Oh, she went on and on, some nonsense or t'other about how she ain't fit to be no child's mama, since she nearly let Sam drown at the dam. And since she can't give a man young'uns, seems no point in takin' a husband. And how Lance don't want children, anyways...."

"What? Where'd she get a crazy idea like that? I love kids!"

Simon shuffled toward the door, his hands in the air, as he said, "Weren't me pitched a fit out here in the barn, had all the young'uns bawlin' like sheep...." In the doorway, he faced Lance again. "I knowed all about your mama and your daddy, young fella. Knowed about that brother of yours, and all that nonsense 'bout you leavin' the seminary."

"But—how?"

Simon grinned. "I might be old, but these ol' ears work just fine, and I heard a thing or two, that's all you need to know. Heard...and don't care. Don't nobody care but *you*. I know Bridget, son, and she ain't gonna care, either. But I can't stand 'round here jabberin' with the likes of you all the livelong day. So, I'm gonna say just one more thing... that li'l gal loves you, and if you let her slip through your fingers, you'll regret it the rest of yo' days."

When he was gone, Lance tucked in one corner of his mouth and kicked some straw across the barn floor. Then, pocketing one hand, he paced up and down the aisle between the stalls, repeating Simon's parting words in his mind. What if he'd been right, and Bridget really did love him? And what if, even knowing the whole of his sordid past, she'd go right on loving him, anyway?

He couldn't know for sure, but Lance knew this: If he didn't at least try, he'd never forgive himself.

Though time and Bridget's constant care had long since healed Sam, the burden of the accident still weighed heavily on her mind. Try as she might, the echoes of a childhood event would not give her a moment's peace....

She'd been nine when Mrs. McPherson had left her boy in Bridget's care. "He's a handful, mine ye," the mother had warned her before heading for town, "so don't take yer eyes off him for a minute!"

Thinking to keep him occupied, Bridget took him to the river, sat him on the big rock overlooking the valley, and handed him a fishing pole. She'd been on her hands and knees digging for more earthworms that he could use as bait when he'd slipped from the rock and into the murky water below.

Though she'd leaped into the river and plucked him out, a wet and wailing boy had greeted his ma when she'd come back from the market. "Ye're not fit to have young'uns in yer care, Bridget McKenna. If there's a God in the heavens, He'll see y'never have another to look after!" Those angry words were what had made her such a fretful nag when her own ma had passed and she'd been put in charge of her siblings. Even now, though an ocean separated her from them, she felt duty bound to watch over them, to meet their every need. Whenever Suisan wrote that one of them needed shoes, or a coat, or warm gloves, Bridget would wrap up the money and send it east.

Trouble was, filling their needs this way, in addition to sending them three-quarters of her pay each month, kept the Atlantic passage fund from growing enough to buy seven one-way tickets. She couldn't remember the last time she'd purchased material to sew herself a shirt or a skirt; in fact, Bridget couldn't remember the last time she'd threaded a needle on her own behalf!

"Not that I'm complainin', mind you," she confessed to Matilda one wintry night when the rest of the family had retired. "It's just that I'm beginning to fear one of my oversewn seams will split or a hem will fall, right in the middle of town!"

The older woman's gradually dimming vision might have missed the murky shadow in the hall outside her kitchen, but her sharp ears picked up the sounds of footsteps. Narrowing one eye, she stared hard at the doorway, trying to determine which of the Magnolia Grange men it might be.

Too tall to be Sam, too flat-bellied to be Claib, too broad-shouldered to be Simon, she reasoned. *And why would Mr. Chase sneak about in his own house?*

It could be no one but Lance.

Matilda had answered to no one but Chase himself in all her years on the plantation. Like his father before him, Chase had given her complete control over the house and its staff. Long before the War Between the States, she'd had the freedom to speak her mind anywhere on Auburn soil and had earned the ears of her employers. She'd been doing it so long now, it came as second nature.

Well, honeychil', she thought, grinning to herself, *you is gonna get an earful out there in the hall to make your eavesdroppin' worth the while*! "Why don't you buy a new dress with the money Mr. Chase gives you ever' week?" she asked Bridget.

Bridget sighed. "Because I send most of it home—for rent and food and peat for the fire. The rest I save so that, one day, I can pay for my family's passage to America."

"Mmm-hmm," the housekeeper said, raising her voice. "Jus' the other day, I heard Mr. Chase sayin' how easy Simon's days was gonna be once yo' brothers and sisters get here to help out."

"Goodness, Matilda," Bridget said, laughing, "why are you shouting? I'm sitting three feet from you!"

Matilda could see that her shadowman was shaking his head, and she snickered before saying, "You ought to ask Mr. Chase 'bout helpin' you bring yo' kinfolk over. Why, he'd probably be more than happy to pay their way, like he done yours."

"I could never ask that of him. He's already been so generous—far more generous than the likes of me deserves."

"Oh, now...you more than earn your pay, so what's this nonsense 'bout you not bein' deserving?"

"Mr. Auburn and Drewry treat me more like a family member than an employee, and that was never part of the bargain. So it seems only fair that I give 'em more than they pay for."

Sighing, Matilda said, "I can't for the life of me figure out why some handsome fella hasn't snapped you up, made you his wife." With a quick glance toward the door, she continued. "Seems a shame, is all, for all that motherly love God blessed you with to be spent on other folks' young'uns."

"You're a dear to say such things, Matilda, but the truth is, I'm not lookin' to marry. Not now, anyway. Maybe not ever. Wouldn't be fair."

"Oh, now you's just talkin' nonsense! Why ever not, when you is as beautiful on the inside as on the out?"

"Because I can't have children."

"Dear Lawd," Matilda said, leaning forward to grab Bridget's hand. "How long you known you's barren, girl?"

"Barren?" The word seemed to stick in Bridget's throat. "Why, I'm not—I'm not barren!" She cleared her throat and started again. "I'm perfectly healthy in every way, so I'm sure that if I tried, I could have as many children as I'd like. But—"

"Y'all is daffy, then. If you ain't barren, you could give yo' husband children."

"No, I can't, because I'd be an unfit mother."

Keeping a close eye on the shadow in the hallway, Matilda chuckled and slapped the table. "Why, as I live and breathe, I don't know when I ever heard such foolishness. You? Unfit?" She growled quietly. "Now girl, I's gonna trust you with somethin' nobody else knows. You can't pass it on, on account o' somebody's feelin's might just get hurt. But the truth is, you is the best mama them children ever had. I mean no disrespect to their dead mama, but, honeychil', you is a hundred times the mother she was. And Miss Drew? Well, she got herself a heart of gold, that one, but you outshine her, too!"

"She didn't let Sam nearly drown."

"You know well as I do that boy is as mule-headed as his daddy. The stories I could tell you about Mr. Chase when he was a boy...? Mmm-hmm, he could try the patience of all the saints in heaven, that one! Seemed ever' time I blinked, he was into one thing or 'nother. Once, whilst I was takin' a bath, he clumb all the way to the top of that big oak and got hisself stuck up there. Took half the hired hands, standing one atop the other, to get that boy down."

"You must have been terrified!" Bridget exclaimed.

"Only for a minute. The fear passed right quick, and ol' Matilda went from worry to fury. Took all the patience God give me to keep from hollerin' what I'd do when finally his feet hit the ground, 'cause I tole him and tole him never to go up there."

"How old was he?"

"Same age li'l Sam is now."

"Aww, so young...."

"'Spare the rod, spoil the chil'. The Lawd didn't write down those rules for His own good health, you know."

"I suppose...."

"Suppose, nothin'. If I'd a'whooped him, like I shoulda, he never would have gone back up there."

Bridget gasped.

"Yes'm, the very next day, there he was again, way at the tippy-top of that ol' tree. Broke his arm that time, fallin', and lay unconscious two whole days."

Another gasp.

"Nobody's fault but my own," Matilda said. "Yes'm, if I'd a'whooped him good...."

Now a sigh from Bridget, and then another.

"Darlin'," Matilda said, "don't you know what an impression you is makin' on those young ones? Why, Sally copies ever'thing you do, and li'l Sam never, *ever* done what he was tol' before you come along. If you can't see that, then you're as blind as poor ol' Tildy." She paused, then added, "I'm old, so it's natural that my eyesight is failin'. What's *your* excuse?"

"It's a lot to be thinkin' on, I'll give you that." Standing, Bridget said, "I'm headed upstairs to take one last peek at Sam and Sally before I turn in." She bent to kiss Matilda's cheek. "And you'd best be doin' the same!"

Lance flattened himself against the wall and held his breath, praying Bridget wouldn't see him in the shadows as she passed on her way to the staircase. He caught a whiff of lavender as she walked by, then counted each step as she climbed to the second floor. "You best be hittin' the hay yo' own self, Mr. Lance," Matilda said, startling him.

He hadn't moved, hadn't made a sound. Why, he'd scarcely breathed! How had she known he was there?

"Ol' Tildy been lookin' out the corner of her eye since afore you was born," she said, chuckling. "Gonna take more than anything the likes of you can think up to fool me. Now, git on up to bed, or do I have to take my wooden spoon to the seat of *yo'* pants?"

"No, ma'am," he said, grinning. "G'night, Matilda."

Lanced closed the front door quietly behind him and headed for his loft room. He'd go to bed, as she'd instructed him to, but it wasn't likely he'd get any sleep. Because he, too, had a lot to think about.

Chapter Ten

The moon glowed white in the black winter sky, sending a single shard of bright light through the tiny window above Lance's bed. A blustery wind whistled through the treetops, making them scrape their fingery branches against the barn walls with a sound like cats' claws.

He counted his heartbeats. Counted the ceiling boards. Counted the ticks of the carriage clock beside his cot. He recited the Lord's Prayer. The Twenty-third Psalm. The Preamble to the Constitution. But none of it could distract him from one inescapable thought.

He loved Bridget McKenna.

Lance spent a few hours plotting his future with her: They'd live in his family's mansion in New York, where nobody had lived for years. There, they'd raise three or four youngsters—more, God willing—and Bridget could grow roses of her very own, like the ones she'd long admired at Magnolia Grange. He'd start that import-export business he'd always dreamed about, and, together, they'd travel the world in search of amazing new things to entice his customers. They'd be so in love that the years would pass quickly, and before they knew it, they'd sit side by side in matching bentwood rockers and watch their grandchildren frolic in the yard....

Leave it to me to have daydreams at night, he thought. And, grabbing his jacket, he headed out to take a mind-clearing walk. His hands deep in his pockets and his chin on his chest, he reached the stream before he realized how far he'd traveled in his fuzzy-headed daze. It would be dawn in a few hours, and a long, hard day of work lay ahead. He knew he should try for a few hours of sleep.

As he headed for the barn, something caught his eye. It appeared to be a snowy dove, fluttering its wings on a stone bench in the garden. It must have been injured in some way, for why else would it be out here so late at night? Unable to ignore the creature's apparent suffering, he eased forward so as not to frighten it, hoping with each careful, cautious step that it would fly away, back to the safety of its nest. He didn't relish the idea of putting it out of its misery.

Upon closer inspection, he realized it wasn't a dove at all, but a letter, its pages fluttering in the breeze like the peace bird's wings. Lance picked it up, but only because the wintry gusts threatened to scatter it around the darkened yard. Glancing around, he collected all the pages, then headed for his room.

The moon outside had been bright, but not enough to allow him to read who had written the letter, or to whom. But in his room, by the glow of his wood stove, he saw Bridget's name on the envelope—it was printed in the same script as her name on the envelope he'd handed her in Sam's room the day after he'd nearly drowned. The crisp, clean script on the first page was smudged in a few places. Had it been the tears of the writer or the reader that had blurred the perfect, precise penmanship?

The better question was, why hadn't Bridget read it in the privacy of her room, where it was warm and dry, rather than on a cold, hard bench in the garden as the winter winds blew? He knew how she treasured any news from Ireland, so what could have happened to make her leave it behind?

Gently, he placed the letter on his pillow, then sat down on the cot to pull off his boots. Lighting the lantern on his bedside table, he lay back on his bunk. Three sheets of paper, each no more than five by seven inches, lay one on top of the other near the neatly penned envelope beside his head. From the corner of his eye, he saw the word "Bridgie," and he smiled softly at the affectionate nickname her sister used. Lying on his side, he fingered a corner of the top page, as he imagined she'd done.

Then, he sat up, and, telling himself it would help to know more about her, so he might find a way to help her regain at least some of her lost joy, he gathered the pages and began to read.

My dearest sister,

Please forgive me for not answering your last letter sooner. I know how you look forward to hearing from us back home because, as you've so often said, we might not have much, but at least we have one another. I feel guilty having neglected you so, Bridgie, for the least I can do is take a moment now and then to tell you how we're faring, thanks to your sacrifices and hard work.

It's good to hear that little Sam is finally better. It has always pained me to hear of anyone's suffering, but when it's a child...well, rest assured I have prayed for him.

Speaking of suffering, it seems I'm not the only one impatient to leave this place, Bridgie, to put memories of the famine and fever behind, once and for all. The last of the Sweeneys and the Boyles have crossed the Atlantic to settle in your New Jersey, while the Gallaghers and the Douhertys have chosen Pennsylvania. I don't expect a one of them will ever return. And why would they? They're free at last from a land traumatized by the British, whose horrible rule has left our beloved Ireland in near ruin. I know God expects us to forgive and forget, but it'll be a long, long time before the English will be forgiven, or what they've done will be forgotten.

As if there wasn't enough hatred of them here, now the animosity has crossed the sea and is taking root on American soil. I have a suspicion, Bridgie, that what they did to our people will haunt us for generations to come. Not only have they scraped this land bare of what grows, but they've cleared it of the people who lived off it, too.

Sorry, dear Bridget, to start out my letter by complaining so bitterly about these things that nag me. As always, you're the one I turn to when my soul aches to be honest. Oh, how I long for the time when we'll sit and talk face-to-face like in the old days! If I'd known how desperately I'd miss you, I'd have taken better care to appreciate you when you were with us.

But enough of my whining!

Da's cough is much improved, though his color is still pale and his eyes don't twinkle quite so brightly. To be honest, I can't say if it's the cough that derailed him or life in general. But at least he's sleeping better, and that's sure to put the apples back in his cheeks, eventually.

Our sisters are still working hard every day at their reading and writing. The boys don't have as much time for studying, but they're doing well, too. Won't it be blissful when, at the end of a day's work, they'll all have time for the things other young people take for granted, like watching the sunsets and the moonrises, and reading by lamplight, and falling asleep with full bellies?

Well, Bridgie girl, there's no point subjecting you to any more of my foul disposition. (By the time you read this, I'll be on top of the world again, so don't fret!) I'll end this letter with the list written by our own Irish Solomon....

If you be too wise,
much will be expected of you;
If you be too foolish,
you will be deceived;
If you be too conceited,
you will be thought vexatious;
If you be too humble,
you will be without honor;
If you be too silent,
you will not be regarded;
If you be too feeble,
you will be crushed.

It was good advice, Bridget, my dear, that Cormac gave to his warriors, and it's as useful today as it was centuries ago, isn't it? In any case, I intend to read it often and see how much a difference it will make in my life during the coming months.

Take care, sister dearest, and know that our thoughts and prayers are with you always.

Suisan

Lance lay there for a long, long time, one hand tucked under his head, the other pressing Suisan's letter to his forehead. Though he was descended from a long line of English blood, he'd been born on American soil, had grown up in a house built by American hands, and had been educated in American schools. Until he'd met Bridget, he hadn't felt much of a connection to the Brits who had come before him.

But he felt it now, in the form of guilt hammering hard in his heart.

His family had money, and plenty of it. But even if he added every cent of his father's ill-gotten wealth to the riches of every other Anglo-American, it wouldn't be enough to repay the Irish for the crimes committed against them.

If he chose to exercise it, Lance had some political pull, too. But not even the strength of Samson would have been powerful enough to undo the bonds tied around Ireland by British hands.

Lance was but one man, and Bridget one woman. Like the star-crossed lovers in the Shakespearean play, they were the unwilling victims of an ancient and deadly feud. Though generations of misunderstanding cost Romeo and Juliet their lives, at least the young couple had gone to their graves having known true, pure love.

Whether or not Bridget would ever admit loving him, given the constraints of their backgrounds, Lance would move heaven and earth to secure a happy future for her.

And he would begin at first light.

Christmas at Magnolia Grange had always been a festive occasion. This year, because they were celebrating both Christ's birth and Sam's full recovery, the season took on an even brighter glow.

From her makeshift bed on the parlor morning seat, Drewry happily instructed the field hands' children to gather holly and pine boughs from the woods, then taught them how to festoon every door and window with a bright green garland.

Matilda baked mountains of gingerbread men and sugar cookies, and Simon and Claib chopped down the tallest tree Bridget had ever seen within four walls. It towered over everything in the parlor, its pointed tip leaning a bit where it touched the ceiling. Sally and Sam strung cranberries on its short-needled branches, and Chase surprised them with a box of delicate hand-blown ornaments imported from Italy's Tuscany region.

A light snow began falling at twilight on Christmas Eve, and the children's delighted squeals could be heard from every corner of the mansion. While Simon readied the Christmas goose, Claib stoked the fire. Matilda's mincemeat pies were cooling in the pie safe as Drewry's delicate fingers picked out carols on the harpsichord.

Through it all, Bridget plastered a gay smile on her face and joined in the frivolity. To do anything else would disappoint the children. But deep in her heart, she hid the truth: Christmas was just one more holiday spent without her family.

No one here could be blamed for the fact that an ocean separated her from her loved ones, so she'd taken great care in wrapping her gifts. For Drewry, she'd embroidered fancy D's and crocheted a lacy border on three linen handkerchiefs. In one corner of Chase's hankies, which were larger than Drewry's and minus the pretty trim, she'd sewn big C's.

She hoped Matilda would like the rose water she'd been soaking for months in a carved glass bottle, and that Simon would enjoy the red suspenders she'd made for him. Of one reaction she could be certain: Claib's bunions would rest well in the soft, blue slippers she'd knitted. Only Sally and Sam would receive store-bought gifts—their own copies of the new McGuffey reader.

For Lance, she had a sweater she'd toiled over for months, squinting into the lamplight after everyone else had gone to sleep. To make it, she'd taken apart her favorite shawl, made from fine Aran wool. Bridget couldn't wait to see it on him, to find out if the ivory yarn set off his eyes the way she thought it would.

That night, the children went to bed without the usual fuss, knowing that by morning, Santa Claus would have visited them.

They burst into Bridget's room just after the rooster crowed, piling onto her bed and pulling at her covers. "Wake up, sleepyhead, it's Christmas!"

Rubbing sleep from her eyes, she yawned and stretched. "Merry Christmas, m'darlin's," she said, gathering them near. "Whilst I'm getting dressed, I want the two of you to get on some real clothes so you won't catch a chill when you go downstairs."

They scampered from her room, and she had to smile as Sam's door, then Sally's, slammed in the children's excitement.

Knowing they'd be up and about with the birds, Bridget had set out their clothes the night before. Had set out her own garment, too. Now, she was as anxious to wear it as the children were to open their presents. *Ye're a grown woman*, she scolded herself silently, *so act like it and exercise some restraint!* After splashing water on her face and blotting it dry, she slipped into the beautiful gown.

She'd never had occasion to wear this Drewry hand-me-down before, and she'd been looking forward to wearing it—not for practical reasons, such as seeing how much to take in or let out, but because she wanted to see how it would feel being draped in such finery.

The satin rustled as she pulled the gown over her head, and the skirts spilled to the floor like a shimmering green wave. Fastening the tiny pearl buttons, spaced no more than a quarter inch apart, took all the dexterity she could muster, and Bridget prayed for the patience to finish before the children returned.

Next, she pulled on a pair of white woolen stockings and stepped into soft, black slippers—another Drewry hand-me-down—and hoped she wouldn't trip while clumping around in shoes that were one size too big.

She was twisting her hair into a thick braid when Sally and Sam burst into her room. "We're ready," Sally announced, followed by Sam's hearty, "Let's go!"

"Hold up one second, young man," Bridget said, "and try to keep your voice down, or you'll wake the whole household." As she spoke, Bridget quickly wound a green satin ribbon, made from scraps she'd cut from the dress, into her braid. "We have to see if yer da and Drewry are up before we thunder down the stairs."

By some miracle, she was able to convince them to give her time to comb their hair, and, when she finished, Bridget took each of them by the hand. "Let's tiptoe down the back stairs and see if Matilda has any treats for us in the kitchen. Surely, everybody will be up by the time we've eaten them...."

"Do you suppose Tildy will surprise us like she did last year?"

"I'm sure of it," she said. And while Matilda kept the youngsters busy with tarts and other tasty treats, Bridget raced back upstairs to wake Chase and Drewry. "It's me," she said, lightly rapping her knuckles on their bedchamber door. "The children are ready and waiting...."

Silence.

"Sir? Ma'am? The wee ones are dressed and looking forward to you joining them in the parlor...."

More silence.

"Well, goodness gracious, sakes alive," she said under her breath. "The pair of 'em are like the livin' dead!" She gave it one more try, knocking harder this time. "Merry Christmas morning!" she said in a louder voice. "There's a couple of anxious young'uns wantin' to know what old Saint Nick brought 'em...."

Finally, the door opened a crack, and one of Chase's puffy eyes peeked through the crack. "Don't tell me they're up already," he said. "It's barely four in the morning!"

"Aye," she said, "up and dressed and rarin' to go."

"Give us fifteen minutes."

"Better make it ten, sir. Sam's already chompin' at the bit. Don't know if I have the strength to keep him from under the tree!"

"All right, then, ten minutes."

She started for the stairs when his gravelly voice stopped her. "And Bridget?"

"Sir...?"

"Thanks. You're an angel."

"Just doin' my job, sir."

"Balderdash. You're a blessing, on Christmas and every other morning of our lives."

Grinning, she headed back down to the kitchen. "Have y'finished yer breakfast, then?" she asked the children.

"Yes," Sam said, and the impatience all but steamed from under his collar. "*Now* may we go into the parlor?"

"Just a few minutes more, darlin'. Yer da and Drewry—"

"—are ready and waiting," Chase finished for her. "What's keeping the bunch of you?"

"How'd they get dressed so fast?" Bridget asked Matilda when they were out of earshot. "I only woke them a moment ago."

A sly grin lit her face as she said, "Don't ask me, honeychil'. I only works here."

When she rounded the corner to the parlor, Bridget saw that Simon had lit every candle on the tree. Everyone was there, dressed in his or her Sunday best and wearing a grin that matched Matilda's. Bridget didn't know what to make of it, but she went along as Chase handed out the gifts, making everyone ooh and aah over what was hidden beneath the tissue paper in every brightly wrapped package.

She hadn't known what to expect when Lance lifted the box top on his present. Certainly not the deep furrow that lined his brow or the tight set of his jaw. When he held up the sweater, his fingers trembled slightly, then he met her gaze and said, "You made this? For *me*?"

She answered with a nod.

"But—when did you have time?"

"Here and there," was her nonchalant response.

"It's—it's beautiful," he whispered. "And you made it yourself...?"

Another nod.

This time, when his eyes met hers, he smiled. "No one has ever done anything like this for me." Then, taking great care to replace the sweater in its box, he got up and crossed the room in three quick strides. "Thank you," he said, his hands on her shoulders. "You don't know how you've touched me."

Bridget licked her lips, suddenly aware that all eyes were on them, and prayed the candlelight would hide her blush. "I—I hope it fits," was all she could think to say.

He raised one eyebrow before tipping back his head to let loose a delightful peal of laughter. "So do I," he admitted, "but even if it doesn't, it's still the nicest present I've ever received."

Lance's amusement dimmed as his face loomed nearer to hers, and his eyes sparkled. "Thank you," he whispered into her hair. "Bridget, I lo—"

"Maybe you should try it on," she interrupted him, "to see if it needs some minor tweakin'."

Nodding, he smiled. "All right, but first, my gift to you."

The silence that had surrounded them died as folks darted this way and that, whispering and snickering under their breaths. Lance walked over to the gold draperies that separated the parlor from the dining room and parted them with one quick *whoosh*.

And there in the doorway stood her father, and, behind him, Caitlin, Aileen, Sean, Cormac, Eamon, and dear, dear Suisan. Was she hallucinating? She got to her feet, rubbed her eyes, and looked again.

"Oh, Bridgie," Liam said, "ye've become a woman in the years gone by. Yer ma would've swelled with pride to see such a vision standin' here."

Try as she might, she could not move or speak. A rush of heat climbed to her ears as her feet thudded slowly forward. As she approached her family, she noticed that every Auburn and all of their staff were standing in a line, grinning like a pack of hyenas. And at the back of the line was Lance, wearing the sweater she'd made him, with a satisfied smile on his face.

She understood in a flash who'd made this all possible. She didn't know how, but it was clear from the expressions on every face—her family included—that this was his gift to her. She didn't know whom to hug first!

The next several days passed in a flurry of activity as Bridget and her kin got reacquainted. By the first of the year, her father and siblings were all settled in cozy cottages behind the mansion, each with a job to do.

Lance refused to explain how he'd managed to bring them all to Magnolia Grange or how he'd kept their arrival a secret until Christmas morning. All he'd say every time she'd ask was, "I wanted this Christmas to be your best ever."

And it had been.

If she hadn't loved him before, Bridget certainly would have fallen hard after seeing all the trouble he'd gone to in bringing the McKenna clan to Magnolia Grange. It had been so exciting, in fact, that it didn't dawn on her until a day or two had passed that it hadn't been just a lot of work—it had been expensive, too.

"Honey, that boy have mo' money than Mr. Chase," Matilda had said when Bridget asked where he would have gotten the funds. "Way I hear tell, his mama—Mr. Chase's sister—married a fella whose pappy owned half of England. An' that daddy of his doubled his inheritance long before Mr. Lance was a twinkle in the man's eye. Now, what you say to that, li'l Miss Bridget?"

Lance was Chase's cousin? And how could he have been wealthy and never given a hint of it? She'd heard of the Yorks. Who in America hadn't? How could he be next in line to inherit the York fortune and not have gloated about it? Bridget couldn't wrap her mind around the idea, because Lance was too soft-spoken, too kind-hearted, too *good* to have come from rich British stock!

"'Member what I tol' you 'bout not judgin' others?" said Matilda. "Now ain't you glad you loved him before you found out?"

"Who says I love him?" Bridget countered, grinning.

"*You* says, with them eyes an' that smile, that's who."

Blushing, she pressed her palms to her cheeks. "Is it really that obvious?"

"Only to folks who can see the two of you lookin' at each other."

"Everyone knows?"

"Everyone."

"And Lance? Am I so transparent that he knows, too?"

"If he don't, then he be blind as a bat!"

Bridget nodded as the room filled with Matilda's laughter.

"He has truly humbled me. I never realized...."

"How powerful love can be?"

"Yes. But how...how will I ever repay him?"

"What a thing to say, girl! He don't expect you to pay him back. He done what he done out of love!"

"I suppose you're right. He's only too aware that I have no money...."

"Weren't no dollar signs in that boy's eyes when he looked at you, Bridget McKenna. You got plenty to give him. He know it, I know it, an' it's high time *you* knew it."

"All I have is my love, Matilda. Is that—is it really enough, after all he's done for me?"

"Honey chil'," the woman said, grabbing her hands, "love is *all* they is. At the end of yo' life, it ain't gonna matter how many jewels is sparklin' on yo' fingers, or how big yo' house is, or how fancy yo' couch is when company comes callin'. All that's gonna matter is how you been loved, and how you loved back."

There was wisdom and truth in Matilda's simple words, and Bridget knew it. "But I don't know how to tell him."

"Sho' you do, darlin', sho' you do."

Bridget got to her feet. "You're absolutely right. And I'm going upstairs right now to pray on it." She punctuated her comment with a noisy kiss to the woman's cheek, then marched resolutely from the room. While she was at it, she'd pray about something that had come to her in the wee hours of the morning: a way to make Lance as happy as he'd made her.

"...And though I'm well aware there's a bit of bad blood between your people and mine, I think we can get beyond it, if we try."

Liam leaned one elbow on the stall's gate and nodded somberly. His brow was furrowed with deep lines that proved he was giving Lance's speech a great deal of careful thought. "I appreciate that y'chose to talk with me before discussin' the matter with m'girl," he said, combing fingertips through his thick, gray beard. "It tells me you respect yer elders, that you'll respect m'Bridget, too."

"I'm no shirker, sir," Lance continued. "I have a sizeable savings, and you can be sure Bridget will never want for anything. Nor will any member of her family."

"Aye, I can already see that."

"I only hope you can find it in your heart to forgive me for what the English did to your people. Breaks my heart to know what my kin—"

"Stop right there, boy," Liam interrupted him. "You've got nothin' to be sorry for. 'Tweren't none of your doin'."

Lance breathed a sigh of relief. "I'm happy to hear you say that, because grudges sometimes get passed down with the family heirlooms. Hate is a powerful emotion, and—"

"Not near as powerful as love. In all you've said, I've yet to hear you say you love my daughter. I'll not give my blessing till I hear the words." He dropped a hand on Lance's shoulder. "You have any idea how long a lifetime is, boy? Ye'll be standin' at God's altar, promisin' to live out the rest of yer days with one woman. If love doesn't bind you, the pair of you will be miserable and wishin' for the end to come before it's natural."

Lance sensed Liam had more to say, and so he held his tongue.

"But if you're in love, you can face any calamity. Two hearts united are stronger than one, any day."

"I love her with all my heart," Lance said, meaning every word.

"Enough to last a lifetime?"

"Two, if she can put up with me that long."

"And y'say yer drinkin' and gamblin' is behind you?"

"On my honor, sir."

"Then if she'll have you, you've got my blessin'."

Lance shook his hand heartily. "Thank you, sir. Thank you. I'll be the best husband I know how to be. Better, even."

When he withdrew his hand, a silver band winked up from his palm. “Sir?”

“Fine father I’d be if I didn’t give a proper dowry for my girl. ’Tain’t much, but it’s genuine. ’Twas her ma’s, and I’d like you to be the man who slips it on her finger.”

Lance couldn’t speak past the lump in his throat; he didn’t even try. And Liam, who sensed the younger man’s plight, laughed heartily. “May God’s grace and a flock of angels be with you when you pop the question, ’cause I rather like the idea of havin’ you for a son-in-law.”

Epilogue

September 21, 1893
New York City

With his hands clasped at the small of his back, Lance surveyed the gardens where he'd played as a boy, smiling as his grandson chased a raggedy mutt named Target across the lawn and his granddaughter rode the wind on a rope swing he'd hung just for her.

His wife slipped up behind him and wrapped her arms around his waist. "What are you lookin' at, m'darlin'?"

In the years they'd been together, she'd lost most of her Irish brogue, but every now and then, it slipped out. Lance cherished every musical note. "Just counting my blessings," he said, turning to take her in his arms.

She stood on tiptoe to kiss his chin. "Your mother says to tell you lunch is ready, and that she's made your favorite."

"Baked ham and sweet potatoes?"

Bridget nodded. "And corn muffins, too."

Having his mother back, the way she'd been when he was a boy, had been the *second* greatest blessing she'd given him.

It had taken months, but, working quietly behind the scenes, with the help of the McKennas, Drewry, and Chase, Bridget had arranged to have his mother released from the institution in upstate New York. The loving care and warm weather she'd experienced at Magnolia Grange had agreed with her, and within weeks, Diana was once again her old self. And she'd been with them for years now.

In the course of their marriage, Bridget had not only given Lance all of his family back, but she'd also given him six healthy children of his own—three of whom were now married with children of their own.

He studied the still-beautiful face so near his own, the face he'd been waking up to see for more than a quarter of a century now, and cradled it in his palms. "Why have the hands of time painted my temples gray and lined my skin with creases, yet left your lovely face untouched?"

"Oh, they've touched me," she said, winking. "It's just my good fortune to be short, while you're tall. Hard to see my wrinkles from way up there. That, and gravity is on my side, tugging my creases to the back of my head each time I look up at you."

Lance bundled her close and kissed her forehead. "You've always been able to make me laugh." Holding her at arm's length, he said, "Do you know what a joy you are in my life?"

In place of an answer, Bridget kissed him, then rested her head on his chest.

Liam had long since met his Maker, but those wise words he'd spoken that day in Chase's barn still echoed in Lance's head. Two hearts united really *were* stronger than one alone. "You'll be a beauty till your dying day," he said.

"So say the eyes of love," she teased, tweaking his cheek. "God knew what He was doin', making our eyes fail just a bit with each passing year, didn't He?"

Lance was not teasing when he said, "I see as clearly today as I did the day I first saw you on the staircase with your arms full of sewing supplies, and the second time, when you'd been comforting that Sheffield fellow after his girl rejected his proposal."

"Ah, but Joy came to her senses a year later. Remember what a pretty bride she was?"

"Not as pretty as you…."

"Wonder what made her say no in the first place," Bridget said.

"Will you think I'm an insensitive lout if I admit that I don't give a fig?"

Laughing, Bridget kissed him again. "How is it you remember what I was carrying that day?"

"I remember everything, from the color of the thread on the spools to the way your sparkling blue eyes set my heart to hammering and the way your long, coppery braid made the blood pound in my ears."

"Flatterer…."

"And those lips of yours, all perky and pouty, why—"

"Lance York," she said, shushing him.

He kissed her long and hard, and when Bridget came up for air, she said, "What's come over you? What if the children see—"

"Let them," he interrupted her, "so they'll know what lasting love looks like!"

She looked into his eyes for a long, silent moment, then said, "I struck a bargain with God the day I arrived in America. I was too young and foolish to know I shouldn't…."

He quirked an eyebrow. "You never told me that before."

"Nevertheless, it's true. I promised Him that if He'd bless me with a love like my parents shared, I'd spend the rest of my days doting on the man He chose for me."

He pressed his lips to hers, then whispered, "Then I'd have to say you kept your end of the bargain, Bridget McKenna York."

Kate Ties the Knot

Chapter One

1855
Currituck, North Carolina

The huge, hollering Irishman had been hot on the boy's heels for half a mile. Eight-year-old Adam Flynn raced into his mother's shop for protection, nearly overturning a dressmaker's dummy as he rounded the corner.

"What's gotten into you?" she demanded. "Haven't I taught you better than to—"

"There y'are, ye thievin' li'l brat!"

The burly, bearded man who filled the doorway reminded Adam of Jack's giant, his fists clenched at his sides, his feet planted shoulder-width apart. The boy had heard stories about J.J. O'Keefe, among them that he'd literally fought for the money to erect his shipbuilding warehouse. Adam sidled closer to his mother.

"Hand over me lunch," O'Keefe growled, extending a meaty palm, "before I hand *ye* over to the constable."

His mother stood with a protective arm around her son's shoulders. "I don't know who you think you are, barging in here and frightening my boy," she huffed, "but I won't tolerate such behavior in my shop."

He matched her angry gaze. "Who I am, ma'am, is John Joseph O'Keefe." His expression and voice softened slightly as he added, "I apologize for stampeding in here like—"

"Like a raging bull?" she interrupted him.

O'Keefe grinned sheepishly. "Well, I wouldn't have put it quite that strongly, but that'll do, I guess."

For a moment, the adults merely stood there, face-to-face, with arms crossed and chins lifted in stubborn determination, as Adam stared gap-jawed, wondering who would break the silence first.

"I know who you are," she said. "You may well have every man in town intimidated, but you don't frighten me!"

When a corner of O'Keefe's mustached mouth lifted, Adam relaxed. But, all too soon, O'Keefe turned his gaze on the boy. "Y'ought to be ashamed of yerself, hidin' behind yer ma's skirts. Are y'a coward, as well as a thief?"

"How dare you! My boy never stole a thing in his life!"

O'Keefe kept his eyes on Adam as he lifted his bearded chin and raised an eyebrow. "Then, maybe ye'd care to explain what he's got tucked under his arm, there," came the gravelly retort. "'Tisn't a fat, red hen," he said, pointing. "I can tell ye that."

She followed his gaze to the lunch pail under Adam's arm. "What?—Where?—Adam! Where did you get this?" she demanded, taking it from him.

He looked from his mother's shocked face to O'Keefe's strangely calm one and back again. Placing a hand on her forearm, Adam said, "I—I didn't know it were his, Ma."

O'Keefe expelled a puff of air, reminding the boy of a fire-breathing dragon. "I feel sorry for yer poor ma," he fumed, "havin' a thief and a coward *and* a liar for a son." His gray eyes narrowed. "Ye know as well as I that ye stole me lunch today, just as ye stole it yesterday and the day before. I saw ye with me own two eyes. Practice behavin' like a man, why don't ye, and own up to yer dirty deed."

Adam had never been afraid for his life before, but he had been plenty scared moments ago, when O'Keefe's big, booted feet had thundered close and hard behind him. But he was safe now, in the shelter of his mother's arms, and he knew it. He aimed a cocksure smirk at the man, fully prepared to continue professing his innocence. What choice did he have? If he pleaded guilty, his ma would punish him by adding chores to his already too-long list.

From the corner of his eye, he noticed his mother staring at him with a sideways, suspicious sort of look. Was she angry? Sad? Hurt? He truly couldn't tell. But, fortunately for him, his ma wasn't one to dwell on a person's shortcomings—especially her only son's. *Especially* if teary eyes and a quivering lip accompanied his apology. Adam held his breath and began working on what he would say.

"Well, don't just stand there, snifflin' like a girl, lad. Fess up!"

The production of tears was forgotten as Adam stiffened his back. "I'm *not* a girl!" he protested, grabbing the lunch pail from his mother. "Here, take your stupid old lunch, if it means that much to you!" Without getting too far from his mother's side, he thrust the container into O'Keefe's hands. "It's probably full of worms, anyway."

His mother pressed a palm to each blushing cheek and closed her eyes. And Adam rolled his. One fleeting second passed before she looked at him.

"Oh, Adam," she said softly, her voice trembling a bit. "What have you done?"

He'd have given anything not to have put that pained, disappointed look on her face. If O'Keefe hadn't been standing there, frowning and shaking his head, Adam might have wrapped his arms around her, admitted how much he loved her, and told her how sorry he was to have caused her pain.

But the big man had called him a girl. And Bobby Banks and the other boys who'd been with him when he'd run off with the lunch were hovering near the door. They'd heard everything....

Standing taller, Adam shrugged and made a face to tell them that a dented, old lunch pail wasn't worth this fuss and bother.

His mother folded her hands at her waist and faced the giant. "I can assure you, Mr. O'Keefe, that nothing like this will ever happen again."

During the long silence that followed her promise, Adam watched O'Keefe carefully. *A minute ago, he looked like he might take me over his knee...and now he looks like he wants to hug Ma.* Adam gulped as he realized the stories he'd heard about the Irishman were true. He really *was* crazy!

As if to prove it, the man aimed his gray-eyed glare at Adam. "Say ye're sorry, why don't ye, so we can put this mess behind us."

Has he ever been a boy? Adam wondered. *Doesn't he understand that saying sorry will shame me in front of all my friends?*

"Don't tell me ye're waitin' for yer ma to do it for ye...."

Adam made a thin line of his lips and crossed both arms over his chest. Those boys peering through the window would see he wasn't a *girl*!

O'Keefe combed beefy fingers through his beard. "So, we can add 'stubborn' to yer list of faults, then," he said. "All right...."

He bent forward slightly and rested his enormous palms on his knees, putting himself at eye level with Adam. "Yer name is Adam, is it?"

With brow furrowed, Adam refused to speak, but O'Keefe didn't seem the least bit fazed.

"How old are y', Adam?"

"Eight." And, for the benefit of Bobby and the boys, he added, "And three quarters."

O'Keefe nodded. "Well, then, Adam Eight-and-Three-Quarters, y'owe me three lunches and the buckets they was packed in." Holding out a palm the size of a dinner plate, he rubbed all four fingers against his thumb.

Adam had seen the gesture enough times to know what it meant. And he'd heard enough about O'Keefe's handiwork in the ring to know he'd better try, at least, to make good on his debt. Suddenly, his mother's protection seemed woefully inadequate. As he struggled for a comeback that might appease the ex-boxer, she stepped from behind the counter, unlocked her cash box, and withdrew a silver dollar. Then, marching purposefully up to O'Keefe, she dropped it onto his upturned palm. "I'm sure that will more than cover your losses."

Is she out of her mind? Adam wondered. *Those old lunch pails weren't worth a whole dollar, not even filled with cheese and sausage!* Besides, he'd heard his ma muttering to herself just that morning about how this last dollar had to last them until old man Andersen paid her for the dress she was making for his daughter.

He watched O'Keefe look at the coin, then up at his mother's face. Just how daft *was* the man, anyway? Hadn't he ever seen a dollar before?

"'Twasn't ye who stole me lunches," he said softly, wrapping his fingers around her slender wrist. "Shouldn't be ye who pays for 'em." He pressed the dollar into her hand, took a step back, and faced Adam. "Don't tell me y'aim to stand there, mute, while yer poor ma fights this battle for ye."

Squirming under the intense scrutiny of O'Keefe's hard glare, Adam looked down at the floor. In the past, folks had never paid much attention to his fatherless status. During the last few weeks, however, having no pa had helped him get away with all sorts of mischief. Why wasn't it working on the Irishman? Flustered, afraid, and ashamed, he blurted out, "I'd pay you back, but I haven't got any money. Besides, wasn't my idea to steal from you in the first place. I wasn't the only one who—"

"I saw yer li'l gang," O'Keefe interrupted him, "and I see 'em now, too." With eyes narrowed, he added, "But it weren't them that ran off with me lunches. So, here's what ye're gonna do...."

His eyes wide as hen's eggs, Adam's swallowed, waiting for O'Keefe to pronounce his sentence.

"Ye'll work in me warehouse until I say we're square."

Adam felt his mouth drop open. "Me? Work in your ware—"

"Mr. O'Keefe," his mother said, "I realize you haven't been in town very long, so perhaps you're not aware that my boy lost his father." She held the coin between her thumb and forefinger. "Please let me reimburse you for—"

"I'm not so new that I don't know who y'are," he said flatly. "Ye're Kate Flynn, widow of one Sean Flynn." His gravelly voice softened considerably when he said, "I'm sorry for yer loss, Mrs. Flynn. Truly, I am."

For a moment, Adam thought he was off the hook.

But only for a moment.

O'Keefe shot a stern glance at him and said, "Not havin' a da is no excuse for stealin'." Meeting Kate's gaze again, he added, "What the boy done was wrong, and it's up to him to make it right."

It seemed to Adam that time stopped while the adults gawked at each other. And then, O'Keefe started for the door. "Tell ye what, lad," he said. "I'll leave it up to ye. Pay the debt, or don't." He shrugged. "Won't be me who sees the Dark Faerie in me dreams if ye don't make things right."

The Dark Faerie? Adam had no idea who or what that might be. He knew from O'Keefe's tone only that it was someone—or something—to be reckoned with. A shiver snaked up his spine as the man opened the door.

O'Keefe paused there in the doorway, then turned and said, "But let me leave ye with this to think on: If ye've even a pinstripe of good left in y'after rubbin' elbows with those ruffians, havin' this debt hangin' over yer head will nag at ye like an ancient fishwife. When ye're ready to ease yer conscience, ye know where to find me."

Conscience? Adam had been hearing the word for as long as he could remember. He wasn't exactly sure what a conscience was. Maybe it was something a boy grew into, like all those other words adults bandied about: responsibility, sensibility, discernment. He'd obviously not grown up enough to have developed one yet, because if he had, wouldn't *one* of his pranks have nagged at him by now?

Sunshine, glinting through the open window, gleamed off the silver dollar his mother had placed on the counter. Obviously, O'Keefe had a pinstripe of good in *him*, because he'd decided against taking the money.

Then, his mother's eyes welled with unshed tears, and she folded her hands, just like she did when she prayed. "Thank you, Mr. O'Keefe," she said, wearing her reserved-for-good-customers smile. She could be painfully to the point when she wanted to be. And, judging by O'Keefe's surprised reaction, she'd made it clear that nothing would make her happier than for him to leave.

"G'day to ye, Mrs. Flynn."

And, just like that, he was gone.

Ordinarily, when Adam was chastised by adults, feelings of anger and resentment swirled in his gut. O'Keefe had been, by far, the toughest adult who had dealt with him. So, it surprised him, as he watched the man cross to his workshop on the other side of the road, that he felt no hint of the typical emotions.

What he felt instead was an uneasy stinging sensation that prickled at his brain. A sign, perhaps, that he was developing a conscience?

"I understand you had company earlier."

Kate Flynn looked up from her sewing. "I imagine everyone within a two-mile radius knows I had a visitor this afternoon," she said, smiling at her elderly neighbor. "Why, even O'Keefe admitted he behaved like a stampeding bull."

Thaddeus Crofton pulled up a chair and helped himself to a cookie. "Way I hear it, Adam had it comin'. He's been making a pest of himself all over town the past couple weeks," he said around a mouthful of the sugary treat. "What's eatin' that boy of yours, Kate?"

She shrugged and met his pale, blue eyes. "I'm not sure. Maybe it's those boys he's been hanging round with, putting ideas in his head." Sighing, she added, "I don't know what to do with him."

"You're gonna let him work off his debt, that's what." The man took another bite of cookie. "A little hard work never hurt anybody, least of all a boy who thinks he's entitled to help himself to what ain't his."

"But he's only eight, Thaddeus. He can't do a man's work."

"J.J. is a decent fellow. I'm sure he won't give the boy more than he can handle."

"But—but that warehouse is no doubt filled with all sorts of dangerous tools. He could get hurt."

Chuckling, Thaddeus reached across the space between them and patted her hand, then pointed at her sewing table, where needles and pins, razors and scissors lay in an orderly row. "He's managed to stay safe around your tools of the trade. Besides, eight is more than old enough to develop some good, old-fashioned horse sense."

She bit her lower lip. "I suppose you're right."

"'Course I'm right. Just ask Mary." And with a jolly wink, he added, "Don't look so worried, Kate. *'Train up a child in the way he should go: and when he is old, he will not depart from it.'"* He smiled. "You're a good woman—strongest I've met. Good mother, too. So, I know you'll do what's right. You always have."

Setting her sewing aside, Kate stood up. "Thanks, Thaddeus," she said, handing him another cookie. "Now, get on back to your own store before Mary puts the sheriff on your trail."

"You're the one ought to be afraid of that wife of mine," he said, tipping the treat as if it were a high silk hat. "She don't take kindly to folks spoilin' my supper, y'know."

The tiny bell above the door tinkled quietly when Thaddeus made his exit, and Kate went back to her work, hoping it would distract her from the worries that had been hounding her of late.

It had all started several weeks ago, one evening after supper, when Adam had shoved his plate aside and propped both elbows on the table. "What *really* happened to my father?" he'd asked.

Kate had looked into his trusting, blue eyes and wondered how much of the truth he could handle. She never lied to her only son, unless one counted lies of omission. Shouldn't she protect him just a little while longer?

"You already know what happened, Adam. Your father was...." Even after seven years, she'd found it almost impossible to say. "...He was shot."

"I know, I know. By a man name of Prentice, during a poker game. But you never told me *why*."

It seemed that ever since the boy had been old enough to hold a two-way conversation, he'd been fascinated with the circumstances of his father's death. Kate had wanted to instill the picture of an upright man in the boy's mind, to ensure he'd have a good example to follow. But to accomplish that, she'd been forced to leave out most of the details of her husband's life—and death.

"He was cheatin' at cards, wasn't he?"

"Oh, Adam," she'd begun, breathing a weary sigh, "you know this isn't my favorite subject. When will you—"

"I'll quit asking when you tell me the whole story."

Her heart pounding, she'd stood up and begun stacking plates. "What makes you think I haven't?"

"Bobby heard his mother talking to Kenny's ma, and she said Pa was a drunkard and a gambler, that he got into lots of fights, and that he nearly killed a man once." Locking her in his intense gaze, he'd looked far older than he'd had a right to. "They say he beat you, too."

A butter knife had clattered to the table as Kate had tried to restrain her shock. Yes, there had been beatings—too many to count—and she still had the scars to remind her. But what kind of mother would she be if she gave her boy that type of memory of his father?

Besides, it had happened years ago and miles away, in Raleigh. After the funeral, she'd packed their meager possessions and headed east to make a fresh start on the North Carolina coast, where no one would know anything about Sean, or her, or her son. So, how had Bobby's mother found out?

"Is it true?"

She'd wiped her brow with the back of her hand. "Is what true, son?"

"All of it—but mostly, that he beat you."

Which is the greater sin? she'd wondered. *Continuing the lie, or saddling him with the ugly truth?* "Your father was...he was a colorful man," she'd said, choosing her words carefully.

"Not as colorful as you," he'd countered.

Kate had been about to ask Adam what he'd meant when he'd said, "People say he beat you black and blue on a regular basis."

Carrying the dirty dishes to the sink, she'd made no effort to mask her anger. "And I suppose Bobby's mother said that, too," she'd fumed. "That woman needs to get out her Bible and read James 4:11!" Closing her eyes, Kate had recited the verse: "'*Speak not evil of one another, brethren. He that speaketh evil of his brother, and judgeth his brother, speaketh evil of the law, and judgeth the law: but if thou judge the law, thou art not a doer of the law, but a judge.'"*

"I'm not a baby, Ma. You can tell me the truth. I can handle it, you know."

She'd tried sidestepping the boy's questions. "Have you done your chores?"

"And I'm not stupid, either," he'd added, shoving his chair back from the table.

From the moment of Adam's birth, everyone had remarked how much he resembled his father. At that moment, with that determined set of his jaw and the slight lift of his left brow, he'd reminded her of Sean more than ever.

"I'm smarter than most kids my age. Miss Henderson told you that last year. So, I'm smart enough to understand what—"

"I'm your mother, Adam Flynn, and I will do what I believe is best for you. And, right now, I say it's best to drop this subject."

He'd stared at the ceiling and whined, "But, Ma!"

"But nothing," she'd said, bracketing his face with both hands. "When I think you're ready for the rest of the story, I'll let you know."

His brows together and his lower lip out, he'd said, "When will *that* be?"

And she'd told him the truth, as she'd known it to be at that moment. "I don't know, son. I know only that you're not old enough right now."

He'd wriggled free of her to say, "I'll bet you got in a few good licks, 'cause you're pretty good at defending yourself!"

Trembling with shock, Kate had aimed an index finger at him. "Adam Flynn, you will not speak to me in that tone of voice. Now, you march straight up to your room, this instant!"

Slump-shouldered and grim-faced, he had obeyed. But from that day on, he'd spent more and more time with Bobby Banks, Currituck's resident troublemaker. Everything Adam had said since that night had been argumentative, everything he'd done, rebellious. Just days ago, flustered and infuriated by his behavior, she'd demanded to know what had gotten into him. He'd responded, "I'm half you and half him. What do you expect?"

The answer had not satisfied her. Quite the contrary. His words—spoken as if from a young man of sixteen or more—had terrified her. What would become of her young son who, until now, had been playful and innocent, loving and kind, if he decided to emulate his father?

Now, alone in her dress shop, Kate sighed. Sewing was not taking her mind off her troubles, as it usually did. *Please, Lord,* she prayed, *clear my mind of these burdensome worries. Either that, or give me the ability to work while I worry!*

She picked up a wedding headdress and started stitching candlewick centers in the daisies she'd crocheted along its outer edges. When the flowers were complete, she'd attach them to a veil of sheer, white gauze that would float all the way down to the gown's hem. It would be a lovely dress.

Kate wondered for the tenth time how Mr. Andersen had secured enough satin for his daughter's big day. Times were hard, and fabrics like silk, satin, and Spanish lace were all but impossible to come by. Yet he'd somehow provided Kate with more than enough material to create the puffed sleeves, the full-circle skirt, and the billowing train.

"Why, Katie, I do believe that's the loveliest dress you've ever made."

She laughed softly. "That's what you say about every dress I make, Mary." Smiling at her elderly neighbor, she added, "I have a kettle on the stove. How about a cup of tea?"

The old woman pulled out a chair and settled her portly frame into it. "Don't mind if I do," she huffed. "Been on my feet since dawn!"

Kate fetched two delicate china cups and saucers from the shelf above the big, iron stove. "I guess you're here because Thaddeus told you what happened this afternoon," she said, spooning tea leaves into the pot.

Mary nodded. "Don't you worry, sweetie. I raised seven young'uns of my own, don't forget. And every last one of 'em got ornery from time to time." Then, she winked. "Adam's no exception. He's just testin' his wings, is all."

Filling the cups with the hot brew, Kate sighed. "I hope you're right."

"Had me a favorite Bible verse when my boys were small," Mary said, and, patting wayward wisps of hair that had escaped her white bun, she held a finger aloft. "*'Take therefore no thought for the morrow: for the morrow shall take thought for the things of itself. Sufficient unto the day is the evil thereof,'*" she recited with eyes closed.

Nodding, Kate smiled. "I'll add that to my list that includes,*'Casting all your care upon him; for he careth for you.'*"

Mary slurped noisily from her cup and pointed at the wedding gown. "Who's this one for?"

"Abigail Andersen."

"Aye, yes," Mary sighed, massaging her temples. "She's marrying Nathaniel Peters's youngest boy, if I'm not mistaken." Wiggling her eyebrows, she added, "Promises to be one of Currituck's biggest shindigs ever. Are you invited?"

"Yes, but I don't think I'll be going."

"Why ever not? You could use a day off." Mary shook a finger under Kate's nose. "You work too hard, if you ask me, Kate Flynn."

"Only hard enough to keep the wolf from the door."

"The wolf? You mean the banker, don't you?"

"Wolf, banker...they're one and the same to me."

"Something you know better than most, way I hear it."

The way she heard it? Was the whole town talking about her past? Suddenly, Kate had an idea. Everyone knew that Mary carried stories the way a bee carries pollen. If she told the woman the truth, it would be dispatched faster than by a *Gazette* reporter, and when the gossipmongers told their tales, at least there'd be an ounce of truth in them.

"It's strange," Kate began, smoothing the silky fabric that lay on her work table, "that my own wedding dress is the reason I'm a dressmaker today."

"Is that so?" Mary got up and waddled over to the stove to top off her tea, then stirred a heaping spoonful of sugar into the cup. "I've known you for years and never knew that."

"I was born in Philadelphia," Kate said, nodding, "and so was Sean."

"Sean—your late husband?"

"Mmm-hmm. As a young girl, I thought he was the most handsome man, but he paid no mind to me. At least, it seemed he hadn't noticed me. By the time I realized that for all his good looks, he had nothing good inside, where it counted, it was too late....

"His father got very sick, you see, when Sean was barely out of college. He'd never been a poor man, mind you, but when he put Sean in charge of the bank, the money started rolling in." Kate rolled her eyes. "My, but that man could be ruthless! Foreclosures, evictions, refusals to loan money to the hardworking folks who really needed it...."

Mary frowned. "What in the world possessed a sweet girl like you to marry a man like that?"

"Well, that's a story unto itself."

Mary leaned forward, her eyes twinkling mischievously. "Thaddeus has already had his supper...."

For the next half hour, Kate kept Mary spellbound with the story of how her young brother had died of the cancer ten years earlier. Treatments and medications, she explained, had all but depleted her parents' meager savings. When the boy died, the modest plot and nondescript headstone that marked his grave had closed out their account.

"Oh, how sad," Mary sighed. "What a shame!" She clicked her tongue. "Thank the good Lord, me and my own have been blessed with everything we need, including good health." Shaking her head, she added, "My heart goes out to your ma. I can't imagine having to bury a child...."

"It was hard on both my parents, but on Ma in particular." Kate took a sip of her tea.

"And on your sister, too, I imagine."

"Yes," she said, remembering her own heartache of watching her brother wither away, then watching his spirit leave him, and, finally, watching the plain, pine box being lowered into the ground. "Very hard."

Mary slapped a chubby thigh. "So, your wedding dress got you started in the sewing business, did it?"

She was a kind woman, Kate thought, to try to lighten the mood with a change of subject. Trouble was, what Mary had heard so far was only the beginning. "Yes, I had no choice but to make my own dress," Kate said. "My father went to Sean, explained he wouldn't be able to meet his bank note for several months, and asked for an extension...just until he could catch up on a few of George's medical bills. Papa was a carpenter, a hardworking man who'd earned a reputation for never shirking his duties. He would have made those payments, if only Sean had given him a chance."

Mary blinked and gasped. "You don't mean to say—"

"He threatened to foreclose on the mortgage."

"You're right. He was heartless!"

Kate had never shared the story with anyone before, and she wondered if she could do it now. *You must*, she told herself. *Because, if you don't, you'll be haunted by rumors...and so will Adam.*

"So, did he foreclose?"

"He asked for my hand in marriage, instead."

"Surely, your pa didn't agree! Why, that would be the same as—the same as selling you!"

Kate remembered the fateful conversation she'd had with her father. "But Pa," she'd pleaded, "I can't spend my life with a hotheaded bully who divides his time between beating people in the saloon and kicking families off their properties!"

Her father's cheeks had reddened, and he'd stared at the floor. "Aw, it won't be so bad, darlin'. He's not the brute people say he is. Been sowin' wild oats, is all. Marriage will settle him down—you'll see." But his smile hadn't quite reached his eyes when he'd said, "Settled *me* down, didn't it?"

"But, Pa, you were never like Sean Flynn!" Kate had insisted. "And what if marriage *doesn't* settle him down? What will become of me then?"

For a moment, her father had said nothing at all—but she'd had a fecling there was plenty he would have liked to have said. "You're right, of course," is what he'd finally said. "Don't know what I was thinking."

Grateful to be free of the horrible marriage prospect, she'd thrown her arms around him. "Isn't your fault I'm so picky, Pa," she'd said, kissing his whiskered cheek. "I want to marry a man like you, who's loving and kind and hardworking and—" She'd stepped back and lain a hand on his cheek to add, "—and more handsome than those Shakespearean actors who came to town last year!"

"You're full of stuff and nonsense, Katie Barnes," he'd said, tweaking her nose. "Now, get on home and help your ma put supper on the table. And tell her to make it quick, 'cause I'm half starved!" Then, he'd gone back to working on the finial for the highboy he'd built.

During the mile-long walk home, Kate had asked herself why her father would even try to talk her into marrying a man like Sean Flynn when he knew as well as anyone what kind of reputation the banker had earned.

That night, Kate had gotten her answer....

"Goodness, girl!"

Mary's voice roused her from her reverie.

"I thought you'd passed out or something, you were so quiet and still," her old friend said.

"Sorry," Kate muttered. "It's just—I've never told anyone this story before."

"I know, sweetie," the woman said, patting Kate's hand. "But you can trust me. Now, I know what some folks say about me behind my back—that I'm a busybody and a talebearer—but you can count on me to keep what you've told me to myself."

Wouldn't that be ironic! Kate thought. *Finally, you open up to the Gossip of Currituck...and she won't spread the story!*

"So, on with it, girl...you made your own dress, did you? And I'll bet it was something to behold, knowing what magic you can work with a needle and thread."

"Not nearly as lovely as this," Kate said, stroking the satin of Abigail's gown, "but at least I walked down the aisle in white."

"Ah, Katie-girl...."

But she continued on, as if the woman hadn't spoken. "I realized that if I didn't marry Sean...." She swallowed hard, remembering the heated argument she'd overheard between her mother and father. "Sean had promised to cancel their entire debt, provided I agreed to become his wife. It was the only way out for them."

"Married a man like that to save your family? You're a true heroine, girl!"

Heroine, indeed! Kate thought. She knew that she'd never been anything of the kind, especially considering the only reason she'd decided to tell Mary the ugly truth was to help her escape the gossip that was upsetting her son. She hoped that once the parents of his friends found out, they'd teach their boys to keep civil tongues in their heads.

But it had been a terrible idea. *If you hadn't gone off half-cocked, as usual...if you'd asked the Lord's guidance in the matter....*

Too late now to pray for divine intervention. Mary already knew everything.

Well, almost everything....

Kate hadn't told her neighbor how Sean had smirked when she'd visited him at the bank the morning after her parents' argument, when she'd whispered that if he truly meant to wipe out their debt, she'd marry him.

"So, I made my dress from a damask tablecloth my grandmother had given me." Kate smiled a little, remembering the way her sister had draped it over her shoulders before the sewing started, and how they'd collapsed in a fit of giggles over a string of horrible puns: "Well, you're all set!" Susan had said.

"Yes, the salt of the earth, that's me."

"After all these years putting up with your silly jokes, this marriage will seem like gravy!"

"Good to know you at least enjoyed the making of the gown, if that happy look on your face is any indicator," Mary interjected.

"Yes," Kate admitted, "I did enjoy that part of it."

"And did you make your veil from this beautiful stuff?" Mary asked, gently touching the lace Mr. Andersen had ordered from Europe.

Kate couldn't help but laugh. "I should say not! My veil was made from the curtains Ma had hung in my bedroom window. After the wedding, I made ruffles of it and sewed them to the collar and cuffs of one of her Sunday-go-to-meeting dresses."

Draining the last of her tea, Kate proceeded to tell Mary how she'd become Mrs. Sean Flynn precisely one month after his so-called proposal. "I was sixteen and he was thirty the day we moved into his room in his parents' mansion. Oh, what a house it was!"

She described the many rooms and their ornate furnishings, the acres of rolling hillside surrounding the residence, and the dozens of servants required to keep it all in order. "Then, one day, about a month after the wedding, Sean informed me we were moving. 'Heading South,'" she said, mimicking his deep, bossy voice. "'Because I can't stand living under my father's control for another minute!'

"He'd bought land here in North Carolina, where he'd been planning to start a whole new business venture—a chain of Flynn banks, one in every major city between Florida and New York. All he could say for months, it seemed, was, 'We'll be rich—filthy rich!'"

"And did it work? Did he get rich?"

"Yes and no."

Mary's brow furrowed.

"See, he made money. Lots of it. But he gambled it all away."

"Oh, Katie...."

"I never wanted anything but a man who'd love me the way my pa loved my ma," she said, more to herself than to Mary. "As long as we had shelter, enough food, and the basic comforts for our children, I didn't care if we had lots of money. The hardest part," Kate admitted, "was going though it all without having my family to turn to. Sometimes, I thought I might die of missing them."

In truth, her biggest fear had been that she'd die—period—during one of Sean's many rages. She remembered vividly the first time he'd struck her.

Never the shy, retiring type, Kate had believed it was her wifely duty to show her husband respect, especially in public. And so, whenever Sean would talk business at parties, after church services, and with friends they met while walking down the street, she'd smile and nod to show others that she supported whatever he said or did—even when she could plainly see that his latest get-rich scheme was nothing but another lofty, ill-founded dream.

One time, she'd made the mistake of questioning him in private. "I don't want to go to Georgia," she'd blurted out. "I want our baby to be born here, in the home we built for—"

"You'll do as you're told!" he'd bellowed, turning his back to her. If she hadn't been so upset, Kate might not have run around to face him head-on. Might never have said, "My father never made any major decisions without first discussing them with my mother."

His blue eyes had glittered menacingly as he'd said, "I am not your father, and you most certainly are not the wife your mother is!" Grabbing her wrist, he'd jerked her against his chest and said through clenched teeth, "But you are my wife, and, God help me, I'm stuck with you now." His eyes had been mere slits when he'd added, "You'll give me obedience, not financial advice. If you dare ever question me again, you'll be sorry."

She'd been raised in a home where gentleness and love prevailed. How dare he put his hands on her as if she were an errant child! She had been the best wife she knew how to be, especially considering the circumstances of their marriage. Hurt, angry, and humiliated, Kate had issued a threat of her own: "If you ever talk to me this way again, *you'll* be sorry!"

A heartbeat later, she'd learned that when Sean Flynn issued a threat, he meant business. For weeks afterward, she'd hidden in the house to hide the bruises and scrapes that were proof of his lesson. Over time,

Kate had learned to accept Sean's drunken binges and the beatings they inspired. What she had never come to terms with were the cold-blooded attacks that had not been whiskey-induced—the ones administered for no rhyme or reason, except to feed his sadistic pleasure. Sometimes, as he'd come at her, Kate had known she was looking into the face of pure evil.

"Katie," Mary interrupted her again, "you're pale as a bedsheet. Are you all right?"

Blinking, Kate refocused on the here and now. "Yes—yes, of course. Sorry to behave like an addle-brained twit." Brightening, she said, "Now, where was I?"

"You were saying that you missed your family when Sean took you away from Philadelphia."

"Oh, yes...." Licking her lips, Kate continued. "Things got progressively worse. The more money Sean made, the faster he spent it. We were in debt up to our eyebrows, and he was forced to shut down six of the seven banks he'd opened. He took to gambling regularly, insisting that if he could get just one good hand of cards, everything would right itself."

"And that's how he got himself shot?"

Kate's eyes widened. "How—how did you know?"

Mary shrugged. "Town this small? Folks talk."

Bobby's mother? Kate wondered. *But, really, what does it matter?*

"Before it happened, Sean was desperate," she continued. "Out of time and out of options. The men in the game with him, and others at the bar, testified that Harland Prentice had accused him of slipping an ace of spades into the deck."

Mary shivered. "The death card."

Kate swallowed. She'd never heard it called that before. "It was for Sean, at least."

"That's enough," Mary said, standing up. "It's one thing to get things out in the open, but it's entirely another thing to beat yourself with the memories." She pulled Kate gently to her and wrapped her in a motherly embrace. "Try to put it all out of your mind, sweetie," she whispered. "He was a brute and a beast, way I hear it, and got his just deserts. When a man takes to whiskey and gambling, he's bound to end up in a bad way." Patting Kate's back, she added, "*'For all they that take the sword shall perish with the sword.'*"

Suddenly, Kate felt an overwhelming need to be alone, and she stepped from the comfort of Mary's hug. "Better get back to work," she said, rubbing her temples, "or the bride will walk down the aisle in a half-sewn gown."

Mary waddled to the door and, placing one hand on the doorknob, said, "I meant it when I said I wouldn't breathe a word of what you told me to anyone. I promise."

Tears stung Kate's eyes, but she blinked them back. "I'm sorry, Mary. It was selfish of me to burden you with—"

"Nonsense! Isn't healthy, keeping things like that all bottled up inside. It's a wonder you haven't popped!"

Kate felt like a weak, spoiled little girl, tattling on a schoolmate for taking too long on the swing. "I haven't done anything to deserve a friend like you, Mary."

The woman pulled open the door. "Why don't you turn in early for a change? You've been lookin' a mite pale the past few days. The extra sleep will do you good."

"Maybe you're right."

"'Course I'm right. I'm always right. Just ask Thaddeus!"

Then, laughing, Mary let herself out, leaving Kate alone to stare helplessly at the ceiling. On the other side of it, her innocent little boy lay sleeping. Innocent for now, anyway. *Bless him, Lord, and protect him from all harm. Guide his actions and his thoughts, and—*

Her prayer was cut off by a question: *Why did you tell Mary all those things?* The answer came just as quickly: *Because you're self-centered and spineless; too weak to handle a little gossip.* She'd had no business talking that way about Sean. Whatever else he might have been, he was Adam's father. And she'd move heaven and earth to protect her son from learning about what kind of man his father had been. What if Mary didn't keep her promise? What if Adam found out?

What have you done, Kate Flynn? What have you done?

With hands folded, she closed her eyes tight. *Forgive me, Father, for coming to yet another important decision without first seeking Your guidance.* And, in a small, trembling voice, she prayed aloud, "Please don't let Adam learn about his father from anything I said tonight!"

Her heart hammering, she rose slowly and headed to her room, knowing even as she climbed the stairs that sleep would be a long time coming this night.

Chapter Two

John Joseph O'Keefe lifted his hammer high, brought it down with a heavy hand, and secured the prow of the two-master. Another week of work, and this fine, little ketch would be ready for the wealthy New York entrepreneur who fancied himself to be a high seas skipper. It had taken a few weeks longer than usual to complete the project, since the rudder, the tiller, and even the winches needed to be attached so that the left-handed captain could manage the rigging with ease.

Behind him, the schooner he'd already finished sat waiting for pickup. It was an impressive craft, with jib-headed sails and extra-long turnbuckles. It had been one of his favorite projects, and J.J. was proud of the work—not because he'd forged the cleats, cam-cleats, shackles, and other fittings himself; not even because he'd included double-strong goosenecks and mast hoops; but rather, because he'd been given free rein to design the vessel's interior, a task that had required him to make full use of his carpentry skills. From cabin housing to hatch cover, from cockpit to companionway, every carefully selected, cut, and carved sheet of mahogany bore his artistic touch. And on the transom—the pièce de résistance—the boat's name was painted in J.J.'s one-of-a-kind, bold, black lettering style: *The Flying Cloud.*

J.J. loved his work, not only because it allowed him to make use of his hard-learned skills, but also because it allowed him to work alone. True, there weren't many one-man operations left—he lost an occasional job to a company whose crew could produce a boat in record time. But J.J. refused to trade peace and privacy for pay. He could earn a great deal more by hiring his own crew, but what would he gain by hiring five men, or three, or even one, to increase his output, if he'd lose the silent solitude he so treasured? Why, the normal day-to-day banter among workmen alone would cost him the memory of the sounds of the sea—the foghorn's mournful *phoomph-phoomph*, its two-note serenade punctuating the splash and hiss of the surf's spray; the gentle lapping of waves pummeling the pilings; the toll of a distant buoy bell.

He inhaled deeply of the salty air and, with eyes closed, held his breath for a moment, relishing its prickly, briny scent. Smiling, he let out his breath, slow and easy. He loved the sea. Always had, always would.

J.J. knew that to some, the ocean was a menacing thing, deep and dark and dangerous, teeming with strange, monstrous beings that lurked beneath the surface, waiting to sink razor-sharp teeth into meaty flesh and bone. But those folks saw only the violent, smoke-gray skies above it, streaked with sooty thunderclouds and silver-white lightning. They knew it as nothing more than a wild and wicked thing that churned the air into deadly williwaws, which blew sailors and fishermen off course and into the waiting arms of Azrael, the Angel of Death.

It was all that, to be sure. But it was more—so much more.

To J.J., the sea was froth and foam and peaceful fog, and sweet, soft breezes that set the halyards quietly clunking against the masts in a syncopated rhythm that had lulled him to sleep many a night.

And, oh, how he loved the sea at night, when black, velvety skies sparkled with ten million pinpricks of starry light, and the milk-white glow of the moon glinted off the water. He loved it just as much in the daytime, too, when the golden glow of the daystar highlighted stout, swollen clouds and brightened the blue-green water, where, among sharp-toothed shark and stinging jellyfish, lived the playful dolphin.

Canoes, boats, ships—however large the vessel, however long it took J.J. to build it—provided him the only excuse he needed to be near to his cherished waters. He knew men who compared the sea to a woman, citing quicksilver mood changes as the reason.

Not J.J.

Oh, he'd always used feminine pronouns—her, she—to refer to the sea, of course. And, yes, he was the first to agree she could be moody—tranquil one minute, stormy the next, or even destructive, disastrous, and deadly—but to compare her to a female? In J.J.'s opinion, that was a dishonor she did not deserve.

The sea didn't behave as it did from a self-centered need to dominate. She did not consciously manipulate or calculatedly control the men who loved her. She had wiles, to be sure, that wooed and won men, but she never used them deliberately—as women used tears, pouting lips, and sullen silences—to get her way.

In fact, she had no "way" at all; she simply existed. A chemist might describe her as a complicated composition of chemicals and gases, which, singly or in combination, reacted to things like gravity and atmosphere in a multitude of ways that had nothing at all to do with man. But J.J. knew it was simpler than that. His presence, or the lack thereof, had no bearing on what she did or didn't do.

What a man saw when he looked into her dark, glittering waves could trick him, could fool his eye...if he let it. On days when she was turbid, no matter how hard or how long J.J. scrutinized her, he'd get a shallow glimpse, at best, of what hid beneath her gleaming, seemingly calm surface. But when the sun was bright and the sky clear, he often convinced himself he could look into the watery world and see all the way to the other side of the earth.

J.J. had experienced a similar sensation yesterday, looking into the widow Flynn's wide eyes. He'd sensed there was far more to her than she allowed the casual observer to see. And he'd had a feeling that, even after careful observation, few would ever get to know the real Kate Flynn.

He hammered the last nail into the prow and ran a calloused hand over the supple curve of the wood. Next, he'd finish up the companionway, and, after that, the foremast. One day soon, a sailor would climb the mast and, shading his eyes with one hand, shout, "Boat on the horizon!"

"Where away?"

"Broad on the port quarter, Cap'n."

"Back the jib, then," he'd roar, reversing the tiller so the stern would swing to starboard. And as he prepared to bear off, he'd add, "Hard a'lee!" and steer through the eye of the wind.

The eye of the wind....

Now, why does that remind y'of Kate Flynn? he asked himself. *And why are ye thinkin' of her, when she's not yer type—not yer type at all?*

The only other brown-eyed woman he'd known up close and personal had been his mother, and he didn't believe another woman had been born since who could match her in any way. Perhaps that was why the fair-haired types had always appealed to him. If J.J. had learned only one thing in his thirty-five years, it was the futility of fighting nature. He had a slew of relatives who had tried and failed. *And the plain and simple truth,* he told himself, *is that they're all as dead as doorknobs this day because of it*!

In the past, whenever he'd been drawn to a woman, it had been because of a pair of big, blue eyes, waist-length blonde hair, a voluptuous figure, or an alluring voice. *The widow has none of those things in her favor, so why in tarnation has she been on yer mind day and night since yer go-round in her shop?*

Shrugging, he tried to focus on his work.

Maybe it's 'cause ye've got a few things in common with her....

For one thing, she'd come to Currituck seven years ago, after burying her husband, and J.J. hadn't been here long, himself. A hard winter's journey across the Atlantic had brought him to New York back in 1851. It had taken him a year to work his way south, searching for a place he could call home.

For another, he'd heard that Kate had arrived with fifty dollars in her purse and nothing in her carpetbag but a change of clothes for her and the boy. J.J. had brought nothing from Ireland but an extra shirt, a few measly punts to exchange for American dollars, and his journal.

Rumor had it she'd turned down three marriage proposals since setting up shop in Currituck, giving no other reason than that she had a distaste for the institution. And J.J. had vowed, after coming close to marrying but managing to avoid the folly, never to get closer than arm's length to a woman again.

As if that weren't enough, Kate had paid cold, hard cash for a building that had been half destroyed by fire—cash that, according to Mary and Thaddeus, she'd earned by scrubbing floors, taking in laundry, and baking pies for the hotel restaurant in town. It had taken years, Mary had said, and though she and Thaddeus had tried to talk her out of buying the dilapidated, old building, Kate had bought it, anyway. She'd been determined, they'd said, to be her own boss and provide a good life for her son.

Many were the times he'd passed her window on his way to the feed and grain and found himself fighting the temptation to watch her scrub the thick, sticky soot from the walls or, with hammer and nails, replace a singed trim board. J.J. had built his warehouse with his own two hands.

If he hadn't seen it with his own two eyes, he might not have believed she had crafted, painted, and hung the dress-dummy sign outside her door. He, too, had designed his own sign.

She'd set up shop on the first floor, set up house on the second; he'd created a living space of sorts in the loft above his vast workspace.

The only real fault gossipmongers could cite about her was that she spent far too much time on her work and not nearly enough of it reading her Bible. J.J. had no right to focus on that miniscule fissure in her character, for he hadn't seen the inside of a church since long before leaving Ireland. He didn't know what kept Kate from the Scriptures, but he knew why he'd fallen from the fold.

As far back as the 1600s, one royal crown or another had degraded his people. Where was the all-loving Father when the victories of Elizabeth the First meant the defeat of Ireland? Where was this powerful Being when J.J.'s ancestors were suffering from starvation and losing their homes at the hands of the English? J.J. had lost everyone who mattered during the horrible potato famine—parents, siblings, cousins, and neighbors—and had no use for a God who seemed to sanction such wretchedness and misery.

He didn't know if Kate had brought her Bible along when she'd left her old life behind, but he certainly had not. What he did know was that she'd packed up and left Raleigh, a place that, according to Mary and Thaddeus, was little more to her than painful memories, sadness, and proof of foolish decisions. It had taken courage to do that. He knew, because he'd done it, too.

Yes, they had much in common. But they had differences, too. Whereas she'd left a bustling city, he'd fled a disease-racked homeland. He'd gone it alone; she'd had a son in tow.

So, where's all this comparin' and contrastin' taking ye, O'Keefe? J.J. demanded of himself. Unfortunately, he had no answer.

If some other fellow had a mind to settle down, fine for him. As for J.J., he knew how to cook and clean and darn his own socks and sew on a button. What did he need with a woman cluttering his house with doilies and knickknacks and bonnets and such?

He'd satisfied his appetite for romance once, and it had left such a bitter taste that he doubted he'd ever hunger for it again. Still, if he did have a mind to settle down, he could do worse than with the likes of Kate Flynn....

Frowning, J.J. shook his head. He needed to clear his mind of the cobwebs of the past and the delusions of the present.

But even as he stepped over the schooner's rail and into the cabin, he had a feeling it would take more than any amount of work he might do to truly get his mind off the lovely young widow.

Kate had seen J.J. around town dozens of times, heading to or from his warehouse, on his way into or out of Mary and Thaddeus's feed and grain, or walking along the dock. She hadn't given his solitary strolls much thought before their confrontational meeting, but something stirred in her now as she watched him moving slowly along the planks.

Kate almost hadn't purchased the narrow, two-story house with its twenty by fifteen-foot backyard. The clapboards had needed a good sanding and a fresh coat of paint, and there had been shingles missing from the roof. The brick chimney certainly hadn't been cleaned once in the years the dwelling had stood on the lot.

Indeed, if the condition of the place was any indicator, it had never experienced a thorough cleaning.

She had first seen the place on a dreary afternoon. With driving rain pounding the ground outside and damp drafts slithering between cracks in the window-panes and sneaking through the floorboards, the place had seemed cloaked in gloom. Kate had hugged herself, whether to fend off the chill or to keep fear at bay, she didn't know. To this day, she wasn't sure what had made her put one foot in front of the other to climb the charred, rickety staircase.

But she thanked God that she had.

It had been while standing by a window, gazing out at the sea—the gunmetal-gray sky, the howling wind, the drenching downpour providing a view unlike anything she'd ever seen—that Kate had decided to invest her savings in the house.

The Atlantic's choppy waves had glowed, as if each had been streaked with white by an artist's paintbrush. Between thick, smoky clouds, patches of pearly white had peeked through, and the mist that rolled lazily toward shore had hovered around dock workers' feet like ashes, disturbed by a whiff of air. *If the sea can look that beautiful in this kind of weather,* she'd thought, *I can only imagine how much more beautiful it will look in sunny weather.*

The view alone had been worth every splinter, every blister, every stiff joint, and every sore muscle caused by the countless hours of backbreaking labor that had turned the house into a home for her and Adam. The ever-changing scene was the one constant in her life—the one thing she could count on to lift her sagging spirits, restore her faith, and renew her energy. She'd come to depend on its restorative powers so much that she'd placed a high-backed rocking chair and a small table near her bedroom window so that she could sit facing the shore. Later, she'd had a small balcony built so that she could climb out her window and enjoy even more of the vista, unhampered by ceiling or walls.

Without fail, the majestic panorama would calm her, soothe her, and remind her who had created the awesome beauty before her. *If God could create this*, she'd tell herself, *He can ease your petty fears*. "Going to the Window," she called it in the privacy of her mind. It was where she'd go to think, and today, it was where she went to pray about Adam's cantankerous, unruly behavior. A gentle May breeze filtered through the open window, lifting the gauzy curtain and riffling her hair.

Resting both elbows on the windowsill, she propped her chin in her hand, took a deep breath, and, closing her eyes, savored the fragrance of spring flowers. When she opened her eyes, she saw J.J., his head down and hands pocketed, standing alone on the dock. He lifted one hand and brushed it through his hair, then let his arm fall limply at his side. His broad shoulders lifted, then fell, and Kate took this as a sign that he, too, had inhaled the sweet scent of the sea. Turning slightly, he tilted his bearded face toward the sky and shook his dark-haired head.

Kate knew very little about him, save that he'd used his fists to buy everything that was his. Well, that wasn't entirely true. She also knew he'd come to Currituck by way of New York after fleeing fever and famine in Ireland. Of course, if it hadn't been for Thaddeus, she'd know next to nothing about him; indeed, she'd know nothing about most of the town's inhabitants, except perhaps the measurements of the ladies whose dresses she'd designed or the leg length of the men for whom she'd sewn trousers. Always one to give credit where credit was due, Kate admitted that her elderly neighbor's lips loosed only when he sipped too long from the bottle of tonic prescribed by Doc Parsons—which the doctor delivered no fewer than two times a week. Where Thaddeus had secured the information was anyone's guess, but Kate supposed that as long as she didn't pass on any of the so-called news, both she and Thaddeus were safe from being branded as gossips.

According to one of Thaddeus's reports, J.J. O'Keefe had never lost a boxing match. Not that it surprised Kate. Even a man with a height and weight to match John Joseph O'Keefe's would be hard-pressed to beat him, for most men lacked the initiative and energy to be champions. And she could see in his no-nonsense stance, his matter-of-fact way of speaking, and his habit of looking everyone in the eye that he had what it took to be a champion.

After each victory, according to Thaddeus, O'Keefe would reward himself with a restaurant meal in the nearest big city, siphoning off just enough from his winnings to pay for his room at whichever boardinghouse he'd call home that day. Upon settling in Currituck, J.J. had spent every moment he wasn't boxing on Buck Bay, working for Emmitt Creed on his fishing trawler. Every cent he'd earned, whether by fishing or fighting, had gone directly into the bank. Thad had reported that within a year, J.J. had saved enough to buy the land near the dock, along with the lumber and nails to build his warehouse.

What is it about Irishmen that drives them so? Kate wondered as she watched him from her window. *Why must they always be the best? And drink and fight?*

Sean had exhibited the same drive and determination to succeed, had dreamed those same ambitious dreams. Whenever he'd been in one of his get-ahead moods—which was most of the time—he'd wear the same "I can do anything" expression that O'Keefe had worn when he'd flown into her shop like a human tornado.

Kate remembered the way he'd branded her with that gray-eyed stare, as if he could read her mind, heart, and soul with one searing glance. She shuddered involuntarily, realizing that if he had been able to read her at all, he'd have known that his mere presence had awakened fears she'd thought had been long buried.

Now, she watched J.J. lean against a thick piling, cross those muscled arms over his chest, and lower his bearded chin. Her brow furrowed as she squinted through the window, trying to get a better look. Was he praying? *Of course not*, she quickly determined. *He doesn't seem the type.* But then, hadn't she heard that the Irish were religious by nature and by birth? Even Sean had turned to the Lord on occasion.... *Pity that it was only when he'd exhausted his money by gambling or his energy by beating me, she thought.*

With her palms resting flat on the windowsill and her elbows pointing north and south, Kate rested her chin on her hands. She didn't understand the emotions rising in her as she continued staring at him, down there on the dock. Something about him seemed to call out to something in her with a heartfelt, desolate plea that told her he was every bit as lonely—and as tired of being lonely—as she. True, he'd huffed and puffed and pawed like an angry bull when Adam had stolen his lunch, but then, his privacy had been invaded, his property violated. Hadn't he had every right to be riled?

The fact that Adam had stolen his lunch struck her with newfound shock. What in heaven's name would she do with that son of hers?

As if he'd heard Kate's silent question, J.J. lifted his head and, without looking left or right, focused directly on her. For a long, eerie moment, they remained locked in the unnerving eye-to-eye connection. She likened the link to a spider's web—strong enough to support the arachnid's weight, yet fragile enough to be torn from its moorings by a gust of wind.

When, at last, the moment ended—and it ended only because J.J. looked away—Kate thought she understood how the eight-legged creatures might feel when the silken latticework that took hours, even days, to construct was quickly and cruelly destroyed without warning. The eye contact between her and J.J. had lasted perhaps three blinks of an eye—more than enough time for an awareness of each other to bind them, mind to mind, soul to soul.

J.J. glanced up again, tilted his head to one side, and pocketed both hands.

Is he—is he smiling at me? she wondered. Then, *Yes! Yes, he is!* Flustered that she'd been caught ogling—again—Kate straightened her back and moved away from the window. Maybe she'd imagined the whole thing. Perhaps he hadn't seen her at all. Perhaps he'd been looking at something else, not her. After all, down there on the dock, he was about fifty yards away. Could he really have seen a woman in a window?

The memory of his smile flashed in her mind. Yes, he'd seen her, all right. Never one to take comfort from false hopes, large or small, she admitted that the moment had indeed happened. Standing up, she smoothed her apron, tucked a wayward curl into her braid, and backed still further from the window.

She and J.J. O'Keefe had lived in the same town for several years. And though little more than a narrow, rutted road separated their businesses, their homes—their lives—his path and hers had never crossed...until Adam had decided to steal the man's lunch.

Chance meetings had a way of repeating themselves. Sooner or later, she and J.J. O'Keefe would bump into each other again—of that, she was sure. And when they did, she hoped the encounter would not be angry or accusatory because, for reasons that made no sense, she was strangely attracted to the burly Irishman.

This was a problem. A big problem. At Sean's graveside, she'd vowed, for the safety and well-being of her son, never to get close to another man. And this man was to be avoided more than most, for he had far too much in common with Adam's father.

"Who is she?" Mary whispered to Thaddeus as the two stood outside the feed and grain and watched the woman riding down the street on a white pony, her head held high, her eyes focused straight ahead.

"You've got me by the feet, Mother...."

Mary took a step closer to her husband. "She looks like an Indian."

"Well," he replied, moving his briar pipe from one side of his mouth to the other, "she's got the look of a squaw, I'll give you that."

"But she's wearing a white woman's dress and high-heeled boots. What do you make of that?"

"There's your answer, Mother," he said, pointing to the shoes. "No Indian in her right mind would trade comfortable moccasins for hard soles."

Just outside the feed and grain, the woman stopped, dismounted, and tethered her horse to the iron ring hanging from the hitching post. Turning to Mary and Thaddeus, she calmly announced, "I am in need of flour and cornmeal. Do you have these things?"

"Y-yes," Mary stammered. "Of course." Gathering her skirts, she climbed the wooden steps. "Won't you come inside with me?"

The woman held up a hand. "Before you go to much trouble," she began, "I must tell you that I have no American dollars. I hope to trade for what I need."

Laying a fat-fingered hand upon her bosom, Mary looked at Thaddeus. "Well, now, I don't know. We've always been a cash-only business...."

Her husband stepped up beside her. "What sort of fool rides into town expecting to get something for nothing? We can't afford to trade baubles and beads for our goods. Why, how could we—"

The woman reached up and removed a small, leather bag from the saddle horn. Opening the drawstring, she dipped a hand inside. "Do you call these 'baubles and beads'?"

Thaddeus took a step forward and, with a gnarled forefinger, poked at one of the gemstones. "Are they diamonds?"

One corner of the woman's mouth lifted in a wry grin. "I could say that they are, for I can see that you would not know a diamond from rock candy. But Running Deer does not lie." Smiling, she said, "These are crystals. I polish them myself."

"They're just beautiful," Mary said with a sigh of admiration.

"And those?" Thaddeus asked, pointing at another type of stone.

"Iron."

"But—but it looks like gold...."

Running Deer nodded. "Some call it fool's gold, and for good reason. It is pyrite," she explained. "Harder, but not as heavy as the real thing. See these grooves, here?"

Thaddeus nodded.

"Real gold does not have such grooves."

He regarded her out of the corner of his eye. "How is it you know so much about things like this?"

Laughing softly, she dropped the stones back into the bag. "A missionary taught me to read and write. Taught me to cipher numbers, too." She shrugged. "I learned these things from books."

"Why, that's just plain wonderful!" Mary said, clasping her hands together. "Thaddeus, she's a believer, same as you and me!"

"Was your family saved, too?" Thaddeus asked.

The warm light in her dark eyes vanished, and she shook her head.

"Why not?"

"They believe in a different god, but they do believe."

"Ain't no god but the one true God," Thaddeus proclaimed.

"I am convinced, but they could not be."

"What tribe are you with?"

"I have no tribe."

"Nonsense. You're an Indian, aren't you?"

She retied the gem sack to the saddle horn and glanced west with a sad, faraway look on her face. "Once," she whispered, "I was of the Algonquin people."

"And you ain't one now? Why ever not?" He paused. "Say, you didn't kill nobody, did you?"

Pursing her lips, she arched one eyebrow. "Not yet."

The old man's blue eyes widened as Kate stepped onto the porch of her shop. "What's all the chatter about?" she asked. "Sounds like a meeting of the magpies out here."

"I am Running Deer," the woman announced, bowing slightly at the waist. "I came in hopes of trading for flour and cornmeal." Her gaze found Mary's, then Thaddeus's, before she focused on Kate again. "It seems I have come a long way for nothing."

Kate had heard the word *bigotry* and could define it, as well. But never before had she seen it with her own eyes. It surprised her that her friends and neighbors—people she thought she knew and understood—could judge any human being because of the color of her skin.

"What's going on here?"

Kate's heart thundered at the sound of Howard Andersen's booming voice. He was Currituck's resident bully and troublemaker. As if Running Deer didn't have enough problems already!

"What're you people doing, standing here jabber-jawing with the likes of this redskin?" he demanded.

"Don't you know they're crawling with parasites, that they're murderin', thievin'—"

"Good morning, Howard," Kate interrupted him. It was a shame, she'd always thought, that such good looks had been wasted on this shallow, conceited Scandinavian. But perhaps his vanity had a purpose other than to annoy those around him. "Where have you been keeping yourself?" she asked him, forcing her voice to express a brightness that she didn't feel. "I haven't seen you at Sunday services in weeks!"

"Why, g'mornin' to you, Mrs. Flynn." He removed his Derby and, smiling, said, "Been busy, but I'm planning to stop by this week. Need to make final arrangements for Abigail's weddin', don't you know."

"And how is Adelaide?" Kate asked.

At the mention of his wife, Howard put his hat back on. Minus the smile, he said, "She's fine. Just fine."

"And the other children?"

"Good, they're all good."

"Seems the only chances we get to chat are when you come to my shop to order a new shirt or a pair of trousers." She'd made him a dozen shirts and nearly as many pants in the years since opening her shop, and she'd altered several dresses for his wife and sewed skirts and blouses for his other daughters, too. "I think you work too hard, Howard!"

But he wasn't that easily distracted. "You part of this little hen party?"

"Hen party?"

He nodded toward Running Deer. "She visiting you, too?"

The Indian woman stared down at her feet. "Actually," Kate said, taking her horse's reins, "she was just about to come inside for a fitting, weren't you, Running Deer?"

Suspicion glinted in the woman's dark, slanting eyes, but she allowed Kate to lead her away, stopping to retie her horse to the post in front of the dress shop.

"See you two later," Kate called to Mary and Thaddeus, then added, "Say hello to Adelaide for me, Howard!"

The trio murmured quietly as the women entered Kate's shop. Kate peered out the window at the white horse. "What a beautiful animal."

"His name is Konawa. It means 'barter' or 'deal.'"

"I have an apple and some oats upstairs. Won't you join me for a cup of tea?"

As Kate pumped water into the tea kettle, Running Deer smiled and said, "I do not know if you are a very brave woman...or a very stupid one."

"Neither, I hope," Kate said, putting the kettle on the stove.

"Are you always so kind? Or have you made an exception on my behalf?"

"If you want the truth, I made an exception, because I rarely have time for polite conversation."

The comment inspired the first of many smiles Kate would coax from the woman, and, before the evening ended, she felt she had made a friend.

For the first time in weeks, Adam's behavior could be described as something other than grumpy and mean. "I liked Konawa," he said over breakfast the next morning. "He let me feed him apple slices."

"Running Deer tells me he isn't particularly friendly with most people, and that you must be very special."

When the boy smiled, his whole face lit up. Oh, how she'd missed seeing the deep dimples in those freckled cheeks!

"Is she coming back soon?" he asked around a mouthful of toast.

Kate overlooked the violation of table manners to say, "I hope so."

"Me, too." Then, "I think it's good that you have a lady friend who's close to your age. Haven't had one of those in a long time, have you, Ma?"

Kate felt the heat of a blush creep into her cheeks. She hadn't had anyone her age to talk to since leaving Philadelphia. "No, I don't suppose I have."

"That's a puzzle," Adam said, looking wiser than his years. "But I think I know why. It's 'cause you're the prettiest woman in Currituck, and the other ladies are jealous. That's why."

Her flush deepened. "What a nice thing to say, Adam."

"Just the truth, is all. And you're the nicest, too." He shrugged. "Can I ask you something, Ma?"

"Of course."

"Would you be angry with me if I went to work for Mr. O'Keefe?"

Angry was hardly the word. More like afraid, worried, concerned—

"He was right, you know," Adam said.

"About what?"

"About not being able to get a decent night's sleep on account of feeling bad about what I did. I don't like feeling guilty." Grinning, he added, "Think it means I have a conscience?"

"Of course you do. Whatever made you think you didn't?"

Leaning his cheek on his fist, he said, "Well, I did just fine before, without worrying what other folks thought... if I made 'em angry or hurt their feelings—"

"You've been considering all that, just because of what Mr. O'Keefe said?"

Adam nodded. "So, can I, Ma? Can I work for him and pay for the stuff I stole?"

Kate took a sip of her coffee, more to forestall the tears than to figure out what she'd tell her son. *He's growing up,* she admitted to herself, *and it's looking like he might just become a good, decent man.*

In her heart, she'd always believed this day would come. But that it would get here this early? And thanks to John Joseph O'Keefe...?

Kate smiled and said, "Yes, son. You may work to pay off the items you stole."

Chapter Three

J.J. did his all-fired best to hide the smile that had been bubbling inside him since first noticing the boy, crouching in the warehouse doorway, as if a rabid dog might live inside. As Adam continued searching the darkened interior for him, looking right and left from outside the building, a gull screeched overhead. Both of the boy's feet left the ground in startled response. With arms akimbo and neck craned, he strained his ears to identify the sound. The gull swooped low, squawking again. Adam ran a hand through dark curls, and J.J. could almost hear the boy's relieved sigh.

'Tis yer fault the little fellow fears his own shadow, O'Keefe, he thought, watching the boy cower beyond the door. *'Tweren't ever yer intention to frighten the child.*

That wasn't entirely true. J.J. had been miffed the first time his lunch had disappeared. Annoyed when the second had vanished. But as he'd watched the third being carried off by the trio of hooligans, J.J. admitted, he'd grown angry. He'd determined, even then, to ignore the matter. *They're bound for prison, no matter what you do*, he'd thought.

That is, until he'd spied the flash of fear and dread in the youngest one's eyes. That alone had inspired J.J. to give chase, thinking even as he ran behind the boy that the "Oh, no!" expression meant that one, at least, might be saved from a future of delinquency.

As a lad, J.J. had survived a similar experience. If it hadn't been for old man McPherson, there was no telling how he might have ended up.

"I—I'm sorry, Mr. O'Keefe, sir," Adam said when he finally spotted J.J. Twisting his cap nervously with both hands, he went on. "I been thinkin' about what you said, and I've come to make things right."

J.J. fought the urge to throw down his sandpaper and pull the boy into a hearty hug. It had been hard for the boy to show up this way, as evidenced by his rapidly blinking eyes and quivering lower lip, and he'd earned a moment of dignity.

"Does yer ma know ye're here?"

Adam nodded.

"And she's all right with ye workin' off yer debt, then...?"

Another nod.

J.J. put the sandpaper in his tool bucket and leaned both arms on the boat's rail. No doubt the young mother had her hands full, trying to keep the two of them fed, clothed, and under a roof. Trying to teach the boy how a man should respond had to be tough, indeed. "Ye're a lad of many moods, I see."

"Sir?"

"Ye weren't standin' this tall the day I caught ye stealin' me lunch. Didn't speak like a boy with proper breedin', neither. Had me convinced ye were just another thievin' punk, bound for a prison cell." Smiling, J.J. winked. "I'm pleased to admit I was wrong—dead wrong."

"I don't hang around with those boys anymore, sir," Adam said, staring at the toes of his boots.

"Why not?"

"Ma says folks will judge me by the company I keep." Without raising his head, he peeked through his long, dark eyelashes. "I don't want other people thinkin' I'm bound for prison."

A lecture like that was supposed to be delivered by a father to his son, not by a woman no bigger than a minute. J.J.'s heart ached for her, as well as for this boy, who reminded him of himself at the same age. Crouching, he pretended to rub some dust from his boot. "So, when would y'like to start?"

Adam licked his lips. "The sooner the better, sir."

J.J. remained child-sized to ask, "Know how to handle a hammer?"

"Yessir. Got my own toolbox," Adam said, smiling for the first time since they'd met. "When things come loose around Ma's shop, I'm the one whacks 'em into place." He punctuated the statement with a proud jerk of his chin. "Got me a cross saw, a pry bar, and a—"

"How 'bout a level and T square?"

"Yessir, got those, too."

"And how's yer arithmetic?"

"I hate it, but I get by."

"Well, remember that the hand that wields the tool is no better than the head that guides it."

Adam tucked in one corner of his mouth, nodding in halfhearted agreement.

Chuckling, J.J. placed a hand on the boy's shoulder. "I think it's best we don't put any strain on yer tools, since y'need 'em to help out yer ma and all. Ye'll use mine, and I have plenty, as ye'll soon see."

The fear that had glinted in Adam's eyes was gone when J.J. added, "Ye'll give me three hours, one for each lunch y'stole. Fair enough?"

"Yessir, fair enough."

J.J. extended a hand, and, for an instant, the boy hesitated to take it. He recovered quickly, though, and thrust out his arm. "So, now that we've shaken on it, we've got a deal. And between good men, a handshake is as binding as any legal contract."

Adam nodded. "I understand, sir."

J.J. spent the next half hour giving Adam a tour of the warehouse, the dock, the boats he was building, and the one he'd just finished. The boy paid wide-eyed attention to every detail, nodding, asking questions, and repeating proper boating and construction terms. *He'll be all right...if he keeps away from those hoodlums*, J.J. said to himself.

At the conclusion of the tour, he grabbed two big mugs from the shelf above the coal stove. "Do y'drink coffee, lad?"

Adam accepted the mug. "Nosir, but I've always wanted to give it a try."

J.J. hesitated, holding the coffeepot over the mouth of Adam's cup. "'Tis only fair to warn ye...I'll not go against yer ma. If ye want a second helping, ye'll need her permission."

"She won't mind. Ma loves coffee. I expect she'll like having someone to share a morning cup with."

J.J. nodded and made a mental note of yet another item to add to his "Good Things about Kate" list. "Gets a mite ripe by this time of day," he said. "Sorry there's no milk or sugar to cut the bitter taste."

Adam mimicked J.J.'s actions, right down to uttering a satisfied "Ahhh" after swallowing. "It is a bit bitter," Adam admitted, "but I reckon that's true about many things in life." He took another gulp. "Guess it's good to get used to things like this while you're a young'un, so you can handle 'em better once you've really become a man."

Too soon to tell Adam he was already on the right road? Yes, J.J. thought so. Better to wait until the boy had clocked all three hours. "Well, let's get busy," he said, leading the way toward the workbench.

To J.J., it seemed he'd grown a three-foot shadow, which could mean only one thing: Adam wanted a man's firm, fair hand every bit as much as J.J. knew he needed it.

But did he want to be that man?

Better make up yer mind right quick, he told himself, *'cause if ye get involved now, y'might be in it for the long haul.*

Did he have the time?

Yes and no.

But did he want to *make* the time? Exercise the patience required to teach the emotionally unsteady youngster about carpentry, shipbuilding, and life?

And what of the boy's mother? She'd been fit to be tied when J.J. had insinuated she hadn't been hard enough on Adam. If the boy went home dirty and sweaty and aching from hard work, it might be like provokin' a mama tiger....

Could he deal with that?

Did he even want to try?

J.J. glanced at Adam and found the boy looking up at him with wide eyes that beamed with boyish innocence. *How long is that gonna last without a man to keep him in line?* he asked himself. Wavering for a moment between protecting his beloved solitude and helping this needy boy, he took a deep breath and then tousled Adam's dark curls. "Ready for yer first assignment?"

"Oh, yessir!"

"All right, then, listen here...."

Adam copied J.J.'s stance and opened his eyes even wider, as if to prove he was paying attention.

"For starters, ye'll quit callin' me 'sir.' Makes me feel like a dodderin' old fool."

"Yessir. I mean, all right, Mr. O'Keefe."

Gently, J.J. chucked the boy's chin. "Not 'Mr. O'Keefe,' either. That was my da's name. We'll be partners for the time being, so ye'll call me J.J. All right?"

Grinning, Adam said, "Right."

Perhaps someday, he'd tell Adam about his boyhood experience with Nate McPherson. For now, J.J. could only hope he was man enough to do for Adam what the old man had done for him.

"Yer boy was admiring this today," J.J. told Kate, standing at a careful distance, "when I showed him round the warehouse."

Kate stepped closer to accept the tiny replica of a many-masted sailing vessel, accurate to the minutest detail. "Why, it's just beautiful," she said.

"'Tis nothin', really," he said, shrugging. "I don't usually make 'em for the smaller boats, but when I get a contract to build somethin' more elaborate, I put together a scale model."

She turned it around to study it from another angle. "I'll bet some folks say it's a lot of unnecessary work, don't they?"

"Aye, matter of fact, some do."

"And, no doubt, it *is* a lot of extra work, but it's not the least bit unnecessary, and I understand exactly why you do it."

"Oh, ye think so, do ye?" he asked, grinning.

Returning his playful smile, Kate nodded. "This is much more intricate, and it requires far more skill, of course. But, in theory, it's a pattern, like the ones I draw up before sewing a dress or a suit." She held up the boat to inspect its underside. "It's nice to have something to look at, something to guide you, when you sit down to work."

"'Tisn't often I run into a body—a female body, in particular—who sees things as I do." He smiled. "But I didn't bring the boat over here to show it off. Not that it wasn't pleasant gettin' yer opinion."

Statue-still, she held the model to her chest. "Then why *did* you bring it, Mr. O'Keefe?"

"Ye seem like a no-nonsense woman to me. Am I right?"

"I'll admit, I've never had much respect for those who don't say what they mean. It's a colossal waste of time, for one thing, and there's always a good chance folks will misread your intentions."

"I'll take y'at yer word, then, and say it straight out: the boat isn't for ye. It's for yer boy."

She smiled gratefully. "I'm sure he'll treasure it."

"Somethin' else, ma'am?"

Her brows rose as she waited for him to speak his request.

"Would ye mind very much callin' me J.J.? Every time I hear 'Mr. O'Keefe,' I expect me da to step up and say, 'What?'"

Kate laughed, thinking that he was quite handsome when he smiled that way. *Pity he doesn't do it more often....*

His smile widened and, holding a thumb and forefinger inches apart, he said, "So, tell me, Mrs. Flynn, do y'have wee duplicates of all the dresses ye've made?"

It made her blush to admit that, on occasion, in addition to patterns, she *had* made doll-sized versions of her creations. "How did you know?"

He shrugged. "Ye just look like the type, that's all."

"What type?"

"Y'know," he said offhandedly, "a woman who's made a place for everything, who can't let a speck of dust settle without gettin' her feather duster out, who—"

"The woman you're describing sounds like a fanatic, Mr. O—I mean, J.J. And I'll have you know that while I'm organized and tidy, I'm certainly not a fanatic!"

Grinning, J.J. leaned closer and whispered, "That's not what yer boy says."

Since Sean's death, being this near a man had made her flinch, as if she half expected to dodge a fist or shut her ears to a cutting remark. Yet, for a reason she couldn't explain, J.J.'s nearness caused no such anxiety. Odd, considering his size! Instead, she felt safe. Protected. "What does my boy say?"

J.J.'s eyebrows rose, and the corners of his mouth turned up in a wry smile. "He says if he puts a thing down, even for one tick of the clock, ye're off and running with it." Chuckling, he added, "Says he doesn't know where most of his things are."

She giggled, then harrumphed. Folding her arms over her chest, she said, "Why, they're—"

"—right where they belong!" they said together, laughing.

A moment of companionable silence passed before Kate said, "I was just about to have a cup of tea. Would you like some?"

"Ordinarily," he said, "I'm a coffee drinker. And Adam says ye're a coffee drinker, too."

"Oh, I love a cup with breakfast. But it's more expensive than this homegrown tea, so I switch mid-morning."

"I'd love a cup of yer homegrown brew, ma'am."

"Won't you join me upstairs, then?" she asked, curtseying before leading him upstairs to her apartment.

Once inside, J.J. looked around approvingly. "I was right."

"About what?" she asked, while pumping water into the tea kettle.

"I'd wagered I could eat off this floor, and there's not a scrap of clutter in sight."

The admiration in his voice and eyes was obvious. Still, the compliment puzzled Kate. Why *wouldn't* the home she made for her son be clean and tidy? The world outside was fraught with disorder and upheaval. Wasn't it her duty to provide the boy with a haven from that chaos?

Life was unpredictable, at best; naturally, she wanted her boy to have a safe harbor from the tumult. "If you love your house, I always say, then treat it like a home."

J.J. nodded. "Me own ma used to say, 'A house isn't a home until a mother's love makes it so.'"

Kate couldn't identify the expression that crossed his face as he said it and chalked it up to the fact that he was a bachelor. As she set the table and poured the tea, they discussed the weather, the clock tower the town elders wanted to build in the center of town, and other local lore. Suddenly, Kate blurted out the question that had been niggling at her since she'd noticed J.J. hovering around her back steps earlier. "Tell me, J.J., what really brings you here?"

His beard hid very little of his blush. "Why, the boat, of course," he said, pointing to the model.

"Please," she said, "have a seat." Then, "Adam is working for you now. You could have given it to him directly—he'll be there again tomorrow."

J.J. turned a chair around, swung one leg over its seat as if mounting a short-legged horse, and straddled it. Grinning, he leaned both arms on the chair's back and met her eyes. "Ye're not one to mince words, are ye, Mrs. Flynn?"

"Waste of time," she reminded him. "And so are distractions...."

J.J. cleared his throat, telling her he'd picked up on her insinuation. "I—I only meant to leave the boat outside yer door, so the boy would find it first thing in the morning. Never expected ye'd be on the porch on a night as chill as this."

Kate often stood looking out at the sea before getting ready for bed. It soothed her, steadied her nerves. Before J.J., no one had noticed.

"Ye seemed to be a million miles away," he said. "Where were ye wishin' ye could be?"

She laughed softly. "Oh, it was nothing as melodramatic as that. It's just...the sound and the scent of the sea are calming to me."

"I feel the same," he said. "Hasn't been easy for ye, has it?"

"Self-pity doesn't pay the bills, so I won't make time for that, either."

"To be honest, I don't feel the least bit sorry for ye. I'm only saying that it can't have been easy, burying a husband, leaving everything behind, starting over in a new place, all with a youngster to raise." He took a swallow of his tea. "I am a bit curious, though...."

She sipped her own tea and waited for him to explain.

"Why didn't ye head back to Philly when ye lost yer man, so ye could be near yer family?"

"I have no family," Kate said, wrapping both hands around her teacup. Staring into the dark, shimmering liquid, she went on, "The accident happened about a month before Adam was born. The news was such a shock that—"

"Accident? What news?"

She took a deep breath and put down her teacup. "There was a fire in the church. Everyone inside was trapped by falling beams. It was wintertime, so they'd shuttered the windows, and...and...."

J.J. placed his big hands atop hers and looked deep into her eyes. "So, ye're alone, too, then," he said, his voice a mere whisper. "One more thing we have in common."

No man had touched her—not since Sean. His palms, pressing against the backs of her hands, were every bit as warm as the cup she'd been holding. And, despite the calluses—or maybe because of them—they felt surprisingly strong. "I'm not totally alone. I have a grandmother."

His eyes brightened. "Well, now," he said, "that's wonderful news. Is she here in Currituck?"

Kate shook her head. “No, she’s never been to North Carolina. After the fire, she went home.”

“Home?”

“To England.”

The color of his eyes now reminded her of a stormy sky. Why had the mention of her grandmother’s homeland changed his demeanor? “Is something—is something wrong?”

Releasing her hands, he stood up and made for the door. “No, not really. Thanks for the tea, Mrs. Flynn.”

“If I’m to call you J.J., you’ll have to call me Kate.”

He opened the door and smiled, but the smile never quite made it to his eyes, she noticed.

“All right, then—Kate it is.”

“Thank you for the model. I know Adam will love it.” She hesitated, unnerved by the sudden change in his mood. “But, wouldn’t you rather give it to him, yourself? So you can see his initial reaction?”

“Maybe ye can tell me all about that the next time I see ye.”

And, just like that, he was gone.

Kate carried their cups and saucers to the sink, rethinking their conversation and trying to determine what she’d said to upset him. It must have had something to do with the mention of England. But what? And why such a drastic, negative reaction? She changed into her night clothes and wondered about it some more. An hour later, she was still wondering about it, wandering from window to window, restless, agitated, and tense, though she couldn’t think of a single reason she should feel this way.

Grabbing her thick, fringed shawl, she stepped onto the little porch outside her window—the only home improvement she hadn’t made with her own two hands, and the only luxury she’d allowed herself in years.

Most of the time, being here had been a comfort, but once in a while—like tonight—the faint scent of soot and charred wood wafted into her nostrils, reminding her that, years ago, a ferocious blaze had chased away the family who had lived here. How strange that at almost the same time in history, a fire had killed her family, hundreds of miles north of Currituck.

If she'd known that neither scrubbing nor painting nor the passage of time would eradicate all of the awful odors and the images they conjured, she might not have purchased the property. For when the reminders assaulted her, she could almost feel the heat, could almost hear the hiss and crackle of the flames as they hungrily chomped through the house, room by room.

Time after time, when the horrible pictures appeared in her mind, she'd throw open the window as far as it would go and pray that God Almighty would send a powerful wind to blow away the haunting images. If anyone else had noticed the odors reminiscent of the fire, they hadn't mentioned them to Kate, so she had little choice but to admit they were nothing but the products of her overactive imagination.

Now, she longed for the crisp pungency of briny air, but no matter how deeply she inhaled, the stench of scorched lumber refused to leave her. As the night cloaked her, Kate wondered why so many people feared the darkness. True, it made it more difficult to see, and, yes, an assortment of predators could be lurking in the shadows. But there was comfort in the thick, inky blackness, too, if one chose to see and feel it—the kind of serenity borne of silence that grows stronger with each passing moment.

Kate likened the hours between twilight and daybreak to a warm quilt thrown by a protective parent over a sleeping child. The dark invoked calm, quietness, and reassurance. It promised peace and contentment...if one dwelt on what was beautiful about it, rather than the fearful thoughts it could inspire.

Above, a bright canopy of stars winked and shimmered like miniscule crystals. Every time she looked up at the night sky, Kate was reminded of her life-loving sister, who would routinely gather petals, or sand, or feathers, and, giggling with glee, fling them skyward. Kate often wondered if, on the day the Lord created the earth, He'd cast the spangles into the heavens in a similar way.

She remembered, too, that when she'd been but a girl, her mother had calmed her nightmares by saying the twinkling stars were God's angels, winking to the humans He'd assigned them to as a sign that all was well.

Another pleasantry of the night was the ever-changing face of the moon. Sometimes, it appeared as slender as a newly trimmed fingernail shaving; other times, it looked as round as a ball. Its lunar light beamed down upon the earth in silvery fronds. "The fingers of God's hand," her mother had called them, "reaching out to give each of His children a reassuring pat on the head as he settles in for a long night's sleep."

Kate felt none of those things tonight. Perhaps it was the eerie wind that soughed, softly yet sharply, from the sea. Or maybe the crisp, late-May air was keeping away her much-needed peace.

The breeze riffled her hair, and Kate shivered. Adam had always been a restless sleeper, and he'd likely kicked off his covers. She'd left his window open a crack, so this chilly wind would no doubt be blowing over him. Climbing back inside through her window, she made her way to his room and saw that, sure enough, he lay on his side, huddled in a knee-hugging ball. Gently, she tugged up the coverlet she'd fashioned from material scraps and tucked it under his chin. Every maternal chord in her sang out as she looked into his sleeping face, and her eyes filled with awe-inspired tears of gratitude. *Oh, how blessed I am to have him in my life,* she thought. *Thank You, Lord, for giving me this precious child to love!* If she accomplished nothing else in her time on earth, at least she would have contributed something worthwhile in the form of this beautiful boy.

Kate knelt down beside his bed and, carefully, so as not to wake him, combed her fingers through his soft, cinnamon-colored curls. A shaft of moonlight sliced through the slight opening in his curtains, slid across the floor and onto his bed, and illuminated his sweet face. Long lashes rested on freckled cheeks, and one corner of his mouth was turned up in the beginnings of an innocent, little-boy smile. *What are you dreaming, little one? Are you chasing a bullfrog? Kicking a ball? Surf fishing?*

He'd tucked one small hand beneath his cheek; the other clutched his feather pillow tightly to his chest. *How can you look so much like your father, yet be nothing like him in any other way?* she wondered.

A dreaded thought reverberated in her heart like a Chinese gong: *What if he is like Sean, but simply isn't old enough yet to show the signs?*

Someday, the freckles peppering the bridge of his nose would fade, and his innocence would fade with them. Soon, his narrow chest would broaden and thicken with mighty muscles. Would a caring heart continue to beat inside it? Now, Adam's long-fingered hands baited his fishing hook with cheese because he couldn't bear to kill a worm. Would those same gentle hands someday clench into angry fists to cause deliberate pain?

He was satisfied now—happy, even—with a roof over his head, enough food for his belly, a modest wardrobe, and a few treasured toys. Would a never-ending yearning for more, always more, drive him to a violent end?

Kate pictured Sean as she'd last seen him: slumped over the green, felt-topped poker table with a dagger in one hand, dollars in the other, bleeding from a bullet hole in his temple, his eyes open but unseeing. "Not that for my boy," she whispered. "Please, Lord, not that."

Adam stirred, and, regretfully, Kate withdrew her hand. But she continued to kneel beside him, her hands folded in prayer, unmindful of the hard, board floor, the chill in the air, the late hour, or her weary eyes. She was content merely to watch him sleep.

When Adam had been but a baby, she'd spend hours this way, convinced that if she hadn't needed a few hours' rest, herself, she easily could have whiled her life away, content to count his breaths, his tiny murmurs, his sweet sighs.

I know that his body will grow, Lord, that his mind will broaden, and that his feet may carry him far from home. I know these things are part of Your greater plan for Adam. But won't You let them happen slowly, please? Let him linger a while as a boy, Lord, before taking him headlong into manhood....

Regardless of the timetable God had set for Adam's life, Kate was not the kind of mother who'd try to forestall these things—not even if, when he became a man, a job, a woman, or a burning desire to see the world took him from Currituck. Someday, she'd give her full-grown son this advice: "If you can remember only one rule, make it the Golden Rule, for it will guide you well in every area of your life."

And maybe she shouldn't wait until he was a man to dispense that advice. Maybe she should give it to him now. *Maybe you should have given it to him long ago....*

Before meeting up with Bobby and his gang, Adam had been a happy, cooperative child who'd needed only rare reminders to do his chores and an occasional prompt to finish his schoolwork. The only orders he'd obeyed since his association with those ruffians had been those barked by Bobby, the leader of the pack.

But lately....

Lately, he'd been doing his chores without a single cue from Kate. And every job, no matter how menial, he'd do as though aiming for perfection. Most of the time, Kate happily admitted, he hit the bull's eye, and even on the rare occasion when he missed, she could see proof of his good intentions on his face and his stance. The evidence was there from the moment he climbed out of bed in the morning until he closed his eyes at night.

Kate's sweet, thoughtful son was back, and she knew there was only one explanation for his sudden and amazing transformation.

She stood up and pressed a light, loving kiss to Adam's temple. "Sleep well, sweet boy, and may the angels bless your dreams."

As she climbed into her own bed, Kate smiled. "And may the angels bless your dreams, as well, J.J. O'Keefe."

J.J. didn't understand the feelings warring inside him, because living by his motto had never let him down before: "Avoid all things English."

Years ago, as he'd said a final good-bye prayer over the graves of his parents and siblings, he'd known he would never return to pray over them again. That very night, as the moon had slipped behind a cloud, he'd crept aboard a ship bound for New York's harbor. He'd hidden for weeks in the bowels of the boat, slipping out only once the sun had long set to scurry in the shadows like the roaches and rats in search of food and water. Thoughts of freedom had kept him alive, helped him endure the nonstop lurching of the boat. The Yanks had fought long and hard against British oppression, and they'd won. He'd needed no more information than that to know he'd feel at home in America.

Provided he could make it there.

If the sailors or their captain found him, he'd be cast overboard. He'd heard stories of stowaways who'd treaded water for days until exhaustion—or hungry sharks—had overtaken them. He'd also hoped not to succumb to some dread disease caused by flea bites, sleeping among the rats, or drinking tainted water and eating spoiled food....

As a boy, he'd had a healthy fear of death. Healthy, because it had prevented him from taking foolish chances, like making shortcuts across the peat bogs, seeing how near the edge of a cliff he could stand without falling into the bay, or sneaking into old man McPherson's store to steal cakes or cookies.

As a young man, he'd feared death because, by then, he'd learned to appreciate what life could offer—the friendship of a father, the kinship of a brother, the love of a good wife, the birth of a child.

But, huddled among the sacks and crates and boxes in the foul-smelling hold of that ship, J.J. had felt no fear of death. There, he'd had but one fear: that he wouldn't make it to the green fields of Americay.

Now, as he lay in his bunk above the warehouse, he closed his eyes, thinking how, even after all this time, it was often difficult to believe he'd made it. *He'd made it!* Clasping both hands under his head, J.J. stared up at the rafters. Shimmering moonlight slanted through the boards above and glinted from nail tips that protruded through the underside of the rough-hewn, lumber-and-shingle roof.

Kate's eyes gleam like that, he thought, half smiling.

And then, he remembered she was half English, and the smile faded. If English blood flowed in her veins, could she be as good and decent as she seemed?

J.J. wanted to believe she could, because in moments like these, when he was alone with nothing but his own thoughts, he liked to pretend that a normal future was possible for him after all; that love and family life could be his again, with a woman like Kate by his side.

Kate O'Keefe.

It sounded good. Sounded right. Sounded like something Danny Flannigan down at Kerry's Pub might have put to music—if the fever hadn't sent the Dark Faerie to take the fiddler, too. J.J. sat up with a start and punched his mattress. How could he even consider life with an English woman, especially so soon after meeting her?

He could consider it because in her soft, brown eyes, he saw all the misery and loneliness of her soul. Oh, she put up a good front for her boy's sake, with her happy face and lilting voice. But the sadness was there, just beneath the surface—and because she'd made the sorry mistake of marrying an Irishman, of all things! That one of his own could raise a hand to any woman boggled J.J.'s mind. How could Sean Flynn have harmed a lass as lovely as Kate?

And, surely, she was loving. What else could account for her marrying the brute to keep her parents' business from going belly-up?

Yes, she was a scrappy little thing; for proof, one needed to look only as far as the way she'd defended that Indian woman on the steps of the feed and grain. He'd been across the street at the bank when voices raised in anger had caught his attention, and he'd stood in the doorway, watching and listening in amazement that someone her size would take on two full-grown men and a woman twice her weight on behalf of the Algonquin princess.

He'd seen Running Deer many times before, pacing up and down Currituck's shore. "Stay away from that one," Abe Peters had warned him. "Her own people won't have nothin' to do with her. They say she's crazy as a bedbug." Shaking his head, Abe had added, "The Ind'ins threw her out of the village, way I hear it, and she's been livin' in a cave over yonder ever since."

"Why do they say she's crazy?"

"Seems she found a map once, hammered into leather by the ancients. The missionary what taught her to read helped her decipher it. More a tall tale, iffin' y'ask me, 'cause it weren't nothin' but a picture of the Sound, only half the width it is now." He scratched his bristly chin. "I tol' her it had to be a mistake. Maybe the man who drew it had failin' eyesight.

"But she weren't havin' none of it. She b'lieved ever' last word of it. Said we'd all best be careful how we treat them trees, 'cause if we aren't, one day, they'll all be gone."

"What trees?" J.J. had asked.

"Why, them cedars over yonder," Abe had said, pointing a gnarled finger. According to Running Deer, a hunnert years from now, there won't be nothin' left but scraggly poles stickin' up outta the sand and water."

J.J. had chuckled. "It'll take folks more than a hundred years to use up that much lumber."

"You ain't followin' me, Irish," Abe had said, shaking his white-haired head. "Runnin' Deer says people ain't gonna be the end of them cedars. The ocean will!"

Frowning at the memory, J.J. shook his head. Crazy as a bedbug? Perhaps. But that was certainly no reason to shun or mistreat her. Kate hadn't feared her. Hadn't treated her poorly. Hadn't snubbed her. Instead, she'd invited her inside, no doubt for a cup of her homegrown tea. He admired her more than he cared to admit.

Half English or not, she was the best thing that had happened to him in a long, long time.

Chapter Four

"I can't believe ye talked me into this, Thaddeus."

"Let's get one thing straight right up front, son: Nobody talks J.J. O'Keefe into anything, least of all a feeble old man like me."

J.J. grinned. "And the only thing feeble about ye, Thaddeus Crofton," he countered, "is yer reasons for askin' me here."

Thaddeus lifted his shoulders in an innocent shrug. "It's a Sunday social, nothin' more. The reverend encourages us to—"

"Gather the flock?"

"Say what you will, O'Keefe. You're as glad to be here as I am to have you here."

It was J.J.'s turn to shrug. "Fried chicken and a slice of Mary's apple pie is why I'm glad to be here."

"Well, you know better'n most that nothing comes free in this life. Consider hearin' the preacher's sermon as payment for your meal."

J.J. planted both boots flat on the floor and crossed his arms over his chest just as Mary leaned forward to peer around Thaddeus. "Will the two of you stop your whispering?" she scolded them gently, squeezing her husband's knee. "I can't hear a word the reverend is saying!"

"Sorry, Mother," Thaddeus said, out of the corner of his mouth. "I was just tellin' J.J., here, that—"

"I *heard* what you were telling him. So did the rest of the congregation!" She flashed him a loving smile. "Now, for the love of St. Pete, please hush."

J.J. stared straight ahead and fought the feelings of jealousy swirling in his gut. He'd never envied another man before in all his days—not the wealthy ones with the power to influence others, not the great orators and teachers, not even those who were bigger and stronger than he. Whether they came by these things by good fortune or the sweat of their brows, J.J. didn't begrudge them what they had. But he envied Thaddeus Crofton, because the old fellow had something that money couldn't buy—the love of a good woman.

J.J. had heard it said that a good mate is chosen by the Almighty on the day a man is born. Unfortunately, the Lord didn't write the intended lady's name on a slip of paper and tuck it into the baby boy's bunting. As a result, some men spent their lifetimes searching for the perfect woman and never found her. Others tried them all on for size, to see if one woman fit better than another—only to find that none fit "best." There were those who'd been kicked in the teeth by so-called love a few times before stumbling into the arms of the real thing. And then, there were the lucky few who seemed to find love without having to look at all.

Thaddeus was one of those.

If J.J. had been a guest at the Croftons' wedding, he knew he'd have witnessed new love just as surely as he was seeing it now, though they'd been together nearly sixty years. They'd shared a bed, a home, and a business, and had raised six strapping sons and two darling daughters. There had been hard times, but even those had been good in their way, and the proof was written on the couple's faces, heard in their voices, and expressed in the sweet, soft words they exchanged.

No, J.J. didn't envy Thaddeus's thriving business, and he wouldn't, even if he didn't have a successful company of his own. Didn't hunger after the man's money. Had no desire to own a home like the Crofton's, or to belong to a tight circle of church friends.

How many times had J.J. told himself he didn't need a woman to cook and sew and clean for him? Too many to count, so he didn't envy Thaddeus those things, either. It was the little things—the gentle touch, the loving look, the almost instinctual way in which Mary straightened Thaddeus's tie, finger-combed wind-blown hair back into place, and laughed at his jokes, even though she'd heard them dozens of times before. Mary, it was plain to see, was a woman in love, and the ways in which she fulfilled the duties of caring for her man were proof of it.

Kate would be that kind of wife.

And what would he give her in return? Only every aspect of his life! The sweat of his brow, his waking breath, his last thought before he slept would be hers, and hers alone.

He looked over at her, sitting there on the other side of the little church with her boy at her side. She was staring straight ahead, nodding and smiling in response to the sermon. Lovely, so lovely—no one could argue with that! Her smile had the power to warm even the coldest night, and if it was true that music could soothe the savage beast, Kate needed only speak a word or two to tame the wildest tiger.

J.J. had been in her home; had seen with his own eyes the precision and orderliness of her life, from the conversation-conducive positioning of furnishings to the colorful carpets and curtains. To the casual observer, it might appear that the blankets and cushions had been placed nonchalantly, but J.J. knew better. Smiling, he pictured her standing in a room, squinting in assessment and chewing her knuckle as she sought the perfect spot to put this doily or that knickknack. And the perfection of her needlework was more proof of her attention to detail. *If she puts that much time and attention into the everyday things of her life, imagine how much time and attention she'd put into loving her man!*

J.J. watched Kate lift her chin, then incline her head. Even from her profile, a person could tell she had eyes as wide and winsome as a doe's, right down to the long, dark lashes. Those eyes had been responsible for the way he'd caught himself daydreaming not too long ago....

He'd been putting the final coat of varnish on a mast when he'd found himself staring off into space, and his brush's dripping the sticky substance on the toe of his boot had brought him back to reality. Grinning like a fool, he'd tried to come up with a name for the color of her eyes, for they weren't brown or blue or green. For lack of a better word, he'd settled for "beautiful."

J.J. closed his eyes so that nothing would distract him from picturing her eyebrows, which arched like the gentle curve of a boat's prow...her high cheekbones...her skin, which promised to be as velvety as magnolia petals. He could tell by the thick bun at the base of her swanlike neck that her hair would likely reach her hips if ever she let it down. And if she did, no doubt, it would billow like a wind-filled sail. Surely, his fingers would meet if he wrapped one hand around her tiny waist.

For all her femininity, Kate was spunky and strong, as evidenced by the way she'd matched his angry glare at their first meeting. Like a mama lioness that hovers over her cubs, she would have fought to the death, if need be, to protect her boy. *This is not a woman to be trifled with*, he'd thought at the time. And, having gotten to know her better, he now knew this to be true.

There was no denying it: Kate Flynn fascinated him. Why else would he be sitting here, sweltering, in this too-small, too-crowded church? He'd vowed never to pay homage to the God who had allowed such savagery to take place in his homeland, yet that vow hadn't crossed his mind when Thaddeus had invited him to the meeting. Remembering what Mary had said about Kate attending Sunday services "no matter what," he'd fixed his mind on one thing, and one thing alone: If he said yes, he could see her again.

Now, as J.J. continued to watch Kate, he tried to ignore the roiling in his gut, the rapid beating of his heart, the sweat that slicked his palms, and the dryness that parched his throat. Grinning to himself, he couldn't help but wonder, *If all this is yer reaction to merely looking at the woman, what might become of ye if ye're ever lucky enough to take her in yer arms?*

Oh, it had been a mistake to entertain *that* thought, for it filled his being with longing. He wanted to protect and provide for her, to comfort and treasure her, to brand her with kisses and touches and promises of everlasting fidelity.... And he wanted her to do the same for him.

J.J. noticed Kate suddenly begin to squirm in her pew, and, with a tiny, lace-gloved hand, she adjusted the bow of her bonnet, the folds of her skirt, and the buttons of her bodice. Then, with no warning whatever, she turned that lovely, wide-eyed face toward him and looked straight into his eyes.

For an instant, they sat there, bound one to the other by an invisible thread, as on that evening in early May, when J.J. had felt someone's eyes on him and had looked up to see her watching from her bedroom window. That night, the connection had lasted a heartbeat, maybe two, but this time, it didn't last even half that long.

Kate had ended the first delightful moment, but it was J.J. who was first to turn away this time. He'd heard it said that the eyes were windows to the soul. If that were true, then Kate had looked straight into his, and he didn't know if he wanted her taking his measure as a man—for what if she were to read all the hard feelings and hatred written on his heart?

❀

Kate tried to ignore the feeling that someone was watching her, and when she finally gave in to the temptation to see who it might be, she was shocked to turn and look directly into J.J.'s eyes.

To her knowledge, he'd never attended Sunday services since moving to Currituck. She wondered what had drawn him to church today, but not nearly as much as she wondered why he'd been studying her so intently. What was that expression burning in his eyes?

She blinked to fight the bewilderment swirling in her head, for he was looking at her in the way he had that night when she'd seen him on the dock. Now, as then, his eyes seemed to be filled with expectation. But expectation of *what*?

As if hypnotized, she kept her gaze locked on his, mesmerized by his presence. *What do you want from me?* was her silent question, and it hammered at her until his expression darkened, as if he were reining himself in. Kate regretted the change in him, and she blinked again, yet continued to look into his eyes. Suddenly, his brow furrowed, and she was astonished at the depth of her disappointment when he looked away. They'd shared something meaningful in that special moment in time, and he'd ended it.

Why did that knowledge make her heart ache so? And why did she miss him, as if he'd left on a long, solitary journey? It made no sense, her feeling this sense of longing, loss, and sadness, especially considering she and J.J. barely knew each other.

Immediately, she corrected herself. She *did* know him, though that made no sense, either. When J.J. had stopped by to deliver the boat model for Adam, he'd been friendly, and their conversation had been warm. Had she been mistaken in thinking he liked her as someone more than just a neighbor?

Sighing, Kate loosened the bow of her bonnet. *Stop behaving like an addle-brained twit!* she told herself, frowning. *You're in the house of the Lord, for heaven's sake!*

She couldn't remember ever allowing anything to interfere with her worship. Whether alone at home or here with her fellow parishioners, whether doing her daily devotions or simply praying as she went about her routine activities, she had never let the everyday frustrations and distractions of life keep her from focusing on her heavenly Father. But not so today! Her mind was fixed on J.J. O'Keefe and would not let go.

Kate felt the heat of a blush color her cheeks, and she stared guiltily into her lap. What could she think, except that she'd allowed herself to *feel* something for J.J., despite her best intentions to avoid doing so? Comparing and contrasting him with her husband had done little more than confuse her further. Her husband had not been a believer, and J.J. was not a churchgoer. The Dublin-born Sean had come to America before his first birthday, while J.J. had spent all but the past few years on the wild, rugged Burren, near Galway Bay.

She tried to dispel the sweet, warm feelings rippling inside her heart at the mere thought of J.J. by telling herself that, surely, he was worse—far worse—than Sean. Because, while her husband had used his fists to beat her into submission, he'd done so mostly when whiskey had dulled his wits. J.J., on the other hand, had stepped consciously and deliberately into the ring, dozens of times, to face every opponent who thought himself strong enough to beat "The Annihilator." And, according to Thaddeus, J.J. had never lost a match, enabling him to line his pockets with money gambled away by men from New York to South Carolina.

And so, Kate decided to implement a strategy. Whenever she had a positive thought about J.J., she'd counter it with a negative one. If she saw him using his brawn to help Mary and Thaddeus unload the heavy shipments that arrived weekly at their store, she'd envision him using that same strength to pound the faces of less powerful men. Whenever she acknowledged the artistry of the hands that turned raw wood into beautiful sailing vessels, she'd paint a mental picture of him using those same hands to render competitors unconscious. Whenever she saw the productive results of the time he'd spent with Adam, she'd remind herself how he'd once earned his living.

But which was the *real* J.J.? The man whose fists had once been the tools of his trade, or the one who now used a chisel and saw?

The congregation stood up in unison, rousing Kate from her reverie. When the strains of the organ swelled and the parishioners' voices pronounced the lyrics of "Amazing Grace," Kate didn't join in, because her mind was not on the music. Instead, like that of an unruly child, her mind wandered. Was J.J. singing over there in his pew beside Thaddeus? And, if so, did his masculine voice sound as resonant in song as it did when he spoke?

Kate didn't know why, but now, her mind recalled the way his eyes had widened when she'd turned and realized he'd been watching her. It made Kate smile just a bit, because his startled expression was proof that he, too, knew how it felt to be caught gawking.

The Fourth of July was hot and steamy, even before the sun came up, but if the citizens of this tiny coastal community noticed, it didn't stop them from celebrating in full regalia. For weeks, while the town's housewives had been busy sewing the banners that now flapped brightly on every porch and storefront, the men had built a multitiered gazebo on the main street in preparation for the holiday festivities.

Now, wooden tables stood in U-formation under the pine trees, covered with dozens of pies and cakes and mountains of cookies to keep the breeze from lifting the tablecloths into the air like red-and-white sails. On the center table sat huge serving platters of fried chicken, roast pork, and spit-charred beef. And, on the left, breads and rolls of every shape and variety were arranged in baskets amid piles of tableware.

The day before, the children of Currituck had shoveled dirt into the road ruts and covered the entire length of Main Street with sawdust to keep the grit at a minimum. Now, all dressed up in her red, white, and blue finery, Currituck, North Carolina, was ready to celebrate America's seventy-ninth birthday.

At the stroke of nine, there would be a parade. Later, the orchestra would gather in the shaded bandstand to play an assortment of toe-tapping tunes, their brass horns and silver flutes gleaming in the sunlight.

There would be a two-legged race, a pie-eating contest, and a muscleman competition. The children had insisted on a dunking booth, and the men had insisted on a kissing booth. And any ladies and gentlemen who had not yet joined hands in the holy sacrament of marriage were eligible to participate in the boxed lunch auction.

Dressed in their Sunday best, the fine people of Currituck greeted one another by tipping white, straw hats...big and small, young and old, male and female alike. Kate hadn't seen J.J. since the Sunday when she'd caught him staring during the service. Afterward, he'd hurried out of the church, forgoing the after-sermon handshaking and well-wishes, and the potluck supper, too. Mary had cross-examined Thaddeus about the Irishman's absence, but all he'd said was, "J.J. is a grown man. I guess he knows whether he wants a chicken dinner or not."

Kate hadn't seen him on the dock, outside his warehouse, or anywhere else in town, for that matter. But, surely, he'd show up today....

She had done a lot of praying about the matter of J.J. O'Keefe and had concluded that if there was to be anything more than mere friendship between them, the Lord would need to send her a clear signal; the man, himself, seemed to have no intention of doing so. She'd certainly never been the shy, reserved type, for if she had been, her business would have died the very week she'd opened its doors. If need be, she'd take the proverbial bull by the horns. But only if need be, and only if she could be certain J.J. was the man God had chosen for her.

Mary Crofton had said that J.J. would participate in the Fourth of July Festival, so Kate had chosen her outfit far more carefully than usual. From scraps of cotton fabric she'd used to sew the Chandler twins' matching dresses and leftovers from a bolt of bright white, she'd made a narrow-skirted gown with a scoop-neck bodice and three-quarter-length sleeves. She'd used red for the outer pleats and white for the inner ones, so that the ivory fabric showed only when she moved, thereby separating the pleats. She'd trimmed the sweeping, scooped neckline and cuffs with tiny, tightly pressed pleats, and, in honor of the day, she'd borrowed a narrow, blue belt from her favorite skirt. Kate believed in balance in all things, and so, to offset her black, button-up boots, she wore a black cord around her neck, tied in a minuscule bow at her throat.

She wound her hair into a sensible bun every morning, not because she liked the style—in fact, she did not—but because it kept the unruly tendrils out of her way as she leaned over her sewing. Today, though, she'd gathered it from the crown forward to form a loose braid, and she'd wound red, white, and blue satin ribbons through it.

She'd baked a pan of apple cobbler and covered it with a blue and white flowered tea towel. As she was positioning it among the other tasty treats, she heard footsteps padding across the lawn behind her. *Adam, no doubt*, she thought, grinning, *come to see if he can sneak a finger of fudge icing from Mary's cake or a cookie from the schoolmarm's plate.* She opened her mouth to tell him he'd just have to wait until after the blessing when a deep voice said, "Looks good enough to eat."

Kate would have recognized that rich baritone anywhere, and her heart soared with relief that J.J. had decided to come. Pretending that the desserts needed rearranging, she kept her back to him and said, "Mr. O'Keefe, I'm so glad you decided to join us today."

"Haven't missed the Festival since I settled here. Why would I start now?"

"That's odd," she said, adjusting the covering on her cobbler. "Neither have I. You'd think we'd have bumped into each other, wouldn't you?"

A warm, heavy hand rested on her shoulder, turning her around to face him.

"That's quite a dress ye're wearin' there, Mrs. Flynn. Made it yerself, I presume?"

J.J.'s eyes glittered in the sunlight, like shards of gleaming glass, as he waited for her answer. Kate's heart was pounding, and she feared he heard every beat. "Yes," she said, one hand to her chest, "from scraps."

His eyebrows rose with confusion. "Scraps?"

She shrugged. "Pieces left over from other people's clothes. Seems a shame to let them go to waste."

A muscle bulged in his jaw before he eased into a smile that sent her heart to thumping again.

"A man has to admire a woman who isn't wasteful."

As he spoke, his gaze slid over her face so slowly, she could almost feel a caress on her forehead, her cheek, her throat. Their eyes locked—his flashing, hers no doubt round with amazement at the brazen seductiveness she saw in his.

"This is becomin' a habit, Mrs. Flynn."

Kate blinked. "This? I—uh,...what's becoming a habit, Mr. O'Keefe?"

J.J.'s quiet chuckle rumbled like the warning growl of a panther. "This starin' into each other's eyes. If we keep it up, we'll set folks' tongues to waggin', sure."

But even as he said it, Kate noticed that he hadn't removed his hand from her shoulder. "Forgive me for saying so, Mr. O'Keefe, but it's no fault of mine. Your eyes are such an unusual color that I can't help staring." She grinned. "That's my excuse. What's yours?"

"Don't need one," he said without hesitation. "If anyone should ask what I'm oglin' at, I'll simply tell 'em the truth."

Her heart skipped a beat. "And—what might that be?"

J.J. took half a step closer and put his free hand on her other shoulder. With his brow furrowed slightly, he took a deep breath, then said, "That I might as well ogle openly, 'cause even when I close me eyes, I still see ye."

The sweetness of his words took her breath away. And then, he whispered, "Ah, but ye're a vision, Mrs. Flynn—the sort, I expect, to inspire men to write poetry."

Holding her breath, Kate searched his face for a sign—even the smallest—that he was toying with her. If she saw as much as a flicker of sarcasm, it would be her turn to disappear, just as he had after church all those weeks ago!

Yet, although she found his scrutiny unnerving, she saw no trace of taunting in his face, and she breathed a sigh of relief. "I seem to recall," she said in a slow, soft voice, "that we agreed not to refer to each other by our surnames, Mr. O'Keefe."

His left brow arched, and she glanced left and right at his hands, then gestured with her arm to the mere inches separating them. "Here we stand for God and all His angels to see, and the whole town, as well!" Shrugging, she added, "Mr. O'Keefe and Mrs. Flynn seem awfully formal under the circumstances, wouldn't you agree?"

For an instant, J.J. merely stared into her face. Gradually, faint laugh lines appeared at the corners of his eyes, and he leaned close, closer, until he could rest his chin atop her head. "I'd be a lot more agreeable if—" He leaned back and looked at her again.

"If what?"

"Well," he began, winking, "whenever I strike a bargain, I like to do something to make it stick."

She smiled. "Like shake hands, you mean?"

He glanced over at the church, where folks were beginning to gather for the parade. Nodding, he pursed his lips. "A handshake would work, but...." His gaze slid back to Kate's face and locked on her eyes. "But I had something a little more...uh, personal in mind."

"A signature, then?" She laughed. "You want me to sign a document that states my agreement to refrain from—"

It suddenly dawned on her where J.J. was headed with his suggestion. He meant to seal their deal with a kiss! How could she have been so dense? Why, now he'd think she'd been flirting openly with him! She searched her brain for something, anything, intelligent that she could say to make him see she wasn't flirting, to make sure he understood she really *was* that dense, when his face loomed closer. Instinct made her close her eyes, and, holding her breath, Kate waited.

It seemed an eternity before his lips touched hers, but when they did, it was as though the heavens had opened up, musicians had begun to play, and a choir had burst into song. Oh, how glorious it felt, being surrounded by his powerful arms and feeling his heart beating against her chest. How different from Sean's kisses this was!

The tittering of several young ladies nearby captured their attention, and Kate's heart ached when J.J. stepped back. With his arms still wrapped gently around her, he wiggled his eyebrows. "Seems we've set folks' tongues to waggin', just as I predicted."

Feeling like a giddy schoolgirl, Kate bit her lower lip and tried to ignore the ladies hiding mischievous grins behind dainty hands. "Um, Kate?" said one.

"Yes?"

"Would you make *me* a dress like yours?"

"It's nothing but scraps, Annie, and—"

"I don't care! If a dress like that will get Hank Bennett to kiss me that way, I don't care if it's made from a burlap sack!"

Resting her forehead against J.J.'s chest, Kate whispered, "Next time you issue me a warning, I promise to heed it."

Oblivious to the gawking girls, he said, "If it's all the same to ye, I'd just as soon y'ignore me." Wiggling his brows again, he added, "'Cause, if ye want the truth, I rather like the outcome."

"Is it true, Ma? Did he—did he really *kiss* you?"

Kate gasped. "Adam! Wherever did you hear such a thing?"

The boy rolled his eyes. "Everybody's talking about it." Leaning closer, he said, "Even Rev. Hall."

And to think I shared my life's story with Mary to keep people from talking! Kate buried her face in her hands. "Dear Lord in heaven...."

Looking between her fingers, she saw Adam slap a hand to his forehead. "So, it's true?"

Phoebe Greene darted up and gave Adam a playful shove.

"Cut it out," he barked.

"Hello, Mrs. Flynn," Phoebe said in singsong. "Adam's mad at me 'cause I told him I saw you and Mr. O'Keefe kissing."

Adam groaned.

"Did you just *hate* it, Mrs. Flynn?"

Hardly! Kate thought, uncovering her face.

She pressed fingertips to her temples as Adam came to her rescue. "I think I hear your mother calling you, Phoebe."

Her hands on her hips, the girl leaned forward. "Fibber," she snapped, her blonde braids flopping as she shook her head. And just that quickly, she was grinning again. "So, was it really, really awful, Mrs. Flynn? I can't imagine letting a nasty ol' boy kiss me." Wincing, Phoebe stuck out her tongue. "Ick!" Then, "Did his beard tickle your face?"

"Like your mother's does," Adam interjected, "when she kisses you good night?"

Kate bit back a giggle. "Adam," she said, feigning sternness, "tell Phoebe you're sorry."

"Sorry," he said.

"Say it like you mean it," Phoebe scolded him. And when he wouldn't, she huffed, "Boys!"

Just then, a high-pitched voice called, "Phoeeee-beeeeee!"

"Goodness, my mother *is* calling me!"

"Told ya," said Adam, grinning and wiggling his eyebrows.

Once Phoebe was out of earshot, Kate drew Adam to her. "Can I ask you something, son?"

"You know the rule," he said, quoting her. "Any question, anytime."

"What do you think.... How do you feel.... Um, I—"

"I like him just fine," he said with a snicker. "Though not as much as *you* do, obviously...."

Feeling the beginnings of a flush, Kate said, "Oh, look! Mr. Fisher is in the dunking booth." Pressing a penny into Adam's hand, she said, "See if you can get him good and wet."

"Maybe I ought to visit the kissing booth, instead, see what all the fuss and bother is about."

Kate called his bluff. "I'm sure your teacher would love that. Why, Miss Henderson told me just this morning that you're one of her favorite students—"

Adam wrapped both hands around his throat, as if the very idea was enough to choke the life out of him. "Last time I looked, Abigail Andersen was in the booth. What's Miss Henderson doing in there?"

"Same as you, I expect—trying to find out what all the fuss and bother is about."

Adam pocketed the penny and ran off, then darted back to hug Kate. "Love you, Ma."

"Love you, too," she called after him. Life was almost as perfect as it could get, she realized. She and Adam had been blessed with excellent health. Theirs was a good, solid home, and, thanks to her business, they had more than enough money to keep the pantry stocked. She'd come a long, long way from Philadelphia to Raleigh to Currituck.

And then, she thought of J.J.'s kiss....

She'd prayed for a sign, after all. How much clearer could the Almighty have been?

J.J. had been about to apologize to Kate if his kiss had embarrassed her when Adam had raced up from out of nowhere. J.J. had stayed back, waiting and listening. The boy was eight, after all, with a young boy's attention span. How long could the conversation last?

He'd made himself comfortable leaning against the bark of an ancient pine, and hadn't been able to believe his ears with he'd heard Phoebe ask Kate about the kiss. Everybody knew that Phoebe was the daughter of Currituck's biggest gossip. Every muscle in him had tensed as he'd waited for Kate's response. "It was wonderful!" he'd hoped she'd say. "The most magnificent moment of my life!" But had he really expected her to speak the words in his heart?

He'd tuned out the actual conversation and pictured her, perched on the edge of Adam's bed, combing slender fingers through her son's hair. It was, admittedly, a bittersweet picture, because J.J. had always wanted a houseful of children who'd throw their arms around him when he came home after a long, hard day. If he could make that dream come true, he'd want it to be with a woman like Kate.

When Adam had scampered off, it had interrupted J.J.'s thoughts, and he'd looked up to see Kate sit back and close her eyes as a dreamy smile further softened her features. *What's goin' through that gorgeous head of yers?* he'd wondered. *Are ye thinkin' of more young'uns just like Adam runnin' through our house?*

Our house? Was he daft?

It was at that moment that J.J. had realized he'd closed his eyes, too, and, by the time he'd opened them, Kate had gone—out of sight, but certainly not out of mind. The truth was, she'd been on his mind every spare moment since his first glimpse of her.

"Psst! Adam!"

He searched for the person who'd whispered his name and spotted Bobby, crouched in the hedges. "What're you doing in there? Don't you know there's a—"

"Shhh!" Bobby insisted. "Git on in here. I have somethin' to tell you."

Adam wedged himself into the small space between the trees and the shrubbery. Frowning, he said, "It's a lot cooler out there."

But Bobby waved his complaint away. "I was at the warehouse this morning."

"J.J. O'Keefe's warehouse? Why?"

"No reason," Bobby said, shrugging. "Just foolin' around." He snickered. "Figured out a way for you to get even with that big, dumb Irishman."

"Why would I want to get even with him?"

Bobby shoved Adam, hard. "Because, dummy, he made you go to work for him, that's why, and got you in big trouble with your ma!"

Adam shook his head. "Nah, I'm not in any trou—"

But Bobby grabbed his sleeve. "Don't give me that. She made you go to work for the big lummox to pay him back for those lunch pails you stole."

"Lunch pails *you* told me to steal, you mean...."

Sneering, Bobby put himself nose to nose with Adam. "What are you, a baby or something? Too yeller to get even? Are you afraid of O'Keefe?"

Adam hung his head. The only thing he was afraid of was being seen as a coward in the eyes of Bobby and his bunch. He'd seen what they did to boys who didn't dance to their tune....

"I saw him writin' in a book," Bobby was saying, "and when he were out, I snuck in there and had me a peek at it."

"What did it say?"

"He come back too soon for me to get a good look."

"Then, why didn't you just take it and run?" *There!* Adam thought. *See how you like being called yeller!*

"Didn't need to, dummy," Bobby said. "Went back later and read it."

"So?"

"So, you'll never guess what's in it."

Adam wanted to admit that he didn't care. Not even a little bit. "What?"

"Poems! Think what would happen to his tough-guy reputation if word got out that he writes poems like a sissy!"

"Nobody would care—"

"He beat my pa once, busted his nose. *Pa* would care."

"Why'd he beat your pa?"

Bobby frowned, then said through clenched teeth, "Pa wanted to fight him; said iffin' he won, we'd have rent money for a year."

Adam chucked. “Anybody with half a brain knows J.J. can’t be beat.”

Bobby filled his hands with Adam’s shirt. “My pa *could so* have whopped that Irishman...if he hadn’t cheated.”

Adam didn’t believe that. Not for a minute! “How’d he cheat?”

With brow furrowed, the boy said, “Well, I don’t rightly know, exactly. But it’s what my pa said after, so he must’a cheated.”

Oh, right, Adam thought, *and everybody in Currituck knows your pa never lies....* “So, how long ago did this fight happen?”

“Three years ago, give or take a month.”

“And your pa is still holdin’ a grudge?”

“We had to sell our cow after that fight, ’cause Pa’d been sure he’d win.”

So, the man wasn’t just a liar, Adam realized—he wasn’t very bright, either, and the proof was, he’d gambled against J.J....and lost.

“My pa says O’Keefe wouldn’t have needed to cheat, ’ceptin’ he’s a sissy. And now, I got proof of it.”

“What did you do with the book of poetry?”

Bobby snapped his fingers. “Couldn’t grab it that second time, either. I tell you, the man walks like a cat. Just more proof, iffin’ y’ask me, that he’s a sissy!”

“So, why are you telling me all this?” Adam asked. But he had a sinking suspicion he knew.

“Well, pal o’mine,” Bobby said, sliding an arm around Adam’s shoulders, “you’re the one who’s over there all the time, vistin’ with your sissy *buddy*. You can take that book and—”

“Me? Why do I have to do it when you already know where it is?”

“’Cause he won’t suspect you, that’s why! Besides, it’s easy to get to. You know that big toolbox in the back of his place? The one with all the different-sized awls in it?”

Adam nodded.

"Well, sir, it's in the table underneath it, in the right-hand drawer." Bobby gave Adam's back a playful smack. "Now that you know where it is, too, you can get it real easy."

"I—I don't think I want to."

Bobby's grin became a grimace. "Nobody asked what you *wanna* do, you mama's boy. I'm here tellin' you what you're *gonna* do."

Adam's heart thundered, and he licked his lips. "And what if I don't?"

"Somethin' awful will happen, that's what."

"Like what?"

Squinting, Bobby scratched his chin. "Like...maybe your ma's shop could catch fire, or—"

"You better not hurt my ma!" Adam growled.

"Now, now," Bobby said, his hands in the air. "I ain't sayin' that's what'll happen. Just pointin' out what *might* take place, is all."

"If anything happens to our house, or her, I'll—"

Bobby was nose to nose with Adam when he snarled, "You'll what, pipsqueak?"

"I—I don't know yet," he stammered, "but—but—"

The bigger boy clamped a hand over Adam's mouth, silencing him. "Don't mess with me, girlie-boy. Who do you think burned down that house the first time? That's right, big eyes. Me."

"But—but why?"

"'Cause the kids who lived there were always askin' dumb questions, that's why."

Adam remembered hearing how, after the fire, the family had been so broke, they'd been forced to move in with cousins in Baltimore. "Seriously, Bobby, what could they have done to make you mad enough to—"

"What are you, a constable? All you need to know is, I want that book, and you're gonna get it for me—or else."

Adam glanced over at the stand of pine trees across the way, where J.J. stood talking with Thaddeus, Mary, and his mother, who clearly cared about the Irishman, judging by the dreamy look on her face.

"This is the perfect time," Bobby said, giving him a rough shove, "while the sissy is busy moonin' over your ma. If you come back here without that book…." He shook a fist under Adam's nose.

Adam crawled out of the hedgerow, got to his feet, and, his head hanging, trudged toward the warehouse. *Right-hand drawer,* Bobby had said, *under the big toolbox….*

"Sorry, J.J.," Adam muttered, "but I'm the man of the house, and I gotta do whatever it takes to keep my ma safe."

As eventide shrouded the sunshine, a quiet settled over Currituck. Main Street was deserted now, save for the occasional stray dog sniffing out scraps under the now bare food table. The bandstand that had throbbed and thumped with knee-slapping music sat silent, and the booths where kisses had cost a penny and the reverend had been dunked stood empty. The basket that had been auctioned for three dollars toward the purchase of a new organ lay on its side, its bright-red bow askew. The contents of fried chicken and cornbread, prepared by Carrie Oken, had been devoured hours ago by Pete Stanford, the highest bidder in the boxed lunch auction. A crow hopped along in the dirt, wrestling with a length of twine that had bound fathers' ankles to sons' in the two-legged race, and a yellow-striped cat snoozed contentedly on a table forgotten by the reverend's wife. The street that had teemed with activity and voices finally rested, for the families of Currituck had returned to their homes to await the final phase of the Fourth of July festivities: fireworks!

A stranger passing through town, glancing into the windows of shops and houses along Main Street, would have seen a toddler and his infant brother napping in the Abbott house, the Williams family gathered around the table for a light snack, the Reverend and Mrs. Hall in the church, setting out the new hymnals, and Miss Henderson in the schoolhouse, taking inventory of the materials she'd need when school started in the fall.

And in the Flynn house, Adam lay on his stomach across his bed, reading from a thick, leather-bound journal propped against his pillow. The first entry was dated January 1, 1830. He squinted and did some mental mathematics. Earlier, he'd heard Mary say, "It's about time J.J. started actin' his age," after hearing about the kiss. "The man's thirty-five years old. If he doesn't start a family soon, his young'uns will still be in diapers at his funeral!"

If it's 1855, and he's thirty-five, Adam calculated, *then J.J. was ten years old when he wrote this poem.* Flattening the page with the heel of his hand, he propped his chin on his fist and read silently:

She is twilight and moonlight,
She is sun on the waters.
She is rain clouds and blue skies,
She is God's sons and daughters.
She is sheep on the hillside,
She is cows on the roads.
Rising from the Atlantic,
She is proud, she is grand.
She is endless beauty.
She is my Ireland.

Adam rolled onto his back, taking the book with him. *You must've done the arithmetic wrong*, he thought, frowning. *There's no way a ten-year-old wrote a poem that good.* With his fingertip, he scrawled numbers on an imaginary blackboard—and the result was the same. He shook his head, acknowledging that J.J. was a smart man, especially considering the way he could handle a measuring stick and figure out how to make ends meet. But he'd obviously been a smart boy, too.

He turned to another page, with an entry written on June 5, 1841. This time, his ciphering told him, J.J. had been twenty-one:

> *Last week, I was the honored guest of sweet Molly McGuire, who wore a long, white, satin dress to wed my cousin, Tim. The preacher wished them many children and a long, happy life, and led us all in prayer for Tim and his new wife. "They'll need our prayers," the reverend said, "to face the road ahead."*
>
> *True enough—and they'll need money for a house and food, too. I prayed for that, instead. I didn't hear the sermon (though, knowing the reverend, I doubt I missed much), so I didn't hear them say their vows or see them exchange their first kiss. But I saw the look Molly gave me as she spoke the final words, for it was a look that's sure to haunt my dreams. She told me with her eyes that Tim was her second choice, and that I'd come a whisker from standing where Tim stood at the altar.*
>
> *I made my vow right then and there: "Don't ever take a wife, for surely you'll regret it all your natural life." If, in a weak-kneed moment, I should give my heart away, may the good Lord numb my brain so I won't feel the pain of it!*

Chuckling, Adam whispered, "Good for you, J.J.!" Then, he turned to the most recent entry, dated July 3, 1855:

Dear God in heaven,

You know that I stepped into the ring with powerful men—men who looked as though they had the brains and the brawn to put me down. But they didn't. You know that I had no bone to pick with them, no ax to grind, no reason to want to see them harmed. Yet harm them I did. You made me strong, and I lifted my fists, bare-knuckled, lowered my body, bare-chested, and looked into their eyes—eyes gleaming with hate. Or determination. Or fear. And I swung with all my might, because I knew no other way. "Do your level best, or don't waste your time." It was one of the best lessons my father taught me, and I'll take it to my grave. You know why I fought to win. So much was riding on it. To lose was unthinkable, because losing was the same as admitting defeat...and not only in the ring. Until now, fighting has been easy, because I haven't wanted much from life but solitude, peace, the contentment that comes from working hard, and the joy of remembering Ireland. And You know that until now, I haven't needed a woman to complete me, because before now, I hadn't met one who could. But that was before Kate. When I looked into her eyes, I saw into her heart, and all the cold places in me warmed.

Adam closed the book and set it aside, knowing as he did that J.J. O'Keefe was in love with his mother. He didn't quite know how to react to that, for without the journal, he wouldn't be as certain of it. The sheriff had arrested Victor Wilson last year for sneaking peeks into first-floor windows all over town. A "peeping Tom," they'd called him—though he'd seen nothing but pies cooling on window ledges and damp tea towels draped across the sills to dry—and had made him spend a night in jail. Vic had been so ashamed that he'd left town when they let him out, and no one had seen or heard from him since.

Adam didn't need to be full-grown to understand that what he'd done was far more unacceptable than looking into windows. J.J. had not intended for his words to be read. Would there be sketches of trees, lambs, horses, and the like if J.J. had wanted others to know his most private thoughts? And would there be pictures of Adam's mother, smiling, praying, and staring off into space?

Oh, J.J. loved her, all right. If the letter to God didn't prove it, the drawings surely did.

Adam had watched as Currituck's eligible bachelors—some never married, some recently widowed—had tried to woo and win her, without success. Kate had done it gently, of course, for that was her way, but she had turned them down. Until Adam had learned the truth about his father, he'd assumed it was because she still loved her late husband.

The day after J.J. had followed him home, demanding repayment for the stolen lunches, Adam had been sitting on the stairs, unnoticed, and he'd listened as his mother had poured out her heart to Mary. There was a tall, oval mirror in one corner of her shop, where her customers could see how fine they looked in the garments she sewed for them, and he'd been able to watch her face in that mirror. He'd known, as the story had unfolded, that she hadn't turned down those marriage proposals because she still loved his father. She'd turned them down because she feared him.

If Adam had heard it once, he'd heard it a hundred times: "Your ma has the prettiest eyes ever!" He'd always agreed—not because they were big and brown, but because they looked at him with such love. Those eyes had narrowed as Kate had talked to Mary; they'd darkened when she'd spoken of the beatings. Adam had attended a wedding or two and was familiar with the vows—how could the man who'd promised to cherish her raise a hand to her?

Adam was a long way off from falling in love, himself, but that didn't mean he couldn't recognize true love when he saw it. If his mother had written pretty words about J.J., he hadn't seen them. But J.J.'s journal? It made things, as the grown-ups liked to say, as plain as the nose on his face.

Would they marry? And, if they did, would they all live here, in the apartment above his mother's shop, or, perhaps, in the loft rooms above J.J.'s warehouse? He hoped they'd choose the former, for while the man's living quarters were clean and roomy, they were hardly homey.

It might be nice to have a pa for the first time in his life—especially one who could teach him so many things. Adam's heartbeat quickened as he added, *Someone who can teach me to handle a boy like Bobby....*

He shouldn't have taken the journal. He'd known that even before slinking into the warehouse. But now it was done, and it was too late to make things right.

Wasn't it?

"You know right from wrong, son," his mother often said. "And, on the occasions when you're not sure, ask yourself what I might say...."

Adam leaped up from his bed and headed for the stairs, quoting another phrase favored by his elders: "It's never too late."

He would put the journal back where he'd found it and pretend he'd never trespassed into the territory of J.J.'s most secret thoughts.

And he'd keep a mighty close eye on Bobby from here on out, too.

"What're ye doin' back here, Adam?"

With quaking hands and hammering heart, Adam shoved the journal into the drawer and said, "Snooping." He opened the drawer where J.J. kept his awls. "I like looking at your tools."

J.J. grinned. “Well, put things back where ye found ’em when ye’re done snoopin’, to keep the sawdust off ’em.”

“Okay....” Then, “J.J., did you ever have a run-in with a bully?”

“Sure. Plenty of times, when I was a lad.”

“Really?”

“Somebody givin’ y’a hard time?”

Adam shuffled to the front of the shop and stood there, his hands in his pockets, staring at his feet. “Sorta....”

“So, ye’re just wonderin’ how ye’d handle a bully, in case ye find yerself face-to-face with one someday?”

The boy’s eyes brightened. “Exactly!”

J.J. sat down on the corner of his battered, old desk. “Now, let me see,” he said, tugging at his beard. “First off, I guess I’d try to figure out if the bully is really worthy of bein’ afraid of.” He met Adam’s eyes. “Is this ‘could-be bully’ bigger than ye?”

“Lots bigger,” Adam admitted. “And lots older, too. But that’s not why I’m scared of him.”

J.J. pretended he hadn’t heard the boy’s open admission. “And is this ‘could-be bully’ the type who makes threats?”

“Yes, he sure is!”

“Ahhh,” J.J. said, nodding. “Then, the next thing ye need to do is ask yerself if this bully is the type who might actually carry out his threats....”

He watched as Adam’s face blanched.

“...and if he’s been in trouble before....”

“What if—what if this bully I might run into someday...,” Adam said, frowning. “What if he claims to have burned down a house, just ’cause he didn’t like the kids who lived there, on account o’their askin’ too many questions. What if this bully is like *that*?”

J.J. had heard stories about the house Kate had bought and repaired. The way he understood it, the sheriff hadn’t been able to make the charges stick because the accused boy had parents who’d insisted he’d been home when the blaze started. "Ye think this bully might set another fire?" J.J. asked him.

Adam only nodded.

"What makes ye think such a thing?"

On the heels of a shaky sigh, the boy said, "'Cause he tol' me so."

He'd seen Bobby around town, strutting up and down the street as if he owned Currituck, and there wasn't a doubt in his mind the boy would carry out his threat. "So, what petty crime did ol' Bobby want you to commit to keep him from burnin' down yer house?"

Adam took a gulp of air, all the proof J.J. needed that he had a good handle on the situation. "He isn't gonna do anything of the kind," J.J. assured him. "Not as long as the two of us are around to watch over yer ma."

A glimmer of hope lit up the boy's eyes.

"But ye're not off the hook that easy, Adam. Only way to beat a bully is head-on. There's a chance he'll wallop ye good, but there's just as good a chance he'll respect ye for standin' up to him."

Adam sighed.

"Let me tell y'a story, lad," J.J. said, pointing to the chair beside his desk. Once Adam had sat, he said, "When I first came to town, I kept runnin' into a fella who didn't like me much."

"But why? Everybody likes you."

Smiling, J.J. said, "Thanks, lad, but 'twasn't always that way. I had to earn the respect of the people of Currituck."

"Does he still live here?"

"That he does. And when he learned what I used to do for a livin', he got himself into a dither over it. He thought sure it was nothin' but talk, and set out to prove I weren't good at me job. Guess he figured a big, dumb Mick like me didn't have the brains to earn bein' called 'The Annihilator.'"

"What's a Mick?"

J.J. chuckled. "Yer innocence sometimes astounds me, Adam. It's what some folks call an Irishman when they want to insult 'im. 'Mc—' literally means 'son of,' and there are many 'sons of' Ireland—McThis and McThat—"

"But your name is O'Keefe."

"Shows how little sense insults like that make, doesn't it?"

Adam nodded, and J.J. went on with his story. "So, anyway, I didn't pay this fella any mind at first, but he must've got bored hittin' me with nothin' but words, and he took to usin' his hands. I didn't want to fight him, 'cause I knew well the damage a professional boxer could inflict. He had a wife and young'uns, and I didn't want to hurt him.

"Then, one day, he caught me off guard, knocked me flat on me back."

"And did you get up and beat him senseless?"

"I could've, but 'twouldn't have been a fair fight. I told him if it was a fight he wanted, then a fight he'd get. But it'd be in the ring, with gloves and a referee. So, we set a date. The day of the fight, we took off our shirts, and he was down ten seconds into the first round."

"It was Bobby's father, wasn't it?"

"It was."

"And now he leaves you alone?"

"We'll never be pals, but we behave like civilized men now. I doubt I put an end to his bullying, but he learned to stay out of me yard. See, a bully will always find a willing victim. 'Tis a part of his nature. Trick is to make sure he knows *ye* won't be his victim."

"So, I have to fight Bobby?"

"Hopefully not. Maybe he's more reasonable than his da, and a stern talkin'-to is all it'll take." J.J. paused, then added, "'*A wrathful man stirreth up strife: but he that is slow to anger appeaseth strife.*'"

"I didn't know you read the Bible, J.J."

J.J. knew that Adam's mother was a believer who was trying to raise her boy by God's Word. She wouldn't appreciate his sharing negative opinions about her Lord and the Good Book with her son. "I don't read it as often as a man ought," he said, choosing his words carefully, "but I know this: the Almighty doesn't mean for us to stand idly by and let others run roughshod over us."

"How do you know that?" Adam asked.

"Haven't y'heard that yer body is His temple?"

Adam nodded slowly. "I think I get it now. Thanks, J.J." He slid down from the chair and headed for the door. "Will I see you at the fireworks show later?"

"Wouldn't miss it for the world."

J.J. watched Adam walk away, standing a little taller than when he'd seen him enter the warehouse for the first time.

J.J. had never seen anything quite so beautiful.

Oh, he'd watched a fireworks show before—three times, to be precise. But the giant, shimmering flowers that bloomed and then rained their colorful petals down on Currituck were nothing compared to Kate Flynn's eyes.

"Where did they get the canisters this year?" Mary Crofton asked, drawing J.J.'s attention from Kate's face.

"Don't rightly know, Mother," her husband replied. "Why, Mary, you're glowin' like a schoolgirl!" Then, he kissed her on the mouth.

"Thaddeus," she said, giggling, "I'm just thankful it's dark, or folks would see me blushing from the other side of the street!"

Leaning forward on the blanket they were sharing with the Croftons, J.J. whispered, "Will the two of you rein it in a mite? There are children about, don't y'know."

Thaddeus grinned. "To answer your question, darlin' wife of mine, I believe the town council ordered these straight from China."

"But aren't *all* fireworks made in China?"

"Most," he said, shrugging. "But I hear tell that some feller by name of Homer Jones ordered himself...."

J.J. tuned out the story by moving closer to Kate, and he slipped an arm around her waist. "Good old Thad," he said, "savin' Currituck from a passel of inferior-grade fireworks."

"Is that so?"

"'Tis."

Kate sighed. "Isn't it romantic?"

"The fireworks, ye mean?"

"Well, in a manner of speaking, yes. But I was talking about Mary and Thaddeus. Isn't it wonderful that they still behave like newlyweds after all their years together?"

So, she's envious of 'em, too....

"I wonder...," she said, her voice soft and dreamy as she stared up at the sky.

"What do ye wonder?"

"What's their secret, do you suppose?" she asked, turning to look in his eyes.

"Secret?"

"How have they kept the spark alive?"

J.J. wanted to wrap her in his arms, pull her to him, and press a kiss to her lips. "'Tis no secret. Leastways, not in my opinion."

Kate sat up and crossed her legs at the ankles. "Go on," she said, her hands clasped in her lap. "I'd love to hear your opinion."

He leaned back, his fingers splayed on the blanket, his arms stiff to support his upper body. "There's nothin' mysterious about it," he said, matter-of-factly. "They were meant for each other. It's as simple as that."

Kate scooted closer. “It can’t be that simple. All around the world, people get married every day, and I imagine all of them believe they’re meant for one another.”

“The difference,” J.J. said, “is that the ones who stick together are the ones put together by God Himself.”

Kate smiled, then remarked, “You surprise me.”

“Oh?”

“I never imagined you were the type.”

“What type?”

“Religious.”

“Just ’cause a man doesn’t spend every Sunday in a pew doesn’t make a heathen of him, Kate. Besides, there’s a difference between bein’ religious and bein’ spiritual.”

They watched the next three firework explosions in companionable silence. As the men lighting fuses on the shore by the Sound prepared the next canister, Kate said, “Have you ever asked Him, J.J.?”

“Ever asked Him what?”

“If a particular lady was the right one for you?”

He looked into her face. “Should’ve once, but didn’t.”

“Disaster?”

“That’s puttin’ it mildly.”

She smiled sadly. “I should’ve once, too, and didn’t.”

“Yer husband, ye mean.”

Nodding, she said, “My ‘keeper’ is more like it. It truly felt like the right thing to do—marrying him, I mean. Turned out to be bad for everybody, Sean included.”

“He got the prettiest, sweetest little wife in Americay...most lovin’, too. How could it have been bad for him?”

Kate shook her head, and J.J. knew she meant to protest his compliment. “Hush, now,” he said, “’cause I’ll not listen while ye dismiss the truth. Ye did a good and loving thing, linking yerself to that no-good Irishman. ’Tweren’t yer fault things turned out like they did.”

Kate tilted her head to one side. "I appreciate your coming to my defense, J.J., but the fact is, I didn't ask God's guidance in the matter. I made the decision, just like that," she said with a snap of her fingers. "I often wonder how differently my life might have turned out if only I'd asked."

"If," he echoed. "Takes but two letters in English to spell the biggest word in any language."

Kate sighed. "I suppose you're right."

"I know I'm right. I'm always right. And if ye're ever in doubt, just ask, and I'll be happy t'remind ye of the fact."

A second ticked by before their voices joined in harmonious laughter.

"Say, what's goin' on back there?" Thaddeus asked.

"You two are making more noise than the fireworks!" his wife said.

"You know, Mary," Kate said, catching her breath, "you're absolutely right."

"I know I'm right."

Kate and J.J. tried to stifle their chuckles, but, in no time, both realized it was hopeless. They rolled onto their sides, laughing even harder than before. Tears filled their eyes as they slowly regained control, just in time to hear Mary mutter, "Young folks these days," which inspired another round of giggling.

"Hey!" shouted Burt Garfield, one of the men operating the fireworks display. "You boys get away from there!" The big, burly fellow stomped toward Bobby and his bunch, intent on picking them up by the scruff of the neck and tossing them boots over brains into the water. "Don't you realize we're working with explosives here? *Gunpowder*?"

"We didn't touch nothin', mister," Bobby said, feigning innocence. "We just wanted to see how you get them rockets to go so high in the sky."

"When you're older," Burt said, "you can volunteer to light the fuses."

"But mister—"

"But nothin'! These are pyrotechnics, boys. One wrong move, and we can all be blown to smithereens. Now, get a move on!" Shaking his fist, he added, "Before I show you how high I can get *boys* to fly in the sky."

Bobby narrowed his eyes and studied his options: run around the big lummox or bide his time. Finally, he shrugged and smiled. "C'mon," he said to his gang. "Mr. Garfield is right. We're bound to get hurt if we hang around here."

"Now *there's* a sensible fella," Burt said, winking. "You can see the fireworks better from a distance, anyway." Shielding the side of his mouth with his hand, he whispered, "All you see from this vantage point is the fiery tail of the rocket, and you're so busy squintin' and coverin' your ears at the awful squeal that you miss the good part."

Bobby frowned. *Grown-ups. Each one's dumber than the next.* "Why do you do it, then?"

"Somebody's got to. At my age, I've enjoyed my fair share of fireworks. Seems fittin' and proper to give others a chance to enjoy the show." Satisfied he'd convinced the boys to move back, Burt added, "Now, get on outta here. We're about to set the fuses for the finale."

Bobby grumbled to himself, but he grinned and led his friends away from the row of hollow, metal pipes that acted like miniature cannons for the fireworks' canisters. Once they were out of Burt's line of vision, Bobby signaled the boys to duck into a stand of nearby trees. "Hunker down here a minute while I figure out what we're gonna do," he whispered.

"I dunno, Bobby," Stevie said. "Mebbe we oughtta listen to ol' Burt. I don't wanna get blown to kingdom come."

"What's wrong? Y'scared?" Bobby glared at the rest of the boys. "Looks like the widdle baby forgot to bwing his widdle bottle." Nose to nose with the smaller boy, he grabbed a handful of shirt. "Or maybe the widdle baby's diaper needs changin'. Is that it, Stevie? Huh?"

"Stop it!" Stevie hollered. "I'm not a baby!"

"Why don't you pick on someone your own size, Bobby," came a stern voice.

All eyes focused on the speaker.

"Well, well, well," Bobby said, turning Stevie loose. "If it isn't Adam Flynn, son of the village harlot."

Adam didn't even know what the word meant, but he could tell by the other boys' reactions that it didn't mean anything good. "You take that back!"

"Who's gonna make me?"

"My mother is *not* a—a—what you said."

"Then what's she doin' kissin' a man who ain't her husband, right in the middle of Main Street for everybody to see? My ma says—"

Adam stepped right up to his opponent. Until that moment, he hadn't realized that Bobby stood a full head taller. "I don't care what your ma says," he growled. And, filling both hands with the bigger boy's shirt, he said, "Take it back."

"If y'know what's good for you, you'll let go of me."

"Take it back, and I will."

Bobby cocked a fist, but Adam was faster, and he wrapped his fingers around the boy's wrist as Bobby said, "Hey, the pipsqueak is pretty fast, ain't he?"

The other boys did not respond, except to stare wide-eyed at Bobby. Adam recognized the look on each of their faces. He'd worn it enough times himself when Bobby had thrown his weight around.

"Get off of me, you miserable little snot-eater, or—"

"Or *what*?" Adam spat.

"Or—or—or I'll turn your face into pulp, that's what!"

"Is that what happened to your ugly face? Somebody bigger than you turned it into pulp?"

Adam's retort inspired quiet snickers from the boys, followed by a sneer from Bobby. "Listen to him, the boy whose ma is a harlot and whose pa got shot cheatin' at cards."

"I hear that, sometimes," Adam countered, "my pa would get so riled up, it took three or four men to pull him off a man twice his size."

Bobby's pupils constricted, and he swallowed. "So?"

"So, folks say I'm an awful lot like him...."

The bully thought that over for a moment. "You're pretty brave for a little squirt who's about to get the beatin' of his life."

Adam shrugged. "Not brave. Determined."

"Huh?"

"Determined not to let you push me around anymore."

"Ha! He's a real buster, ain't he, boys?"

But the boys said nothing.

"Did you get that book, like I tol' ya?"

"I did."

"So, where is it?"

"I put it back."

"What? Why?"

"'Cause it was wrong to take it, that's why."

"Liar. You never got it in the first place."

Adam provided a quick description of J.J.'s journal, and Bobby sneered. "All right, so you saw it. Don't mean you took it and then put it back."

Now, Adam described a few of the drawings he'd seen inside.

"Go back and get it!" Bobby ordered.

"You're not the boss of me."

A myriad of emotions flickered over Bobby's face as he struggled to free himself from Adam's grasp. Once Adam had let him loose, he said to his pals, "We're missin' the fireworks. Let's get out of here."

With the exception of Stevie, the boys, some with hands pocketed, others with their arms crossed over their bony chests, sauntered past Adam. Frankie hesitated, his gaze wavering between amazement and admiration, as if unable to decide whether to stay or to head out with Bobby.

"And you'd better not set fire to my mother's shop!" Adam bellowed. "I'll tell the sheriff what you said about burnin' it down before, and you'll go to jail for the rest of your life!"

"Sheesh! You must be plumb outta your mind," Stevie said. "Ain't nobody ever talked to Bobby like that and got away with it."

"That's just 'cause nobody ever tried before." Adam held his ground, pretending fear wasn't pounding in his heart.

I sure hope you were right, J.J., he thought as the boys disappeared into the darkness, *'cause it sure won't be fair if Ma pays the price for what I did just now.*

"Somethin's wrong," J.J. said, peering into the darkness. "I can feel it in me bones."

Kate sat up. "I don't see anything amiss."

"'Tisn't what I saw that's botherin' me; 'tis what I heard. That last one...it sounded different from the rest."

Kate was on her knees now, her elbows cupped in her palms, looking for the source of J.J.'s distress. "What? What was different?"

"I do declare," Mary huffed, "you two are worse than a couple of rowdy young people." Her smile and Thaddeus's vanished when they read the expression on J.J.'s face. "What is it, son?"

Thaddeus never got his answer, for J.J. stood up quickly—ready for what, no one knew.

"Hey, down in front!" someone hollered. "It's like tryin' to see around the sidc of a moving barn!"

But J.J. ignored the complaint. "Somethin's wrong. Sounded like—"

Suddenly, there was a bright flash, a loud explosion, and an agonized bellow, followed by another blast, and then another.

"The canisters!" J.J. rasped, and he was off and running before anyone could question his words.

He thundered across the grass toward the beach, his big, booted feet splashing along the water's edge as he headed for the spot where Burt and the others were setting off fireworks.

"Stay back, O'Keefe!" a man shouted as he passed. "There's nothin' you can do for him."

"Go in there," said another, "and you're likely to end up in the same fix!"

J.J. paid them no mind. In the fleeting seconds it took to cover the last of the ground, his mind whirled back to a day in Ireland when one of his pals had gotten ahold of a small, antiquated cannon. Connor's rage had grown infectious and had spread through the countryside like the fever. Armed with nothing more than crude weapons—hand-forged pikes, knives, clubs, and rocks—they'd practiced for one short week, running defensive maneuvers the Pikesmen would employ against the Brits. They'd had but a dozen cannonballs, and though they'd had no idea how many might have been duds, the men had decided to test one. Because J.J. had been young and quick and strong, he'd been assigned to move the thing from place to place. And, when it had been time, he'd rolled the ball into the cannon's barrel, hit the ground, and prayed as the call was sounded. "Ready—*fire*!"

They'd waited as the stench of sulfur from the match had dissipated, as the wick had fizzled and sizzled, and as the red-hot glow had moved toward the gunpowder. And, when the smoke had cleared, Connor had been lying on his back, arms akimbo. It had been a grisly, bloody sight—one that had made every man present grimace and turn away. Every man but J.J., who'd knelt beside his lifelong friend. "I'm a goner, John Joseph," Connor had said. And, though J.J. had known it to be true, he'd denied it. "Promise me y'won't let 'em tell me ma how I ended up, for she'll see it in her dreams till she draws her last, sure."

With the image still bright and clear in his mind, J.J. ran up to Burt, who was staring dumbly at what was left of his arm. "Are ye daft, man? What were ye thinkin', pokin' yer arm down that shaft?"

Burt managed a feeble grin. "Young'uns," he managed. "One of 'em…." Then, mercifully, he passed out cold.

J.J. lifted him like a mother lifts a baby and headed for Main Street. "Run ahead and tell Doc to get ready," he shouted to no one in particular, "and somebody fetch a bottle of whiskey." He glanced at Burt's ashen face and added, "'Cause the man's gonna need all the numbing he can get."

Chapter Six

"Strange you should ask me that."

J.J. shifted in his chair at the sheriff's remark. "Strange?"

"Well, it's been two, maybe three, years since I've heard it mentioned. Then, not two hours ago, a boy comes in here asking the same questions you're asking now." Sheriff Walker looked up from his whittling to meet J.J.'s gaze. "You can see why I find that strange, can't you?"

J.J. eyed the man warily. What was strange, in his opinion, was that Ernest Walker wore a tie every day of his life. What was strange was that he didn't wear a cap or a Derby or one of those wide-brimmed things the fellows out West were sporting these days, but rather a tall, black stovepipe hat. As if on cue, Sheriff Walker took it off and hung it on one knee. "What's past is past, J.J. Nothing I can do—within the bounds of the law, that is—about any of it. Besides, it's all hearsay and mumbo-jumbo, and you know it."

"Bobby wanted Adam Flynn to take part in one of his petty crimes, and when the boy refused, that hooligan threatened to burn down Kate's place."

The sheriff had been lounging in his high-backed chair, looking for all the world as if he hadn't really heard a word of J.J.'s report. But at those words, he sat up and planted both boots on the floor. "He *what*?"

"Ye heard right, Ernie. Now what do y'aim to do about it?"

The blade of Sheriff Walker's whittling knife scraped over his whiskers as he considered his options. "Y'know, we never did figure out what happened when that house burned down."

"Ye're sure it wasn't an accident?"

"Not a chance. The place reeked of whale oil." Leaning his elbows on his knees, he turned his tall hat upside down, right side up, then upside down again. "It was the stench that woke Mary Crofton. If it hadn't been for her caterwaulin', there's no tellin' how much damage that fire might have caused. She had the whole town wide awake inside of fifteen minutes, and the bucket brigade had the blaze under control an hour later."

"Too late to save the house, though."

Walker nodded. "At least the family got away with their lives...."

"I heard that Norris and one of his granddaughters got burned up."

"That's what most folks think. Not me. I've always contended they died some other way."

"If the fire didn't kill 'em, what did?"

"Oh, the fire did 'em in, all right." Sheriff Walker gave J.J. a quick once-over. "You ever been in Kate Flynn's place?"

"Twice. Once in the dress shop, once in the kitchen above it."

"Did you get there by way of the front? Or by the back steps?"

J.J. didn't see what difference it made and said so.

"If you'd gone up by way of the inside stairs, you'd have noticed a door at the top of the staircase. A door with a big slide-bolt on the outside of it. Whoever set that fire threw the lock first."

Wincing, J.J. said, "So, the grandfather and the girl were—were trapped?"

"Now, don't get me wrong," Sheriff Walker said. "Trevor Norris wasn't the type of man you'd want running for mayor." Twirling one silvery tip of his handlebar mustache, he said, "But he paid his bills and didn't trouble folks." He took a deep breath. "What reason did Bobby give for settin' that house ablaze?"

"Said the kids asked too many questions."

Walker slumped in his chair. "Never put two and two together before," he said, staring out the window. "That Indian woman said she saw the boy that night, but I didn't pay her any mind." He shrugged. "Even her own people say she's crazy as a loon."

"Running Deer?"

"That's the one. All these years, I more or less figured she had somethin' to do with it. Which is why ever' time she sets foot in town—which ain't often, I'll admit—I've always got my eye on her."

"Anything like that ever happen before?"

"The fire, you mean?"

J.J. nodded.

"Nah. Small stuff, maybe...eggs on people's clapboards, soap in the windows...mischief, mostly. Except—" His blue eyes darkened as the brows above them knit in a serious frown. "Stolen purses, break-ins at the hotel, and...." He frowned. "And then there was Miss Henderson's cat—"

"Killed?"

"Set afire."

Wincing again, J.J. shook his head. He'd never been overly fond of felines, but he'd never harm one, either. "What kind of mind prompts someone to do something like that?"

For a moment, neither man spoke, and the only sound was the steady *ticktock, ticktock* of the big clock inside the door of the sheriff's office. "What kind of grades did Miss Henderson give Bobby?" J.J. asked, breaking the silence.

"You're makin' me look bad, O'Keefe." One side of the sheriff's mouth lifted in a somber grin. "You ever get bored building ships, maybe you ought to think about signing on with a detective agency."

"Had my fill of that sort of stuff in Ireland, Ernie, but thanks for the compliment."

"Bobby was only about seven years old when that cat died. Missed too much school to earn decent marks, but even when he showed up, he didn't do much more than raise a ruckus." He shook his head. "Who would've thought a boy that small could hate that big?"

J.J. ignored the girls' childish taunts as he headed for the dress shop. He figured he had it coming, kissing Kate out in the open the way he had the day before.

"Kate and J.J., sittin' in a tree," they chanted, "K-I-S-S-I-N-G. First comes love, then comes marriage...."

J.J. knew what came next, and, as he rounded the corner, he completed the verse in his head. *...then comes Kate with a baby carriage!* The picture that flashed in his head made his heart ache with longing.

But he had to stop dreaming about what *he'd* like and start focusing on taking care of Kate. Nothing was more important than her protection and well-being, and who knew where that lunatic Bobby might be lurking. J.J. hoped his plan would guarantee her safety.

He owned two work shirts, both blue, plus a white one for special occasions, and he needed a fourth like he needed more whiskers in his beard. But since he couldn't think of a logical excuse to be alone with her—one that wouldn't start gums to bumping, anyway—he decided to have her measure him up for a new one.

Kate was leaning over her worktable, a fat pencil behind one ear and three straight pins between her teeth, when he walked into the shop. The corners of her mouth lifted in a warm smile when she turned and saw him standing in the doorway. "Mmm!" she said, keeping her teeth closed around the pins. Then, pointing to a nearby stool, she said, "Mmm-mmm!"

"Hello, yerself," J.J. said, grinning. "Maybe I should come back later. Ye look, and sound, mighty busy."

She pulled the pins from her lips and stuck them in a tomato-shaped pincushion on the worktable. "Don't be silly. I'm never too busy to visit with a friend."

Ah, Kate, he thought, *what I'd give to be more than just yer friend.* "Got me an official invite to Abigail Andersen's wedding, and when I took a look at m'only good shirt, I thought I'd better see about gettin' me a new one."

"You're here to hire me to make you a shirt?"

He smiled. "Why d'you look so surprised? It's what ye do, isn't it?"

"Well—well, yes," she stammered. "It's just—I—I never expected to be measuring you up for—"

He closed the gap between them in three strides. "If the prospect of bein' that near me causes ye such apprehension, I suppose I could ride on over to Sligo, see if there's a seamstress there who needs the work...."

Kate's cheeks reddened, and her eyes widened. "I'm not afraid of you! It's nothing like that, really."

But J.J. knew better. She was afraid, all right—afraid of what people would say if the two of them were seen alone again. And who could blame her, after yesterday? "Easy, now," he assured her, placing one hand on her shoulder. "I've as much right to be here as any other customer." He pointed to the shop entrance. "The door's standin' wide open, and so are the curtains."

Kate fidgeted with the lacy trim of her apron pocket, then tucked a curl behind her ear. "You're right, of course," she said. "So, tell me, have you seen Burt Garfield today?"

"Last I heard, he's holdin' up. Doc says he lost a lot of blood. It's doubtful he can save Burt's arm, but at least the fool man didn't blow himself to smithereens."

Kate raised her eyebrows in pity. "What do you suppose he'll do for a living, with only one arm? He surely can't be a blacksmith anymore."

"Why can't he?"

"Well, wouldn't it be dangerous, working around fire and molten metal and all? Besides, how would he hold his tools and work on the anvil at the same time?"

"You know better than most that folks can beat incredible odds...when they've a mind to." J.J. smiled. "If Burt wants to keep smithin', I reckon he'll find a way to make it work."

"Easy for you to say, Mr. I've-Got-Both-Arms."

"One-masted ships sail just as well as two-masters. It's just a matter of the right rigging." J.J. slid the sack from his shoulder and pulled out the wooden arm he'd made. "I worked all night on this. When the time's right, I'll give it to him."

Kate inspected the stitching that secured the leather harness to the wooden arm. "You made it?" Her eyes danced with awe and wonder, and she smiled. "You made it *last night*?"

J.J. shrugged as she grabbed her notebook. "What's that for?" he asked, settling onto the seat of a tall wooden stool.

"I have all my records in here—the names and sizes of practically everyone in town." She opened to a random page, then leaned in closer so that he could read along with her. "See?" she asked, pointing to the top line. "This one is Kay Green's. The very first time she asked me to make her a dress, I jotted her measurements in here. That way, anytime she wants something else—a skirt or a blouse or even a coat—I can make it without asking her to come back for a fitting every time. I already know the distance between her shoulders and her ankles, between her knees and her ankles—"

"What if the distance around her middle changes?"

"You mean, if she was going to have a baby or something?"

J.J. pictured Kay Green. First of all, the woman was well beyond childbearing years; second, it was her love of pie and cake that puffed her belly. "Yes, something like that."

"Well, if I happen to notice a change, I might ask her to stop by so that I can adjust the numbers." Kate turned to a blank page and wrote J.J.'s name at the top.

"Y'have lovely penmanship, Kate." Almost as an afterthought, he tacked on, "No surprise, though, since every single thing about y'is lovely."

Kate felt herself blush as she laid the book on her worktable and scrawled tidy column headings with her pencil: "Shoulders," said one; "Chest," said another. "Now, then," she began in a crisp, businesslike voice, "would you mind standing on that box over there so I can measure...." Giggling, she cut herself off and, looking up at him, said, "On second thought, maybe you should stay right here, and *I* should get up on the box."

My, but she's a vision, J.J. thought, stepping up onto the wooden platform. "I'll stand anywhere ye tell me to." *I'll do anything it takes to be near ye....*

Kate took a cloth tape measure from her apron pocket. If not for the bold, black numbers printed on it, J.J. might not have known what the peculiar disk-shaped thing was. "Why go to all the bother of wrappin' it up that way," he asked, "when it's one of the things y'use most often?"

"Too messy to just toss it into a drawer," Kate explained, hanging it around her neck.

Even if her answer hadn't satisfied him—and it most definitely had—Kate wouldn't have needed to say another word. For, all around him, bolts of cloth, spools of thread, needles of varying widths and lengths, and scissors of assorted sizes were arranged in an orderly fashion. Precision, he was beginning to understand, was synonymous with Kate Flynn.

Standing behind J.J., Kate held one end of the tape measure against his shoulder bone, unrolled the tape, and pressed it to the other. "Thirty-five," she said, mostly to herself, and jotted the number in her book. Quick as a bunny, she scampered around in front of him to size up the length of his arms.

"Long as I'm here," he said, "there's somethin' I feel I'm obliged to tell ye—"

"Thirty-six," she muttered, and, after adding that to her book, she met his eyes. "Lift your arms, please." When he did, she wrapped the tape around his chest. From there, she moved on to his biceps and wrists, then to the length of his torso.

Oh, how he loved having her so near! But, thinking she hadn't heard him, J.J. opened his mouth to repeat himself.

"So, what, exactly, have you been meaning to tell me?" Kate cut in while holding the tape around J.J.'s neck.

"Last thing I want to do is worry ye, Kate, but ye might be in danger, and—"

"Seventeen," she said distractedly.

She pressed the tape to the front of his shoulder and, sliding the length of it between her thumb and forefinger, followed it down, stopping several inches below his hip. "We don't want your shirt coming untucked, now, do we?"

J.J. caught her wrist. "And we don't want ye gettin' hurt, now, do we?"

Kate tucked in a corner of her mouth and looked him in the eyes, reading stern concern that caused her self-assured smile to vanish. "Well, out with it, J.J. Or are you conducting some sort of test to see exactly how long it will take you to scare me *completely* out of my wits?"

Groaning, J.J. said, "That's the last thing I wanted to do." Glancing from the open door to the wide window, he added, "Isn't there someplace we can go—where we can be alone?"

Kate gasped, then covered her mouth with one hand. "Why? Is the news so horrible that you expect me to faint dead away?"

"No, of course not."

She lifted her chin. "Then why can't you tell me here?"

He looked toward the door again. "Because the wrong person might walk by, overhear us...."

"Adam is next door, helping Mary take inventory." The barest hint of a smile brightened her eyes. "She promised to pay him in peppermint sticks—two for every hour he works."

J.J. did his best to soften his expression. "'Tisn't Adam I hope to avoid."

She bit her lower lip. "J.J.," she said, looking down, "would you mind...?"

He followed her gaze to her wrist and immediately released her. "Good grief!" he rasped. "Look what I've done! Ye're likely to get welts—bruises, even!" He met her wide eyes, then cupped her chin in his palm. "Oh, Kate, m'darlin', can y'ever forgive me?"

She paid no mind to the redness his fingers had caused on her creamy skin. Smiling, she took the offending hand in hers and pressed it to her cheek. Then, she led him to the shelves lining the opposite wall, where she'd stacked bolts of material in order by weight and color. "What sort of shirt did you have in mind?" she asked. "Cotton? Flannel?" Sending him a saucy grin, she added, "Something fancier, maybe? Like silk?"

What did he care what the shirt was made of? He deserved horsehair after what he'd done to her! Kate was so tiny, so fragile and delicate, and she'd spent years married to an abusive man. What must she think? "Kate," he said, "I'm so sorry." His heart aching, he struggled to reclaim a degree of his formerly stoic demeanor. "How can I convince ye that I'd never—"

Kate's flirty grin vanished, and, in its place, came a warm, loving expression. "John Joseph O'Keefe," she began, "for all your size and strength, you're nothing but a big softy. If I were a betting woman—and, I assure you, I am *not*—I'd wager it gives you grief to squash a bug under your boot." Tenderly, she stroked his arm. "Don't ask me how, but I'm as sure as I can be that you'd never hurt me—not in any way." She took his hand and wrapped it around the same wrist he'd held moments ago. "Now, tell me, won't you, what has you so upset?"

This wasn't the first time he'd had to fight the urge to wrap her in his arms and hold her so close that not so much as a breath of air could pass between them. He suspected it was far from the last time he'd feel the urge, either. "Might we find a less conspicuous place?"

"Of course," she said, patting his hand. "Let's go upstairs and have a cup of tea." She glanced at the clock. "It's nearly noon, so I'll fix you a sandwich." Without turning loose his hand, Kate headed for the back stairs. "I baked a ham yesterday," she said over one shoulder, "with sweet potatoes, butter beans, biscuits.... You'd think I was cooking for a whole army instead of just Adam and me!"

J.J. had come here to tell her to be careful, to lock her doors and windows, to remain alert when she walked around town, and to make sure she never went anywhere alone. He'd anticipated a few tears and a little nervousness, which would require him to reassure her. *How did things get so turned around that she's offering comfort to me, instead?* he wondered. Overcome with emotion, J.J. gently tugged Kate's hand, and when she turned to see why he'd stopped, he said, "Kate, I might as well tell ye right up front that I don't know what's wrong, but m'gut tells me—"

Even though she was standing a step higher than J.J., Kate had to look up a bit to meet his eyes. "Maybe you got hold of some rancid meat yesterday at the Fourth of July Festival...."

Spoiled food had nothing to do with the sensation roiling in his gut! The urge to hug her gave way to an incredible yearning to kiss her. *Patience, man*, he cautioned himself, gritting his teeth. *There's a time and a place for everything, and this is neither the time nor the place for—*

Kate leaned forward and, standing on tiptoe, kissed his brow. "Well," she said, matter-of-factly, "you don't have a fever, you'll be happy to know."

"Fever?"

"It must be something else that's upsetting your stomach."

'Tisn't my stomach that's upset, he thought, remembering the gentle touch of her lips pressed to his forehead. But Kate chattered the whole way up the stairs, taking his mind off the matter at hand—for the moment, anyway.

"The lips," she was saying, "are so much more sensitive than the hands. Much better for taking a person's temperature." On the landing, she said, "I know tradition dictates that mothers and wives should hold a palm against the face to test for fever, but—"

She stopped talking so suddenly that J.J. worried she'd twisted her ankle or something. As it turned out, she'd simply decided, by looking at him, that he'd heard enough about fevers and palms and lips. Grinning at her uncanny ability to read his moods, J.J. shook his head.

"Speaking of hands," she said, "you're welcome to wash yours in the basin, there, while I put the water on to boil.

And, while he did, Kate made a sandwich, set a place for him at the table, and then tucked a napkin into his collar. "There's plenty more where this came from, so, please, don't be shy to ask for seconds."

Did Kate understand the power she wielded over him, standing this near, talking softly, doing loving, wifely things? She sat down across from him and stirred a spoonful of sugar into her tea. "Are you testing me, J.J.?"

"Testing ye?" He picked up the sandwich.

"To see how patient I am."

He didn't get it and said so.

"You aren't here because you need a shirt—though I'm delighted to make one for you. And you aren't here for the free meal, either."

"I'll have ye know, I haven't eaten since the Festival yesterday—"

"And you're not here for the tea, since you prefer coffee, so—"

"Did y'ever stop to consider maybe I stopped by simply because I enjoy yer company, Kate?"

Groaning, she pressed both hands to her temples. "J.J., please, just spit it out! You have my word, I won't swoon!"

He combed his fingers through his hair. "All right, then. How much do ye know about what happened to the people who once lived in this house?"

"I know there was a fire, that they lost everything. That most of the family made it out safely—except for a little girl and her grandfather."

"Do ye know how the fire started?"

"Thaddeus thinks a lantern overturned, because Mary smelled whale oil." Kate frowned and leaned both elbows on the table. "What does any of this have to do with me and my safety, J.J.? I didn't buy the house until the Norrises were long gone. The place had been empty more than a year when I moved in, and it took two years to make it truly livable."

J.J. remembered how, soon after he'd settled in Currituck, he would sometimes see her as he passed by; and how, each time, he'd hear her singing as she scraped or scrubbed or painted. "Didn't ye think it odd there was so little damage done to the downstairs?"

Kate tilted her head. "Why, yes, as a matter of fact. I've often wondered about that."

"I'm recallin' one of our earlier conversations, when ye said how much ye dislike it when folks beat round the bush."

One brow rose on her forehead, and she smiled, a quiet signal that he'd already violated her rule. "Then, let me get right to the point. The fire wasn't an accident, Kate."

"What—what do you mean? Of course, it was. Everyone in town says so."

"Whale oil was the fuel, all right, but it didn't come from any overturned lantern. Someone doused the place with the stuff, then threw the bolt at the top of the stairs. The child and her grandpa might have survived, too—if they'd been able to get out of that room."

Kate gasped. "How absolutely horrible!" Then, in a small voice, "But—but who would do such a despicable thing?" And a second later, "You know, don't you!"

"I've talked with Ernie Walker about it."

"But why, J.J.? Why would you have any interest in a fire that happened even before you came to town?"

"Because," he said, taking her hand in his own, "I've been led to believe that history might repeat itself."

While she stared in silence for a moment, he thought, *She's some kind of woman. Just look at her, sittin' there, tryin' her best to be brave.* When Adam had first told him what Bobby was planning to do, J.J. hadn't cared a hang if the ruffian was thirteen or thirty—he'd wanted to wring his neck. But a quick walk on the dock had calmed him down and cleared his head. "Violence begets violence," he'd told himself. There were better ways to deal with the likes of Bobby Banks.

But, now, seeing the fear and misery written on Kate's face, J.J. found himself fighting the murderous urges again. She should be happy, smiling, calm, and at peace at all times, not wringing her hands and chewing her lips, worrying about the safety of her son and herself. J.J. wanted to throttle anyone who threatened her security, and if Bobby thought himself man enough to think up such dastardly deeds, maybe he was old enough to be punished like a man for his crimes.

And J.J. was just the fellow to do the punishing.

Kate sent him a weak smile. Under other circumstances, she'd have said, "You're not hungry? Let me wrap up your sandwich, so you can eat it later." If she hadn't been trying so hard not to cry, she probably would have told him how much she'd enjoyed having him over for lunch.

But she hadn't said a word in minutes, and he found himself loathing the boy who'd done this to her.

J.J. knew what he had to do.

And he knew what it might cost him.

He longed to take Kate in his arms and whisper words of assurance into her ears. He started to tell her not to worry, that things would be all right—that he'd *make* them all right. But a sob ached in his throat, and he sat there, mute and helpless. How could such feelings of tenderness simmer in his heart alongside the vengeful, boiling bloodlust coursing through his veins?

"Ye can finish measuring me for that shirt another time," J.J. said, on his feet now. "Thank ye for the sandwich. And the tea. And the companionship. And I'm sorry, Kate—sorrier than ye'll ever know that I had to be the one to break this ugly news to ye. Sorry about what I did to yer pretty little wrist, too."

He left without saying good-bye, without giving her a hug or kissing her one last time, and something told J.J. he'd regret that down the road when they locked him up for what he intended to do.

Ye may never be lucky enough to call her yer own, John Joseph O'Keefe, but ye'll do yer level best to see that she's safe.

If that meant eliminating the reason she was afraid—and paying for it with his own life—so be it.

"Where are you headed in such an all-fired hurry?"

"Step out of the way," J.J. said sternly. "I've business to attend to."

Despite J.J.'s warning tone, Sheriff Walker blocked his path. "What kind of business?" He frowned and crossed his arms over his chest, eyeing the Irishman warily through his gold-rimmed spectacles.

J.J. tried to evade the man. "It's none of yer concern, Sheriff."

"I've been a sheriff nearly as long as you've been alive, O'Keefe. I know trouble when I see it, and there's trouble written all over your face."

J.J. clenched his teeth. "I'm askin' ye politely as I know how. Let me by."

"You headed over to that boy's place?"

Grinding his molars together, J.J. asked, "What boy?"

"Back off, O'Keefe. There's no evidence linkin' Bobby Banks to any crime."

"No evidence? There are dead pets and terrified women all over town. Now, some might consider killin' cats and stealin' purses to be nothin' more than childhood pranks, but I don't. And even for those who don't find that behavior intolerable, burnin' down houses with people still inside—"

"Like I said," the sheriff interrupted him, calm as you please, "there's no proof Bobby had anything to do with that stuff. So, I'm telling you to back off."

J.J.'s forefinger popped from his fist as if fired from a pistol. "Ye're the man with the badge," he steamed, poking the finger into the sheriff's chest. "Tell me ye're doin' somethin' to *get* the evidence ye need, and I'll back off."

Sheriff Walker gave the offending finger a casual glance. "I could haul you in right now, if I had a mind to—"

"On what charges?"

"Assaulting an officer of the law, for starters."

This wasn't solving anything. While he and Sheriff Walker were facing off, J.J. realized, Bobby could be off doing God knows what. He pocketed both hands and tried another tack. "Sorry," he muttered, shaking his head. "Don't know how ye stomach police work, Ernie, keepin' yer temper while criminals like Bobby get away with murder."

Sheriff Walker eyed him for a moment. "What say we start this conversation over from the beginning?"

J.J. nodded.

"So, tell me, O'Keefe, where are you headed in such an all-fired hurry?"

J.J. took a deep breath. "To me warehouse," he fibbed. "I've got a boat to build for a big Virginia banker."

With a one-fingered salute, the sheriff sauntered down the walkway. "Have yourself a fine day, J.J.," he said over his shoulder.

"And the same to ye, Sheriff."

J.J. felt that the mighty hand of God had affected this little scene. Being stopped by the sheriff had probably saved him from doing something he'd regret for the rest of his life. *Thank Ye, Lord, for bein' at m'side and on m'side.*

"*Vengeance is mine; I will repay, saith the Lord,*" he reminded himself. If there was an ounce of truth in the verse, J.J. believed Bobby was in for a rude awakening.

And soon.

❀

“What’re you doing, Adam?”

The boy knew without looking who had asked the question. Taking a deep breath, he rolled his eyes. “What does it look like I’m doing, Phoebe?”

“I dunno,” she said in a singsongy voice.

In spite of himself, Adam peered over his shoulder as she dug the toe of one dainty shoe into the ground.

“Are you building a raft?” she asked, then popped the tip of one blonde braid into her mouth.

Adam sat back on his heels and looked at his creation. Logs of this size were scarce in Currituck, and it had taken him more than a week to gather enough wood for the project. And then, there had been the matter of lashing them together. He’d spent two more days braiding scraps of twine, picked from the trash bin behind the Croftons’ store, and a yet another week tying together the odd-sized pieces of hemp he’d found here and there.

Phoebe wrinkled her nose. “Aren’t you afraid it’ll tip over?”

“Tip over? Ha! There are enough pegs in that thing to sink a battleship!”

And it was true. He’d found hundreds of old, rusted nails in a wooden barrel behind Owen Roberts’s workshop. The carpenter had had no use for them and gladly let Adam haul them away. There were perhaps two dozen straight ones in the bunch, but most of them were bent, and some had no head. One by one, Adam had laid them on a flat boulder and hammered them into submissiveness.

The mast itself was constructed of two unwieldy tree limbs, laid out in the shape of a cross and tethered with his best length of rope. It hadn’t been easy standing the thing up all by himself, but he’d managed to wedge it into the round hole he’d sawed in the center of the raft.

There was a bit of play in the fit, but he'd learned by watching J.J. that wood swelled when wet.

His easiest task so far had been the sail. He'd seen a picture of a Viking longboat in one of his mother's books, and he'd patterned his sail after the Norsemen's. Once, it had been a blanket on his bed. Now, held to the wood by dozens of nails, it caught the gentle east-northeast wind and set the mast to creaking and squeaking against its rope tethers with every slight turn.

Trouble was, the whole thing had teetered and tottered and threatened to topple with the first good puff of air. That's when the nails had really come in handy. Using every scrap of lumber he'd been able to wheedle from Mr. Roberts, he'd secured the nails at forty-five degree angles—all fifteen of them—between the mast and the raft floor. There had been four nails left over when he'd finished, so he'd banged those in, too, just for good measure.

Blinking flirtatiously, Phoebe asked, "Where are you going on your raft?"

"Across the Sound."

"Does your mother know?"

"'Course she does," he said. "I told her I'd be leavin' soon as I got the thing built." It wasn't the whole truth, but it wasn't a lie, either.

The girl's round, blue eyes widened with adulation as her voice took on a whispery, reverent tone. "You mean, you didn't even need her permission?"

His chest and chin out, Adam nodded. "Man doesn't need permission to do what he knows he's capable of."

Phoebe looked toward the Sound. "Why would you go there? It's nothing but sand and—"

Adam stood up and faced the sea. "Have you been there?"

She pouted prettily. "No...."

"Then how do you know what's there?"

A little shrug was her answer.

"Just think—there might be diamonds in those rocks! Or a gold mine. Or pirate treasure, buried in the dunes. Or—"

"Or, maybe," Phoebe giggled, "you're just a silly boy who reads too much."

"Reads too much? Why, I don't even like reading my speller," Adam countered, dropping to his knees once more. "I think I hear your mother calling," he added, tugging at a rope.

"You're just trying to get rid of me."

"If I thought it'd work," he said dully, "I'd tell you it was Santa Claus calling."

From the corner of his eye, he saw her frown. But, just as quickly, the girl's face brightened. "Can I help?"

"Nothin' you can do."

"I could make some sandwiches and bake biscuits for you to take with you on your trip. I could put them all into a jar with a nice, tight lid, so they'd stay dry." She paused. "Well, I could...if you wanted me to."

Actually, Adam thought her idea didn't sound half bad. "Will you make the sandwiches and cookies yourself?"

She grabbed a fold of her skirt and held it out until the fabric formed a semicircle. "Any simpleton can pile meat and bread together," she said, giggling. "Why, I bet even you could do it, Adam Flynn!"

Adam shook his head. Girls, he grumped. "I just don't want your ma askin' questions, is all, about why you're cookin' and bakin' all of a sudden."

"What's your favorite, shortbread or oatcakes?"

Adam's mouth began to water, and he licked his lips. "I guess I'll leave that up to you. But if you really want to do it, you'd better get crackin', 'cause I'm leaving tomorrow at first light."

"But, Adam," Phoebe said, looking up, "there's a storm coming! I heard my grandfather say the last time the sky looked this way, a williwaw blew through town."

"Aw, the old man's worryin' over nothin'. A little rain ain't gonna hurt me."

"Have you ever heard what a williwaw can do?"

"Can't say I have." In all honesty, Adam didn't know what a williwaw was.

"Why, it can blow a whole town away, and flood it, too. Just think what a storm like that could do to your rickety little raft."

"Rickety? My raft ain't rickety. She's sturdy as—"

"It won't hold up in a williwaw. You'd better wait until the storm passes."

"You ain't my ma, Phoebe." On his feet now, Adam said, "I'm goin', and that's that."

Sighing, she started to walk away. "Well, it's your life...."

"That's right," he called after her.

Adam looked at the angry, darkening skies overhead and shivered.

J.J. was hunched over his forge, pumping the bellows to increase the heat. The lump of iron he held in his tongs glowed a bright cherry-red as he laid it on the anvil to pound it into the shape of a cleat. From the corner of his eye, he noticed Bobby Banks loitering near the door, and he had an idea.

"Hey, there, lad. Come on in."

The boy swaggered into the warehouse, his hands pocketed, eyeing everything he passed. He stopped a few feet shy of the forge as J.J. shoved the cleat back into the coals, then tromped on the bellows pedal again. Flames leapt up and licked the underside of the cleat, as well as the tongs.

"Looks mighty hot," Bobby said.

J.J. gave the iron a few pinging whacks with his hammer. The cleat had to be smoothly rounded if a sailor's knot was to slip on and off easily. Most folks squinted when they got this near the fiery intensity of a forge, for it threatened to singe the skin and blind the eyes. Not Bobby Banks. He seemed rooted to the spot, his lips slightly parted, and he breathed heavily, mesmerized by the glare.

"Don't stare at it, lad," J.J. warned him, "or it'll strike ye sightless, sure."

Blinking, the boy roused himself from a self-induced daze. He swallowed, then repeated, "Looks mighty hot."

"Well, don't ye worry none. I know how to put out a fire."

Bobby met J.J.'s eyes. "How—"

"Why, y'drown it, o'course." He punctuated the response by driving the fire-red tongs, cleat and all, into an iron-handled, wooden bucket of water. It spattered and sputtered and hissed like the call of a giant snake, creating a billowing plume of thick, snow-white smoke that, for a moment, blotted Bobby from view. It took no more than an instant for the spume to fizzle as the cleat cooled. Bobby had gotten J.J.'s point, as evidenced by the frightened and fearsome expression on the boy's face.

J.J. had never seen such raw, unbridled hatred—not even in the eyes of the most cold-blooded English landlord. This boy hadn't reached his fourteenth year, and yet his face displayed a loathing that seemed to have no particular source, no particular target, but burned hotter than the cleat had burned in the forge. What fueled his heartless malice?

He was a dark and dangerous being, villainous to his core. J.J. had never looked into the eyes of true evil before, but he was looking at it now, and it shook him to the marrow of his bones.

Chapter Seven

Adam had seen a few storms, some of them serious, but nothing that compared with this one. *You should have listened to Phoebe and waited for it to pass*, he thought.

He'd left at dawn, thinking that the ominous, gray skies overhead meant nothing more serious than a few lightning strikes, some thunder, and maybe a gust of wind or two. But this?

The sucking undertow of great, crashing waves drove him farther, farther from shore, and he lifted his head, squinting past the stinging rain that pelted his face. *If I could just get a glimpse of the dock,* he thought, *maybe I could steer myself back.*

The raft was the only thing between Adam and sure death. He was glad he'd spent as much time as he had constructing it. Glad he'd connected each log to the next one carefully, with sturdy hemp. But how long would the knots of those mismatched pieces stay together? How many more jolts could they endure before snapping?

"If a job's worth doing, it's worth doing well." He hadn't taken J.J.'s advice seriously at the time, but, right now, it seemed like the most important lesson he'd ever learned, and he was glad, too, that he'd finally taken it to heart.

Adam gripped his lifeline tighter. He'd never been more afraid for his life—not when J.J. had chased him through the streets of Currituck, and not even when he'd stood toe to toe with Bobby Banks on the Fourth of July.

Adam had sensed distant danger when setting sail at dawn. Something had told him to turn around, to make the trip another day. But the adventure of it—and the fact that he'd stupidly bragged to Phoebe about it—had spurred him on.

Now, with one cheek pressed hard against the rough wood of the deck, Adam held his breath as yet another wave crashed over him. *Thank You, Lord,* he prayed when it didn't wash him overboard. *And thank You for giving me the good sense to lash down my supplies before leaving.*

The craft rose on a hissing, spitting wave. Lightning exploded behind the tattered, gray clouds. A powerful thunderclap rattled his bones. "Dear God," he whimpered, closing his eyes, "please help me get home. Help me—"

The angry sea surged yet again, lifting the tiny craft high, higher, until Adam could see nothing but smoky sky all around him. The ropes holding the raft together creaked and groaned. Yes, he'd done his best to build it right—but right enough to stand up to a beating like *this*?

The watery world all around him became, in his mind, a monstrous living creature, gurgling and growling as sea swells surged up the beast's muscular arms. Waves curled like powerful fists and pounded down with the force and fury of a giant. The Atlantic was Goliath, and Adam was David. But, unlike David, Adam had no weapon to hurl in self-defense, nothing to protect himself against the power of the sea.

If you'd listened to Phoebe, he thought again, *you'd be home now, safe and sound, warm and dry.*

But it had seemed like such a short distance across the Sound! Convinced he could travel over the narrow strip of water in no time, Adam had decided to take the chance that he could make it over and back again before the rains began. *So much for outwitting nature!*

Every now and then, the storm calmed a bit, and, during those fleeting moments, Adam could see the shore, J.J.'s warehouse, the slate roof of his mother's dress shop, and other stores tucked along Main Street. Each chimney that poked up along the horizon reminded him of the hats that lined the shelves of Mr. Gentry's menswear store.

If I make it back in one piece, he silently promised God, *I'll never miss Sunday school again. And I'll always ask Ma's permission before doing anything so foolish*!

Not once in his nearly nine years on earth had Adam seen a williwaw—Phoebe's grandfather's name for a hurricane—but he'd heard plenty of stories about the floodwaters that drowned everything in their paths. J.J. had said, "It's the winds that terrify sailors. All over the world, they have strange names for the mighty winds. In the Orient, they call 'em 'typhoons.' In Africa, they're 'harmattans,' and they say 'monsoon' in the Middle East. But by whatever name, they're wild and violent and bent on destruction...."

Surely, this was a hurricane, though Adam hoped and prayed it was not—for if the tales he'd been told were even partly true, he was doomed.

If he died, who'd fetch wood for his mother's stove? Who would carry her groceries and help her wrap cloth around wooden blocks?

Adam pictured her, the wind mussing her hair as she stood at the door, a shawl pulled tightly around her shoulders as she watched with worried eyes for her boy's safe return.

Lying on his stomach, Adam pressed his face into the crook of his elbow and struggled to blink back hot tears. *Oh, great*, he thought, punching the raft, *just what you need right now—more water in your eyes*! He willed himself to stop crying. He'd be nine in a few months—too old to cry.

Still, the tears came, because Adam wanted to be around for his birthday. If he had to meet his Maker, he could think of far better ways to do it than by drowning during a gale!

The truth was bitter and ugly: He had no one but himself to blame for the fix he was in. Adam went from listing ifs to citing maybes....

If he'd listened to Phoebe...if he'd asked his mother's permission...if he'd at least told someone where he was headed, he might have been talked out of taking the trip....

Then, maybe he wouldn't be riding the wild waves now. Maybe he wouldn't be afraid for his life. Maybe his mother wouldn't be home alone, worrying about him.

Adam knew he had no choice but to lie still and wait it out. He hoped the angry sea would soon tire of toying with him.

It was surprisingly cold for a summer day, and Adam was surprisingly tired—tired of holding fast to the ropes that kept him from being eaten alive by the hungry waves, tired of holding his breath as each one pummeled him, tired of worrying which gust of wind would be the end of him.

He'd probably swallowed a gallon of the Atlantic's salty water, and his sickened stomach churned like the swollen sea. He yawned, downing yet another mouthful of the briny liquid. If he was exhausted enough to yawn, could sleep be far behind?

Stay awake, he warned himself, *or you'll end up as fish food for sure*!

Just then, he spied the end of the rope he'd planned to use to tether the raft once he'd reached dry land. He crawled toward it on his belly, and when he got hold of the rough hemp, he said through chattering teeth, "Thank You! Thank You, Lord!" For it was more than long enough to lash himself to the deck.

Adam wrapped the rope tightly around his middle, threaded the end through the loops holding the logs together, and breathed a sigh of relief. Now, at least, he had a small chance of surviving this ordeal. Now, he might not be gobbled up by the ravenous sea, should fatigue overtake him before he made it home again.

Home.

It had been a mistake to look toward shore. Adam's heart sank to realize that the riptide had pushed him miles away. The storm had a life of its own; it had become a villainous entity that had kidnapped him and was holding him for ransom, far, far out to sea—miles from his mother, from his warm bed, from....

"Oh, J.J.," Kate cried, "will he ever wake up?"

J.J. wanted to give her an answer that would calm and reassure her, but Adam had been unconscious for twelve hours.

"The longer a person remains in this state," Dr. Parsons said, removing his stethoscope, "the less likely he'll come out of it."

A moment of silence ticked by before Kate found her voice again. "Nonsense. He's a strong, healthy boy. He'll be fine." Tidying her son's covers, she added, "You'll see...."

J.J. watched with careful eyes as she perched on her son's bed, alternately laying cool compresses across his bruised forehead and running her fingers through his hair. She hadn't left his side since J.J. had carried Adam up the steps, and signs of weariness were becoming evident on her pretty face.

"Kate," he said softly, resting a hand on her shoulder, "let me take over for a while. Have a bite to eat; get some rest."

"I can't, J.J. I have to be here when he wakes up."

"You'll be useless to him if you keel over from exhaustion," the doctor said.

Kate shook her head. "I'll eat and sleep when I know he's out of danger."

J.J. and the doctor exchanged worried glances. "I have several other patients to see yet this evening," Dr. Parsons said. "That storm did more damage than the last one."

J.J. pictured the usually tidy streets of Currituck, now littered with chunks of wood, soggy paper, and mud. Several houses on the north end of town had been destroyed. Piers had been torn away. Porches were missing. The entire backside of the church was gone, and many of the headstones in its graveyard lay like wounded soldiers in the muck.

The little row of buildings that included his warehouse had miraculously been spared, though the wind had torn a door from its hinges, and he'd have to replace several shingles. How odd that the brutal blasts had blown the dock away yet had left the boat he'd berthed in the harbor in perfect condition.

The citizens of Currituck had known that the storm was approaching, but its severity had still managed to catch them unawares; high tide had magnified the effects of the nor'easter. Yes, Dr. Parsons would have patients to see tonight, and he'd no doubt remain busy for days to come, stitching up wounds and patting pumice onto the bruises and abrasions of survivors.

Owen Roberts, the carpenter, had asked J.J. to lend a hand building coffins—six of them, to be exact—for those who hadn't survived. J.J. knew that he ought to be getting to work on them, but he didn't want to leave Kate alone.

"See that she gets something to eat," Dr. Parsons instructed him as he packed up his medical bag. "And try to get her to lie down before she falls down."

"I'll try, but ye know Kate...."

The doctor shook his head. "Well," he said, frowning as Kate put a new cloth across Adam's forehead, "I know you'll do your best."

When the doctor had gone, J.J. slid an arm around Kate's shoulders, but she didn't seem to notice. His heart ached for her. She had no one in this world but her son. If something happened to him—

J.J. preferred not to dwell on Kate's state of mind were the boy to take a turn for the worse. He went into the kitchen instead, put on a kettle for tea, and rounded up some ingredients to make a batch of soup. Maybe the scent of onions and ham would rouse her appetite. *But even if it doesn't, she'll be havin' a bowl when it's done!* he determined.

Minutes later, he set a cup of hot tea on Adam's bedside table. Since Kate didn't seem capable of taking her eyes off of her son, J.J. decided to take matters into his own hands.

Sitting down beside her on the edge of the bed, he wrapped her in his arms. "Ah, Kate, m'darlin'," he said, "ye're tremblin' like the last leaf of autumn."

She melted against him like butter on a hot biscuit. "I've never been more frightened in all my life," she admitted in a whispery voice. "He looks so small, so helpless, lying there all bandaged up."

Rubbing soothing circles on her back, J.J. nodded. "I know...."

But, really, what did he know of a mother's love for her child? He'd known many kinds and depths of love—for his family, his work, his Ireland, *his Kate*. Yet, at this moment, as the Dark Faerie hovered near Adam's door, he could only imagine what it would be like to love in the all-consuming, unconditional way of a parent.

Kate sat back and took J.J.'s face in her hands. "If not for you, I think I'd go mad."

He could see how hard she was trying to keep her emotions in check. "Nonsense," he said, smiling a bit.

"Ye're the strongest person I've ever known. Ye'd be fine, with or without—"

"J.J.," she interrupted him, as tears welled in her eyes, "he wouldn't even *be* here if not for you. And for Phoebe, for telling us where he was." She bit her lower lip to stanch a sob. "Thanks to you, at least he has a chance." Resting her cheek on his chest, she said, "How does it feel to be a hero?"

"I wouldn't know," he admitted, wincing. "I did only what any man would have under the circumstances."

Kate sat back, her gaze all but drilling holes into his eyes. "Any man wouldn't have risked his own skin to save a boy from drowning."

"Sure, he would have, Kate. How could he *not*?"

"Doc saw the whole thing from his window. Said he was sure that if the wind didn't get you, the waves would, and—"

"Doc talks too much." J.J. brushed the hair from her eyes, then said, "Will ye do somethin' for me, Kate?"

"You know I will."

He lifted the teacup from the nightstand. "Have a sip, won't ye? I added a spoon of honey, just the way y'like it."

He felt her stiffen.

It started quiet and slow, like the distant, plaintive lament of a lone wolf. Not a moan, exactly, but certainly not a cry. It was a sad, sorrowful sound, reminiscent of those dreadful days in Ireland, when his sister Erin lay dying, and his mother, too weak to comfort her, grieved helplessly.

Kate's shoulders lurched twice, three times, and then she froze, holding her breath, clutching at a wrinkle in his shirt. J.J. felt her warm tears against his skin, and he wanted to sob, himself. He hadn't known how to soothe his brokenhearted ma, so how could he hope to ease Kate's utter sadness?

With ease, he could heft entire logs and stand them upright once he'd hewn them into masts. But what good was physical prowess to him when he was powerless to offer Kate the smallest solace?

J.J. had filled his journal with words that painted pictures, set scenes, and made moods, yet he couldn't think of a single thing to say to give her a moment's respite from her misery.

And so, he simply held her tenderly, his big hands patting her back and massaging her shoulders. He hoped that his love for her would radiate to her by way of his fingertips.

Some minutes later, her sobs subsided. "I'm sorry," she said on a ragged sigh.

"Sorry?" A joyless chuckle crackled from his throat. "Whatever for?"

"I've gotten your shirt all wet."

A feeling surged over him—a sensation that reminded him of the tales told by Irish sailors about the tranquil, tepid waters of the South Seas, waters that foamed and frothed over a man like gentle hands, and soft, sultry winds that ruffled and fluttered like the whispery wings of angels. He wanted—needed—to define this feeling, to give it a name. Less than a second passed before a word came to mind.

Love.

Deep, abiding, and overwhelming, it made him feel helpless and Herculean at the same time. Weak, because, for all his muscular might, he did not possess the strength to fight it. And strong, because he knew it would enable him to endure any hardship, persevere through any pain. His body might well live on without it, but his heart and soul would not.

Love.

Or...was it *Kate*?

J.J. honestly didn't know where one left off and the other began. In his heart, in his head, the two were synonymous.

"Good thing it's summertime," Kate said, her breath warming his chest, "or you'd catch a chill walking around in that damp shirt."

Nothin' can chill me. Not the wicked winds of winter, not the snow from the mountaintops, nor the icy blasts of the Northlands. I'll always be warm as long as ye're near me, Kate.

Kate sighed and snuggled closer to him. "Why, J.J., that's the most beautiful thing anyone has ever said to me."

Either she was a mind reader, or he'd said aloud the words stamped onto his soul. He looked at her face, into eyes so round and brown that he likened the feeling to staring into a pond at midnight, when the moon dipped low in the sky and kissed the rippling ebb tides that danced at the shoreline with shimmering, silvery light. *Ah, Kate, m'darlin', I could live the rest of me days lookin' into yer lovely face, for I love ye with all that I am and all I'll ever be.*

Kate sat up and dried those lovely eyes on the hem of her apron. "You have the heart of a poet, John Joseph O'Keefe."

So, he'd spoken his thoughts aloud *again*?

She reached for the teacup and sipped daintily. It made a glassy *rat-a-tat* when she put it back on the saucer held by her other trembling hand. "Sweetened to perfection, just as you promised."

If only J.J. could promise her that Adam would wake up, and that, when he did, he'd be his usual robust and rowdy self. If only he could promise a fortune-filled future, a life free from everyday fears and frustrations. He wanted to give her security. Surround her with safety. Shroud her with happiness. Because she deserved all that—and more.

Suddenly, J.J. was painfully aware of how very little he had to offer her. A huge and hulking warehouse, filled with half-built ships and bottomless boats; two rooms above that were empty, save for a narrow, creaking cot and a rickety table and chairs; a history of violence; the earned courtesy of the Marquis of Queensbury....

"He looks so peaceful, doesn't he?" Kate asked, taking his hand.

Nodding, he gave hers a gentle squeeze.

"He wouldn't look that way if he were in any pain," she said, meeting his gaze. "Would he?"

J.J. read the hope and expectation shining in those wide, innocent orbs. "He's restin' easy, darlin'," he said gently. "And so should ye. Ye're lookin' a mite pale."

Kate waved away his concerned remark, then sighed. "Life can sometimes be hard, can't it?"

"True enough, but it's easier to bear when y'have a friend to lean on."

Kate placed the cup and saucer back on the nightstand. "Please don't say that."

Her voice sounded so soft, her eyes looked so sad. "Don't say what?"

Long eyelashes dusted her cheeks as she looked down at her hand, resting lightly upon his knee. "Please don't say you're just a friend, because you're so much more than that."

Could she possibly mean...? Because if she did, his world would be—

J.J.'s heart thrummed, each hard-beating throb more emboldening than the last, as he took her face in his hands. "I'm nothin' but a thick-headed Irishman, Kate," he said, his eyes blazing into hers, "so I'm afraid ye're gonna have to be a bit more precise...."

She smiled, and he read admiration, appreciation, and adulation in her gaze. "Tell you *how* you're more than a friend, you mean?"

Nodding, he licked his lips. Would she say it?

She began haltingly. "I think—I think maybe—I might have fallen—"

"Oh, why don't you just kiss her, J.J.?"

Stunned into silent shock, they focused on the boy's storm-battered face.

Kate wrapped her son in a desperate embrace. "Adam!" she cried, gently kissing his cheeks, his forehead, and the tip of his nose. "You're all right. You're all right!"

"No, I'm not," he protested, holding up a hand to fend off her motherly ministrations. He looked at J.J. "Well, don't just stand there," he pleaded. "Make her stop. I didn't survive the storm only to be smothered by my own ma!"

Swallowing a sob of relief, J.J. laid a hand on Adam's shoulder and gave it a fatherly squeeze. "Sorry, son, but I'll not stop her. She earned every smooch, worryin' over y'as she did since I pulled ye out of the drink. The storm didn't kill ye, so, surely, a few kisses won't hurt ye none." He paused, raised an eyebrow, and added, "Consider yerself lucky she's not smackin' the cheeks you sit on, instead. Ye deserve a whoppin' for sailin' into the eye of the storm like ye did, without so much as a word to anybody."

When Kate faced him, J.J. half expected her to scold him for chastising her son. Instead, what he read in her shimmering eyes set his heart to pumping with relief, joy, and expectation.

She loves you, he realized. *Kate Flynn loves you!*

Bobby Banks loved it when a plan came together.

It was long past dusk when Bobby sauntered down the street with his hands in his pockets, whistling "The Riflemen of Bennington." An appropriate tune, he thought, since O'Keefe hailed from the British Isles.

He'd never cared much for the Irishman, a fact that had little or nothing to do with the way the man had pulverized his father in the ring. Bobby didn't like *any* man who was able to read his thoughts, and O'Keefe seemed to have mastered the art. Still, he could take the man or leave him…

…until lately.

All that had changed a couple of days back, when, as was his custom, Bobby had been prowling around town, looking for something to do…and someone to do it *to.* He'd paused in the doorway of J.J.'s warehouse, watching as O'Keefe hammered a misshapen lump of iron into a cleat that would someday hold fast a ship's line. He'd been in the workshop many times before, but never when the Irishman was about. That day, the man had actually invited him inside.

He should have suspected something was afoot.

The friendly greeting had quickly turned ominous, and Bobby hadn't understood why the ex-boxer had aimed that gray-eyed glare at him, or why his lip had curled with disgust. But he'd had no trouble understanding that the man believed him responsible for what had happened to the Norris family.

There was only one way he could be so certain of a thing like that. Mealy-mouthed Adam Flynn had told O'Keefe about the threat. Bobby despised Adam. *Little squirt made me look like a fool in front of the boys,* he fumed silently, narrowing his eyes. By blatantly disobeying a direct order, Adam had caused the rest of the gang to question Bobby's authority. No one had ever stood up to him that way, let alone a twit half his size!

Clenching his jaw, Bobby shoved his fists deeper into his pockets. The little snot would pay for crossing him.

Adam's mutinous act had turned out to be—what was it the grown-ups called it?—a blessing in disguise. Bobby hadn't needed the journal, after all, because he'd devised a new scheme—one that would take care of O'Keefe…and Adam, too, once he learned that his so-called hero had burned to death in the bowels of his own boat.

Two birds with one stone. Life didn't get much better than that!

He'd been watching O'Keefe for days now and knew even before the man climbed the stairs that he'd leave those coals glowing in the forge. Dousing them would mean he'd have to start a whole new fire in the morning rather than conveniently fanning the embers into bright, new flames.

Bobby knew where the man kept his coal scuttle and where to find the short-handled shovel to scoop out the glowing coals, and the moment the Irishman was out of sight, he slipped in through the back window he'd unlocked during an earlier visit and headed straight for the supplies. Holding his breath, he winced, fearing O'Keefe might have heard his boots hit the floor. He winced again each time the shovel scraped through the coals. When he felt he'd filled the bucket halfway, he scurried back out the way he'd come in, darting from shadow to shadow like a two-legged, blond rat. It wasn't until he was standing outside again that he breathed a sigh of relief.

Time's a-wastin', he warned himself, heading for the dock. He couldn't allow anyone to spot him, because how would he explain a coal scuttle filled with hot coals?

His eyes on the prize, he headed straight for O'Keefe's latest project—a beautiful schooner, still resting in its construction support on the dock. He'd seen the man at work on it dozens of times and knew that the Irishman took great pride in the ship. Well, his cocksure expression would change tomorrow, when he set foot aboard *Freedom Sails....*

Bobby boarded the boat in one neat leap, landing on two feet on its polished mahogany deck. Crouching, he ran through the hatch—and his boot heel caught on the top step.

Down the ladder he went, his elbows and knees, hips and shoulders thumping the walls and rails, until he came to an abrupt stop that forced the air from his lungs, flung hot coals in all directions, and left him in a twisted heap of arms and legs.

Startled, Bobby lurched and blinked as the now empty scuttle landed with a clatter, and the hatch slammed shut behind him. When he caught his breath, he whimpered quietly, trying to assess his injuries—not an easy task in the pitch dark. There didn't seem to be a place on him that didn't ache, and he knew, even without benefit of light, that he was bleeding—bleeding badly. On the way down, he'd snagged himself on something—a nail? a hook?—making it impossible to determine if the gluey, wet substance along the leg of his trousers had come from the gash in his thigh or the wound on his palm. Wincing in pain, he moved his fingers down the outer seam of his pants, inching ever closer to the source of this most excruciating agony.

His thumb touched something sharp and jagged. "Your bone!" he bellowed. "It's your thigh bone!" Waves of nausea and lightheadedness washed over him. "That stupid Mick," he muttered through clenched teeth. What was he thinking, building a ladder that steep? And why had he left something so sharp poking out to snag an unsuspecting kid?

It wasn't supposed to happen this way! The plan had been to scatter coals across the floor so that they'd burn slowly; so that, when O'Keefe came down the ladder to investigate the source of the smoke, he'd plunge headlong through the gaping, burning hole, straight through to the murky waters beneath the dock, where Bobby had seen a rusting anchor embedded in the mire.

"Stupid Mick," he said again, as dizziness overtook him. Struggling to breathe, Bobby closed his eyes and surrendered to unconsciousness.

❃

J.J. poured himself a cup of strong, black coffee, intent upon finishing Burt's wooden arm that night.

Placing his mug on the far corner of the workbench, he perched on the high-backed stool that faced the windows and picked up a hank of leather. Following the pattern he'd sketched, J.J. used brass brads to secure one end of the harness to the wooden arm. A snip here, a stitch there, and he'd be ready to line the hollowed-out insides with cushiony shearing wool. It would be a poor substitute for a real arm, but, at least when Burt strapped it on, he'd be able to use the clamp, positioned where fingers ought to be, to hold things steady while his good hand measured, pounded, and sawed.

J.J. leaned back, propped his feet on the table, and used a short-bladed knife to bevel the edges of the leather. Bits of tanned hide fell into his lap and onto the floor. No matter—he'd sweep it up when he was gathering the rest of the shavings and sawdust from his pride and joy, *Freedom Sails*.

A movement outside caught his attention, and J.J. looked up from his work.

The sight on the other side of the window stunned him so much that he nearly cut off his thumb. He threw down the leather and the knife as both his booted feet hit the floor running.

Freedom Sails was on fire!

J.J. was out of the warehouse in an instant and covered the distance between the yard and the newly built dock in record time.

"J.J.!" he heard Thaddeus yell. "Where you goin' in such a rush?"

Without missing a step, J.J. pointed along the shore.

"Good heavens," the old man said. "Mary! Pass the word—fire at the dock! We need to form a bucket brigade, starting at the water's edge!"

J.J. barely heard the order, for his mind was fixed on the boat. He was on board in seconds, squinting into the chalky, choking smoke, trying to identify its source. Tying a neckerchief over his mouth and nose, he raced across the deck and noticed that the hatch was closed. *Why on earth?* he wondered, throwing it open.

Instantly, he was engulfed in a thick cloud of lung-clogging smog. Instinct made him crook an arm to cover his face, and he stepped back. But a low, moaning voice urged him forward again. Someone was down there. "Who?" and "Why?" never entered his head. All J.J. knew was that he had to get to him fast.

"J.J.!" Thaddeus bellowed. "Are you mad? You can't go down there!"

But J.J. was deaf to everything but the faint cries coming from below. He plunged into the roiling, rising cloud and, blinded by the eye-burning haze, felt his way along the wooden handrail as he moved down the ladder.

Everything in him shouted, "Turn around! Get out!" A week ago, when he hadn't had much reason to live, when he hadn't known that Kate Flynn loved him, he'd have paid no mind to the warning. But this night? Only the small voice, weakly calling, "Help...help me...," urged him onward.

His boot touched something, and he crouched down. "Thank God," said the voice—a voice he recognized. "Bobby? Bobby Banks?"

It all came together so fast, J.J. didn't know what hit him. Despite the smoke, there was enough light from above for him to see the coal scuttle, lying on its side. He saw the glowing pieces of coal, eating through the floorboards. Had the boy come down here to burn the boat? To trap him in the bowels of his own creation?

Bobby's keening cry grew weaker, quieter, telling J.J. there was no time to ponder guilt or innocence or the reasons for his latest madness. And so, he knelt down in the pool of blood and, with a great grunt, lifted the boy in his arms.

J.J. cringed, not at the boy's limp weight, but because all four of his limbs poked out at odd angles. Bobby had one good arm, though, and, with it, was clinging to J.J. for all he was worth.

J.J. knew he shouldn't open his mouth, shouldn't waste precious oxygen trying to speak. But the overwhelming sense that Bobby needed to hear his voice outweighed reason. Whether the boy had set fire to the Norrises' house, or killed the schoolmarm's cat, or threatened Kate and Adam, or caused this blaze, tonight, he was just a terrified boy in horrific pain. "Easy, lad," he said, struggling to climb the ladder. "Ye're gonna be fine."

Those few words were all J.J. could manage before the smoke choked off his airway, but it was enough, it seemed, to ease the boy's mind. Topside at last, J.J. willed himself to put one boot in front of the other, to get the boy away from the smoke. He trudged a distance of a hundred yards or so before his knees buckled, and he sank slowly to the dock, cradling Bobby in his arms. Then, spent and wheezing, he leaned back against a piling.

The clock tower in the village square counted out the hour—midnight. The members of the fire brigade went efficiently about their business as a crowd gathered around J.J.

"Well, looky there," someone said. "If it ain't Bobby Banks."

"Battered and bruised and bleedin' like a stuck pig," said another voice.

"So, there's justice in this old world after all...."

"Shut up, the lot o'ye," J.J. growled. "Can't ye see he's in a bad way? Somebody fetch Doc Parsons and the boy's pa."

"Pa?" Bobby rasped.

"Hush, lad," J.J. said, placing a gentle hand of restraint on one bloody shoulder.

"Did I get it done right? Is the Mick gone?" Bobby murmured deliriously.

So the boy *had* set the fire on purpose!

J.J.'s breath caught in his throat, and it took all the strength he could muster to say, "Hush, I said. Y'need to save yer strength." His gaze traveled the length of the boy, from his sweat-dampened, blond hair to the gaping wound in his thigh. J.J. had seen exposed muscle and bone before, yet the sight still set his stomach to rumbling. At least the boy had stopped struggling, had quit trying to sit up.

J.J. looked into Bobby's face, where tear tracks had washed clean swaths through the soot.

The boy's eyes, wild with pain, focused on J.J.'s eyes. "W-why'd you save me?"

"Because it was the right thing to do."

"Even though—?"

"Even though," J.J. echoed.

Bobby nodded once before taking a deep, rasping breath, then tensed from head to toe.

"Hold on, lad," J.J. grunted. "Help is on the way."

He'd seen the lad going into the church from time to time. Had Bobby learned enough during his infrequent visits to save his soul? Had he repented at some point? J.J. hoped so, because it didn't look like Bobby would live long enough to experience regret...or redemption....

A sob ached in J.J.'s throat as he looked into Bobby's blue eyes, for though they were wide open and staring, they saw nothing. He hung his head. "God's mercy on ye, lad," he said. "I'll say a prayer for yer immortal soul."

Chapter Eight

They buried Bobby two days after the fire, with no one in attendance but Rev. Hall, J.J., Kate, and Bobby's parents, Amos and Beatrice. His tombstone stood stock-straight, marking his final resting place with stone-cold granite. To the right, another stone read, "Beloved Brother," and on the left was one that read, "She will be missed." On Bobby's stone, the mason had carved, "Robert B. Banks, December 15, 1841–July 15, 1855"—and nothing more.

Amos Banks stepped away from the plot, then turned and reached for J.J.'s hand. "Heard what you tried to do for my boy."

Kate watched J.J.'s fingertips tighten and his brow furrow. "Sorry I didn't get to him sooner," was his craggy response.

"Risked your own skin to save him. Thank you for that."

Sobbing, Beatrice Banks stepped up beside her husband. "You probably think my boy was bad. No point denying it. We both know it's true. But—"

"—but he was our boy," Amos finished, then fished a flask from his pocket and tilted it to his lips. "Wouldn't blame you if you judged me harsh," he said, screwing the top back on.

"Ain't for me to judge," J.J. said. "That's 'tween ye and yer Maker."

As Bobby's parents walked away, Kate extended her hand to J.J. "How about if I warm a bit of the soup you made for me the other day?" she asked.

Smiling sadly, he hugged her for a moment, then led her from the cemetery.

"You look tired, J.J. Maybe you'd rather go home and get some sleep?"

"Can't," he admitted. "I've tried." In a lighter tone, he added, "If I slept, I'd only dream of y', anyway, and I'd much rather be with the real thing."

Kate stopped and stood in his path. Wiggling a finger under his nose, she said, "Come here, Mr. O'Keefe." And, when he leaned closer, she pressed a lingering kiss to his lips.

"What was that for?" he asked afterward, grinning. "Not that I'm complainin', mind ye."

"For your being you." Kate resumed walking. "I forgot to tell you something the other day when Adam came to." On the heels of a deep breath, she said, "I know what folks must be saying, what they're probably thinking, considering the way we were—um, entangled...on the Fourth.

"I've always conducted myself like a proper lady, following God's rules—and man's, too—to the letter. And, to be honest, I don't know if what I'm about to say is a violation of either."

"Not likely," J.J. interrupted her. "Ye're as pure as new-fallen snow. Anything in yer head is surely fine with the Almighty."

Kate had been thinking about this for days, even since before he'd kissed her at the Festival. From the first story she'd heard about him, Kate had decided to keep a safe and careful distance from this man with a violent past. *Get too close*, she'd warned herself, *and you're liable to be the next one he pummels...and not for money, either*!

It hadn't taken her long to figure out that John Joseph O'Keefe had the gentlest soul, the sweetest temperament, and the kindest disposition of any man she'd ever known, including her dear, departed father. Kate had discovered that J.J. was a practical man, too—realistic to the bone and logical to the end. He'd seen the advantages of his size and power, and, realizing he could put them to good use, satisfying men's lust for blood and gore, he'd earned enough to build a burgeoning ship business.

But the moment he'd been able to, J.J. had set aside his gloves and stepped out of the ring. Amos Banks had goaded him into one last fight, but Thaddeus had told Kate that it had upset J.J. so badly, he'd sworn he'd rather die than repeat the scene.

Then, J.J. had stomped into her life, all bluster and blow, demanding retribution for stolen lunches and the pails they'd been packed in. Kate had thought him petty and cheap that day for scaring the wits out of her boy just to reclaim a few slices of bread and three dented lunch tins. She'd thought him a heathen, but she'd been wrong about that, too, for his steadfast faith in God had motivated everything he said and did.

Adam had been a joy to be around since J.J. had come into their lives. Indeed, her son wouldn't be alive today, if not for the burly Irishman!

She could plainly see that J.J. needed little more than a few creature comforts to keep him happy. *Freedom Sails* hadn't been constructed to add to his own coffers. Rather, he'd built it at his own expense to carry the produce and products of the town's hardworking citizenry to northern ports, where a handpicked crew would sell goods on their behalf and return with a tidy profit to help build their businesses.

Ever a shrewd businessman, ever a poet, J.J. believed that the beauty of the small, seacoast village might attract tourists one day. "They'll come in droves," he'd teased, "and build houses right on the beach, so they can get an eyeful of all the beauty the sea holds."

"Houses on the beach, indeed!" Kate had said, laughing. "What sort of fool would build on a foundation of sand?"

"Ah, Kate," he'd sighed, "ye're probably right. But a man can dream, can't he?"

Only a moment ago, he'd said he dreamed of *her*. "J.J., will you show me the boat?"

He halted. "It's a wreck, thanks to the fire. It'll take weeks to get her back into—"

"I'll keep that in mind."

"But, I thought ye had somethin' to tell me...."

"I can say it on the boat as easily as I can say it here. I've wanted to see your handiwork; this way, we can kill two birds with one stone."

His arms slid around her, and he pulled her close. "Ye're a source of constant joy in me miserable life, do y'know that?"

"And you in mine," Kate said, pulling away. "Last one there is a rotten egg!" She hiked up her skirts and ran as fast as her legs would carry her, feeling young and impetuous and playful for the first time in many years... feeling womanly and wanted and loved for the first time in her *life*.

J.J. could have caught up with her in three strides, she knew, with those long, strong legs to help him along. Smiling, she thought, *How like him to let me win.*

Kate bounded up the plank connecting the dock to the boat's deck, then leaned against the rail. "Thank you," she gasped, breathless.

Halting next to her, J.J. gathered her close again. "For what?"

"Oh, nothing." She shrugged. "Just for being you."

"Ready for a tour?"

"I am," she said, putting her hand in his.

For the next ten minutes, J.J. captured her attention by identifying the ship's parts by their proper names—the stern, the bow, the bowsprit, the beam, and so forth. "It's beautiful," Kate said when he'd finished. "You're a true artist."

"Take hold of this," he said, handing her a rope.

"What is it?"

"The main halyard. I want ye to fasten it to the cleat, here," he said, pointing to the squat, iron T on the rail.

"But, J.J., I don't know the first thing about—"

"Then it's high time ye learned." And, guiding her hands, he taught her to "make fast," looping the rope around, then over and right, crossing under and left, and finishing with a tug.

"It's almost exactly the way I tie knots when sewing."

"Makes sense. It's strong and sure and trustworthy." He pulled her close. "And so are ye."

"J.J., stop," she said, batting her lashes flirtatiously. "You'll give me a swelled head, comparing me to the likes of a knotted rope."

Chuckling, he held her near. "'Twasn't meant as a physical comparison, darlin', 'cause Lord knows ye're far shapelier than a length of hemp." His hands on her shoulders, he said, "Ye're everything a woman ought to be, Kate, but, in me humble opinion, there's just one thing wrong with ye."

Pouting, she said, "What thing?"

"Well, how'd ye like yer people to be buried beside mine?"

With wide eyes, she said, "What?"

"Bear with me, Kate. 'Tisn't easy for a dumb Irishman to say what I'm about to say...."

She smiled.

"All right, then, try this on for size: Kate O'Keefe. Now, tell me that doesn't have a fine ring to it!"

"Does it come with a fine, *gold* ring?"

Clasping Kate's hands between his own, J.J. looked toward the sky and, exhaling a great huff of air, closed his eyes. "Praise God Almighty!" he bellowed, driving both fists heavenward in a gesture of joy and victory. Then, in a calmer voice, he added, "I have a little somethin' for ye...."

"A present? But it isn't my birthday, or—"

"It's the first day of the rest of our lives," he said, uncovering a waist-high wooden crate. He grabbed a crowbar to pry off the lid, then lifted a strange-looking machine from inside.

"J.J., this is for me? How sweet!" Then, "I'm sorry to be so dense, and I hope I don't seem ungrateful by asking, but—what is it?"

"Why, it's a sewin' machine, of course, straight from the foundry."

"A—a sewing machine?" Kate walked a wide circle around it, smoothing her hands over the graceful curves, the slick, black enamel, the sleek, oak drawers, and the heavy, iron legs. "But—how does it work?"

"Near as I can figure, ye put the string up here and weave it through this loop and that little arm, there, and when ye tromp on the pedal, the needle goes up and down, and...." He spread his arms wide. "And ye're sewin'!"

Kate clasped both hands beneath her chin. "My! Whoever would have thought it possible?"

"Way I see it," J.J. continued, hugging her from behind, "ye're gonna need all the time-savin' devices money can buy."

Leaning into him, Kate asked why.

"So ye'll have plenty of time for—"

Gasping, she faced him. "For children? *Our* children?"

His face ruddied with the beginnings of a blush, and she threw her arms around his neck. "What ever did I do in my life to deserve a man like you?" Then, she took a step back and frowned.

"What? Y'haven't changed yer mind, I hope—"

"Of course not. You're about to lose a button," she said, tapping his collar. "Good thing I'm a bit forgetful."

"Forgetful?"

Kate removed the threaded needle she'd poked into her sleeve. "I keep it there when I'm working, so I won't lose it among my other sewing notions." Grinning, she shrugged. "Now, stand still, so I won't poke you."

In a moment, the button was tight and sure, and Kate wound the extra thread around it several times. "What did you call it—a half hitch?"

J.J. nodded.

"Well, there you have it, then. A button fastened with a half hitch. But don't let it give you any ideas."

"Ideas?"

"When you say 'I do' at our wedding, you'll be hitched *all the way*. Got it?"

J.J. threw back his head and laughed. "Got it."

Kate's smile softened, and so did her voice. "Remember on the Fourth of July, when you kissed me under the pines?"

"Only every other minute or so."

"When we were making that silly promise to call each other by our first names?"

"Ah, Mrs. Soon-to-Be-O'Keefe, I love the way yer mind works. Y'wouldn't be suggestin' we seal this deal with a kiss, now, would ye?"

"I insist on it."

A moment later, when J.J. came up for air, Kate combed her fingers through his hair. "Nice?" she asked, tilting her head.

"Very."

"Well, that's just a small sample of what you'll get, once we've tied the knot for real...."

Follow the Leader

Chapter One

September 1868
Freeland, Michigan

"Hup! Two, three, four. Hup! Two, three, four."

The troops obediently followed their leader, who was walking backward and giving instructions in singsong.

Focusing on something behind the leader, the shortest soldier said, "Uh, Sergeant?"

"No talking in formation," the commander growled playfully.

"But, sir, there's—"

"No 'buts,' recruit. Remain in formation or—"

Thump.

He turned to see what he'd hit—a tick too late to stop what the collision had started.

The shortest soldier plowed into the leader, the two behind him marched into each other, and the young woman, arms moving like windmills, landed on her derriere amid a tangle of skirts as books, slates, and chalk rained down around her.

"Oh, bother!" he said, whipping the cap from his head. "I—I'm sorry, ma'am. Didn't see you standing there. I—we...." He extended a hand to help her up. "Are you all right?"

"Oh, I think I'll live," she said, taking his hand. Brushing dust and grit from her blue velvet skirt, she smiled. "If it'll make you feel better, you and your little army can help me pick up my things."

Had she—had she *winked* at him? No woman, not even Rita, had ever done that before!

He looked at her then. Really looked at her. She had the loveliest smile he'd ever seen. It brightened her big, green eyes, and everything else around her, too. It took a great deal of concentration to look away from the delicate face to fulfill her request, but he found the presence of mind to begin stacking books in his arms. One by one, each item disappeared into her seemingly bottomless canvas bag.

He felt obliged to explain—if not for this adorable young woman, then to encourage good manners in his children, who'd clustered around him, watching closely. Clearing his throat, he ran a hand through his hair and grinned. "We play 'soldier' on family outings," he began. "It helps me keep 'em together. I'm afraid I simply wasn't looking where I was going."

She peered around him at the inquisitive faces of his children. "No harm done," she said.

"C'mere, kids," he instructed them, placing one hand on the blond boy's shoulder. "The little fella here is Timmy." His free hand rested on top of the girl's head. "This pretty brunette is Tricia, and the big guy's name is Tyler."

The woman slung the bag handles over her shoulder. "It's a pleasure to meet all of you," she told the children. "And it was an experience," she added, looking directly into his eyes, "meeting you." She held out one white-gloved hand. "I'm Valerie Carter."

First, she'd winked, and now she was offering her hand? He'd never met a woman quite like her before. Tentatively, he shook it. "Paul Collins," he said, still wondering why her name sounded so familiar.

They stood in silence for a moment, staring into each other's eyes, her hand nearly hidden in his. Timmy coughed. Tricia sighed. Tyler cleared his throat. All three children were grinning when Paul glanced over at them, reminding him to release her hand. "Were you on your way in or out when I—"

"In," she said. "I'm trying to get a head start." Valerie paused, as if wondering whether or not to tell him more. Then, she shrugged and began her explanation. "I'm the new teacher. Monday will be my first day."

His dark eyes widened, and his eyebrows rose. "Well, now, isn't that a coincidence?" he asked his children. "Miss Carter is new here, too." Paul faced her again. "We just came back to town, ourselves. That's why we're here—to enroll the children in school."

She gave the children her friendliest smile, then gathered her skirts and started up the steps of the schoolhouse. "Let's go inside," she suggested, "and get better acquainted." The huge brass doorknob squealed as she turned it, and the heavy oak door creaked as it swung open.

"It's very dark in there," Timmy whispered, staying close to his father's side. "How will I ever learn to read, Pa, if I can't even see the books?"

Valerie's merry laughter brightened the room even before she struck a match to light a lantern. Adjusting the flame, she said, "How's that, Tim?"

The boy grinned shyly and shoved both hands deep in his pockets. "Lots better, ma'am."

"Don't you just hate rainy days?" she asked Tricia. "They're so...." Valerie paused, wrinkling her nose as she searched for the word that best fit the day's mood. "They're so gloomy."

"Yes, ma'am," the girl agreed, focusing on the scuffed toes of her high-buttoned shoes.

Valerie unceremoniously plopped her bag onto the dusty desktop. "This is my first visit to the school, too, you know." Her hands on her hips, she surveyed the one-room space. "Now, where do you suppose the 'brand-new student' forms are?" she asked no one in particular. Rummaging through drawers and shuffling with shelf contents, she frowned. Then, clapping her hands once, she said, "Guess we're just going to have to make one of our own."

She pulled out the battered wooden chair behind her desk and sat down. Taking a sheet of paper and a pencil from her bag, she gestured toward the neat rows of desks. "Please, won't you all sit down?"

Obediently, each Collins did as she'd instructed, including Paul, whose knees nearly touched his earlobes as he tried to balance his considerable frame on the tiny wooden chair.

"What's your full name?" Valerie asked Tyler.

Sitting up straight, the boy said in the deepest voice he could muster, "Tyler Joshua Collins, ma'am."

"What a fine, strong name."

The serious face brightened. "Pa says I'm strong as a horse."

"That's good to know. It'll be good to have a strong young man around to carry in wood when the snow comes. Would you mind being my helper?"

A grin curved his lips upward. "Not at all, ma'am."

"How old are you, Tyler?"

"Be eleven soon, ma'am."

"Let's see," she said, squinting and tapping her chin with the end of her pencil. "That should put you in level five. Maybe even six. Am I right?"

"Yes, ma'am. I finished my fifth year up in York."

"Pennsylvania?"

The boy nodded. "I was born here in Maryland, but we moved to Pennsylvania when I was one."

She smiled. "I guess you don't remember much about it, then, do you?"

Tyler grinned. "Don't remember a thing."

"We have something in common, because I don't know anything about Freeland, either." She met Tricia's eyes next. "If I had to guess, I'd say you're about nine. Am I close?"

Her head bobbed up and down. "I'm eight. Almost." Glancing at her father, she added, "Pa says I'm big for my age. Gonna be tall, like Ma was."

Like Ma *was*? Valerie pretended not to have heard the obvious reference to a deceased mother. Her heart ached for the children. For their father, too. She knew how much it hurt to lose a loved one, but to have lost someone as important as a mother at such a young age.... "You're in your third year, then?"

Tricia nodded. "That's what the teacher back home said."

"This is home now," Timmy pointed out.

Valerie couldn't help but notice the sadness that enveloped the little family at the boy's simple statement. She wondered what event had inspired the move from Pennsylvania to Maryland. "That leaves you, Timmy," she said, her voice deliberately cheery to change the mood. "Have you gone to school before?"

"No, ma'am."

"Level one, then," she said, smiling. Turning her attention to their father, Valerie added, "Mr. Collins, you can be very proud of them. They're fine, mannerly children."

"Thank you for the compliment, ma'am, but Mrs. Collins is responsible for their good behavior." His voice was a near whisper when he said, "She died during the war. I, u...I expect that'll be helpful information if you're to deal with my young'uns on a daily basis."

Suddenly, she felt the need to busy her hands and began rearranging things on her desk. Yes, it was helpful information. These children would most definitely need extra care and compassion. A little more of her time than the children who had two parents.... When she met his eyes again, she said, "I'm sorry to hear of your loss."

Valerie didn't know it was possible to feel so many emotions at once. She experienced confusion, embarrassment, and pity all at the same time.

He grinned sheepishly, twisting his soft, black hat in his hands. "I've had nearly five years to get used to the fact. I suppose I could have put it a bit more gently...."

"Mr. Collins, there's absolutely no need to apologize. That horrible war...." Valerie's voice trailed off as she pictured her home, destroyed and smoldering. "The War Between the States cost me everything I held dear. Freeing the slaves was the only good thing to come of it, in my opinion, and if you ask me, the pigheaded menfolk who run this country should have been able to accomplish that without so much bloodshed!"

"Ma was gonna get us a baby," Timmy interjected, "but she had to give it back to God."

Just when you think you're the only one in pain, Valerie said to herself, *someone comes along and shows you things could be worse.*

"God must'a liked Ma a lot," Timmy added, "'cause He kept her and the baby, too."

From the corner of her eye, Valerie saw Paul sit a bit straighter in the tiny chair. Saw him throw back his broad shoulders. That he'd reacted physically to the plain truth five years after his wife's death told Valerie the wound was still quite painful.

She wished for the courage to look him straight in the eye and tell him he'd done a fine job being both father and mother to his children, that the proof glowed in their loving eyes. She wanted to tell him that she'd known men in similar circumstances who had moved heaven and earth to replace their deceased wives as soon as humanly possible.

Valerie glanced at the books on the corner of a desk that desperately needed dusting. At the windows, which probably hadn't been washed in years. At the large, faded blackboard in the corner, which could use a good scrubbing. The floor was gritty with dirt, and the desks and benches.... She had a lot to do, and very little time in which to do it. "Well," she said, standing up, "I have enough information for now. I'll see you all on Monday, bright and early, right?"

"Right," Timmy said, his voice shrill with eagerness.

"Do you have slates?" she asked as she escorted them to the exit.

The children nodded. "Pa made us pack 'em real careful so they wouldn't break during the move," Timmy offered. "Ma bought 'em for us with her egg money before...."

Valerie put her hand on the boy's shoulder, sensing he couldn't complete the awful sentence. "Good! Then I'll see to it that each of you gets a brand-new piece of chalk first thing Monday morning," she said. "We'll consider it my 'welcome back to Freeland' gift to you."

"I think we'd better head on home," Paul told the children, "and let Miss Carter get busy putting her school in order." He opened the door. "Thanks for your help," he said, setting the felt hat atop his head.

She watched them walk down the steps and across the dusty road before they disappeared into the woods just north of town. The clouds that had darkened the sky earlier were gone now, and the sun shone in the September sky, brightening the day and her spirits alike. Taking a deep breath, Valerie headed back inside to survey what Mr. Collins had called "her school." In two short days, the empty seats would be filled with children.

Valerie's heart beat a bit faster at the prospect of being the person who'd teach them to appreciate all the wonderful things an education could add to their lives. If she could make a positive difference in even one young life, she'd have earned her salary.

She had no way of knowing that she'd already made a difference in three young lives...and one older one....

❀

"She's mighty pretty, Pa. Do you s'pose she's a good teacher?"

Paul thrust his hands deep into his pockets. "She seems real smart to me, Tim." He walked behind his children, picturing their new teacher's happy face. Hearing her light, melodic laughter. Wondering whether her chestnut-colored hair felt as soft as it looked. And pondering what sadness had dimmed the gleam in those big, green eyes. It surprised him to realize he wished he was a boy in school again.

The children ran on ahead, toward their new home. The house hadn't been occupied in years, but Paul and the children had made it livable. Each had worked in a specific room, scrubbing and sweeping until the place sparkled. Still, despite the cleanliness, something was missing....

Paul had wandered the rooms alone each night, listening to the rhythmic sounds of his slumbering children and trying to determine exactly what he'd neglected to do, what he'd forgotten to bring with them from York that would make this house a home, like the one in Pennsylvania had been. They'd been in Freeland for nearly a month, yet he hadn't been able to find that missing piece to the puzzle.

He sat down in front of the hearth with his Bible open on his lap, distracted by the soft, soothing spatter of rain against the windowpanes. Paul leaned back in the creaking rocker and closed his eyes, remembering how, on nights like this, Rita would sit across from him, knitting or darning socks, while he whittled a toy for the children or repaired a harness, both totally content and at peace with their lives. The ache of missing her throbbed harder than ever in this new-yet-old place, and Paul wiped the annoying tear that rolled down his cheek.

He was tired. So very tired. Even his sigh, as silent as the raindrops that slid down the windowpane, sounded tired.

But he hated the thought of going to bed. Climbing onto the narrow feather mattress alone roused an ache deep inside him that hurt every bit as much as a hammer's blow. He'd lie there, hour after hour, praying that sleep would rescue him from his loneliness, from his memories.

But it wouldn't.

And so, Paul had developed a ritual to avoid retiring for the night—one that involved closing windows, locking doors, turning down lanterns, and checking on the children. When the last chin had been tucked in, though, he'd have to admit that with the sunrise would come the promise of a long day's work. He needed his sleep, he knew, and so, reluctantly, he'd slip between the crisp, white sheets that Rita had embroidered with bright blue flowers, remembering that she was gone forever.

Now, Paul glanced around the room that he'd shared with her during those first happy months of their ten-year marriage. They'd lived on the old Collins farm barely two years when Rita's father had suffered a heart attack. If she and Paul hadn't returned to Pennsylvania to help out, the old man would surely have lost his farm and also his life. Paul had rented the Collins property to a friend, who was to see that things were cared for until he and Rita could return. How could he have known that the return to Maryland would never happen in her lifetime?

Their years in Pennsylvania had been happy ones, thanks especially to Rita. Knowing how her husband missed his family, and how it must have hurt him to have left the farm behind, she'd worked diligently to make the dark, drafty house beside her father's a warm, bright place. With Rita beside him, Paul had barely noticed the faded wallpaper or the imperfections in the windowpanes that distorted their view of the fields beyond.

But after that soldier's bullet had ended her life, the house had seemed to shriek with flaws and failings. Rooms that had felt light and airy thanks to Rita's ruffles and embroidery turned instantly gloomy. In place of her sweet greeting at the end of a long, hard day, Paul heard groaning floorboards and squealing hinges. Instead of the aromas of sweetbreads and hearty soups, the musty smell of grit met him at the door. He couldn't bear life in Pennsylvania without her.

He prayed that in Freeland, where their love had begun, he could come to terms with a widower's lifestyle.

He quickly discovered that the little house hadn't changed in the ten years they'd lived up north. It was still sturdy and strong, and he'd tried to arrange the furniture inside it as Rita might have, hoping it would bring him peace and contentment in those solitary hours after the children were asleep.

But nothing he did eased the ache or made him miss her less. Except for the warmth of his children's love, his world was mostly cold now.

And Paul doubted that anything would ever truly warm him again.

The sun had just peeked over the hilltop when he heard their voices. Having been up for hours, he had already milked all three cows, gathered a dozen eggs, and fed the two horses. It was time to replace that slat in the barnyard fence; he'd work until the children called to him.

They'd no doubt found the pan of biscuits warming on the stovetop and the pot of oatmeal beside it. They'd eaten and dressed, performed their indoor chores, and then come running, as Rita had taught them to do every morning, pretending they had no idea where he might be. *Praise the Lord*, he thought, *that some things, at least, never change.*

From where he stood, high atop a grassy knoll overlooking Freeland's town square, Paul could see the white church steeple gleaming in the morning sunlight. He remembered helping his father hang the old bronze bell; remembered, too, helping replace the greased paper in the arched windows with colorful panes of beveled glass.

Paul shook his head sadly. The memory of it ached, even after so many years had passed. He sent a prayer heavenward, thanking God that his father hadn't lived to face the fact that his only son didn't want to walk in his footsteps. If only Paul could have spared his mother the same pain.

"Fine! Hire a new pastor if you like," she'd cried, weeks after his father's funeral. "I can't bear to stay if you won't be in charge." And with that, she'd made arrangements to return to Chicago, where she'd been living with her sister ever since.

He'd never explained his reluctance to stand behind the pulpit to his mother—or anyone else, for that matter—partly because she hadn't asked, and partly because he didn't completely understand it himself. Paul didn't know what God had planned for his life, but he did know what God *didn't* intend for him to do....

The day before their wedding, Rita had tearfully confessed, "I'm not good enough to be a pastor's wife. Planning luncheons and church socials, counseling and helping, nursing and teaching...." Giggling past her tears, she'd blushed and hugged him. "I'm too selfish to share you!"

"Our love isn't selfish," he'd assured her. And nearly every day of their marriage, they'd comment on how much they cherished their time alone as the playful debate seesawed: Did she love her role as wife and mother more than he loved his position as husband and father?

A clap of thunder slapped him rudely back to the present. He'd been letting his mind wander again—something he'd been doing a lot of since Rita's death. But it was no wonder, when everything, it seemed, reminded him of her. He went back to working on the fence.

"Pa!" Timmy called. "Where are you?"

He leaned on the shovel and rubbed his stubbled chin, glad to have his mind solidly back in the present and far from the haunting, hurtful memories of Rita. "Over here, son."

The boy ran up and threw his arms around Paul's waist. "Breakfast was delicious, Pa. Every time I eat one of your biscuits, I wonder how you learned to cook so good."

Paul let the grammar error slide. "It's your ma's recipe." Even that reminded him of how much he missed her, for she'd insisted he learn the basics of cooking and cleaning and shopping. "You must always be prepared," she'd said, "for what lies ahead." It was as though she'd known, somehow, that he'd need those skills someday. Silently, he thanked her, then wished her from his mind. He waited for the pain to subside, though he didn't really expect it to. Five years of experience had taught him that no amount of wishing or hoping or praying could blot her from his memory.

The children came home from school chattering and giggling, sounding happier than they had in a very long time. During supper, all they could talk about was school. And Miss Carter.

"She has green eyes, Pa," Timmy said. "I never saw eyes that color before."

Paul nodded, remembering that he'd had a similar thought in front of the schoolhouse after knocking her down. Eyes as green and bright and shimmering as emeralds....

"And when the sun shines on her hair, it looks like a copper kettle, but in the schoolhouse, it's brown." Timmy pursed his lips, trying to find a color that would explain his teacher's hair. "It reminds me of—"

"Chestnuts," Paul said, absently stirring a spoonful of sugar into his coffee.

Timmy nodded, then propped his elbow on the table, resting his chin on a chubby fist. "I wish I was old like you, Pa."

Paul met his youngest son's eyes and laughed. "And why is that, Tim?"

"'Cause then I could ask her to marry me." The boy sighed. "She's the most beautiful lady I've ever seen."

Up to that point, Tyler hadn't said a word about Miss Carter. "Ma was prettier," he said now. "Her hair was the color of wheat fields, and her eyes were bluer than the sky."

Paul's heart pounded as he thought, *And her smile as sweet as the angels' in heaven....*

Suddenly, Timmy's eyes filled with tears. "Why can't I remember Ma?"

Paul placed his hand over the boy's. "You're trying too hard, Tim." He looked to heaven for the strength to say what his son needed to hear. Pressing his big hand over the boy's heart, he said, "Your ma is there, deep inside you."

"But shouldn't I be able to remember her all the time?"

At that moment, Paul envied his son a little bit, for he'd have given the best tooth in his head to get through just one day without memories of Rita assaulting his mind. "Now, what's this?" Paul asked, wiping a tear from the child's cheek. "My big boy, crying?"

"I'm not a big boy!" Timmy shouted, burying his face in the crook of his arm. "I'm only six, and I want my ma!"

Paul stood up and lifted Timmy's chin, then squatted beside the table to make himself child-sized. "Tim," he said in a soothing voice, "your ma is happy with God in heaven, and she wants us to be happy, too, right here, together."

The boy leaned against his father's massive chest. "What's God want our ma for, anyway?" he demanded. "He's got all those angels to keep Him company. He doesn't need her, but we do!"

Tyler put his arm around his brother's shoulders. "We all miss her," he said, sounding much older than his years, "but it's like Pa said: she's happy in heaven. She doesn't want to come back, so we have to learn to live without her."

Paul met his oldest son's gaze, then looked at Tricia's sad face. Clearly, she agreed with her older brother.

"Is that what you've thought all this time?" he asked them. "You've thought your ma *wanted* to leave us?"

The children said nothing but stared blankly at their half-emptied plates.

Paul stood up again and walked to the fireplace. *Lord*, he prayed silently, *help me comfort them....* When he faced them again, he spoke softly: "Your ma never would have left you by choice. She loved the three of you more than life itself." *Right up until that soldier's bullet ripped through her,* he ranted mentally.

"You told her to stay inside, where it was safe. If she hadn't gone out there to get the quilt from the clothesline...." His daughter stamped one foot. "She should have loved us *more* than that dumb old thing, even if her mother *did* make it."

Tricia was right, and he'd had the same thought a thousand times since that awful day. It was good, he realized, that the children's true feelings were finally coming out. He held out his arms, and they filled them. Blinking back hot tears, he whispered hoarsely, "I'm sure if she'd known what was out there, she wouldn't have gone outside," he said. "She never would have willingly left you, especially not for a dumb old quilt."

He kissed Tricia's cheek, then said, "Tyler's right. We all miss her." Clearing his throat, he closed his eyes and prayed for the strength to say what had to be said, once and for all: "It's time to get on with our lives. She would have wanted it that way." He paused, hugged the three of them tightly, and added, "Why don't we start by getting these dishes cleaned up?"

Tricia moved first, followed by Tyler, and, finally, Timmy.

Paul slumped into the rocker and picked up his Bible. "You shouldn't have talked about Ma," he heard Tricia whisper to her brothers. "It makes Pa sad. Every time one of you brings up her name, he looks like he's going to cry." She concluded by saying, "We all miss her, but he misses her even more."

It seemed all he did lately was pretend. He pretended to be strong for the children. Pretended he didn't miss Rita so much that it ached. Now, he pretended he hadn't heard Tricia's remarks.

Her words, like a cold slap in the face, made him face the hard truth. He didn't want to believe he'd been so lost in his own misery and grief that he hadn't seen how deeply Rita's death had affected the children. But Tricia's words were proof that he'd been wallowing so long in a deep sea of self-pity that he'd seen only his own pain.

Rita had told him once that he could do anything he set his mind to, and with her encouragement and love, he'd believed it. Without her, however, he was unsure, afraid of the future. So, he'd returned to Freeland, where they'd started their happy life together, hoping to reclaim some of that certainty and joy. What he hadn't realized until Tricia's little speech was that he'd been looking straight at happiness all along—in the loving eyes of his children.

Trust the Lord, he told himself, *and He'll pull you through, just as He's done since you were a boy.* He turned to 1 Corinthians 10:13 and silently read, "*God is faithful, who will not suffer you to be tempted above that ye are able; but will with the temptation also make a way to escape, that ye may be able to bear it.*"

Leaning back in the rocking chair, Paul smiled. And for perhaps the first time since Rita's death, he wasn't the least bit tempted to feel sorry for himself.

Chapter Two

She hadn't expected to like Freeland.

Richmond was home. Had always been home, even after she'd buried her family, even after she'd walked away from the smoldering remains of what had been Carter Hall.

The very idea of leaving Virginia had terrified her, but Valerie had grown weary of struggling to survive on meager wages, having been born into luxury and having lived most of her life surrounded by elegance. Teaching in Freeland's one-room schoolhouse would certainly prove an easier life than waiting tables in the swank Southern Belle Hotel, so, at her cousin Sally's advice and insistence, she'd headed north to Maryland.

Freeland was the town that, decades ago, had become home to Valerie's favorite uncle. He'd spent most of his life traveling throughout the eastern countryside, peddling his adaptation of the grist mill. He had been on his way home from demonstrating the handy contraption at a county fair when his carriage had overturned, pinning him underneath.

Valerie's Aunt Betsy had become a rich widow on that terrible, stormy night. Alone and afraid, she'd returned to Richmond. Just as Richmond was the place of Betsy's roots, Freeland was the only home Sally had ever known. Just weeks before her father's tragic death, Sally had taken a husband and set up house on the outskirts of town.

It was from Valerie's home in Virginia that Aunt Betsy had written to inform Aunt Sally of the many tragedies that had befallen the Carter family: the deaths of Valerie's father, brothers, and mother; the destruction of their import-export business; the demise of the grand old plantation. Sally must have gotten busy the moment she'd torn open that letter, because before Valerie had received the official invitation to come and teach in Freeland's little school, Sally had already arranged lodging, welcome-to-town visits from neighbors and fellow church members, and a one-way ticket on the Baltimore and Ohio Railroad.

That letter had changed Valerie's entire life, and now she gently tucked it back into her bureau drawer, giggling to herself as she thought of how all of Sally's work would have been for naught if she'd refused to move to Freeland.

Valerie had been born and raised in her father's mansion. The modest cottage, situated just behind the schoolhouse in the center of town, had no pantry, no summer kitchen, no keeping room, no majestic staircase. But Valerie loved it just the same because it was *hers*. She especially loved the wide, covered porch that ran the width of the tiny house, and the first thing she'd done after unpacking her bags that late-August day was to move the comfortable bentwood rockers flanking the flagstone fireplace onto the porch. In Richmond, it had been a Carter family tradition to sit on the veranda after dinner, sipping mint tea as each family member shared in turn the events of his or her day.

And Valerie was continuing the ritual. Each night, after a light supper, she tidied her small kitchen before relaxing beneath the slatted, white-enameled ceiling and listening to the soft sounds of twilight.

Nearly a month had passed since her arrival. She missed Richmond. She missed family gatherings after church on Sundays. She missed Mama and Papa and her brothers, Lee Junior and Delbert. She missed standing on the docks and inspecting huge crates that bore treasures from the Orient and Africa and Europe. She missed old Garth, whose stories had entertained her from the cradle, and Delilah, who'd been her cook, maid, and dearest friend for as long as she could remember. The old Negro couple had taught Valerie practical things—how to tie a slipknot, how to bake bread—and spiritual things, too—how to say the Lord's Prayer, how to forgive a transgressor.

Her father had owned several thousand acres of land, known throughout the South as Carter's Hall Tobacco Plantation, and it was from his oak-paneled study that he'd run his import-export business. Contrary to Southern tradition, her father had stoutheartedly refused to own slaves. The blacks who'd worked for him had been hired hands, with the same rights and privileges as the whites who'd worked alongside them. They'd been paid fair wages and given clean little homes in which to live, as well as a few acres of good, productive land where they'd raised laying hens, milk cows, and vegetables.

When the War Between the States had broken out, her father had refused to wear a uniform of either color, saying that since the good Lord had seen fit to free him from the bonds of sin, he'd not enslave man, woman, or child of any skin color. The philosophy might have been tolerated up North, but in Richmond, the new Confederate capital, his words were blasphemy.

Her brothers had fought for the South, much to her father's dismay. The only positive thing to come from the day he was shot was her knowledge that he'd never learn they'd both died defending slavery.

On many occasions, Valerie's mother had told her that she'd inherited her father's inner strength—although Valerie had the impression that her mother hadn't intended it as a compliment. That strength had come in handy when she'd packed her few remaining possessions and boarded the Baltimore-bound train. Riding in the jolting, rattling passenger car, she'd silently thanked her father for having instilled in her the ability to accept life—and everything in it—at face value. "Keeps you from going off the deep end, wishing for things that can never be," he'd advised her.

Valerie realized that from the moment she'd stepped off the train, Freeland had lived up to its name; Negro and white, and Spanish and Oriental, lived, worshipped, shopped, and went to school side by side, in peace and harmony. Her father would have loved it here.

Since she would be teaching the children, she'd already met nearly everyone in town; it had taken very little time to feel welcome. In a matter of days, she'd come to view her students like she would her own children. She saw to it that each of them ate a healthy lunch, made sure they were all properly dressed for the weather, and supplied them with slates, chalk, and books. If their parents couldn't afford the tools, Valerie paid for them herself.

In particular, though, Valerie had developed a special fondness for the Collins children. They were intelligent, open-minded youngsters, ready to learn and eager to please. It had become a real struggle not to show favoritism to the three motherless children.

She'd seen their father on only one occasion since the day she'd enrolled his children. He'd come to town one afternoon for supplies and had stopped at the schoolhouse on his way home to have lunch with his children. She remembered the way their faces had lit up at the sight of his large, muscular body filling the doorway. Just as memorable was the adoring expression in his eyes as he'd looked at each one of them.

This was a special man, and Valerie knew it. He worked hard and long in his fields every day, as evidenced by his sun-kissed face and calloused hands.

Yet he obviously made time for his children, for Timmy, Tricia, and Tyler seemed to be the happiest, best-behaved, best-adjusted children in the school, despite their tragic loss.

She couldn't deny that Paul was a handsome man, with his huge, soulful, brown eyes and the wild mass of dark curls on his head. If she could change anything about him, Valerie would see to it that he smiled more often, for he was especially good-looking when he did. Perhaps, when she got to know him better, she could find a pleasant, noncommittal kind of way to tell him how his smile affected those around him...but only to encourage him to smile more often, of course.

Enough daydreaming! she scolded herself. *The man has neither the time nor the inclination to notice you, Valerie Ann Carter. With that big farm to run and three kids to raise, it's a wonder he has time left over to breathe!*

The admission didn't stop her from daydreaming, however, and as she listened to the katydids' song and the locusts' twang, she rocked in quiet comfort. Freeland wasn't Virginia or Richmond or even Carter Hall, but it surely had started to feel like *home*.

Rev. Gemmill prayed fervently for the good weather to hold until the annual picnic at St. John's the following Sunday had ended. Early in the week, Valerie spoke to Mrs. Gemmill and asked what she could do to help out.

"Can you cook?" the pastor's wife asked.

"Why, yes. I can."

"Good! We need pies. Lots of 'em. Bake as many as you have time and fixings for. And since you're unmarried, make a box lunch, too. We auction them off, you know, and this year, the money raised will go toward a new organ for the church," Mrs. Gemmill said.

On Monday night, Valerie baked four pies, and on Tuesday, four more. By Friday, fourteen pies lined her table, buffet, and serving cart. Bright and early on Saturday, she fried up an entire chicken, baked fluffy biscuits and a chocolate cake, and whipped up a batch of cider for the boxed lunch. The only container large enough to hold it all was her sewing basket, and she carefully tucked the food items onto the nest she'd made from a red gingham tablecloth. Then, as an afterthought, she tied the whole thing up with a wide, pink satin ribbon.

Now...what to wear to the picnic on Sunday?

Valerie had salvaged only four dresses from the terrible fire that had destroyed Carter Hall. She'd worn the blue one with the white piping along its hem and sleeves nearly every day since school had started. Certainly, the children were as bored looking at it as she was with wearing it....

On the morning of the picnic, she smoothed her pink skirt, adjusted the bow of the matching bonnet, and pretended to listen to Rev. Gemmill's sermon. As the town's schoolmarm, she was more or less expected to be present at Sunday services, so, of course, she'd go through the motions.

Her body would, that is—but her mind and soul would not. If she hadn't been good enough to secure God's ear as she'd begged Him to spare her father's life, to save his business; if she hadn't been good enough to deserve an answer to her pleas for Him to save her mother and her brothers, she certainly wasn't good enough now. So, if a word or a phrase from Scripture managed to weaken her decision not to listen to Him, Valerie focused on other things, like planning a lesson for her students or redesigning a dress. Today, she mentally rearranged the ruffles on her skirt into a bustle in the back....

Valerie's favorite dress was an emerald gown of cotton twill. It had a six-inch flounce at its hem and black velvet swirls on the lapels of the short, matching jacket. The white bodice boasted twin ruffles, as did the long, cuffed sleeves. Tiny pearl buttons formed a delicate flower on the high collar, and a wide, black satin belt, tied in a big bow in the back, draped down the skirt and nearly reached the hem. But it was far too heavy for a picnic.

After church, she'd change into the white eyelet. Simple in material and design, it could be embellished with a colorful apron without looking gaudy. And if she wore it with her navy pinafore, she could carry her threadbare blue purse without looking like a ragamuffin.

It wasn't like Valerie to spend a lot of time in front of the mirror, but she did so this afternoon. This would be her first appearance at an official Freeland event, and she wanted to make a good impression so that Sally and her husband wouldn't be embarrassed for having recommended her for the job as the town's teacher.

Ordinarily, Valerie tucked her long hair into a twist at the nape of her neck. Today, however, she let it fall softly over her shoulders, held back above each ear by her mother's ebony combs. She didn't like to think of herself as a vain woman, but she had a reputation to uphold as the teacher of the community children, so the dab of rose cologne she dotted on her wrists had nothing whatever to do with the possibility that she might have a chance to visit with Paul Collins.

She draped the fraying velvet straps of the drawstring purse over her arm and headed for the kitchen to grab her pies and walk over to the churchyard. At the door, Valerie stopped dead in her tracks. "How ever will you get all these pies to the church?" she wondered aloud.

"It'd be my pleasure to help you," said a deep, resonant voice.

"Mr. Collins!" she said, a trembling hand at her throat.

"Sorry if I startled you." Removing his black cap, he added, "You look mighty pretty today, Miss Carter."

She felt herself blush at his compliment. "I—I was just trying to figure out how I'd get all these pies over to the—"

"So I heard," he interrupted, grinning. "The young'uns suggested we stop by and see if you needed a hand." With a jerk of his thumb, he indicated the wagon behind him, where his children were giggling and wriggling with anticipation of the day ahead.

The schoolhouse was situated down the street from the center of Freeland, where the church, post office, and train station sat on one side of the railroad tracks, the livery stable, feed store, and hotel on the other. It would have been a lovely, quick walk, carrying a pie in each hand. But fourteen pies would require at least seven trips! "I'm much obliged," she said.

Paul opened the creaking screen door and stepped into the clean, sparsely furnished room. "Tyler," he called, "you and Tricia come on in here and help us load these goodies onto the wagon."

The children were beside him in a whipstitch, and Valerie handed them each a gingham cloth-covered pie. "I'm so glad you were thinking of me this morning. I don't know what I'd have done without you!"

Tyler and Tricia exchanged a puzzled glance, then looked at their father, whose flushed cheeks and downcast eyes told Valerie it had been his idea, not the children's, to see if she needed help getting to town. Her heart fluttered in response.

Paul cleared his throat and, balancing a pie on each big hand, held the door open with his elbow. "After you," he said, smiling at her.

Even with three of them, it took two trips to move the desserts from her kitchen to his wagon. "Sakes alive," Timmy said as Paul climbed into the front seat, "how many pies did you bake, Miss Carter?"

Laughing, she said, "Too many!"

"No such thing as too many pies," Paul corrected her, extending a hand to help her up.

She took his hand and, as on the day they'd met, noticed its gentle strength. She took her place beside him, tightly gripping the handles of the basket that held the boxed lunch. A small hope thrummed inside her. *If I were still a praying woman,* she thought, *I'd pray Paul would bid highest on my lunch.* Because, as everybody knew, the lady who had prepared the lunch was obliged to share it with the gentleman who bought it....

Heads turned and whispers floated as they rode into town. "Seems we've set tongues to wagging," Paul observed, a wry grin lifting one corner of his mouth.

It was Valerie's turn to blush. She gripped the basket handles tighter and lifted her chin. "Well! If they've nothing better to discuss than with whom I hitch a ride into town, maybe the reverend can find some chore to occupy their time!"

Valerie thoroughly enjoyed the sound of Paul's laughter, and she decided, right then and there, to make it happen again...and again...by day's end.

Paul parked between two other wagons beside the church, jumped down, and tied his horse to the hitching post. Then, walking around to Valerie's side of the wagon, he reached up, wrapped his big hands around her waist, and put her gently onto the ground. "Now then," he said, "let's see about putting those pies someplace where *we'll* be sure to find them."

Paul, Valerie, and the children headed for the rows of makeshift tables in the churchyard, which the ladies of the parish had covered with tablecloths of every color and pattern. Just beyond stood the food tent, and the foursome deposited Valerie's pies inside. It was during their final trip to the wagon that Paul stopped beside a table that had been set up beneath a large oak. "Is this one to your liking?" he asked Valerie.

When she'd spotted it on their first pass, Valerie had thought it would make for the perfect place to enjoy the meal, and she might have suggested it to him...if it wouldn't have seemed terribly forward and presumptuous. For all she knew, he'd already planned to share the day with someone, but knowing *she* was that someone made her heart beat doubly fast. "This is just fine," she said. "There's a lovely breeze, and plenty of shade," she rambled, "and we're just near enough to the food and the band."

The musicians were adjusting their fiddle strings and tuning their guitars just beyond the clearing. Paul glanced in their direction and grinned. "So we are," he said. "So we are."

All morning, as she visited with her students and their families, Valerie found herself looking for Paul. It never took more than a few moments to spot him, for he stood head and shoulders above the rest of the crowd. Once, as she was scanning the faces in search of his, she caught him staring at her, and she had to remind herself what she'd read about deep breathing being the latest cure for shortness of breath. Valerie inhaled a huge gulp of air, held her breath, then exhaled slowly. Yes, her heart had indeed ceased its nonsensical fluttering, but whether it was because she'd practiced the latest in medical advice or because Paul had focused his attention elsewhere, Valerie didn't know.

Rev. Gemmill put an end to her wondering when he began marching through the crowd, banging a soup ladle on the bottom of a pot. "Attention, everyone! May I have your attention, please?" The round-faced preacher hopped onto the platform at the front of the food tent and waved his arms high in the air. "It's time for the most highly anticipated event at our annual picnics," he announced, a big grin on his pink-cheeked face. "The boxed lunch auction!"

Whistles, applause, and hoots of pleasure resounded through the churchyard.

"Now, now," he said good-naturedly, "let's keep it down, or we'll never get this over with. Mrs. Gemmill," he said, gesturing for his wife to join him, "won't you hand me the first lunch?"

The stout little woman marched up the steps, stood beside her husband, and lifted the first lunch from the table beside her: a tidy white container tied up with a big red bow. "Lucy Johnson made this one," she said, holding it up for the crowd's inspection.

"Now, let's not forget that the bidding is open to unmarried gentlemen only," the pastor chided, a teasing glint in his eye. "I'll open the bidding at five cents."

"Ten cents," called Charlie Smith, his forefinger in the air.

"Fifteen!" countered Bill Brown, waving his straw hat.

The lunch sold for fifty cents, and a blushing Lucy Johnson left the tent on the arm of a strutting Seth Powell.

When eight lunches had been sold, Valerie realized that she didn't know how many unmarried folks lived in Freeland. Suddenly, she wished she'd paid more attention to Paul and less to the activities, for she had no idea how many boxes he'd bid on.

Suddenly, Valerie saw her own basket lifted up by Mrs. Gemmill. "Goodness, this thing weighs a ton!" she said, laughing. "What's in here, girl, salted rocks?" When the laughter died down, she added, "This lunch was prepared by our very own lovely schoolteacher, Miss Valerie Carter."

"Well," the pastor said, "since it outweighs all the others by half, I'll start the bidding at ten cents."

"Thirty!" hollered Bertram Johansen.

Tom Lowe shouted, "Thirty-five!"

"Three dollars," said a deep voice from the back of the crowd.

Muffled whispers and gasps floated forward as the shock of the high bid sank in.

"Did I hear *three dollars*?" the reverend asked.

Heads turned as the parishioners searched for the man who'd offered to pay such a steep price for a simple boxed lunch.

"You heard right," said the voice.

"Why, Paul Collins," said Mrs. Gemmill, "I was wondering why you hadn't bid on any of the others. Have a hankerin' for salted rocks, do you?"

Laughing heartily, Rev. Gemmill held the basket high. "Sold," he said, "to the man with the big, fat wallet!"

When Paul met her gaze, Valerie knew in an instant that while she'd been watching the auction, he'd been watching *her*. She smiled and willed her heart to stop racing as he made his way through the crowd.

"Guess they'll want us up there," he said, his voice so quiet and shy it reminded her of Tyler's. Without warning, he grabbed her hand and led her to the platform. Just before they reached it, he leaned close to her ear and whispered, "Fried chicken is my all-time favorite."

She read the teasing glint in his dark eyes and smiled. "How'd you know what was in my basket?"

"I can smell my favorite meal a mile off." Then, he got into the short line of fellows who'd bought lunches, grinning at the good-natured taunts of his fellow Freelanders.

"You're mighty generous," Valerie said when at last they sat down at their table. "Why, I'll be the talk of the town since my lunch went for more than twice what any of the others—"

"Let's just hope it tastes as good as it smells," Paul said with a teasing glint in his eyes.

Unable to continue looking into those big, brown eyes, Valerie glanced around. "Where do you suppose the children are?" she asked, spreading a fuzzy blanket of red plaid on the ground.

Paul nodded toward the trees. "Over there, eating pie."

Smiling, she knelt beside him and began taking things from the basket: chicken, buttered biscuits, sweet pickles, chocolate cake. "I hope you like the cider," she said, sitting back on her heels. "It's my mother's recipe, and she didn't use much sugar. It may seem a bit tart if you're used to—"

"If it isn't sweet enough," he said, "all I'll need to do is look at you."

She'd just placed a red-and-white checkered napkin across her lap, and in response to his unexpected compliment, her hands froze in the middle of smoothing it. "So tell me, Mr. Collins, how you ended up in York, Pennsylvania."

"Went up there ten years ago," he said, biting into a drumstick, "when my wife's father needed help running his farm. It was supposed to be a temporary move, but he never really recovered." He tore off a piece of a biscuit and popped it into his mouth. "I hear you're from Richmond?"

She nodded. "My great-uncle helped found Freeland."

"Is that so?" Paul studied her face for a moment. "My mother was born here."

"He talked about Freeland every time he visited. Perhaps I'll recognize her name...."

"Leila," he said, almost reverently. "Leila Morris."

"Was she any relation to Isaac Morris?"

He grinned at her excitement. "He was her great-grandfather. Why?"

"Isaac Morris once owned all this land." Her hand waved across the lawn. "Everything that's now Freeland, and everything that surrounds it. He sold it to John Freeland in 1790. Mr. Freeland opened the first general store. The first post office...."

Valerie continued, thrilled to have someone to share her love of history with, to know someone who seemed as interested in it as she. "Mr. Hoffman at the general store told me that his family owned the first paper mill here. Did you know the Hoffman Mill sold the government the paper on which our first currency was printed?"

"Well, I'll be." Paul continued to study her flashing, intelligent eyes; her lilting, cheery voice; the feminine way she sat there, her legs tucked beneath her on the blanket; the delicate way she nibbled at her chicken and sipped her cider. After a moment, Paul blinked, realizing he'd been staring.

"I'm sorry. I'm boring you," she laughed.

"I'm not the least bit bored," he admitted easily, helping himself to a chicken thigh from the basket. "Seems to me you're just the type to be teaching our children."

She met his eyes. "Why, thank you, Mr. Collins."

He wanted to tell her to call him Paul. Paul *darling*. Grinning, he said, "I was just stating a fact. And please, call me Paul."

It wasn't until the pastor announced the last square dance that Paul and Valerie realized their lunch had lasted two hours. Quickly, they shoved the remaining food and utensils back into the basket and folded the blanket. "Do you like hoedowns, Mr. Collins? I mean—Paul?"

The mischievous glint in her eyes made him grin. "I don't mind 'em, I suppose, but I'm afraid I'm not very good at dancin'."

She rested the basket against the trunk of the tree they'd been sitting under and held out her hand. "Well, why not let me be the judge of that?"

He'd never met a woman like her. If there was a thought in her head, it popped right out of her mouth. She had a mind of her own, that was for certain! Paul put his hand in hers and let her lead him to the dance floor. He felt like a giant beside this petite woman.

As she half ran ahead of him, he watched her purposeful yet feminine stride. Though small-boned and trim-waisted, she was far from delicate. That much was evident in the power of her grip. She moved like a deer, each tiny foot landing precisely where she wanted it to. He paid particular attention to her dainty, white-slippered feet. *Lord*, he prayed, *don't let me step on those tiny toes; I'm liable to mash 'em flat.*

He wondered exactly how old Miss Valerie Carter was. Eighteen? Twenty, perhaps? And then he wondered what a lovely young thing like her saw in a tired old man like him—a thirty-five-year-old widower with more responsibilities on his shoulders than hairs on his head. But before he could formulate an answer, folks had lined up on the planks of the makeshift dance floor. When fiddle, banjo, guitar, and jug played the opening notes to "Old Joe Clark," toes started tapping.

Valerie felt wonderful in his arms. She looked wonderful, too, in her pretty white dress, its full skirt swinging around her slender ankles as she kicked across the floor away from him, then back to him again. He took the other ladies in his arms when the caller said he should, but he paid them no mind. He could think only of when it would be Valerie's turn to dance with him again.

"Swing your partners," the caller sang, "do-si-do."

And they swung and do-si-doed until the music stopped.

"You said you weren't very good," she said, fanning her face with one hand, "but you're a marvelous dancer." She stuck out her foot. "Not one scuff!"

He was laughing. *Laughing*, of all things! That was something he hadn't done since he didn't know when. Paul bowed low. "Thank you, m'lady."

Then, like Cinderella's ball, it was over. Darkness had begun to fall, and with it, the picnic noised quieted. Good-byes and See-you-laters filtered across the church lawn as the parishioners hopped into their wagons and onto their horses and headed home.

"Can we give you a lift?" Paul asked Valerie.

"It's just a short way...."

"But we're going right past your house." He wanted them to spend a few more minutes together, and, judging by the expectant look on her face, so did she.

"Well, I suppose these aren't the most sensible walking shoes."

Relief surged through him as he helped her onto the wagon seat.

"Nice day, wasn't it?" Tyler asked as they rolled slowly up the road.

Paul looked at Valerie and smiled. "Very nice day, son. *Very* nice."

Chapter Three

It was obvious that Paul had no intention of hurrying to Valerie's place. The children, who'd been babbling excitedly when they'd boarded the wagon, now leaned quietly against the rough-hewn sideboards. "All that fun and excitement seems to have tuckered them out," Valerie said, peeking over her shoulder. "Timmy will probably be asleep before you get him into—"

"I hate to see the day end," Paul interrupted her.

She glanced at his profile, silhouetted by the setting September sun. It was a face of angles and planes that served to accent his strength of character. The steady *clip-clop* of the horse's hooves kept time with the crickets' chirps in the field alongside the dusty road, lulling her into a calm, happy mood.

Then his dark eyes met hers. "I can't remember when I've enjoyed a lady's company more."

She held his gaze for a moment, then stared at the now-empty basket on her lap. She wanted to say, "I've *never* enjoyed a man's company more." Instead, she said, "I enjoyed the picnic, too."

His soft chuckle blended with the hoofbeats and insect sounds and owl hoots, reminding her how often he'd laughed as they'd shared her boxed lunch. He'd never met a woman who could mimic cows and birds...and even Rev. Gemmill, and he'd told her so as they were eating. He'd never met one who deliberately made silly faces, either. "All the women I've known," he'd said, "are far too busy trying to impress folks with their proper manners to show the world who they really are. It's as though they don't realize the true definition of etiquette is never making another human being feel uncomfortable." He'd smiled. "I can't count how many times today I saw or heard you put folks at ease." Remembering his words, Valerie was glad for the semidarkness that hid her blush.

She was glad, too, for the comfortable conversation they shared. When he told her how his young wife had been killed, it took every ounce of self-control to keep from giving his hand a sympathetic squeeze. In fact, Valerie came so close to resting her fingertips on his forearm that she could feel the heat of his tanned skin against her palm. But on the chance that he might read the gesture as a show of pity, she held more tightly to the basket handles instead.

Paul, on the other hand, didn't hesitate to grab her hand when she told him that the war had taken her loved ones, the family business, and Carter Hall. "The Lord has surely blessed you with a sturdy constitution," he said, smiling compassionately, "for you've weathered life's storms well."

She wanted to snatch back her hand and say that the Lord had had nothing to do with the person she'd become. Her strength—if, indeed, she possessed any—had been inherited from her father, not granted by God! She'd give Him credit for one thing, and one thing only: allowing everything of value to be stolen from her.

But she didn't snap at Paul, and she didn't take back her hand. The poetry of his words and the warm light from his eyes touched her like few things had before. If she were still a believer, Valerie might have prayed right then and there that God would open this man's heart to her, for she sensed that he had much in common with her father. But thanks to all the death and destruction she'd witnessed, she didn't pray—*wouldn't* pray—because life had taught her the pain that resulted from believing in childish, blind-follower fairy tales.

Logic and reason were what she believed in now. "It is what it is," her father had loved to say, and common sense told her that Paul Collins was kind and compassionate, a loving father, a gentleman. Hard work, drive, and determination were responsible for the man he'd become, not *God*.

She heard him *tsk-tsk* to stop the horse before parking the wagon alongside the white picket gate that opened to her front walk.

"Well, Miss Carter, you're home, I'm sad to say."

Thankfully, night was closing in, for it hid yet another blush. "Thank you so much for the ride. For the lovely time today."

He looked over his shoulder. "You were right," he said, the nod of his head inviting her to peek into the wagon bed. "They're plumb tuckered out."

Valerie smiled at the angelic faces of his sleeping children.

Paul leaned closer and sniffed the air. "Roses?"

Just as he inhaled her sweet scent now, Valerie had inhaled his scents of fresh hay and bath soap all day long. She wanted to close her eyes and take a last long drink of them so that later, when she was alone, she could exhale slowly and remember his crisp, manly musk. Faint shards of moonlight slanted across his chiseled features. She'd never seen longer, thicker eyelashes in her life. And the brown curls that poked out from beneath his cap glimmered with silvery highlights. Valerie warned herself to tread carefully. *How would it look if I let myself fall in love with the father of my—*

"I've been smelling roses all day," he said, "and it dawned on me just now that the wonderful aroma was coming from you!"

—students? she continued. *Especially when—*

"You looked very pretty today," he added. "If the parishioners held a contest, I'm sure you'd have won the prize for prettiest lady at the picnic."

For a fleeting moment, Valerie wished that she wasn't Freeland's only teacher, that he still hadn't gotten over the loss of his wife, and that she hadn't been hardened by the ruins of war....

She licked her lips, acknowledging that there were many other logical reasons why she shouldn't feel this way about him, especially considering she'd known him for such a short time. Gathering the basket and her skirts, she whispered, "I—I'd better go inside so you can get those poor, exhausted children into bed." She was nearly standing, ready to jump down from the buckboard, when he wrapped his big hand around her slender wrist.

"There's a church social next Saturday. Will you do me the honor of accompanying me, Miss Carter?"

She'd seen that look before on the faces of the boys in her class—when they missed an assignment, arrived late at school, or asked permission to leave early. It was the wide-eyed, innocent expression that pleaded for her approval, for her affirmative response.

This was proof, she thought, staring into his velvety brown eyes, of the inappropriateness of forming an attachment to him. She searched her mind for a polite yet firm way to say no. Not a single idea materialized, though, and she slumped back onto the wagon seat, hoping the action would pump blood into her brain and stimulate her idle imagination. "I'd like that," she said, surprising herself. "I'd like it very much, Mr. Collins."

"Good," he said, grinning as he gave her wrist a little squeeze. Then, he hopped down from the wagon and hurried around to her side and, after placing her basket beside a huge wooden wheel, held out his arms. At the church, when he'd gripped her waist to help her down, he'd released her the moment her feet had touched the ground. This time, he held on to her as his gaze fused to hers. "Now then, tell me what it'll take to get you to call me Paul...."

She hadn't realized until that moment just how cold and lonely her life had become, how alone she'd been. Oh, how good it felt, how *comforting*, to stand in the warm circle of his arms! "I'll call you Paul," she began, "if you'll call me Valerie." She hesitated. "But...need I remind you how many tongues we set to wagging today?"

"Most all of them, I reckon."

"Then, you'll agree, I'm sure, that for your children's sakes, as well as our own, we should reserve the familiar addresses for...." Valerie didn't want to presume too much. Or too soon. "...Only for those very rare occasions when we might find ourselves alone."

One eyebrow rose high on his forehead as he considered her words, then nodded, a lazy smile softening his features. "Ah, dear Valerie, I have a feeling it's going to be a very long week," he said as his face moved slowly, slowly closer.

Logic, reason, and the many arguments she'd outlined for keeping a careful distance from him vanished from her mind as she steadied herself for their first kiss. But when his lips finally made contact, it was with her cheek. She hid her disappointment behind a fake yawn.

"A mighty long week," he repeated, chuckling as he drew her into a light embrace.

Once the kids were tucked into bed, Paul sat in the rocker, staring blankly into the flickering fire, his Bible open on his lap. The bright, coppery flames reminded him of the way the sunlight glowed in Valerie's hair.

"What got into me today?" he prayed aloud. "I was acting like some fool youngster head over heels in love for the first time in his life."

And why not? he asked himself. He wasn't a grizzled old man. Yet. And Rita had been gone for nearly five years. The time had come to get back to the business of living life again—for the children's sakes, as well as his own.

He remembered the night not so long ago when he'd promised they'd do just that. They'd needed to hear the words every bit as much as he'd needed to say them, for every moment since had been brighter. Laughter filled the house once more, and no sad crying woke him in the dark of night. They'd taken him at his word; it *was* time to put the past behind them—the sad parts of it, anyway.

So, today, with Valerie, he'd tried to practice what he'd preached. He owed them that much. Owed it to himself, too.

Her laughter echoed in his mind. Her smile, serene and lovely, shone at him each time he closed his eyes. And those eyes, glowing with life and intelligence, glittered more brightly than any gem he'd ever seen. She wasn't afraid to ask questions, and she didn't fear answers, either. He'd watched her from afar, and up close, too, marveling that no matter whom she talked with, whether man or woman, infant or grandparent, she roused the same interested response.

He'd read about the Northern Lights that lit up the heavens like a miraculous glow; the same beauty was enjoyed by all viewers, whether in Canada, Iceland, or the Arctic. Valerie's personality was like that!

Her joy was contagious, inspiring everyone to seek her out. She didn't seem to mind in the least, even though, all through the day, children and adults alike demanded her attention, interrupted her conversations, and disturbed those rare moments of solitude she so obviously enjoyed.

Perhaps she was an angel, sent to the earth to dispense happiness and high-spiritedness, to dispel gloom and doom wherever she went. Her joy was all the more amazing for emanating from a woman who'd suffered many tragedies.

He'd noticed a most curious thing, though. When he'd said grace before their picnic meal, the "angel" hadn't folded her hands, bowed her head, or closed her eyes. When he'd finished the prayer, she hadn't said amen. It seemed strange, because he'd seen her in church every Sunday since moving to Freeland. Surely, she was a follower....

Of course, she's a follower! he rebuked himself. No one but a follower of Christ could be moved to tears by the sight of an eagle, as she had during their lunch, or stunned into awed silence by a sleeping infant, as she'd been when they'd first arrived at the churchyard. No one could have brought pure joy to so many unless the light of God was shining brightly within her.

She'd spent more than half of her first week's salary on supplies for the school. He'd overheard her say in the general store, "Education should teach equality first and foremost. How can we accomplish that if one child has a slate, and another has none, simply because one family can afford it and another can't?"

In just over a month, Miss Valerie Carter had earned a reputation for having a soft touch. No child's tears went unheeded. No student's needs went unmet. If a mother needed flour in order to prepare a healthy lunch for her child, it mysteriously appeared on her porch. If a father had no money to buy shoes for his son, making the long walk to school impossible, a pair of boots in exactly the right size appeared outside his door.

"Where would *I* get the money to do the work of old St. Nick?" Valerie would scoff when asked if she'd played a part in the little miracles.

But Paul had been in the store when she'd purchased a pair of tiny black boots. "What're these for?" Greta had wanted to know as Valerie counted out the coins that made them her boots—at least temporarily. "You got some tiny tootsies there, Miss Carter, but they ain't squeezin' into these here shoes!"

She'd blushed furiously, fumbling with her purse strings, and said, "I have a nephew in Richmond, you see, and his birthday is coming up...."

Paul had known immediately that she was fibbing, and he'd silently judged her, for all untruths, he believed, were unholy. But the very next day, when Emmet Saunders had stopped by to deliver the load of wood Paul had ordered, he'd said, "Strangest thing happened 'bout three days ago, when my boy come home whinin' 'cause his boots was too small. Still, off to the schoolhouse he went next mornin', where Miss Carter wrapped his blisters in bandages and told him not to worry, 'cause he'd get new shoes right soon. And don't y'know, the very next day, there's a pair o' shiny boots just his size out on the porch, an' the boy's callin' me a hero. Didn't have the heart to admit it, Paul, but I never bought 'em!"

The story had forced Paul to reevaluate his rigid opinion about tall tales. Seeing how the "miracle" had affected Emmet and his family had taught Paul that the good Valerie had done outweighed the slight fib she'd told. And she'd done the deed without embarrassing Emmet and his family.

Yes, God lived in her, all right. And he'd see to it she started admitting it, by golly!

Chapter Four

It was harvest time, and Valerie hadn't seen any Freeland farmers—or many of their children—in weeks. The town earned its reputation for producing the best corn and wheat in the state, but doing so required long, hard days in the fields. Though she'd lived through harvests at Carter Hall, she'd never missed school because of them. But these after-war times were hard, and some of her students, the older boys in particular, were needed at home.

She learned the meaning of the phrase "burning the midnight oil," for it took her hours to produce an abbreviated version of the day's schoolwork for the farm boys, who'd be too exhausted after a hard day's work to complete a full lesson. But no sacrifice was too great for the sake of her students.

Most lessons were delivered to absent students by brothers, sisters, or neighbors. Children without siblings, or those who lived too far away to get their work from friends, found themselves face-to-face with their pretty young teacher no less than once a week. And, since acres and miles separated the farms, Valerie was often forced to make her deliveries at suppertime. As often as not, the lady of the house would insist that Valerie join the family for a tasty, hot meal. Halfway through the harvest season, she'd helped wash so many supper plates and cups that her hands were growing dry and red.

If Valerie did more than was expected for her pupils, she went far past the call of duties for their families.

She'd shown Otto and Helga Kratt's mother how to add and subtract, explained the Boston Tea Party to Gregg Pratt's mom, loaned Katrina Albert's mother her collection of Shakespeare's works, and even taught Frank Calvert's mother to read and write. Though Valerie swore them all to secrecy, the whole town was talking about how God had blessed them the day Valerie Carter had decided to make Freeland, Maryland, her home.

Paul Collins, in particular, knew how lucky they were to have Valerie in their lives, for she gave his motherless children special, individual attention—and she did it so matter-of-factly that they never felt any different from youngsters with two parents.

When the harvest ended, Paul began delivering lunch to his children again, and, if the weather allowed, the Collins family would munch their meal together under the big maple in the school yard. Though he never missed a word from his children's mouths, his seat facing the window-wall of the schoolhouse allowed him to watch as Valerie erased the morning's lesson from the big blackboard and replaced it with another, stacked books on the shelves, and rearranged the desks in neat, straight rows.

In church, deliberately choosing a pew across the aisle and a few rows back enabled him to see Valerie during Sunday services. He knew that she shopped in the general store very early on Saturday mornings, so he adjusted his regular shopping day and time accordingly. More often than he cared to admit, he found himself daydreaming, and Miss Valerie Carter was always the subject of his musings. Fumbling for excuses to talk with her, Paul believed his conversations swung from the mundane to the ridiculous: weather, fences that needed repairing, a pesky, loose board on his front porch....

Never in his life had he been so unfocused. Never had he been so easily distracted. He buried his nose in his Bible every evening, praying that the Lord would show him why he thought of Valerie first thing every morning; why she came to mind so many times each day; why, oh why, he pictured her sweet smile and heard her musical voice sing in his memory the last thing every night. He thanked the Lord that no one else had noticed.

Or so he thought....

At breakfast one Saturday morning, Timmy asked, "Pa, why do you stare at Miss Carter all the time?"

He'd been sopping gravy with his biscuit and nearly dropped the bread in his lap. "I don't stare," Paul said, his voice cracking with defensive frustration.

"Not *all* the time, anyway," Tyler teased. "Only when he's awake...."

To hide his flush of embarrassment, Paul reached for the milk pitcher, though his glass was nearly full.

Tricia giggled as he topped it off. "Maybe you're in love, Pa."

Tyler groaned. "Pa...say it ain't so!"

"Papa loves Miss Carter," Timmy said in singsong, "Papa loves Miss Carter...."

"Timmy! Enough of that nonsense!" Paul thundered. "You've put off gathering those eggs long enough. Now get busy!" Facing Tyler, he narrowed his eyes. "Have you stacked that firewood yet like I told you to? And Tricia, did you mend that shirt I brought you yesterday?"

Quietly, the children shuffled off to do their chores. He heard their giggles, muffled by hands over their mouths, and as the kitchen door was shut, he couldn't suppress a smile of his own. But as hard as he tried to ignore it, Timmy's question gonged in his mind for the rest of the day. Why *did* he stare at Valerie all the time?

When she'd first come to Freeland, he'd overheard talk in town. "Spoiled little rich girl," folks had called her. Not many had expected her to be much of a teacher. Not many had expected she'd be much of anything, in fact. But talk these days was more along the lines of, "How'd we ever get along without her?"

She'd singlehandedly whipped the ramshackle little house behind the school into shape, wielding hammer and sawing wood as well as any man. She didn't complain, like other women, when sugar was in short supply, or when they were out of lace at the general store. If anyone needed her for anything, she was there, lickety-split. No wonder Freelanders respected and admired her. No wonder they loved Valerie Carter.

But did *he*?

Paul decided he'd better give the question a good deal of thought...and a whole lot of prayer.

Early one gray October morning, as DeWitt Frank swept the steps of his general store, his wife's high-pitched hollering disturbed his tranquil mood. "Have mercy," Greta shouted, holding her nose and pointing at the raggedy dog that had trotted onto the porch. "Shoo dat mutt away. He schtinks to high heaven!"

DeWitt swished his broom in the canine's direction. "Go 'vay," he ordered it. "Go, now. Scoot! Ve don't need der likes o' you schmellin' up der store!"

The dog sat on its haunches, cocked its head, and whimpered pathetically.

"Vhat're you vaitink for?" Greta demanded. "Git him gone before he scares avay our customers!"

DeWitt was about to bop the pup with his broom when Valerie rounded the corner.

"Don't!"

Paul, who'd just finished shopping in the store, hefted a fifty-pound bag of flour onto the buckboard, then folded his arms over his chest and stood back to watch the scene unfold.

"He's gotta go, Miss Carter," DeWitt explained. "Ve don't know vere he's been...."

"Und ve doessn't care," Greta interrupted him. "He can't schtay here schmellin' like dat! Schmack him, De-Vitt! Go on, giff him a goot one, right on der rump!"

Valerie, unmindful of its filthy fur, wrapped the terrified dog in a protective hug. "What's the matter, boy?" she crooned. "Is everybody picking on you?" She shot an angry glare at Greta. "There's absolutely no need to beat the poor creature."

Greta scowled. "Fine, den," the gray-haired old woman snapped. "You take responsibility for da ugly beast. Zee if I care. But if he bites you, don't come cryin' to me!" she added before stomping into the store and slamming the door behind her.

Valerie opened her mouth to defend the dog to DeWitt. "Don't look at me," Greta's husband said, his hands raised in mock surrender. "I chust vork here." With that, he, too, disappeared into the store.

"Well, looks like it's just you and me, boy," Valerie whispered to the dog. She sat down on the top step of the porch to evaluate her new friend. "Burrs and mud... and I'll bet you have a whole colony of fleas living on you, too," she said, scratching his chin.

Suddenly, she stood up and ran toward the street. Patting her thighs, Valerie called, "C'mon, boy! Wanna play follow the leader?"

Its eyes bright and ears perked up, the dog stood on all fours, then bounded down the street behind the surefooted little woman.

Grinning, Paul shook his head. As much as he would have liked to see how things turned out for the dirty mutt, he had no time for such shenanigans today. He had business at the bank, the blacksmith's, and the feed and grain store. Paul climbed onto the wagon's padded seat and whistled his horse to attention.

As he headed for his next stop, he grinned, aware that no other woman would have defended the mangy mutt. No other woman would have weathered Greta's wrath to save its sorry hide. And, he acknowledged with a chuckle, no other woman would run through the center of town with a stray dog yipping happily at her heels.

An hour later, when he walked around to the back of her house, she was soaked from head to toe. The dog, standing in a steaming tub of clear water, actually seemed to be enjoying its bath. "You look better already," he heard her say. "I might just keep you once I get you all cleaned up. What do you think of that?"

"I think he'd be a fool not to love the idea."

He'd startled her. Paul could see that much in her wide, green eyes.

"Sakes alive," she said. "You must be part cat—I didn't even hear you coming."

Laughter rumbled deep in his chest, but Paul swallowed it. "This is quite an undertaking. You sure you're up to it?"

Valerie brushed her damp bangs from her forehead, the back of her hand leaving a trail of bubbles on her pale, smooth skin. "He's a dog," she pointed out, "not a Bengal tiger. I realize menfolk don't put much stock in a woman's ability to do things for herself, but I think I can handle—"

"I never meant to imply you couldn't handle it," he interrupted her. "I just wondered if you'd given any thought to how much work he'll be."

Valerie sighed. Dipping a soup ladle into the tub of clear water, she began rinsing suds from the dog's back. "Work?" She grinned, blowing bubbles from her upper lip. "You call this work? Why, I'm having the time of my life!"

Paul laughed. If it had been anyone else covered with suds, he might have disagreed. He grabbed one of the towels Valerie had stacked on the small wooden stool beside the tub and draped it around his neck. Then, hoisting the dog from the water, he fluffed its fur. The mutt, glad to be on dry ground again, shook out as Paul squinted to protect his eyes from the water droplets flying every which way.

"Oh, dear," Valerie said, smiling as she filled the ladle with water, "you're all wet." With no warning, she added, "But not nearly wet enough." And then she doused him.

Her childlike glee was contagious. "So, you like to play rough, do you?" he asked, picking up the half-filled tub of sudsy water. "Let's see just how rough you like it!"

Squealing like a schoolgirl, she dodged left and right, holding her skirts slightly up in front of her, running in circles and hiding behind trees until he finally got his vengeance.

"You look like a drowned rat," he said, his hearty laughter bouncing all around her yard.

"I feel like one, too," Valerie admitted, blinking as water dripped from her soaked hair into her eyes. Then she sneezed. And sneezed again.

A feeling of fierce protectiveness swelled within him. Immediately, Paul wrapped her tightly in the second towel and draped his arm around her shoulders. "We'd better get you inside where it's warm before you catch your death of cold," he said, leading her toward the house.

The pooch, padding along happily beside them, seemed to take for granted that he was home, that Valerie was his mistress now. The minute his paws crossed the threshold, he lay down in front of the woodstove as if he'd been doing it since he was a pup.

Paul took a thick quilt from the back of a chair and bundled Valerie into it. Next, he built a roaring fire in the potbelly stove, filled the teapot with water from the kitchen pump, and proceeded to brew her a cup of strong, hot tea.

Valerie was still shivering after she downed the first cup.

"Stand up," he said, taking her hands in his own. "Let's get the blood moving in those puny arms of yours." Vigorously, he rubbed her upper arms. He'd expected her to fuss and refuse his help. Instead, she complied without a word of complaint. She looked tiny and vulnerable, facing him in her small kitchen. She'd always seemed brave and forceful, strong and capable. But the way she stood now, surprisingly quiet and shy as he rubbed her shoulders, made him realize she had a fragile, delicate side, as well. Impulsively, he pulled her into a hug and tenderly pressed her cheek to his chest. It felt good to have her in his arms—so good, in fact, that Paul decided it must be where she belonged. At least, this was where he wanted her to be.

All through the night, Valerie thought about that tiny fragment in time when she'd stood, wrapped in Paul's warm embrace. It had seemed impossible at the time, but she could have sworn that he'd trembled. Surely, it had been no more than a reaction to the coldness of his damp clothes....

He'd stoked the fire and fixed her one last cup of tea, and, after making her promise to eat the leftover soup and biscuits he'd found on the stovetop, he'd left.

And Valerie knew she'd see that wide, handsome smile in her dreams.

The dog refused to leave her side, even for a moment, and Valerie quickly discovered she rather liked having a furry shadow. She shared her supper with him, then settled down in front of the fire, her new pal snuggling against her feet. "Tomorrow, we're going to find something to call you. You're a scruffy old thing, but you deserve a proper name."

After a moment, she said, "Wait—that's it! I'll call you Scruffy!"

The dog woofed, as if in agreement, and rested his head on her knees.

Valerie blew out the lantern flame and climbed into bed. "G'night, Scruffy," she whispered into the darkness, then drifted off to sleep.

She dreamed she'd been walking in the woods and a tree had fallen on her legs, pinning her to the mossy earth. Tossing and turning, Valerie struggled to wriggle from beneath the broad trunk. Would she be permanently paralyzed? A powerful ache in her thighs woke her as the first rays of sunlight peeked through the shuttered window. It took a moment to put the dream together with reality. "Scruffy, you big lummox," she half scolded, laughing, "move over! You've cut off all circulation in my legs!"

Yawning sleepily, the dog obliged. Valerie rubbed her legs vigorously to get the blood flowing in them again.

The act reminded her of the way Paul had rubbed her shoulders the night before. The dream of the fallen tree was immediately forgotten, for she preferred to remember other, sweeter dreams she'd had during the night—dreams of quiet chats over picnic lunches, long buggy rides on sultry summer evenings, playful games of water tag on crisp, fall afternoons, and the happiness that exists between a perfectly matched pair.

What are you thinking? she suddenly admonished herself. *He's hardly the ideal mate for you...or you for him!* She did admire most everything about him, from his loyalty to the children to his dedication to the farm. He was smart, sweet, and funny, too...when he chose to let his guard down. His only flaw, as she saw it, was his doggedly determined devotion to God.

Didn't Paul realize that even without God, things would be exactly the same? Hadn't he ever asked himself why, if his God was so all-fired powerful, He hadn't spared Paul's wife and her unborn baby? Couldn't he see that prayer didn't change anything, or that no amount of faith would alter life's course?

Valerie had been a follower once. But that was long ago, when she'd been young and naïve. She'd grown up since then. Grown up a lot. Time had taught her that blind belief is a dangerous thing, for it gives one hope; and hope, she believed, would only disappoint you in the end.

Yes, she'd been one of the faithful, and when civil war had looked probable, she'd prayed it wouldn't happen. When it did, she'd prayed that the men in charge would do whatever they could to put an immediate stop to it. Of course, they hadn't, so she'd prayed that no one would be hurt. But the war hurt everyone, it seemed, in one way or another. It was a rare day when a friend or neighbor wasn't mourning a loved one killed in some horrible, bloody battle.

The war had destroyed her father's business, and then he'd been gunned down for harboring helpless, hungry slaves. Regardless of their ages, those who'd lost their lives in the War Between the States were husbands and fathers, sons and brothers. Her faith and prayers hadn't convinced God to protect her father or her brothers, or to protect her mother from grieving herself into an early grave.

While she'd still had the plantation, Valerie had prayed for the strength to run it in the way her father would have wanted. But the smoke and flames that had greedily devoured Carter Hall had been visible for miles after the Yankees had passed through...and God hadn't helped her douse them.

She believed God hadn't answered her prayers because He hadn't heard them.

Standing in the ashes of the only home she'd ever known, she'd realized there was one thing, and one thing only, that she could believe in: herself.

Yes, standing in the protective circle of Paul's arms had felt wonderful, but how could she put her trust in a man who blindly followed a Being who allowed such suffering and misery?

On the night she'd rescued Scruffy, she'd admitted to herself that she was falling in love with Paul Collins. But she'd also loved her father, brothers, and mother—all God-fearing people—and look where their blind faith had gotten them! Valerie couldn't bear to love and lose again. It was as simple as that.

Paul didn't understand Valerie's suddenly evasive behavior. If she saw him on the street, she crossed to the other side. If she realized he was in the same shop, she'd leave her goods on the counter and dash away like a scared rabbit. She must have sensed that he'd chosen a church pew with a clear view of her, for she began arriving late so that she could sit out of sight, way in the back. Though she'd agreed weeks before to meet him at a church social, she'd never showed up for it. And though she'd always been one to meet fears and confrontations head-on, she now avoided his eyes.

He missed her bright smile. Her teasing winks. Her silly jokes and her delightfully playful laughter. "Maybe you're in love," Tricia had said. And that was the simple truth. The proof was the big, gaping hole her absence made in his heart.

Paul prayed about it nearly as much as he thought about it—admittedly, a considerable investment of time.

Late one chilly October night, when the children had been tucked safely in bed, he held his Bible to his breast and closed his eyes. "Dear God," he prayed, "help me understand what this lesson will teach me."

Suddenly, the quilt Rita had made, stitch by stitch, slipped from his lap onto the floor. Paul gathered it up and folded it neatly before hanging it over the arm of his chair. Stroking its soft, colorful squares, he remembered happy times with his wife. He hadn't thought of her nearly as often, nor missed her nearly as much, as he had before meeting Valerie. A stab of guilt cut through him. How could he so coldly and willingly set aside her memory? How could he so callously blot her from his mind? The answer was simple: He'd put Rita's death out of his mind because Valerie reminded him how much he'd missed *living.*

Valerie had taught his children to live again, too. Taught them that it was all right, even respectable, to laugh and play and enjoy life, even though their mother was gone. "Nobody expects you to forget your ma," he heard her telling them one day when he surprised them at the schoolhouse, "but if she knew the three of you were sad-eyed all the time, it would just break her heart."

Paul suspected the children missed their extra time with Valerie as much as he did. Once a week, at least, she'd stopped by the farm, her wicker picnic basket overflowing with cookies, sourdough bread, a hot-from-the-oven fruit pie, or vegetables she'd grown and simmered into delicious soups and stews.

And books...oh, how she could make a story come to life! Paul had loved listening as she read to his children, for Valerie's zest for life wasn't just evident in her lyrical voice—it was contagious.

He'd never thought he'd love again. At least, he'd never thought it was possible to love like *that* twice in one lifetime. But just as Valerie had proved him wrong about putting Rita's memory in its proper place, she was proving him wrong about the human heart's capacity to love....

Grinning, Paul slapped his knee. *That's it!* he decided. He'd been feeling guilty for wanting to move forward with Valerie—it seemed a betrayal of his love for Rita. In truth, he recognized, it was the pure, sweet love he'd felt for his wife that made him yearn for that special kind of closeness again.

His Bible fell open to Psalm 107:6: "*They cried unto the Lord in their trouble, and he delivered them out of their distresses.*" It was as plain as the book in his lap: God had heard his cries, and Valerie was the answer to his prayers.

He closed the Good Book and placed it gently on the mantle. "Just one problem left to solve, Lord," he whispered, his smile fading slightly as he stroked the Bible's black leather binding. "How do I get Valerie back again when I don't know how I lost her in the first place?"

Chapter Five

As she descended the wide plank steps of the church, Valerie managed to nod politely in response to the good mornings and howdy-dos of fellow Freelanders. Was Paul Collins to blame for her confused, distracted state of mind? Valerie couldn't be sure....

She told herself it only *seemed* that he'd stared at her all during the service, and that he hadn't *really* been grinning and winking and wiggling his eyebrows at her. He was far too devout a Christian to misbehave like an unruly schoolboy, especially right in the middle of the pastor's sermon about giving the Lord nothing less than one's best!

Her father's old saying gonged in her mind: "Facts are facts!" Either Paul had been making eyes at her all through the Sunday service or she was losing her mind.

Walking along the redbrick path that led from the church steps to the road, Valerie smiled and placed a white-gloved hand over her fluttering heart. Facts were facts, all right. Paul Collins had been flirting with her from his aisle seat, right there in front of his children and the entire congregation. She'd nearly reached the end of the fence that surrounded the churchyard when the *clickety-clack* of tree twig against pickets made her realize that, at some point during her short walk, she'd picked up a small, fallen branch.

Flushing slightly at her own silliness, Valerie dropped the stick. Suddenly, the giddy, girlish response to his grins and winks disappeared, and, in its place, the list of his positive attributes grew. He was tall, handsome, hardworking, responsible...decent and good, too... and a wonderful, loving father.... He deserved a woman who would share his life—every aspect of it, down to and including his love for the Lord. And Valerie could not—*would* not—blindly follow the One responsible for her solitary status in the world.

She found herself standing at her gate, staring blankly at the front of her cottage. *How did I get this far without realizing it?* she wondered. *You're acting like a moon-struck schoolgirl who's never been in love before!* As she shoved the gate open and stomped up her narrow, cobbled walk, Valerie admitted that she *hadn't* been in love before. At least, she'd never experienced anything quite as intense as this....

Lately, as she'd corrected homework papers, Valerie had needed to forcibly blink Paul's charming grin from her memory. And just the other day, amid the *whisk-whisk* sounds of her sweeping, she'd found herself leaning on the broom handle and grinning like a simpleton, remembering the way he'd drenched her with Scruffy's rinsewater. Now, as she entered her dim, quiet kitchen, she had to admit that if she hadn't tilted her own head to get a better view of him during the church service that day, she wouldn't have known that he'd been watching her.

She listened for the reassuring *click* that told her the big oak door had shut out the rest of the world. Safe in her own little domain, she leaned against the door and took a deep, cleansing breath. *Get ahold of yourself. You know better than to get involved with a man like that*, she told herself.

But...a man like *what*?

If she had a mind to settle down with one man for the rest of her life, she could do far worse than the likes of Paul Collins—that much she knew. A future with a man like that would be filled with peace and contentment, joy and laughter. No, he would never be able to give her a mansion or buy her a gilded carriage, but he'd make sure they had a roof over their heads—one that never leaked. He'd see to it that his children never wore rags or limped around in too-small boots, even if it meant working round the clock to buy what they needed. His family would never go hungry. Would never be cold. And his supply of warm embraces and reassuring words would be never-ending. A man like that....

Valerie took another deep breath. The mantle clock told her she'd been daydreaming about him for five minutes straight. Clearing her throat, Valerie slipped off her gloves, one finger at a time. Then, with a flick of her wrist, she untied the blue satin bonnet bow beneath her chin and headed for her bedroom. It wasn't until she slid open her bureau drawer to put away her gloves that she saw the picture that always brought tears to her eyes.

She took off her bonnet, picked up the heavy brass picture frame, and blinked at the frozen images of her family, captured forever in hazy brown. Her father and mother, stern in their stiff-collared clothes and plastered-down hair, were standing side by side behind their three children. Valerie, a mere ten years old at the time, was sitting between her brothers, Lee Junior and Delbert, whose lopsided grins told everyone who viewed the aging photograph that they were proud of the couple with their hands clamped protectively on their sons' shoulders.

Slowly, Valerie carried the picture into the parlor, sat down in her cushioned rocker, and let the tears roll freely down her cheeks. She couldn't remember the last time she'd really cried over her family. For a few moments, she couldn't figure out why a few innocent winks from Paul Collins would remind her of how much she missed them.

When the realization set in, she hugged the photograph to her breast and sobbed uncontrollably. She'd always had an independent spirit. It had gotten her into trouble often as a child, for it had spurred her to investigating places and things and creatures that "could be dangerous," as her mother would often warn. She'd never been a clingy girl, preferring to walk along Richmond's busy streets on her own rather than remain connected hand in hand to either of her parents. But that independent spirit had never led her far from home or hearth; even as a youngster, Valerie had sensed that love, protection, and everything else she'd ever need would come by way of those two sturdy, dependable people.

She cried because she missed them...and because she missed being part of a loving family.

A man like that....

Memories of chatting with her father by the fireside, helping her mother decorate the house for Christmas, and gathering willow branches and turning them into fishing poles with her brothers filled her mind. She remembered carriage rides into town. Moonlit walks. Playing hide-and-seek with her brothers. Valerie didn't just miss her family. She missed family *life*, and it had been Paul who'd reminded her that she was completely and utterly alone in the world.

And why was she so totally alone? Because his precious *God* had turned a deaf ear to her and, one by one, had taken from her all those she held dear.

She stood up quickly and headed to her bedroom, where she gently placed the photograph on her dresser before marching to the kitchen to prepare herself a midday meal. She'd have cold, thinly sliced roast beef with bread and butter pickles on the side, along with a slice of the sourdough bread she'd baked the night before. And she'd wash it all down with a cup of strong, hot tea.

Valerie put a lot of effort into her meals. Somehow, setting a proper table made eating alone seem a little less bleak. So, as she waited for the water to boil, she smoothed the white linen tablecloth and put a silver knife and spoon to the right of the rose-patterned plate, a matching fork to its left. The cup and saucer, she placed just to the right of the knife's tip. She folded a soft napkin into a neat rectangle and placed it in the center of the dish as fresh tears welled in her eyes.

Valerie dropped into her chair and buried her face in her hands. It wasn't like her to give in to self-pity. What had gotten into her?

She blamed the bright, sunny day. Then the crisp, autumn breeze. The pastor's long-winded sermon. The children's angelic voices singing "Amazing Grace."

But it was the photograph, she knew, that had stirred her long-resting emotions. Angrily, she admitted she'd still be surrounded by the loving people in the photograph if Paul's all-wonderful God had only answered her prayers!

Were my prayers that unreasonable? she ranted silently, staring at the tin kitchen ceiling. *You parted the seas, turned water into wine.... You had the power to save them! Why didn't You save them?*

It had been over a year since she'd buried the last of her family, and she'd thought that the worst of her grieving had ended. She'd cried bitterly at their funerals, cried angrily at their gravesites. In time, the tears had come less often and with less intensity. She'd been in Freeland for months now and hadn't had reason to shed a single tear. *So why*, she asked herself, *are you weeping uncontrollably now*?

Tears, in her mind, were a symptom of inner weakness. And weakness made her angry. She could abide sadness and tears in others, especially in children. But not in herself. Tears of anger were the worst kind of all, for they were rooted in self-pity. And self-pity, her father had taught her, was the single most destructive human character trait.

With calm deliberateness, she took the teapot off the flame, wrapped the roast beef in oilcloth, and slid the bread into the wooden breadbox. Once the pickles were back in their Mason jar, she rinsed the bowl they'd been in. Then, after brushing crumbs from the bread plate, she put the lovely dishes back into the cupboard and returned the tablecloth and napkin to the sideboard drawer. She knew better than to cherish these material possessions, for she'd seen how quickly and cruelly things could be snatched away. But these few pieces of china, the beautiful white linen tablecloth, and the three matching napkins were almost the only things she'd managed to salvage from the fire that destroyed Carter Hall. These, and the photograph....

She untied her red gingham apron and hung it on the peg beside the door, then headed for her bedroom. When she came out again, she was wearing old boots and a threadbare dress. Her thick, dark hair, fastened with a ribbon atop her head in a ponytail, was mostly hidden by a wide-brimmed straw hat.

Scruffy was sitting on the porch when Valerie stepped outside. "Well, how long have you been back?" she asked the dog. "You were nowhere to be seen when I got back from church." She squatted to ruffle his sandy-colored fur. "You haven't been up to no good, now, have you?"

Scruffy licked Valerie's cheek and gave a breathy bark.

"Try to stay close to home," she said as she headed for the shed out back. "I don't want to be hollering for you like some fishwife come dark...."

She'd get her vegetable garden cleaned up this afternoon if it was the last thing she'd do. Taking her work gloves from the high shelf just inside the shed, she scanned the semidark space in search of her spade. Just as she reached out to grab it, a horrible, high-pitched scream made her blood run cold.

❀

Though Valerie's house was tucked snugly out of sight behind the school, it sat in the hub of Freeland. The Northern Central Railroad tracks paralleled Main Street, and every store along the road was within walking distance. At times such as this, while running in the direction of the frightening scream, Valerie almost wished she lived high on a hill, out of earshot of the town's bustling activities.

"What is it?" she asked, breathless from her run.

Greta, her face half hidden behind one of her large, calloused hands, dabbed her blue eyes with a lace-trimmed handkerchief. "I found diss tacked to my door chust now," she cried. "Dose men who killed Yonson, it iss from dem."

"Johnson?" Valerie pictured the ever smiling face of the town blacksmith, Abel Johnson. "Abel Johnson is dead? But how...?"

Greta swallowed a sob. "Dey hanged him. Dey vas here in der middle of der night," she explained tearfully.

Valerie took the note from Greta's trembling hands and read silently: "*If you want to keep living in this town,*" said the precisely lettered threat, "*you'll forget everything you saw.*"

Valerie's heartbeat quickened. "Greta," she whispered, "what exactly did you see?"

The older woman sniffed loudly. "Dose men. Riding on big horses, wearing white robes...." Her blue eyes darted back and forth as she scanned the street for possible eavesdroppers before casting a sidelong glance in Valerie's direction. "You vouldn't tell anybody...?"

Valerie shook her head. "Of course not. I'd never put you and DeWitt in jeopardy, but—"

"—but notink! Surely, you've heard of the Vite Bruderhood!"

Valerie nodded. She'd heard of them, all right. They were a savage pack of men who hid their identities beneath white hoods and robes. According to an article in the *Gazette*, the secret society, which had begun organizing its members almost as soon as the Civil War ended, had stayed deep in the South, near Pulaski, Tennessee, its town of origin. They called themselves the Ku Klux Klan. The Pale Faces. The Constitutional Union Guards. The Order of the White Rose. Whatever name they went by, they'd taken it upon themselves to continue the tradition of slavery, despite the fact that so many men had given their lives to put an end to the ugly institution. The Klan firmly believed in white supremacy and believed just as firmly in their right to do whatever they deemed necessary to protect the purity of their race.

"I vas never so afraid in all my life," Greta sighed. "Dey vas terrible to look at."

Valerie led the trembling older woman up the steps and into the quiet seclusion of her feed and grain store. "Let me fix you a cup of tea," Valerie offered, puttering in the tiny kitchen behind the curtained storefront.

Greta sagged into the seat of a straight-backed wooden chair and rested her elbows on the table. Holding her head in her hands, she said, "Dey vould haff been scary enough in dose pointed hats wit' dose big eye holes cut into dem. But dey had skulls on dere saddle horns, too!"

According to the *Gazette* article, the white-robed uniforms and saddle skulls represented the spirits of dead Rebel soldiers. Valerie pictured the gang on horseback, all wearing the dreadful costumes. Even in the bold light of day, they would have been terrifying. She could only imagine how frightening the scene might be, shrouded in darkness.

"Und da torches. Huge, bright fire sticks dat lit up der sky. Ve never even heard dem coming," Greta continued, "'cause dey had wrapped da horses' hooves wit' blankets. Suddenly, dey vas everywhere. All 'round Yonson's shop und up und down der street."

Valerie had always slept deeply. She remembered wishing her house were far above the melee of town sounds, as she'd run toward the sounds of Greta's screams. Now, she altered her wish. If she'd heard something, perhaps she could have gone for help. Perhaps she could have done something to stop the Klan before—

"Dey beat him wit' sticks und clubs," Greta was saying. "Und when he fell to de ground, dey kicked him, over und over. He vasn't even conscious when dey put dat rope around hiss neck...."

Telling that part of the story upset Greta more than anything else she'd said so far. Valerie sensed that if the woman kept what she'd seen to herself, she would see it for the rest of her life every time she closed her eyes. "Don't keep their dirty secret," Valerie urged her. "Talk about it. Tell me. Tell everyone you know!"

She put a mug of steaming tea down in front of Greta, then patted a chubby, work-hardened hand. But Greta's stony, tight-lipped expression made it clear that she had no intention of saying another word.

"It just amazes me how men can be so pigheaded," Valerie said. "This country isn't even a hundred years old yet, and already they seem to have forgotten why it was established in the first place!"

Greta took a slow sip of her tea, then met Valerie's gaze. "Dey mean vhat dey say," she whispered. "I should not haff told you vhat I saw. Now you could be in danger, too. Good ting DeVitt iss busy out back. He vould be furious witt me if he knew I told you...."

Gritting her teeth, Valerie sat down across from Greta. "It's wrong to keep quiet about what happened. You should tell the sheriff what you saw. Because if you don't, Abel Johnson won't be the only Negro man to die at the Klan's hands."

Greta sat, wide-eyed and open-mouthed, staring at Valerie. After a long silence, she said softly, "Dat may be true enough. But I cannot risk it." She sandwiched Valerie's hands between her own. "Please don't make me sorry dat I spoke to you as a friend, Valerie. Tell me you'll keep my secret."

"But what about Abel's family?" Valerie pressed. "Don't you think they'd like to know the truth?"

Greta's tear-rasped voice cracked. "Dey vere dere. Dey saw de same t'ing dat I saw."

Against her better judgment, Valerie nodded her assent. She had to respect the old woman's fear, even if she didn't understand it.

"Vill you pray for me und DeVitt?" Greta asked, her voice quaking with emotion.

Valerie wanted to tell her friend the absolute truth—that the last thing in the world she'd do was pray for their safety. She'd seen the futility of prayer too many times. But, knowing that some folks drew strength from it, Valerie nodded, deciding not to shake Greta's already tentative hold on faith. She rose and headed for the door. "You're sure you don't want me to get the sheriff?"

"I chust vant to forget vhat happened to Yonson."

"If only we could...."

Tomorrow, like the rest of the folks in town, she'd watch as Abel's wife and three small children joined his parents and siblings in the funeral march down Main Street.

No, they would not forget.... "Well, I'll be here if you need to talk."

Getting home meant crossing the street and walking past Abel Johnson's blacksmith shop. Chills ran up and down Valerie's spine as she neared the giant oak where Greta said they'd killed him. As she got closer, she saw the hemp rope, its ragged end swinging lazily in the breeze, that had been the Klan's murder weapon.

Valerie fumed. Keeping quiet about such madness, such violence, would only encourage those horrible men to commit similar crimes. A secret like Greta's would only give them courage to strike again and again, knowing that their frightening power could silence even the strongest-willed citizens, like Greta and DeWitt. Such silence guaranteed the Klan's return.

Valerie had been born and raised in Richmond, and her Southern pride flowed in her veins, pumped in her heart, echoed in her head. She'd lost everything to the horrible War Between the States and had witnessed the slaughter of humans, livestock, and pets at the hands of the Yankees. But even she understood the difference between the ravages of war and the senseless brutalization of innocent, hardworking Americans.

Today, the Johnson family would mourn their beloved Abel.

Valerie couldn't help but wonder which family would mourn a family member tomorrow.

Chapter Six

All too soon, Old Man Winter would blow frigid winds across the land and blanket Abel Johnson's grave with pure, white snow.

Until now, Valerie had passed her cousin Sally's house often, wishing that she and her family were home from their European holiday. She was glad now that Sally hadn't been in Freeland at the time of the grisly event.

Few townsfolk risked talking about the night Abel died, since no one could be sure that a friend, neighbor, or relative hadn't been one of those who'd donned the awful masks and robes to hang him. Ardith Johnson, unable to hire anyone to run the blacksmith shop, had been forced to sell it—and everything in it—for half of its true worth. The Johnsons had lived in the comfortable yet humble rooms behind the shop. Before Abel's murder, Ardith had browsed and bought things from the dress shop, the feed and grain, the hattery. Now, to make ends meet, she and her three young children lived on the drafty top floor of the Freelander Hotel. "I always been a dandy cook," she confided in Valerie one dreary rainy afternoon, "but who'da thought I'd be doing it for money someday?"

Ardith was a lovely young woman who worked long, hard hours without ever missing a Sunday service or a meeting at the schoolhouse. Yes, life was hard, the spunky lady admitted. "But we're all healthy. We got a roof over our heads an' plenty o' food in our bellies. The good Lord saw to it we'd be taken care of when He took sweet Abel home to Him."

The good Lord, indeed! Valerie fumed silently. *Why should those darling children and that wonderful woman have to live without Abel? Where was the good Lord when those murdering madmen tore through town, terrifying and killing an innocent citizen just because of his skin color?*

Valerie had said just that to Greta one day while waiting for the old woman to box up her grocery order. And Paul Collins had overheard every word of Valerie's rampage.

"*'O ye of little faith,'*" he said softly, interrupting her tirade.

She was growing a bit tired of his self-righteousness. How dare he quote Scripture to her simply because he presumed her to be faithless?

"Matthew chapter six, verse thirty," Valerie responded without hesitation.

Surprised at her immediate recognition of the age-old verse, Paul grinned. "*'Watch ye, stand fast in the faith, quit you like men, be strong.'*"

"First Corinthians chapter sixteen, verse thirteen. Believe it or not, Mr. Collins, I was raised in a strict Christian household. I know the Bible quite well," she snapped.

Confused by the fury of her response, Paul stopped grinning. "I'll concede that you've suffered many tragedies, Miss Carter," he said, assuming her uppity tone, "but the Lord isn't to blame for—"

"Then perhaps you'll be so kind as to tell me who *is* to blame," she interrupted him.

Without a word, he placed a hand on her elbow and guided her from the store to the school yard, where they sat on a narrow wooden bench beneath a weeping willow.

"Why I let you lead me here, I'll never know," she said, looking straight ahead and primly folding her hands in her lap.

"You followed because you're hoping I can provide you with the answers you're seeking. You're hurt and confused by your many personal losses. And in your loneliness, you want a place for that anger. You want someone to blame, and you've chosen the Lord."

Valerie stared down at her hands, unable to meet his eyes. She suspected that they would hold the same warmth and kindness she heard in his soft voice. And at the moment, she preferred to deal with facts, not emotions. "Greta told me that your father was a minister, and that you studied to be one, too," she began. "I'm sure you understand the grief and emptiness and anger one can feel when exposed to many losses. But please don't presume to understand why I feel as I do about God. You could never understand."

"Why not?" was his quiet question.

Valerie met his dark eyes. "Because you're a good man. Too good, in some ways."

That statement inspired a soft chuckle from him.

"Don't laugh at me, Paul. I'm serious."

His smile diminished. "I wasn't laughing at you, Valerie. I was laughing at the notion that I'm too good."

Ignoring his denial of her comment, she dropped her voice to a near whisper and said, "Others have lived harder lives than I, yet they continue to believe. To trust and have faith. Why? Because they're *good*. You're like that, Paul. You've suffered losses—hard and painful ones. Yet you've never doubted God's power. Your faith in Christ never faltered."

He took a deep breath and shook his head. "You're dead wrong on that score," he said after a moment. Before she could argue the point, he silenced her by going on to explain. "After I buried Rita, I was angry. Furious, in fact. Inwardly, I ranted and raved because I'd prayed myself hoarse, yet the suffering and pain of those I loved seemed to go on and on." He began counting on his fingers as he continued, "A heart attack took my father without warning. My only brother and his family were killed when their wagon overturned in the river. My sister's husband died at Gettysburg, and grief drove her to an early grave. My wife and unborn child were killed by a soldier's stray bullet intended for a deserting soldier, leaving my other children motherless. And for what? Why hadn't the Lord interceded? Why hadn't He done something to save her and our baby?"

Valerie saw the pain, still bright in his dark eyes, that his memories awakened. "I'm so sorry, Paul," she said. "I never meant to open old wounds."

As though she hadn't said a word, Paul closed his eyes and recited another Bible verse. "*'God is faithful, who will not suffer you to be tempted above that ye are able; but will with the temptation also make a way to escape, that ye may be able to bear it.'*"

"First Corinthians chapter ten, verse thirteen," she said. "Once upon a time, I *did* have faith. I trusted and believed, and, like you, I prayed myself hoarse. But God didn't answer. What was I to think, except that I wasn't deserving of an answer? He looked into my heart and my mind, heard my thoughts and doubts, even as I prayed, and saw how undeserving I was. *That's* why He didn't answer my prayers, Paul. *That's* why He allowed everyone I loved to be taken from me."

Paul sighed, long and loud. "You couldn't be more wrong. Life has made you strong, but I believe that your strength has hardened your heart to the Lord's true message."

Valerie opened her mouth to argue, but he pressed on. "You say you're not good when, in reality, you have more good in your little finger than most of us have in our entire bodies."

She wrinkled her nose over that one, and he watched her bite back bitter tears, which touched a long-forgotten chord in his heart. Rita had been a woman who cried often and easily. She'd been sheltered from pain and suffering to the extent that every time they touched her, even in a small way, tears somehow soothed her.

Valerie wasn't like that. She'd stiffened her back to tragedy instead of giving in to it. She'd marched headlong into life despite all she'd lost. Somehow, he had to make her see that the strength she took such pride in was God's gift to her—His way of sheltering her from further pain and suffering.

Paul wanted to hold her close. To soothe her with gentle kisses and tender touches. To tell her what a rare and valuable person she was. *All in good time,* he told himself. *All in good time.*

"You think no one knows who's been putting food and clothes and shoes on the children's doorsteps?" Paul said instead. "You think folks don't realize who paid for all those wonderful books that have lined the schoolhouse shelves since you came to town?" He took her hands in his and clasped them tightly. "You think we aren't aware it's been *you* buying slates and chalk and paper and pencils, and telling the children the supplies are being paid for by the school district? You did those good things because you believed they needed to be done.

"What's more, you've made great personal sacrifices to do these things. And you did them in a quiet, Christian way, so that no one felt beholden, so that no one was embarrassed by a lack of money." After a long pause, he added, "The only question is, how does that great big heart of yours fit into that tiny little body?"

"But—but I was so careful to stay out of sight!" Valerie stammered. "I didn't want anyone feeling beholden to me—"

"It's my personal belief that Mr. Daniel Webster studied you before he defined the word *good,*" Paul said, smiling when his comment turned her cheeks bright pink. "I can't assume to understand all you've gone through to make you believe as you do, but I can tell you this: the Lord loves you. He knows what you've suffered, and He understands your anger. He *made* you, don't forget…."

She took a deep breath and glanced in the direction of the store. "Greta will think I've lost my mind," she said, giggling nervously. "I paid for my groceries, then walked away without them!"

"You can pretend our little conversation never took place, if you must," he said, "but you can't pretend you didn't hear me. You *are* a good woman, Valerie Carter, and God sees the goodness that originates from your heart. Someday, you'll believe that."

"Thank you for your kind words," she said, one hand on his forearm. "I don't deserve them, but thank you, anyway."

"Don't you own a mirror?"

Her brow furrowed with confusion.

"Can't you see what a remarkable woman you are?" The question made her blush again.

"Paul, please—I—"

He held up a hand to silence her. "Do me a favor, will you?"

She nodded.

"I know you have a Bible in your house, hidden away somewhere. Dust it off and read my favorite verse, Romans 8:35." With that, he stood up, turned on his heel, and headed for his buckboard, which had been loaded with supplies and was waiting near the steps of the feed and grain. He didn't look at her again until he urged the horse forward, and when he did, Paul knew without a doubt that he loved her.

❀

Weeks passed before she saw him again. She missed his easy smile. His sparkling, coffee-colored eyes. The insistent, wayward curl on his forehead that refused to stay tucked beneath his black felt cap. *Why,* Valerie thought, smiling, *I even love that silly cap that he probably wears to bed!*

She'd done what he'd asked of her, albeit not immediately. She knew exactly where she'd stored the Good Book. When she finally lifted the fire-blackened lid of the huge oak trunk, she sank to the floor and wept bitter, lonely tears. These few articles were all that was left of her happy, close-knit family.

Valerie carefully lifted the Bible from its resting place so as not to loosen any of the pages charred by the fire that had leveled Carter Hall. Slumping into her rocker and leaning against the headrest, she held the Bible to her cheek. It still smelled faintly of smoke. The odor, along with the softness of the leather cover against her cheek, took her back in time to the day she'd tried desperately to forget—but couldn't.

She'd just returned from her mother's burial.

Mama would have no marker for her grave for a very long time because the Yankees had destroyed the stonemason's shop. So, Valerie had fashioned a crude, wooden cross the night before the funeral and, using her father's pocketknife, had carved,

Here lies Mandy Carter,
beloved wife and mother.
1825–1863

She hadn't remembered to take a hammer, however, and had been forced to hunt the cemetery grounds for a large rock to use, instead, to pound the cross into the ground. She also hadn't thought to make a point on the end of the cross, and it had ended up taking her nearly an hour to get the marker to stand upright by her mother's grave.

There wouldn't be any of the typical after-service chatter over pie and coffee, for the good folks of her church had much to do, thanks to the Yankees. And it had been just as well, because Valerie had needed to prepare herself. When she'd finished and had begun walking home, she'd realized that it would be the first time in her life that she'd go home to an empty house. The first time in her life she'd be totally alone. She'd refused all offers of a ride home, preferring instead to walk the three miles in quiet solitude.

Valerie hadn't noticed the flaming glow on the horizon until she'd made the final turn that would lead her to the manor house. At first, the orange haze had confused her. She'd read about comets and meteors and such, and she'd wondered, for a moment, if maybe one had fallen to earth. But the closer she'd come to the house, the more aware she'd become that no comet or meteor had caused the day sky to glare in that way.

With tears in her eyes and a sob in her throat, Valerie had run as fast as her booted feet would carry her—down the magnolia-lined drive, across the bridge that crossed a small tributary of the James River, which divided Carter Hall in two, and past the grassy knoll, which led to the wide, welcoming porch....

But the porch was gone.

And so were the heavy, oak double doors.

Yankee soldiers were everywhere, it seemed—some on horseback, others standing, a few sprawled on the lawn like Fourth of July celebrants watching a fireworks display.

Valerie had frozen in her tracks, mesmerized by the flames eating her home and her heritage, board by board and brick by brick. It wasn't till the last ember had died, in the wee hours of the morning, that she'd realized her cheeks had been singed by the powerful heat of the blaze. Soot had grayed the lace trim of her black mourning dress, and flecks of ash had gathered on her shoulders and in her hair.

The soldiers, bored now that the best of the show had ended, had wandered off to see what valuables could be hoisted from the ruins. And Valerie, dazed and confused, had stood shock-silent in the rubble that had once been her mother's lovely, ornately decorated parlor.

When a Yankee soldier had asked her why she was crying over things that represented slavery and oppression, Valerie had marched right up to him and, despite the fact that he'd towered over her like Jack's giant, slapped his face with all the strength she'd been able to muster.

"Slavery was *never* tolerated at Carter Hall!" she'd shouted. "My father gave his *life* defending his workers' freedom!"

She'd shoved the burly man, then had pointed over his shoulder toward the remnants of the tidy white cottages that had flanked the long, winding drive. "See those houses over there? Once, there were twenty of them, and every farm hand had a garden plot behind his house. And a tool shed. They earned fair wages and were free to come and go as they pleased. And see there?" she'd asked, pointing again. "That was our schoolhouse, and all of our field hands and their children learned to read and write there, regardless of the color of their skin!"

"Sorry, miss, that the stench of smoke and charred wood has filled your pretty green eyes with tears...."

She'd never been a violent sort. Why, it had always made her heart ache if Lee Junior or Delbert had so much as squashed a spider beneath his boot heel. But the arrogance of this man, defending an army that had destroyed everything she'd held dear, had made her want to commit violence. Instead, Valerie had summoned the last of her calm. "What city do you call home, soldier?"

Smiling uncomfortably at her angry interrogation, he'd answered, "Boston."

"When you return North to a family that loves you and a home that doesn't have a 'stench of smoke and charred wood,'" she'd hissed, "will you sleep well, knowing what you've done here on Southern soil? Do you truly believe in what you fought for, soldier? Or did you put on that pretty blue uniform just to collect a dependable salary at the end of every month?"

He'd been standing there, blinking like a simpleton, when two of his buddies had called him to join them. Suddenly, as if the shame of war and the hatred that inspires it had enveloped him, the soldier had slung his pack over his shoulder. Tears had misted in his own bloodshot eyes, and he'd said softly, "I know 'sorry' won't do you any good now, but I'm mighty sorry, just the same."

And he'd left her standing there, the last in a long line of proud Carters, alone and surrounded by the shadowy remnants of Carter Hall Plantation.

Valerie had waited until the line of Bluecoats had disappeared into the wooded glen at the north end of the property before tiptoeing through what had been the keeping room, where her father used to tell her stories about when he was a boy, then around what had been the kitchen, where only a few blackened bricks from the wall-wide fireplace had lain in a sloppy heap. She'd wandered into what had been her father's library, where the walls were once lined with green, maroon, brown, and black leather-bound books of all shapes and sizes.

A few books had survived the fire.

Among them had been the family Bible.

It had still been warm and smoldering when she'd picked it up, its cover dulled and dirty, its gold-edged pages singed and curled, and she'd clutched it to her breast and fallen to her knees, sobbing so loud and so hard that she'd wondered if the Yankees would turn about-face to see what wounded animal to put out of its misery.

She'd held the Good Book in both hands, raised it to the heavens, and cried aloud, "Why, Lord? *Why*?"

She had waited, but no answer had come. But then, she'd needed no booming voice to resound from the clouds. She'd known why God hadn't answered.

It was because she hadn't deserved an answer.

She'd lived a life of luxury from the day she was born. Surrounded by riches, Valerie had never wanted for anything, not even for a moment. Perhaps, the Lord thought she'd grown selfish and self-centered, that she should have shared more of her riches with those less fortunate.

The truth was, she'd never even thought of it. Her father had struggled his whole life to protect her from the ugly things in the world, and she'd never seen—let alone experienced—pain and suffering. Mama was her warmth, and Papa was her strength. Lee Junior and Delbert, her protectors.

Then, one by one, they'd been taken from her.

Forever.

If not for her grandmother's entries in the front of the Bible and those few treasures she'd dug from the smoking ruins, Valerie would have nothing but memories of them.

So, yes, she had avoided fulfilling Paul's request to look up the Bible verse, at first, because she'd touched the Good Book before and knew it would only awaken carefully buried feelings of pain and loneliness. Worse, it would awaken carefully buried feelings of anger—anger toward the God who had allowed all her suffering to take place in order to teach a hard lesson to a selfish young woman.

Now, something she remembered about Paul's tone of voice made her open the Bible. Automatically, as if she hadn't avoided the verse these many months, she turned to Romans 8:35 and read aloud in a trembling voice, "'*Who shall separate us from the love of Christ?*'"

Only you can do that, said a tiny voice deep within her heart. Silently, she read the last two verses in chapter eight: "*I am persuaded, that neither death, nor life, nor angels, nor principalities, nor powers, nor things present, nor things to come, nor height, nor depth, nor any other creature, shall be able to separate us from the love of God, which is in Christ Jesus our Lord.*"

Not even my own stubborn, hardened heart? she wondered.

Valerie closed the Bible so softly that it made no sound at all, then leaned back in the rocker and closed her eyes. A sense of being surrounded by love and acceptance rolled over her like a giant, gentle wave. For the first time in years, she knew peace in her heart, and she fell asleep, smiling the sweet, contented smile of a carefree baby.

Chapter Seven

It was the worst winter on record, with ice, wind, and snow that piled up to the windowsills. Richmond often became cold between November and February, but Valerie couldn't remember ever seeing anything quite like this.

When the first snow fell in early December, she felt like a small child trying hard to act grown up, for every few minutes, she found herself standing at the window overlooking the back yard and grinning foolishly as the faded green grass turned into a white blanket of snow. From the front porch, Valerie continued to watch in awe as the flakes floated from the sky and alighted, whisper-soft, one atop the next, on the ground. And, like a child sneaking cookies before supper, she waited until after dark to step out into it. By then, six inches had accumulated on the ground.

She chased Scruffy through the snow, tossed snowballs at him, and allowed him to kick showers of it at her. Lucky for her, the evidence of their romp was hidden by morning beneath another six inches of snow. The world took on a whole new look, covered in white—it was hushed and velvety, peaceful and pure.

That snowfall caused the school to close for the first time that winter—and additional snowfalls caused it to close seven more times that same month. The awesome beauty of the snow had diminished along about the fourth snowfall, even in Valerie's snow-awed eyes.

By Christmas, Freeland was white for as far as the eye could see. Valerie had never had a white Christmas, and she looked forward to waking up to a snowy landscape on that great morning.

Freelanders, she discovered, made a big fuss over the day. For weeks beforehand, prayer groups, choir rehearsals, and decorating and baking parties abounded. Gifts of homemade jellies and preserves, delicious breads and cakes, hand-carved wooden decoys, and more were exchanged among friends and neighbors. The presents went back and forth so quickly that Valerie jokingly said it was the gift exchange, and not Mother Nature, that caused the high winds whipping up and down Main Street.

Church services the Sunday before Christmas were reverent yet festive. Hymns and carols sung by the children's choir warmed the little church building almost as surely as the crackling fire in the huge potbelly stove, and Rev. Gemmill's sermon made the parishioners feel as if they were there in Bethlehem beneath the great star, awaiting the birth of their Savior.

Valerie happily joined in the rituals and customs of Christmas in Freeland, for she was more than the town schoolmarm—now, she was a real member of the community. Freeland had become much more than just the place where she lived. It was home, and the people who lived there were her family.

The anger she'd harbored in her heart after losing her parents, her brothers, and her home had lessened, day by day, gradually being replaced by the warm acceptance of God's love. Paul had been right when he'd told her she didn't have to earn that love, but Valerie felt a strong sense of duty toward the Lord, anyway. And with that duty, she felt an obligation to spend the rest of her days earning the Creator's forgiveness; just as she believed He understood that grief and loneliness had caused her spiteful anger, she believed He deserved nothing but her best.

So, now, when she attended a church service, Valerie listened intently to Rev. Gemmill's sermon. She started and ended every day by reading God's Word. And between the hours of sunrise and sunset, Valerie found herself conversing more easily with Him.

Prayer came naturally now that she'd found her way back to Him.

And she'd found her way back thanks to Paul Collins.

No one could have given her a greater gift, and she loved Paul all the more for it.

So, on Christmas Day, when Rev. and Mrs. Gemmill opened the church, where turkeys and hams, vats of stuffing and yams, and huge bowls of mashed potatoes and gravy lined the long, narrow tables in the church cellar, she sought out his handsome face. That wasn't an easy task, since every Freelander, it seemed, showed up at precisely the same time for the biggest Christmas party Valerie had ever attended.

Early in the day, she was chatting with Greta when Paul and the children whisked her away to the far corner of the meeting room, where they insisted that she shut her eyes tightly and let them lead her into the church's foyer. When at last they told her to open her eyes, she found herself looking at the prettiest rocking chair she'd ever seen.

"I carved the spindles," Tyler crowed, pointing at the rods connecting the sturdy legs to one another, "and Pa caned the chair's seat and back."

"It was me put the little iron brads on the feet," Timmy chimed in. "Used Pa's hammer an' did 'em all by myself! An' Tricia made the cushion so it would match the curtains in your parlor."

Valerie ran her fingertips along the smooth arms of the oak rocker. "I don't think I've ever seen a lovelier piece of furniture," she said, settling into it. "And I know I've never sat in a more comfortable chair."

Paul's grin, which broadened with her compliments, lit up the room. "The young'uns told me they once saw you hammerin' the rockers back onto the chair you have now," he said, twisting his cap in his hands. "It was their idea to make you a new one...."

And what a perfect gift it was. Valerie knew that it had taken many hours to cut and carve and polish the honey-gold wood. The fact that they'd gone to such trouble and given so much time for her brought tears to her eyes.

"Golly, Pa," Timmy said, wrinkling his nose, "I thought you said she'd like it." He gave the matter a moment's thought, then added, "And didn't *she* just say that she liked it?"

Valerie wiped her eyes and tried to compose herself.

"Don't you know nothin' 'bout women?" Tyler whispered to his little brother. "She likes it just fine. It's just that women sometimes cry when they're happy. Ain't that so, Pa?"

"*Isn't* that so?" Tricia corrected him. "Right, Miss Carter?"

Valerie sniffed and nodded. "That's absolutely correct, Tricia." She focused on Timmy and said, "Tyler is right, too, when he says that sometimes women cry when they're happy. And I want you to know that I'm happy now. Very, very happy."

Timmy's blue eyes widened. "Well, don't that just beat all."

"It does seem ridiculous, doesn't it?" Valerie agreed.

Paul laughed and mussed Timmy's hair. "Go on over there and get in the food line," he said to his children. "Save Miss Carter and your old pa a place, won't you?"

Once the children were out of earshot, Paul squatted down beside Valerie and took her hands in his. "I hoped you'd like it."

Being eye to eye with him, Valerie could not mistake the glow of love that emanated from his face. "It'll bring me hours of comfort," she said. "It's such a thoughtful and generous gift. I don't deserve—"

Paul held up a hand. "Why are you always forcing me to shush you with those silly notions of yours?" he asked. "You *do* deserve it! Why, you've been...." He paused, searching, it seemed, for the right words. "You taught my young'uns to smile and be happy again. What a wonderful addition you've been to their lives!"

Valerie waited breathlessly, hoping he'd add, "You've been a wonderful addition to *my* life, too." When several seconds ticked by without a word between them, she said, "Speaking of the children, I suppose we ought to join them...."

His eyes never left hers as he nodded his agreement. "I suppose," he said, still holding her hand as she stood up. He released it only when they began to cross the room.

They walked, side by side, to where his three children were standing in a gaggle of other youngsters waiting to get their share of the Christmas meal. "We thought you were gonna sit there all day," Timmy said, his tiny finger teasingly poking his father in the tummy. "Tyler says you're 'moon-eyed' over Miss Carter. What's it mean, Pa?"

Paul's face flushed. He looked from Valerie to his son and back again, twisting his hat in his hands the whole time.

"It means," Valerie said, deliberately and calmly, "that he likes me." She winked at Paul. "Which is very good news to me, because I like him, too."

Greta, who'd been standing in line ahead of them, turned suddenly. "Da two of you ain't foolin' nobody," she said, clucking her tongue. Then, elbowing Paul's ribs, she winked. "Mebbe ve vill haff a June vedding, yah?"

Paul's blush deepened, and Valerie looked away to hide her own flushed face. But not for long. She felt obliged to rescue him from Greta's well-intentioned yet intrusive joke. "Oh, Greta," Valerie teased, "there can't be a June wedding, because Mr. Collins and I have taken permanent vows of chastity."

Greta chuckled. "Yah. Sure. Und dere's a man in der moon who eats green cheese all da day long, too!" With that, she stepped up to the food table and began filling her plate.

"You're going to sit with us, aren't you?" Timmy asked Valerie.

She glanced at Paul and saw the same question in his dark eyes. "Why, I'd love to join you for dinner," she said, smiling.

No one said another word about Greta's comments as they ate. It felt good, Valerie thought, sitting across from Paul at one of the smaller tables and listening to the sweet chatter of his children. It felt familiar and warm. It felt *right*.

The day went on merrily, with moments of prayer and time for games, as well as a special nativity performance put on by the children. But all too soon, the farewells began to float around the homey basement space of the church. Valerie had made sure to spend some time with all of her students and their families. She'd done her share of serving food and cleaning up. She'd played games and sung songs and prayed. Surrounded by all this warmth, she hated the prospect of returning alone to her little house. She wished the day never had to end.

As she shrugged resignedly into her cloak, Paul stepped up behind her and smoothed the dark, woolen garment over her shoulders. "I thought I'd walk home with you," he said, quickly adding, "so I can carry the chair for you, of course."

Valerie smiled, glad he'd sought her out. Glad he wanted to spend these last few minutes of this very special day alone with her. "How thoughtful, Paul. That would be lovely," she admitted.

They trudged along the snow-covered street, chatting about the delicious foods and playful games that were part and parcel of a Freeland Christmas as they went. Now and then, Paul put the chair down to renew his grip on it. Once, when he did, Valerie sat down, telling him she needed a short nap after all the pie she'd eaten. Much to her surprise, he lifted her, chair and all, and resumed walking and talking as though she were still moving alongside him. Only when she threatened to jump over the side of the chair did he stop and let her down.

Inside her home, Paul held the chair as Valerie lit a lantern in the parlor. "Where would you like me to put it?" he asked.

Valerie bit her lower lip and scanned the room, then shoved her old rocker aside. "I can read and sew and grade papers in it," she said, "right here by the warmth and light of the fire."

He slid the new chair into place. "Guess I ought to get back to the church and round up those young'uns. They'll probably be sound asleep before I get 'em home."

Valerie recalled how Paul's children had fallen asleep in the back of his wagon after the church picnic the previous summer. "It's been quite a day," she said. "I'm sure they're exhausted."

Paul took a few hesitant steps toward the door, then turned to face her. He opened his mouth to speak, but no sound came out. With one hand on the doorknob, he took a deep breath. "What Greta said," he began, "...I hope it didn't embarrass you too badly."

Valerie licked her lips. *Embarrass me?* she thought. Why, the woman couldn't have paid her a greater compliment than to suggest Valerie was wife material for a man like Paul! "Of course, I wasn't embarrassed," she admitted quietly. "In fact, I was quite flattered."

Paul sighed, then smiled. "Good," he said. "Because, I must admit, the idea is appealing...."

Blinking, Valerie took a gulp of air as he crossed the room in two long strides and wrapped her in his arms. "Merry Christmas, Valerie Carter," he whispered into her hair. "A very merry Christmas."

She looked up into his handsome face. "And the same to you, Paul Collins."

When he kissed her, she thought she knew what it would feel like to float on a summer breeze. To ride a wave on a stormy sea. Yet there, in the protective circle of his strong arms, she felt safe and secure.

She felt *loved.*

"There are worse things," he said, holding her at arm's length, "wouldn't you say?"

Still reeling from the surprise of his kiss, Valerie took a deep breath. "Worse than what?"

"Worse than being with a man like me, a time-worn, work-hardened father of three."

He read the long silence that followed as a polite rejection and loosened his hold on her. *Too much, too soon,* he told himself, taking half a step back. Just because *he'd* thought and prayed endlessly about this moment didn't mean that Valerie was ready to respond affirmatively right away to his half-baked proposal.

He looked into her pretty face. Into her bright, long-lashed eyes, which glowed like emeralds in the soft lamplight. At the tendrils of shining hair that refused to stay pinned in the bun she'd twisted atop her head. This time, when he kissed her, he wanted the kiss to say what he didn't have the courage to speak aloud: *If the day ever comes when you love me even half as much as I love you, it'll be the answer to a prayer.*

"I have a little something for you, too," Valerie said after their kiss, breaking away and ducking into her room. "I didn't bring it to the church because I had two brothers, and I remember how awkward men can feel when they're the center of attention."

They stood on either side of her new rocker, Valerie grinning nervously as his big hands tore away the red bow and white paper from his present. For a moment, he only stared at it. "No one ever knitted me a jacket before."

"I thought it would help keep you warm as you tend the animals on cold winter mornings...."

Smiling, Paul shook his head. "You're amazing."

Blushing, Valerie said, "I hope it fits."

He held the thick, gray-green knit against his chest. "It's perfect. But it must have taken months to make, what with all your other duties...."

She shrugged. "An hour or two, here and there." She paused. "But if it had taken months, it'd have been worth every moment."

Paul draped the jacket across one arm of the rocker and stepped around the chair to take her in his arms. "It's one of the most thoughtful gifts I've ever received, and it'll keep me warm even when I'm not wearing it."

The month of January brought frigid temperatures and four more blizzards. By February, every road and walkway looked like a tunnel that had been carved between six-foot snowdrifts. The skies seemed endlessly white, with snow clouds looming overhead and threatening to dump even more of the dread white stuff on the tiny town. By March, the few folks who were able to brave the slick streets complained to Greta in the feed and grain about the horrible weather conditions. Even

Mr. Talbot groaned that in all his years, he hadn't seen such a winter. "An' I'm nigh-on to a hunnert years old!"

"Ole Mudder Nature must be mad as a hornet vit us to be punishing us so diss year," joked the shopkeeper.

But Valerie found nothing funny about the harsh weather. She hadn't seen her students in weeks.

Worse, she hadn't seen Paul in weeks. She missed him more than she'd imagined it possible to miss anyone.

One morning, as the first light of day peeped over the windowsill, Scruffy's barking caught her attention. Valerie got out of bed, dressed quickly, and headed outside.

"What's all the racket about?" she asked the dog.

Scruffy only continued to whimper and paw at the ground.

Once she reached his side, Valerie understood. "Why, you silly thing, you. You'd think you'd never seen a crocus before!" she said, patting his head. "Isn't it wonderful! It's a sure sign that spring is right around the corner."

Hunkering down, she leaned nearer the cluster of purple- and yellow-striped blossoms. Their faint fragrance wafted into her nostrils, and she stayed there on her hands and knees in the cold snow for what seemed like an hour before she'd had enough of it.

"Lose somethin'?"

The rich, masculine voice startled Valerie such that she lost her balance and ended up facedown in the flower bed. "Josh Kent," she scolded, ignoring his hearty laughter, "you scared the daylights out of me. What're you doing here at this hour?"

"I heard that mutt of yours all the way down to the jailhouse," the town sheriff answered. "Thought maybe something had happened to you from the way he was carryin' on."

Valerie stood up and brushed the snow from her hands and knees. "I suppose I ought to thank you for your concern," she said, smiling, "but I'm grateful you decided to become a sheriff instead of a doctor. What a bedside manner you'd have!"

Josh's laughter floated around her snow-covered yard. "Don't suppose you'd have a cup of coffee for a sleepy old bachelor, would you?"

"No, but I could whip one up, if you don't mind keeping me company while I do."

Josh followed her up the walk and into the house. "Don't mind a bit. It's not every day a fella has an opportunity to chat with a pretty young lady."

And chat they did. About the dreadful winter. About the spring thaw. About preparations for the upcoming Easter celebration at the church. She'd been in Freeland six months, and Josh had been one of the first citizens to welcome her to town. He made a point of visiting her regularly, just to see if she needed lamp oil or firewood. She was surprised to learn, there at her kitchen table, that Josh played the part of Jesus in the Passion play every year.

"Well, I figure they picked me that first year because of my beard," he said, stroking the hairy growth on his chin.

But Valerie knew better; she'd heard him sing. "It's that baritone that sold them on you. I'll bet you could sing opera if you had a mind to."

Under his thick, dark beard, Josh blushed. "I do enjoy making music with this here instrument God gave me." He told her there was no one to sing Mary Magdalene's part in this year's production. "Missy Putnam used to do it, but she moved on up to Shrewsbury when she married that Marcus boy." He swallowed the last of his coffee, then leaned closer to Valerie. "Don't suppose you'd be interested in the part, would you?"

Valerie giggled and held a hand to her chest. "Me? Why, I couldn't carry a tune in a basket."

Josh shook his head. "Now, don't you be modest with me, Valerie Carter. I've stood in the pew in front of you at church, an' I don't recollect ever hearin' anybody sing 'Rock of Ages' quite as pretty as you."

Valerie tucked in one corner of her mouth. "That's different, Josh. It's easy to sing when your voice is just one in a crowd. But when it's the only one...."

"Why not give it a try?" he prompted her. "Bein' in the play is a real hoot, I'll tell you. An' the reverend's wife cooks a special dinner for anyone who's part of the Passion play...."

Valerie had sung several solos at Harvester Baptist in Richmond, but she had been younger then. Younger and braver and....

"So, whaddya say, Valerie? Will you do it?"

Sighing, she rolled her eyes.

"We'll have to cancel the whole thing if we can't find somebody to do those songs," he persisted. "They're central to the story, y'know...."

"What about Emma Thompson? She has a lovely voice."

Josh shook his head. "Nope. She just gave birth to twin boys, remember? Why, I doubt she'll have time to *attend* the play, let alone be part of it."

"Sue Rosen?"

"Now, I don't like soundin' mean-spirited, Valerie, but why on earth would you want to do that to all those innocent folks? Sue sounds more like a squeaky hinge than a gal when she sings."

"There must be someone—"

"Looky here. The real reason I stopped by, Valerie, wasn't to see what your old dog was a-barkin' about. It was to ask if you'd agree to do this favor for us. I'm on a mission, y'might say. See...I'm the official choir spokesman."

She raised her brows and blinked in shock. "You mean...?"

"Yup. The reverend himself asked for you. Now, how can you turn down an invitation like that?"

Paul had never heard anything more beautiful in his life. He'd been told that, in years past, Missy Putnam had always done well with the melodies for the Passion play, but, listening to Valerie's rendition of the songs, Paul thought he knew what the poets meant when they wrote about angels' voices. The sound issued from her as smoothly as wind slipped through the willows. She sang with her eyes closed, her hands clasped in front of her, and her soft, melodic tones caught everyone's full attention. Even the babies stopped crying, as if the sound of Valerie's voice was soothing them into sleepy silence.

For a moment, as Valerie stood there in front of her fellow parishioners, wearing the blue gown and veil fashioned for her by Jan Bugg, Paul got a picture of her snuggled in the oak rocker he'd made for her, cradling an infant in her arms as she hummed sweet lullabies into its innocent face.

He blinked himself out of the daydream and chastised himself severely. She'd been through a lot in her short life. If he wanted her as his own, he'd have to be patient. He'd have to take his time.

Paul smiled. He wasn't a rich man. He didn't live in a mansion or own a plantation, and, very likely, he never would. He didn't have much money in the bank. But he had time.

Time was the one thing he had a whole lot of.

When the Passion play ended, it took a full fifteen minutes for Paul to elbow his way up to the front of the church to see Valerie. Even then, the two of them were surrounded by the rest of the choir. He sent a silent prayer heavenward. *Lord, if it's Your will, I'll ask her to marry me. Just show me the way so I'll do it according to Your plan for her life and mine.... But first, You have to do me a favor and clear the way, please.*

It didn't surprise him in the least when he and Valerie suddenly found themselves alone at the front of the church. "You were wonderful," Paul said, his fingertips grazing her cheek.

"I was scared out of my wits."

He laughed. "That was *fear* I heard? Why, I thought the tremolo was part of your natural voice."

She laughed, too. "Don't I wish!" Then, "Do you really think I did all right? You don't think I was too loud? Or too quiet? Could you understand all of the words? The lyrics are so lovely, so meaningful, don't you agree? I'd hate to think I'd rushed through them, because folks should get the full impact of what the writer was trying to express," she rambled nervously.

"Well, haven't *you* come a long way in a short time?"

Valerie drew her brows together as she removed the blue veil from her head and draped it over her arm. "I beg your pardon?"

"Just a few months ago, you were positive the Lord hadn't answered any of your prayers because He didn't love you; today, you're concerned that perhaps one of His children missed the true message of the songs. Do I take that to mean you now believe yourself worthy of His love?"

For a moment, she only stared at him. Then, a slow, easy smile spread across her face. "Yes," she whispered. "I believe it now. It's a wonderful feeling, and I have you to thank for helping me find my way back."

Paul shook his head. "You'd have found your way on your own, eventually, I'm sure."

"Well, that's neither here nor there, now, is it?" she asked, winking. "The fact of the matter is, your persistence softened my cold little heart."

He slipped an arm around her waist and led her down the center aisle of the church toward the double doors, thinking of a day in the future when they'd be taking the same walk. He grinned. "Let me remind you that your heart may be a lot of things, Valerie Carter, but cold is surely not one of them."

Chapter Eight

Now, class," Valerie said, "turn to page forty-eight in your geography books, please." She waited patiently, listening to the quiet shuffling of feet as the children reached under their chairs for their books before flipping through the pages to find the one she'd indicated.

She couldn't help but smile, for she loved each and every one of them almost as much as she would had she given birth to them herself. It felt so good to have them all back at the same time that she found it easy to put the miserable winter out of her mind.

If only Abel Johnson's murder were as easy to forget, she thought, distracted for a moment by Abel Junior, who was sitting up front and grinning for her approval.

Valerie couldn't put her finger on it, but she felt an ominous presence in town. She'd felt it very strongly ever since Abel was hanged by the Klan. For a reason she couldn't explain, she believed the Klan members responsible for his death had moved into Freeland quietly, the way rattlers slither under rocks, ready to strike, unbeknownst to those who tread by. The feeling had diminished some during the harsh winter, but she suspected that was because the Klansmen didn't like nasty weather any more than the good folks of Freeland did.

All through the day, as she taught her students about the geography of Europe, as she showed them how to multiply and divide, as she read to them from *Great Expectations*, her fear grew inside her. And though she prayed it away every time, it came right back, like the bad penny her grandmother had always teased her about.

Valerie suspected that whatever was causing her turmoil couldn't be shed as easily as a bad penny.

Less than a week later, her worst fears were realized.

Ardith Johnson, who'd been working as a cook at the Freelander Hotel since Abel's death, had finally saved up enough money to move into a small house at the end of Main Street. After the family had been forced from their home, Rev. Gemmill had allowed Ardith to store her furniture in the church basement, and when the day came to take up residence in her new home, half the men in the parish showed up to help her move in, while their wives provided cool, refreshing drinks and filling sandwiches. By the end of the day, the congregants of St. John the Baptist church were only too happy to let the reverend lead them in a "Praise the Lord this day is over!" prayer.

Valerie could see Ardith's new house from her front porch, and as she turned out her lamp for the night, she couldn't help but grin with satisfaction as she looked across at the warm glow in the windows. It was only fair and right that Ardith and her children had a chance to turn things around for themselves. It was God's answer to the prayers of Ardith's friends that had given them that chance. Her final thought after a day of worry was the satisfaction of answered prayer.

In the middle of the night, her deep, peaceful slumber was disturbed by a shrill scream. Valerie pulled on her robe and rushed to the window to look outside into the darkness.

There, in the middle of Main Street, was a row of men on horseback. Their white hoods and robes matched the coverings on their horses, and the torches they held cast an eerie glow over the town.

"Put up the cross!" shouted the man out front. A large, oddly shaped medallion hung from a thick chain around his neck, marking him, Valerie supposed, as the leader of this pack of savage men. Two of the others jumped down from their horses, while a third man held the reins. In the blink of an eye, a huge, wooden cross had been jammed into the ground in front of Ardith's house.

"Get the coal oil!" the leader hollered. "Soak it! Soak it good!"

Again, his band of evil men followed his orders.

"And now," the leader said, "let the light of Christ burn bright. Let them see and understand that it is not God's plan for niggers to be equal to white men or to live among us." He touched his torch to the foot of the cross and leaped back as flames shot skyward.

Valerie had never seen a more horrifying sight. That anyone could connect the crucifix upon which the Lord Jesus had given His life for all mankind with something as vile and wretched as this turned her stomach.

"Bring the nigger woman here before me!" the leader ordered. "She will be taught a lesson about God's hierarchy on this night!"

Are they going to kill Ardith as they killed Abel? Valerie wondered frantically. *Will her children be forced to watch their mother suffer at the hands of these barbarians, just as they watched their father murdered?*

Valerie could not stand by and allow such a thing to happen. Hurriedly, she stepped into a skirt and boots and, without even bothering to close the door behind her, dashed into the street.

"Stop it!" she cried, running toward the men. "Stop right now!"

The leader crossed both arms over his broad chest. "Go back into your house, Miss Carter," he said. "This is no place for a young lady."

"I will *not* go inside!" she shouted. "I won't let you touch a hair on Ardith's head!"

His laughter grated in her ears like sandpaper. "Little lady," he said, "there's not a blessed thing you can do to stop us."

Two of the Klansmen half carried, half dragged a kicking, screaming Ardith from her new home. Her children ran behind him, crying and reaching out for their mother.

Valerie ran to them and hugged each one. "Go back inside," she said in as soothing a voice as she could muster under the circumstances. "I won't let them hurt her."

Abel Junior, tall for his twelve years, said to his siblings, "Get on inside, now, or I'll tan your hides. I mean it. Scat, now!"

His little brother and sister inched backward, their fingers in their mouths and their dark eyes wide with fright. "Go on!" Abel Junior repeated. "And lock that door behind you when you get inside!"

"You should go with them, Abel," Valerie said.

"I ain't leavin' my ma. If they plan to do her harm, they'll have to do it over my dead body."

She saw that the boy meant business. "Well, stay beside me, then, and do as I say, you hear?"

Abel nodded.

Together, they scrambled for the burning cross. The Klansmen had already bound and gagged Ardith to a tree nearby, and tears were streaming down her smooth, mahogany-colored cheeks.

Valerie ran forward to comfort her, but brawny arms stopped her. "That's about far enough, Miss Carter," said the leader. "We're about God's business, here. This ain't no place for a woman."

"This isn't God's business," she shrieked. "It's the devil's work you're doing!"

Again, his nasty laugh grated in her ears. "You see why females must never be allowed a voice in the church or the government?" he asked his followers. "They don't know what's good for 'em—even the ones what teach our children!" Then, to Valerie, he said, "All right, Miss Carter, it seems you aim to witness what we must do. But you'll do it from the sidelines." He handed her off to the nearest Klansman. "Hold her tight, now," he instructed. "I don't want her interrupting my work."

"Let go of her, you big oaf!" Abel shouted. "Let go, or I'll kick you to the end of the street!"

"Why, you little nigger brat!" the Klansman growled. "I'll carve you up like a Thanksgiving turkey if you try." He shoved Abel hard, and the boy ended up in the arms of another Klansman.

"Hold him, too," the leader said. "Maybe it's good that he sees what we're about to do here. It'll teach him what's in store for him if he steps out of line...."

Side by side, Valerie and Abel, held tightly by the white-robed madmen, watched in silent horror as the leader took a long, thick whip from his saddle horn.

Lord, Valerie prayed silently, *guide my tongue. Tell me what to say to stop this madness!* And in the same moment, a Bible verse came to mind: "*'O God,'*" Valerie shouted, "*'the proud are risen against me, and the assemblies of violent men have sought after my soul....'*"

The leader slapped the ground with his whip. "Quoting psalms will not help her. This much I assure you, Miss Carter."

"*'...And have not set thee before them,'*" she continued in an even louder voice. "*'But thou, O Lord, art a God full of compassion, and gracious, longsuffering, and plenteous in mercy and truth. O turn unto me, and have mercy upon me; give thy strength unto thy servant....Show me a token for good; that they which hate me may see it, and be ashamed.'*"

It was as if Valerie had not spoken at all. The crack of the whip rang out as the vile thing cut through the cotton of Ardith's white nightgown. The woman did not cry out in pain, as the Klansmen were surely hoping she would. Instead, she stood tall, threw back her shoulders, and quoted a Scripture verse of her own: "*'I will love thee, O LORD, my strength. The LORD is my rock, and my fortress, and my deliverer; my God, my strength, in whom I will trust; my buckler, and the horn of my salvation, and my high tower.'*"

"Shut up!" the leader bellowed. "Shut your yap, nigger woman, or I'll tear every inch of the flesh from your bones, I swear it!"

Ardith's eyes blazed into his as she said, "*'I will call upon the LORD, who is worthy to be praised: so shall I be saved from mine enemies.'*"

"You think so, do you?" the leader yelled. "We'll just see about that!" Again, the wicked slap of the whip tore at Ardith's skin. And again, she did not cry out.

Abel struggled against the grip of the man who was restraining him. "Let my mama go!" he cried. "She ain't done nothin' to you. Why you doin' this? Why?"

The leader stomped over to the boy and glared down into his face. "Why, you ask? I'll tell you why." He pointed past the glowing orange cross to his fellow Klansmen. "We have been called to put the ungodly in their place, that's why. And *you*, boy, are unclean and ungodly."

Just as the leader reached out to grab Abel's throat, a loud voice stopped him. "Don't make me pull this trigger," it said.

The eyes behind the white hood met the angry face of the sheriff, who gave another order. "Untie that woman. Untie her now."

Except for the men holding Valerie and Abel, the Klansmen formed a circle around Josh, their rifles and shotguns aimed at his heart, at his head, at his chest. "You wouldn't shoot me, Josh Kent," the leader said, his voice full of arrogance.

"I will if I have to. Oh, I imagine your puppets here will get off a couple good shots, and I'll likely bite the dust in the process." The sheriff's lopsided grin froze on his face. "But the first bullet outta my little six-shooter here is aimed at your left eyeball. Seems a shame for the both of us to die on such a pretty night, now, don't it?"

No one moved.

No one spoke.

No one dared.

"Uncock your weapons, gentlemen." Josh directed his next comment to the Klan leader in a calm, quiet voice. "If I have to ask you again, I'm afraid there's gonna be a nasty ole bloodstain on that nice, white sheet of yours...."

The faceoff lasted only long enough for the leader to see that Josh was serious. "You'd really die to save this nigger woman?"

"I would," Josh said without hesitation. "Now, untie her."

The leader never took his eyes off Josh. "Do it," he instructed his followers.

"And turn them others loose, too," Josh added.

The men holding Valerie and Abel looked for guidance. When the leader nodded, they pushed their hostages to freedom.

"Don't think this is the end of things," the leader said, mounting his horse. "We have a mission, and we aim to see it through to the end."

As the pack of men rode away, Valerie ran to Ardith and untied her wrists. "Are you all right?" she asked, hugging the woman.

Ardith nodded. "I thought I was a goner for sure," she said, her voice trembling. "If you hadn't come out when you did.... You saved my life, girl."

Valerie ignored the comment. "Abel," she said, "take your mother inside and get her a cool drink of water. I'll be in soon to clean her wounds. Go on, now."

Without a word, Abel led his limping mother back to the house. He returned to the doorway for a moment to smile weakly and wave to Valerie. "God bless you, Miss Carter. You saved my mama." With that, he closed and locked the door.

Valerie ignored Abel's comment, too. "Josh," she said, "thank the good Lord you got here when you did. It was *you* who saved Ardith and Abel's lives. You're a hero!"

"Let's have none o' that. I was standin' there long enough to hear you puttin' it to 'em."

"But it was your authority that made them—"

"If you hadn't stalled 'em, I couldn't have done what I did. She'd've been dead long before I got here if you hadn't come out and raised such a ruckus."

Valerie took a deep breath. Only then did she realize she'd been trembling. "I'm going to see about Ardith's injuries. I'm sure she has some tea in the cupboard. Will you join us, Josh?"

She noted a slight tremor in the brave sheriff's hand as he ran it through his thick, dark hair.

Grinning from ear to ear, he holstered his gun and fell into step beside her. "Why, I'd be right proud to share a cup of tea with the bravest woman I've ever met."

All was quiet in town during the following week. The Freelanders, thanks to Josh, had heard what Valerie had done in the dark that night, and, one by one, they'd made it a point to congratulate and thank her.

All but Paul.

What she'd done had been brave, indeed. But it could have cost her her life. For days after he heard the news, he berated himself. If he'd asked her to marry him at Christmas, like he'd planned, she'd have been safe in his house when the incident occurred. On the other hand, he had to admit that if she had been his wife on that terrible night, Ardith Johnson might not have lived to see another day. He wavered between admiring Valerie's bravery and being angry that she'd put her life on the line. Because, bluntly, when she'd stood up for Ardith out there, all alone in the street, she could have been killed. Her death wouldn't have been an accident, as Rita's had, but it wouldn't have been any easier to bear.

He avoided her for two weeks, not knowing how to face her. He was more proud of what she'd done in defending Ardith than he'd ever been of anyone. If only that good feeling would squelch the residual fear of losing her.

Why can't she be more like other women? he wanted to know. *Why can't she be satisfied with a simple life of darning socks and baking pies? Why does she have to be so all-fired involved in life?*

But even as he asked these questions, Paul knew that if Valerie was more like other women, he never would have fallen so completely cap over boots in love with her.

Her independent spirit meant she'd be a true partner, and he knew that, too. She'd never whimper and whine when life tossed its worst at them. She wouldn't stand aside and let him bear the burdens of getting by, day by day, by himself. No, Valerie would shoulder her share. She'd insist on doing so, in fact. She wouldn't notice if Suzie Jackson wore a hand-me-down hat to church. Her conversations wouldn't center on recipe collections and quilt patterns. She wouldn't need to boast about the good deeds she'd done for the church, because the good deeds would be out there in the plain light of day for everyone to see.

Yes, Valerie would be a true partner. And Paul yearned for that—someone who would not only have a hot meal waiting for him when he returned from working the fields all day, but would also have an opinion waiting for him, too. Some of her strength of character would rub off on his children, he knew, and it made him smile just thinking about it.

Most of what he wanted from life, he wanted for his children: A roof over their heads. Three square meals a day. Clean clothes on their backs. But what he wanted for himself was simpler still: a life with Valerie. He'd learn to live with the outbursts of indignation at injustice that prompted her to do things like she'd done for Ardith. Maybe, just maybe, it was part of God's plan for him to teach her a little of what he'd learned about patience.

The very idea made him chuckle. Valerie had come to town freely admitting she'd fallen by the wayside in matters of faith, but when she'd finally found the righteous path again, she'd begun walking straight down the middle of it. No twists and turns in Valerie's road to the Lord! More likely than not, God's plan wasn't for him to teach her about patience at all. More likely than not, God intended to teach *him* a few things—through Valerie.

Paul remembered wishing on the day he'd met her that he could be a boy in school again. If it was true that God would use her to teach him a few things, Paul sensed that the lessons would be learned and never forgotten, and he believed learning would never be more interesting...or fun.

The planting season, like the harvest, very nearly emptied the classroom, much to Valerie's dismay. But living in a farm community required a teacher to be inventive. To be original. To find unique and special ways to ensure that her students wouldn't miss a single lesson.

And so, just as she'd done during the harvest, Valerie started making weekly trips to the absent students' homes, as well as accepting supper invitations to the same tables that had welcomed her before.

She'd nearly finished her meal of fried chicken, mashed potatoes, and snap beans at Andy Cooper's house when she noticed his dad glaring at her from across the table. She blamed his hard days in the fields for his angry, hateful expression. She blamed her many sleepless nights of devising special lesson plans for her heightened sensitivity. She blamed the uncharacteristically hot weather, the lack of rain....

Stodgy and standoffish, Henry Cooper had never been an outgoing man, and Valerie considered herself lucky if she got a polite hello out of him after Sunday services. On previous visits to the Cooper farm, she'd found his wife warm and friendly...but only as long as her husband wasn't around.

Valerie could blame the stars and the moon and the sun, if she wanted to, for Henry's nasty disposition. But she knew in her heart why his beady, brown eyes bored into her as they did, and she knew exactly when it had started.

The previous week, in the leather goods aisle at Greta's, she'd been trying to decide between a pair of brown or black work gloves when Ardith had come into the store. The three women had chatted a while and paid no attention to Henry, picking through the bin of shirts in search of one large enough to hide his huge belly.

It was when he'd turned to give her a full view of his face that Valerie had looked into his eyes and recognized him as the leader of the white-robed gang. The man under the sheet who'd shouted orders like a drill sergeant had had a huge belly, too. Suddenly, Henry had hollered at Greta, "You don't have much of a selection for anybody who's not a beanpole. Next time you put in an order, consider that, why don't you?"

Listening to that voice was like trying to digest ground glass, because it was the very same voice that had ordered Ardith's beating, the voice that likely would have ordered the widow's murder, had Josh Kent not shown up when he did.

Valerie and Ardith had exchanged quick glances. It was obvious by the fear widening the older woman's eyes that she, too, had recognized Henry as one of her captors.

"*'The Lord is known by the judgment which he executeth,'*" Ardith had whispered, quoting Psalm 9:16; "*'the wicked is snared in the work of his own hands.'*"

Valerie had grinned at the appropriateness of it. "And by the words from their own mouths," she'd whispered back.

Henry had glowered in their direction. "Women," he'd huffed angrily, "got nothin' important to say. At least you're thoughtful enough not to waste your breath sayin' it loud and wastin' others' time."

"*'Be not far from me; for trouble is near,'*" Ardith had said.

"You'd better stop that," Valerie had warned her, "or he's liable to—"

"Liable to *what*?" Henry had demanded.

They'd been so busy giggling and whispering that they hadn't heard his approach. Valerie had stood straight and cleared her throat. "Why, Mr. Cooper," she'd said, "I was just telling Ardith what a lovely time I had out at your place last fall. You're very blessed to have such a devoted family."

Frowning, he'd shaken his head and stomped out of the store.

"Have a nice day, Mr. Cooper," Valerie had called after him.

She'd barely heard his grunt of displeasure.

She'd certainly had no idea what it had meant.

At least, not until now, as she sat across from him at his own supper table.

Valerie knew it like she knew her own name. When or where or how, she didn't know, but Henry Cooper meant to make her pay for interfering with his murderous mission.

Chapter Nine

Two uneventful weeks passed, yet Valerie knew better than to let down her guard. She prayed hard and often that if and when Henry struck, she wouldn't be near any of her students.

Every time Andy Cooper was absent from school, she worried his father would take that opportunity to seek vengeance.

But she couldn't let such concerns distract her from her duties. Two of her students, David Garvey and Laura Harper, would graduate this term, and she had a lot to do to get them ready for the big day. The two students agreed to stay after school a couple of days a week to catch up on the work they'd missed during the planting season.

When David had indicated his desire to continue his education, Valerie had contacted some friends in Virginia and secured him a scholarship at the University of Richmond. When he finished college, he'd return to Freeland as a veterinarian. He worked hard to complete his extra assignments.

Laura, on the other hand, was happy just to be finishing school. She was getting married in less than a month, and most of her attentions were focused on final wedding plans.

The three of them were gathered around Valerie's desk one afternoon when what sounded like a herd of stampeding cattle interrupted their studies. Valerie peered out the window to see what had caused all the noise and gasped to see the Klansmen riding boldly in broad daylight.

"Hurry!" she exclaimed to David and Laura. "Go out the back door and run home as fast as you can. Tell the sheriff the Ku Klux Klan is paying me a social call."

"I won't leave you here alone with them," David insisted. "They're crazy. My pa says they'd kill at the drop of a hat. But what do they want with you?"

"They are crazy, indeed. Which is precisely why you both must leave. If you really want to help me, you'll fetch the sheriff, and you'll not waste a minute doing it!"

Valerie shoved them out the back door, hoping the Klansmen hadn't yet surrounded the schoolhouse. It seemed like an hour passed from the time she'd heard the horses' hooves to when the white-robed men burst into the schoolroom.

She was seated behind her desk as they approached her. "Well, gentlemen," she said coolly, "to what do I owe the pleasure of your company this afternoon?"

"You're stirrin' up trouble," the leader said, "tellin' folks not to listen to our message, tellin' folks we're crazy as bedbugs an' such. And I aim to see you stop it."

"Are you threatening me, Henry Cooper?"

He stood stock-still—amazed, she presumed, that she knew his identity.

"No threats necessary, ma'am. What we bring are promises: You stop bad-mouthin' us, an' we'll leave you alone."

She stood up slowly and rested the palms of her hands on the top of her desk. "And if I don't?"

Henry snickered quietly. "If you don't...." He glanced around the room at the shelves lined with books. At the blackboard. At the neat rows of desks. "If you don't, you can kiss all this good-bye."

She'd expected him to threaten her, personally. Never in her wildest imaginings had she thought he'd destroy the schoolhouse! "Your own son is getting a fine education here in this building," she said, coming out from behind her desk to face him squarely. "Someday, Andy will grow up to be a fine man. He's a smart boy. He could go far in this world, provided you don't do something stupid, like interrupt his education to further your—your *mission*." She spat out the last word to show him her distaste for him and all that he stood for.

"You have a choice, Miss Carter: stop spreading lies about this organization, or *we'll* stop *you*."

"'*For so is the will of God, that with well doing ye may put to silence the ignorance of foolish men,*'" she recited, boldly meeting the men's eyes peeking through the holes in their horrible hoods. "I will continue to do what I believe in my heart to be right."

"Mark my words," Henry said, his voice full of venom, "we will do what we must—"

"...to fulfill your mission. Yes, I recall your saying something similar the night all of you big, strong men overpowered one helpless woman and her child. Well, you mark *my* words: if anything happens to this schoolhouse, or to as much as one page of any book on these shelves, I'll know who was responsible. I'll gladly testify—"

"Won't be necessary," came the voice of Josh Kent. "Law says when an officer of the court witnesses a violation, he can make an arrest on the spot. No witnesses required."

Valerie smiled. Josh was becoming her knight in shining armor, one heroic deed at a time.

The sound of his pistol being cocked cracked the silence of the room. In seconds, rifles, shotguns, and handguns echoed the sound. "I said it before, and I'll say it again: take note of where the barrel of *my* gun is aimed, Cooper. And just for the benefit of you boys in the back... that would be dead center in his hard, little heart. And unless you believe his heart is hard enough to stop a bullet, you oughtn't be standin' behind him thataway."

The eyes in the hoods' holes widened.

"One shot, and you're gonna have to call a special meeting to appoint yourselves a new boss."

Henry lowered his weapon and gestured for his men to do the same. "By gosh, Henry," one said, "this is gettin' to be a bad habit. I ain't a-goin' to be part of terrorizin' women an' children no more." With that, he turned on his heel and stomped out of the schoolhouse. Two more Klansmen followed close behind.

Henry whirled around and shouted after them, "Go on and run off, ya yellow-bellied cowards. The rest of us will protect the white race in spite of you!"

"Protect it from *what*?" Josh demanded. "Seems to me the only thing threatenin' us is dunderheads like you. Now, why don't you climb back up on your ponies out there and ride on home? Have yourself a nice, hot supper and a good night's sleep. With any luck, you'll wake up tomorrow with the sense God gave you and put all this nonsense behind you, once an' for all."

When nobody moved, Josh took a step forward. "Go on, now, git. All o' you, before I get mad an' do somethin' ornery."

The four men still standing behind Henry filed out of the schoolhouse, one by one. Two of them added their hoods and robes to the pile of those left behind by the first men to flee, leaving only Henry and two devotees to ride away in full costume.

"You ain't seen the last of us," Henry hollered as he rode off. "Not by a long shot."

"It's gonna take a long shot," Josh hollered back, stuffing his gun into its holster, "'cause you ain't got the courage to do anything out in the open, up close."

When they were gone at last, he draped an arm over Valerie's shoulders. "Little Missy, ain't there *anythin'* you're afraid of?"

His protective embrace opened the floodgates, and she let herself lean against his strong chest. "There,

there," he soothed, stroking her hair. "It's over...at least for now."

"I feel responsible somehow."

Valerie frowned. "Why, Paul, that's just silly, and you know it," she said matter-of-factly. "You were nowhere nearby on either occasion. Why would you feel responsible?"

Paul had to give her that. Even on his fastest horse, he couldn't get from his farm to the schoolhouse in less than thirty minutes.

He couldn't remember feeling more frustrated. The woman he loved had twice been in jeopardy, and there hadn't been a blessed thing he could do but listen afterward, helplessly, as the sheriff bragged about what a stouthearted little lady Valerie was to go head-to-head with the bad guys the way she had.

Again, he found himself wishing he'd proposed to her back in December.

But he didn't wish to have her as his wife simply to protect her. He wanted her because—*because I love her*! he admitted for the hundredth time.

And this time, he was determined to do something about it. Which was why he'd saddled up his big, black mare and made her gallop at full tilt all the way to Valerie's house.

She'd been peeling peaches when he arrived. Now, after several minutes in her tiny kitchen, watching her peek into the big, bubbling kettle to check on her canning jars and lids, he felt his impatience mounting. He wanted to take her in his arms and ask her to marry him.

She looked pretty, as usual. The white apron she wore ruffled daintily around her shoulders, and she'd wrapped her flowing hair with a red bandanna, accenting her cherubic face.

Paul didn't know which was sweeter—the sugary peaches boiling on the stove or the woman who'd smiled and invited him inside.

After pouring him a glass of lemonade, Valerie put him to work ladling fruit into the wide-mouthed jars that covered her kitchen table. When he splattered juice on his trousers, she stood behind him and wrapped a linen towel around his waist. Having her arms around him felt as normal and natural as breathing, and Paul was sorry when she finally tied the knot at the small of his back and stepped up to the stove to stir the peach pot.

He decided to leap right into the subject of her second altercation with the Klan. "If you were a cat," he said sullenly, "you'd already have used up two of your nine lives."

Valerie giggled. "Well, then, I guess we're both glad that I'm not a feline, aren't we?"

"It's no laughing matter, Valerie. You've got to stop barging into situations that put you in danger."

She put her hands on her hips and narrowed her big green eyes at him. "Now, you wait just a minute, Paul Collins. Let me remind you that on neither occasion did I voluntarily enter into a confrontation with the Klan. I appreciate your concern, but I resent your talking to me as if I were your responsibility. You're not my husband, and—"

"Yet," Paul interrupted her.

Valerie blinked absently at him. "What?"

"I'm not your husband. At least, not yet."

She busied herself rearranging jars on the tabletop.

"I'd have asked you to marry me months ago if I'd known you'd go and get yourself into trouble at every turn."

Her hands stopped in midair above the table, and a tiny grin formed on her face. "Trouble? That's all it would have taken to get you to pop the question?"

He put down the ladle and met her gaze. "Are you saying that if I'd asked you to marry me, you'd have said—"

"Miss Carter!" called a tiny voice from the other side of the door, "Mama sent me over to borrow a cup of sugar."

"Come in, Florence," Valerie said, holding the door open for the little girl. "What's your mother up to today? Cobbler? Cake?"

Florence giggled. "She sent Pa to pick a basketful of grapes, and now she's a sugar-cup short of turnin' 'em into jam. She said to promise you a jar in return for the loan."

Valerie handed the child a large, sturdy mug filled with sugar. "You tell your mother it's a deal!"

Florence eyed the table covered in jars. "What're *you* makin'?" she asked.

"Peach preserves," Valerie said, buttering a thick slice of bread, then slathering it with a spoonful of preserves. "Here," she said, handing it to Florence. "Let me know if it's any good."

At the little girl's bright-eyed grin when she took a bite, Valerie handed her a jar to take home to her mother.

Seeing Florence made Paul remember his own children, and he prepared to head home, albeit a little reluctantly. As Valerie was packing up three jars of preserves for him to take home, he whispered into her hair, "We're going to finish that conversation, Miss Carter. And soon. You can count on it." With a wink and a grin, he waved a quick good-bye and left her standing there, alone, in her kitchen.

She thought about his parting comment long after all the peaches had been canned and the jars had been stored away in her tiny root cellar. Long after the canning utensils had been washed up and put away.

Just before sunset, she settled into the rickety, old rocker on the front porch to watch the sky turn orange and purple. Thanks to Paul, she felt like the wealthiest woman in Freeland. She couldn't name another lady in town who had *three* rocking chairs! Later, as the night sky twinkled with stars and fireflies, Valerie decided that if Paul had been serious—if he did really plan to propose to her—she'd have no choice but to say yes. And she'd say it loudly and quickly, so he wouldn't have even a moment to change his mind.

The scene in the church basement on Christmas Day unfolded behind her closed eyelids: three loving children and one loving man, all of them needing her every bit as much as she needed them.

The Lord had blessed her, for sure. But how long would He test her patience? How long until Paul would say the words she longed to hear? *Paul, Paul, why persecutest thou me?* Valerie thought, smiling wryly.

At long last, graduation day arrived. Valerie had sent invitations to everyone in town and hoped they'd all show up for the school's first real ceremony.

She decorated the schoolhouse with red, white, and blue banners in honor of the occasion. It was such a lovely day that she dragged out every bench, chair, crate, and box from the schoolhouse and stood them in neat, orderly rows in the shade of the oak grove behind the school. David Garvey and Laura Harper had prepared short speeches to inspire and encourage the classmates they were leaving behind, and the younger children had written a play in honor of the graduates.

Songs had been rehearsed.

Awards had been printed.

Diplomas had been penned.

In less than an hour, Valerie would stand at the lectern and introduce two students who had come to mean so much to her during her first year as Freeland's schoolmarm. For their sakes, she hoped every seat would be filled.

She'd made a huge bowl of fruit punch and baked two cakes and six pies. Greta had volunteered a smoked ham, and Mrs. Gemmill had promised to bring her famous baked beans.

At last, the long-awaited moment arrived. David, wearing a stiff-collared shirt and a neat, black bow tie, sat straight and tall in one of the two ladder-back chairs that faced the audience. Laura, her hair tied up in a pretty, pink bow, wore a lovely white dress and matching pinafore. As Valerie, in her white-trimmed navy frock, took her place behind the podium, Rev. Gemmill cleared his throat and coughed to command silence from the crowd.

"Ladies and gentlemen," Valerie began, "I am so pleased to see how many of you turned out to share in this wonderful day with David Garvey and Laura Harper. They have worked hard to reach this goal, and I'm sure it means a lot to them to know they have your support and congratulations.

"David will be leaving us soon, as some of you know. He'll be gone for several years, and we'll miss him greatly."

David blushed when she smiled approvingly at him.

"When he returns, we'll most likely present him with a shingle that reads, 'David Garvey, Doctor of Veterinary Medicine.'"

She waited for the applause to fade away before continuing.

"Laura Harper, soon to become Mrs. Jonathan Hall, will remain here in Freeland, I'm happy to say. She's agreed to be my teaching assistant, so your children will have the benefit of not one, but two teachers!"

Again, she waited for the applause to fade before going on.

"Soon, each and every child in our little school will sit where David and Laura are seated now," Valerie continued. "I'm certain of that. We're fortunate to have such dedicated and hardworking young people among us who will someday contribute to our little community in the same way their parents and grandparents before them did.

"They'll achieve that end because of you," she said, gesturing toward the audience. "You built this school. You hired me. You see to it that your children come here every day. Your unfailing dedication as parents, relatives, neighbors, and friends is directly responsible for Freeland's promising future."

She reached under the podium and retrieved two black album-like booklets, then held them up for all to see.

"In these leather bindings," she said, "is the official proof that this young man and this young woman have completed their primary educations. But the true proof of all they've learned is in the eyes and minds and hearts of David and Laura.

"David Allen Garvey," she said, slowly and deliberately, "will you please join me at the podium?"

David walked stiff-legged across the lawn and came to stand beside Valerie, grinning and blushing like a small boy, even though he was head and shoulders taller than his teacher and outweighed her by at least fifty pounds.

"This is your diploma, David," she said, placing it in his outstretched hands. "I am so very proud of you!"

She hugged him and blinked back tears of joy, then said, "Laura Ann Harper, it's your turn...."

Laura tiptoed gracefully toward the stand and, looking down, smiled happily.

"You've earned this," Valerie said, handing the girl her diploma. "I'm proud of you, too."

Laura gave Valerie a tight hug. "Thank you, Miss Carter," she said. "I couldn't have done it without you." Then, she held her diploma high in the air and squealed with girlish delight.

❃

Paul had taken a seat in the last row, though he'd arrived early enough to sit up front. His children, preferring to sit with their friends, were clustered in the middle rows, where they could whisper and giggle without disturbing the adults around them.

He'd sat back there so he could watch Valerie.

When she'd taken her place at the lectern, he'd feared his face would crack from the width of his proud smile. She looked lovely in her feminine dress; her thick, chestnut-colored hair refused to stay pinned in the proper schoolmarm's bun. She was so at ease in front of these people—smiling and meeting their eyes, gesturing with her delicate little hands, and adding emphasis to various statements now and then with a nod of her head.

Her sweet voice, as clear and crisp as the blue sky above, had carried her message of congratulations to everyone present. And her pride in David and Laura's accomplishments had shone brightly in her big, green eyes. Even from way in the back, Paul could see the soft curve of her long eyelashes.

During Valerie's speech, she'd met his eyes once and had sent him a smile so glorious that he'd thought his heart would burst with love. She was so many wonderful things all wrapped up in one tidy package—strength and warmth, intelligence and grace, beauty and love. And if he had his way today, he'd add another adjective to the list: his.

Chapter Ten

Valerie applauded the new graduates, and the rest of the townsfolk joined her.

While neighbors and relatives congratulated David and Laura, Valerie waved at Paul. Grinning, she half ran to join him at the back of the crowd. He'd walked across the little bridge above Licking Creek that separated the school yard from the road and was standing beneath the maple where they'd shared many sweet conversations. Valerie was glad he'd chosen this place, far from the gleeful crowd, where they'd be able to share a precious moment of privacy.

When Valerie had a little more than ten feet to go before she would grasp Paul's warm, welcoming hand, she froze. Her wide, loving smile of greeting faded instantly, replaced by a mask of disbelief and terror.

Paul had no time to register her fright. He was still wearing that wide, welcoming grin when the dull thud of the club connected with his skull.

Valerie opened her mouth to scream for help, but two white-hooded men rushed at her from either side. One clamped a huge, sweaty hand over her mouth, rendering her silent; the other held her arms. A third man suddenly joined them and jammed a dirty rag in her mouth. As Valerie squealed and struggled to free herself, she saw Paul drop limply to the ground.

And then, helpless to overpower her oppressors, Valerie watched the bright afternoon turn dark as the men yanked a burlap sack over her head.

Her feet, shuffling and scraping as she tried to escape, made no sound on the soft, grassy lawn.

Her screams, muffled by the gag, went unheard.

Then, Valerie felt herself be hoisted over one man's shoulder, carried away like a helpless kitten, and deposited none too gently into the back of a wagon that was filled with what felt like hay.

The ride was long and hard. She tried to pay attention to the noises she heard as they bumped along. Cows mooing. Horses whinnying. Crickets chirping. Locusts buzzing. All so clear, so ordinary—yet not one told her where these men were taking her.

She didn't need a detective's mind to know *who* had taken her. Henry Cooper, no doubt, had ordered her abduction. But once he got her where he wanted her, what would he do with her? Would he torture her? Would he beat her and then hang her, as he had tried to do to Ardith Johnson? Or was the whole kidnapping merely a ruse to frighten her into succumbing to his demands to stop spreading negative reports about the Klan?

"*Ye shall not need to fight in this battle: set yourselves, stand ye still, and see the salvation of the Lord with you.*" Repeating 2 Chronicles 20:17 in her mind brought her a small measure of comfort. A very small measure.

Valerie searched her memory for more Bible passages that would help her remain strong, verses that would help her stand firm once the wagon stopped and her captors announced their demands.

Ephesians 2:5: "*By grace ye are saved.*" Psalm 25:2: "*O my God, I trust in thee:...let not mine enemies triumph over me.*" Proverbs 15:3: "*The eyes of the Lord are in every place, beholding the evil and the good.*" Jonah 2:7: "*When my soul fainted within me I remembered the Lord.*" Deuteronomy 20:1: "*Be not afraid of them: for the Lord thy God is with thee.*"

Valerie clung to that last one from Deuteronomy, repeating it over and over in her mind. It had a somewhat calming effect.

Until the wagon stopped.

Valerie wanted to trust the Lord to protect her, but she knew that no one had seen these men steal her away; they'd clubbed Paul and left him there, alone and unconscious. She hoped someone had found him by now and was tending his head injury.

She whispered a prayer for his safety and well-being: "*'Be not afraid of them: for the LORD thy God is with thee.'*" Then, she said it again with conviction as rough hands grabbed her and yanked her from the wagon. She was led over a grassy area and on to a patch of gravel that crunched beneath her feet for about three steps.

She was on solid ground now.

Hard and...smooth?

The air around her became suddenly chilly, and the pinholes of light that had been filtering in through the burlap bag went out.

The men's movements, their footsteps, and even their whispered commands echoed loudly.

We're in a cave! she realized, fighting to control her terror. *No one will ever find me—or hear me—in here....* "*'Be not afraid of them...,'*" she prayed fervently, silently. "*'Be not be afraid....'*" She realized that if she let them see her fear, she might never get out of this mess alive.

"Take that thing off her head and let her loose."

Valerie recognized the voice as Henry Cooper's.

"But she'll know who we are," said another man.

"Not if you keep your hoods on," Henry barked.

Soon, blinking in the brightness of their torches, Valerie stood face-to-face with her abductors. She bit her lower lip to keep it from trembling.

"Not so brave now that you don't have your highfalutin sheriff around to protect you, are you?" Henry asked, his voice smug with hatred.

Valerie found herself unable to speak. What would she say? That she *was* brave? That she *didn't* wish Josh would show up?

"I warned you to keep your vile comments about the Klan to yourself. What's that old saying? *'Physician, heal thyself'*?" Henry laughed long and hard. "Let's put a twist on it, why don't we? Teacher, listen and learn. You taught the children to obey direct instructions but never learned the lesson for yourself."

"No one saw you kidnap me," Valerie said, finding her voice at last. "What sort of example can you set for the others who might oppose you if no one knows what you've done? You can't very well volunteer this information. If you could do that, you wouldn't need to hide your identities behind those horrible masks."

The eyes behind the gaping holes in Henry's hood grew increasingly fierce and angry. "That's where you're wrong, missy. We have ways of spreading the word. Folks'll know what happened to you, all right. And they'll know *why*."

She'd never been this afraid for her life. Not when she'd gotten lost in downtown Richmond at the age of six. Not when she'd wandered away from a family picnic and had had to climb a tree to escape a black bear. Not even on the day the Yankees had set fire to Carter Hall. Those things had been accidents. Matters of happenstance. Events that had occurred according to no particular plan to harm Valerie Carter. But these men had a deliberate plan, and she was at the center of it.

"How can I be such a great threat to your mission?" she asked, suddenly angry. "I'm one voice. One woman. What damage can I do to you or your movement?"

Henry gave a short, nervous laugh. "In better days, I'd have agreed with you, little lady. But, unfortunately, you've got more power than you know. Some of my men have gone soft, thanks to your sorry little message about equality and freedom. And some of 'em believe that nonsense you've been quoting from the Constitution.

"We've lost over a dozen members since you started your anti-Klan campaign. People had been falling into line left and right, with hardly a backward glance. But now...." Henry shrugged and shook his head. "Seems they don't want to offend Uppity Miss Carter. Maybe they're afraid you'll quit teachin' their young'uns, afraid they'll never find another teacher as gullible as you to work as hard as you do for the tiny salary they give you."

Henry was angry, all right—angry at her powers of persuasion, at the number of friends she'd made in town. But if she'd persuaded any of them, it had been only because she'd quoted what God and the country's forefathers had deemed right and true, and they'd agreed!

"What are you afraid of, Henry? That some Negro or Jew will stand beside you and, by contrast, make your ignorance shine like a beacon for all to see?"

With the back of his hand, Henry slapped her. Hard.

Two of his followers stepped forward, as if to defend her.

"Get back!" Henry barked. "Or there'll be some of that for you, too!"

The pair hemmed and hawed, uncertain whether or not to obey.

"Put that rag back in her mouth. I've heard about enough from her for one day."

While his followers hunted up the rag to do Henry's bidding, Valerie filled the cool, quiet air with questions: "How did you get so filled with hate, Henry? What happened to turn your soul black and your heart to ice? What makes you so sure your message is good and holy?"

The other men looked at him hard, as though, suddenly, merely hearing Valerie's simple questions, they were wondering the same things.

"Get that rag in her mouth, I tell you!" Henry growled. "If I have to do it myself, I swear I'll stuff it so far down her throat, she'll choke before we have the chance to hang her."

"Hang her!" one of the men shouted. "You never said anything about hanging her. We were only supposed to bring her here to teach her a lesson about being quiet and obedient. I told you the night you hung Abel, I'd not take part in any more killings, or in the beating of white women, Henry."

"I'm with you," another man said. "Killin' niggers ain't worth goin' to prison or swingin' at the end of a rope."

"It *is* worth your lives," Henry shouted, his crazed voice echoing through the hollow interior of the cave. "If you're not willing to give your life, you don't belong in this army. If you're not willing to lie down and die for the cause, you don't deserve to call yourself a Klansman."

"Maybe you're right," said the first man.

"Not maybe—definitely," agreed the second.

The pair of them marched out of the cave, tossing down their robes and hoods.

That left Henry only three followers.

"Get out there and make sure they understand what'll happen if they don't respect the oaths they took when they joined up," he told two of them. "The fires and the noose can be set up just as easily where they live, y'know."

The men hurried outside to deliver the warning. During the next hour, the soft shuffling of feet, an occasional clearing of a throat, and several deep sighs were the only sounds in the damp, chilly cave. But the Klansmen never returned.

"No matter," Henry said. "We can summon up as many reinforcements as we need that fast," he added, snapping his fingers, "by sending a one-line telegram to Tennessee. Those lily-livered cowards are of no worry to us. All of 'em know where they stand...and where they'll fall if they cross us." He glared at Valerie. "If we're feelin' real Christian in the mornin', we might just come back with some food for you."

Then, with a wave of his hand, he bid his last soldier follow him out of the cave. They took their lanterns with them, removing all light and the warmth, as well.

Valerie slid down the cold, rock wall and huddled against a boulder, shivering. The man who'd put the gag in her mouth hadn't done a very thorough job. She wondered if it had been an accident, or if he'd been reexamining his conscience, too.

Carefully, so she could drag it back between her teeth should the men reappear, Valerie deposited it on the ground beside her.

Goosebumps pimpled her forearms. Her heart thumped wildly. "Our Father, who art in heaven," she prayed through her tears, "deliver me from evil...."

When Paul came to, he was looking up into the worried faces of his children and the sheriff. "What in tarnation happened to you?" Josh asked him. "You've got a knot on the back of your skull the size of a goose egg."

Paul winced with pain as he tried to sit up. Last thing he knew, he'd been walking toward Valerie in the school yard. "How'd I get here?" he wanted to know, squinting around at the interior of Doc Gifford's office.

"Your young'uns came and got me," Josh said, "and I fetched the doc once I saw how far out of it you were."

"How long have I been out?"

Doc opened his pocket watch. "Nearly two hours. Think you can stand up?"

It took Josh and Doc supporting him, but Paul managed to get to his feet. He stood there for a moment, wobbling on limp legs. Suddenly, he remembered the last thing he'd seen before everything had gone black—Valerie's terrified, wide-eyed expression. She'd seen something she'd tried to warn him about. But what? "Where's Valerie?"

Doc shrugged. "Dunno. Nobody's seen her since the graduation ended."

Paul struggled to free himself from his friends' grasp. "She's not at the schoolhouse?"

"Nope," said Josh.

"What about her house? Has anyone looked there?"

Josh only frowned. "Now, why didn't I think of that?" he said, sarcasm ringing in his voice. "Give me a little credit, Paul—that was the first place I looked!"

"But—"

"Sit down, Paul, before you fall down," Doc said. "Say something comforting to these children of yours. They've been hovering over you, worried sick, since they found you under the oak tree in the school yard."

Paul slumped onto the cot against Doc's office wall and looked into their faces to see the same terrified expressions they'd worn when they'd seen the Yankee bullet rip through their mother. Before he said another word, he had to reassure them that he was all right. "C'mere, you guys," he said, holding out his arms. The children piled into them and snuggled close. "Your old pa is fine," he said. "I've got me a headache the size of a watermelon, but I'm just fine." He kissed their foreheads. "Now, what say you take this nickel here," he said, digging in his pocket, "and run over to Greta's. See if she'll fix me up with a nice, cold bottle of root beer to make my headache better."

The children scrambled to their feet and headed for the door, happy to be doing something—anything—to help their father feel like his old self again. When the door banged shut behind them, Paul met Josh's gaze.

"She hasn't been seen or heard from since the graduation?"

"That's right, Paul," Josh said. "I've been all up and down Main Street, askin' about her." He shook his head and shrugged. "Nothin'."

Paul held his head in his hands. He'd been on the verge of asking her to marry him. Right on the cusp of making her his for the rest of his life...if he was lucky. "Well," he said, running his hands through his hair, "you must have some idea what happened. Tell me what you think."

Josh and Doc exchanged worried glances. "Might not be a good idea, Paul. We know you're kinda...soft on Valerie."

Paul shook his head. "Soft? I'm crazy in love with her, man! If I hadn't taken this hit on the noggin, she'd have this ring on her finger by now!" Paul reached into his shirt pocket. Slowly, tenderly, he unfolded a red bandanna. Inside, a simple gold band glittered in the lamplight.

"Well, I'll be," Doc said.

"Would ya look at that," Josh added.

"I have a right to know what your suspicions are," Paul insisted.

"Do ya reckon she'd a'said yes?" Josh asked, a slight smile slanting his mouth.

Paul nodded. "Yes, I think she would have. At least, I surely hope she would have...."

Again, Josh and the doctor traded serious glances. "Guess we might as well tell him the worst of it," Doc said.

Josh took a deep breath, sat down on Doc's rolling stool, and leaned his elbows on his knees. "It's like this, Paul.... We found footprints in the flower garden near her porch. Big prints. Lots of 'em. And the tracks of at least a dozen horses. Shod horses, mind you." He stared at the floor between his booted feet, as if telling Paul that the rest of it hurt him as much as he knew it would hurt Paul. "Somebody was watchin' her, Paul. On more'n one occasion, from the looks of things."

"The Klan...."

Doc nodded. "Who else?"

"We followed their trail. Led us right to the hitchin' post beside the school. And the wagon tracks...." Josh frowned and stared out the window. "The wagon tracks lead up into the hills."

Paul stood and headed for the door. "Well, what are we waiting for? Let's go and find her!"

"Sit down, you fool man," Doc said. "There's more. And you're not going to like this last piece of news one little bit."

Paul's head swam and his legs felt rubbery. He did as Doc suggested.

"We followed the wagon tracks into the hills. But that's where they end. We can't be sure which direction they headed in once they parked the wagon."

Paul glanced out the window to see that the afternoon light was already beginning to fade. Again, he held his head in his hands. Not one living soul had ever seen him cry. Not when the heart attack had taken his father. Not when he'd received the news about his brother. Not even when a bullet had ripped through Rita. But now....

Josh and Doc shuffled from one foot to the other, not knowing what to say or do to comfort their friend.

Valerie could only hope the quiet scraping noises she heard weren't the sounds of a bear. Or a snake, on its way home to seek warmth from the cool, night air. In the light of day, she had no fear of such things. But then, there was little to fear from things one could see....

Henry had left enough slack in her bindings to allow her to move her hands. The gag she'd removed from her mouth still rested on the ground beside her.

She almost physically swallowed her fear and noticed, dismally, that even the simple act of swallowing had grown difficult. That puzzled her, until she recalled a newspaper story she'd read about savage Indians out West who tortured settlers by binding them with damp strips of rawhide. As the strips dried, they tightened, strangling their victims...slowly.

Henry had tethered Valerie in just that way once his loyal devotees had fled the cave. He'd bound her wrists and ankles, then looped the strip twice around her neck.

Already, she felt its deadly strands drying, tightening, cutting off her breath.

Stay calm, she told herself. *Think!*

Was that water she heard dripping in the distance? She strained to identify the sound coming from somewhere deep in the belly of the cave, then started crawling toward it. If she could find the steady water supply, she believed, she might be able to lie beneath it so that it would drip on the bindings and keep them damp.

Scraping across the rock-hard cave floor, she tore her dress and stockings, and knew she was bloodying her knees, too. One foot landed with a *splat* in a tiny puddle. "Praise the Lord—water!" Leaning against the wall, she allowed the cold liquid to drip onto her bindings one icy plop at a time.

Sleepiness threatened to overtake her, and she knew she needed to fight it. If she gave in to slumber, she might slump to the floor, out of the water's path. And if that happened, the rawhide ties would dry as she slept, and....

Valerie thought of Paul. About his hint at marriage. She'd gladly tie herself to him for a lifetime, if he asked.

Her mother had always said, "Love is the tie that binds." Valerie grinned sardonically. *Mother's words have a totally new meaning today*, she thought.

Her eyelids drooped as drowsiness set in.

Suddenly, a high-pitched squeak echoed through the cave. Then came more of the scraping sounds she'd heard earlier, followed by a flurry of flapping wings.

Bats! she realized, ducking instinctively.

But she was in no danger from the bats, she knew. The only peril she faced was in the form of rawhide strips.

She prayed the Twenty-third Psalm. She said the Lord's Prayer. She sang "Amazing Grace" with more conviction than ever before. She counted all the way to three thousand five hundred and sixty-six.

She also recited the Gettysburg Address. She'd clipped it out of the newspaper because it had moved her, and she'd memorized it for the same reason. If she'd known little things like this could help pass the time during a kidnapping, she'd have memorized the Preamble to the Constitution. The Bill of Rights. The *entire* Constitution, for heaven's sake!

She hadn't eaten since morning, and the hunger pangs were becoming more pronounced.

Why doesn't someone come? she ranted silently. Even the Klansmen would be a welcome sight at this point.

Well, almost.

At least she'd know once and for all where she stood with them. Whether or not they planned to hang her. Or turn her loose. Or beat her the way they'd beaten Ardith. Or....

The possibilities frightened Valerie even more than the actual threats had. She said a prayer that when the time came, she'd be strong and brave, that she wouldn't give them the satisfaction of knowing how terrified she was.

She said another prayer for Paul's safety.

And, despite her best efforts to avoid it, she drifted off to sleep.

Chapter Eleven

Valerie slept so deeply that she was temporarily oblivious to the fact that her bed was made of stone.

Her dream took her back in time—took her south to the wide, warm plantation known throughout Virginia, Carter Hall.

But the beauty of the vast landscape burned up before her very eyes, and, as she dreamed, Valerie could feel the fire's residual heat. She stood stock-still in the ashes and listened as a soft wind sighed through the row of pines lining the farm road; listened as it echoed across the mansion's foundation, where the housekeeper, Marjorie, had recently dusted the polished wood floors for her mother's annual Christmas ball.

There, where bright fires had once licked pot bottoms in the keeping room's hearth, the crackling power of the Yankees' torches burned instead.

Valerie cried softly, almost silently, as she stepped through the remains of Carter Hall, picking her way through the debris in search of something—anything—she could take with her, something to remind her of this house and the people who had called it home.

Smoke plumes rose up from the sooty earth and threatened to choke the life from her, just as the blaze had choked the life from Carter Hall.

She was grasping her throat when she awoke. Grasping her throat and sobbing. Immediately, she realized that her leather bindings had begun to dry as she'd slept. She patted the cave floor in search of the puddle....

Finding it, she sighed with relief, understanding fully why the treasured liquid had so often been called "life sustaining."

As she lay back and let the droplets fall, one by one, onto the ties that bound her, Valerie shivered and recalled her dream.

She supposed she'd been reliving that awful day from her past because the events of it had terrified her so much. They had changed the entire course of her life, just as the events of these past two days and nights had.

Perhaps the nightmare had returned here, in the chilling bleakness of the cave that was her prison, because it offered the promise of warmth, even if the memories were cold.

Valerie remembered stepping into an icebox with her father once. A train had pulled in at the station near the docks in Norfolk, Virginia, and she'd stood aside as her father inspected a shipment of fruits and vegetables from the Caribbean. Huge chunks of sparkling, translucent ice had lined the walls of the boxcar, and the floors, wet with puddles, had stunk of remnants of shipments past—fish, meat, poultry, and vegetables from faraway lands. Being in that cold place had reminded the young Valerie of the evening fogs that so often blanketed the streambed near Carter Hall, though the air in the boxcar hadn't clung to her in the same seemingly mystical way.

Being imprisoned in this cave made her think of that boxcar, though the frigid temperature had no man-made cause; it was from the powerful hand of Mother Nature.

Valerie blinked into the semidarkness and welcomed this second morning of life. Obviously, since the Klansmen hadn't returned as Henry had threatened they would, it seemed they intended to leave her in the cave to starve to death—that is, if she didn't choke first.

She shook her head to clear the frightening thoughts from her mind.

Well, she had no intention of just lying down to die. She'd fight to live, even if it killed her!

It took Valerie the better part of an hour to struggle to her feet. Once she'd achieved a fully upright position, she leaned for a moment against the chilly cave wall to secure her footing and catch her ragged breath.

First, she canvassed the cave floor, which seemed to span endlessly between her and the cave's entrance. The ground was smooth and flat. She took a few unsteady jumps forward, then stopped, deciding instead to take tiny, shuffling steps like the Oriental girls on the Richmond docks, who dressed in kimonos and wore tiny thongs on their feet. It was slow going at first, especially since she was forced to consider that without her arms free to protect her, a fall would probably leave her unconscious until....

Valerie swallowed, feeling the pressure of the leather strip around her neck. Her energy, she believed, would be far better spent planning her survival.

Sunshine brightened the sky outside the mouth of the cave, and with the light came warmth—warmth that would dry her damp skirt and petticoat, warmth that would dry the leather, too....

She didn't have a moment to waste.

She surveyed what lay beyond the cave and saw, perhaps a hundred yards from where she was standing, a field of white daisies. She hobbled toward it. On the other side, she hoped, there'd be a road. A well-travelled road.

She moved forward, glancing back once she reached the edge of the field. From here, the entrance to the cave looked like a yawning giant. Should she return to what she knew for certain, or head for parts unknown?

Either way, whether out here in the bright sunshine or inside the gloomy cave, the leather would surely dry and tighten and....

Valerie dropped to her knees and prayed, "'*Be not afraid....: for the* Lord *thy God is with thee....*'"

When she looked up, the horizon, even with all its uncertainty and potential pitfalls and dangers, looked far more welcoming than the ugly, black mouth of the cave. She was tired. Every muscle and joint ached. She was hungry and thirsty. And frightened.

All she wanted was to lie down and sleep, to put this miserable moment in time far, far behind her.

She'd rest here, surrounded by the lovely white blossoms, but for a moment....

Paul, Josh, and Doc led the search party.

The moment the men of Freeland heard what had likely happened to their beloved schoolmarm, twenty-three of the town's strapping gents had picked up rifles, shotguns, and sidearms to join the hunt. They'd been at it since the night of the town's first graduation ceremony. Since then, they'd seen two sunrises.

They'd combed every square inch of the roadside where Josh had seen the last of the wagon wheel's tracks. With the help of two saplings growing alongside the road, Paul pulled himself up an embankment. From his new vantage point, he was able to survey the countryside in all directions.

Shielding his eyes from the sun with one hand, he scanned the horizon, praying as he did for some sign that the Klansmen had brought Valerie in this direction.

Almost immediately, he noticed a broken branch in the brush up ahead. And beyond that, he saw a fallen, rotting limb that was crushed—possibly by a large, booted foot. "Over here," he called to his fellow searchers. "I think I've spotted something."

Hurrying ahead, he looked for other signs and clues that humans had been where usually only wild things tread. And he found them: broken branches. Crumpled underbrush. A smashed wildflower. A footprint in a patch of caked mud. The evidence was everywhere, and he hooted with glee.

"Look at that," Josh said, pointing at the cave. It seemed they all saw it at once, and they ran full tilt toward it, into it, only to find an empty, hollow, echoing chasm.

"She's been here," Josh announced, putting one knee on the floor as he bent to pick up a grimy rag. "Get a whiff of that," he said, handing it to Paul.

Taking it, Paul inhaled, eyes closed, then whispered, "Roses...."

"There's only one way she could have gone," Doc said, standing in the opening and clutching his black medical bag, "and that's straight ahead." He held up a scrap of leather. "We've got to assume she's been tied, so I don't suppose she could have gone very far. I'll bet if we head in that direction," he added, gesturing ahead, "we'll catch up to her in no time."

"She could have been moving all night," Josh said. "No telling how far she'd get in that time."

"She mighta got turned round in der voods," DeWitt put in.

"Not if her wrists and ankles are bound," Paul said, marching up the gradual incline that led toward the field of daisies. "I was right," he said almost immediately. "You can see that she's been taking small steps...."

The others gathered around to have a look at the tracks Valerie had made.

Hope filled Paul's heart, and he had to restrain himself from running ahead. "She's too smart to have tried moving through here in the dark," he said. "She'd have waited for first light. If she started out this morning, she can't be more than a few hundred yards ahead of us...."

The men fanned out and moved forward, not letting an inch of ground go uncovered. In less than thirty minutes,

Josh whistled to get the others' attention. Once he had it, he pointed at the deep-blue mound just beyond the clearing.

Paul's eyes followed Josh's directions until he, too, saw the mound.

Blue.

Deep, dark blue.

Like the dress Valerie had worn to the graduation ceremony.

No, not *like* the dress she'd worn—it *was* the dress she'd worn....

Paul raced toward the small mound, not stopping until he was beside her. "Valerie, honey," he panted, pulling her onto his lap, "are you all right?"

Woozily, she grinned up at him. "Well, it sure would be nice to scratch this itch on my nose. Can't reach it, though," she said, giggling, "'cause I seem to be all tied up at the moment."

Paul smiled. Only Valerie could use humor in such a moment. Gently, Paul cut the binding from around her neck, followed by the ropes that bound her wrists and ankles. But when she was finally freed from her restraints, much to his surprise, she didn't scratch her nose at all. Instead, she threw her arms around his neck and kissed his cheek.

"My, but you're a sight for sore eyes, Paul Collins! Now, would you mind helping me up?" she said. "I dearly love daisies—they're my all-time favorite flower, as a matter of fact—but I don't relish the prospect of spending another moment facedown in a field of them!"

The search party held back and gave the two a few moments of privacy before joining them. When they finally did, Josh folded his arms over his broad chest and asked, "What's the story here?"

Valerie sighed. "Well, Josh, I hope you have plenty of time, because it's a long, strange story."

And then she fainted.

❀

The Klan's hold on Freeland wasn't as tight as everyone had imagined. In fact, the stranger who had come to town to solicit recruits for the movement left town on the same day that Henry Cooper was arrested for abducting Valerie. "We have too much important work to do," the man whispered between the steel bars on the window of Henry's jail cell, "not to leave any witnesses." He adjusted the cinch on his saddle as he concluded, "We trusted you with this regiment, Cooper, but you proved yourself unworthy of that trust. You were sloppy, and it cost us. We'll continue on as planned, and the movement will grow stronger without the likes of you."

Because Valerie couldn't bear to see the Cooper family lose their only means of support, she didn't press charges against Henry. Neither did she name any of the other Klansmen who had abducted her. In place of gratitude, Henry met her with the same hate-filled eyes as before. Somewhere within him beat the heart of the old Henry Cooper—the Henry who, before his involvement with the Klan, had been a kinder, gentler man. Still, his heart was ashamed of what the new Henry had done and somehow talked him into selling the farm. No one knew where the family would go.

No one much cared.

The last anyone saw of the Coopers, they were heading north as the wedding march for the newly graduated Laura Harper began. Valerie missed seeing the procession down the center aisle because she couldn't make herself go inside the church. Instead, she stood on the porch, her eyes fixed on Andy Cooper's sad face. She watched it grow smaller as the distance between him and the only home he'd ever known grew. Just before he disappeared from view, he raised his hand and waved a final good-bye. "I'm sorry," he mouthed silently. "I'm so sorry...."

Valerie knew she'd see that pained expression in her mind's eye for a long, long time.

Paul stepped outside in time to see what she'd seen. "What are you doing out here all by yourself?" he whispered, cupping her elbow. "You're missing the whole wedding."

Once she'd settled beside him in the pew, he held her hand and stared straight ahead, pretending not to notice the tears that were rolling down her cheeks. Her tears weren't caused by the emotional nature of a wedding ceremony, as those of many other women were. No, Valerie's tears were for Andy Cooper.

Paul gave her hand a little squeeze. He'd made few commitments in his life but took them very seriously. Now, he made a new commitment—he promised himself he'd do everything humanly possible to make sure Valerie would never have cause to cry again. That was one promise he aimed to keep.

He'd discussed his hopes of marrying Valerie with the children as recently as the night before, and they'd seemed as excited and pleased about the plan as Paul himself. *No time like the present*, he thought.

Rev. Gemmill's voice droned on as he read from the book of Genesis. Paul leaned closer to Valerie and said softly in her ear, "Marry me."

For a moment, he suspected that she hadn't heard him, for she continued to stare straight ahead. Blinking. Silent.

"Did you hear me?"

He watched her smile and nod, then felt her give his hand a little squeeze.

"Is that a yes?"

She nodded again and gave his hand another little squeeze.

"Look at me when you say it, then."

When she did, her green eyes brimmed with unshed tears. This time, he knew, they were tears of joy.

"Yes," she whispered.

"Yes, what?" he teased.

"Yes, I'll marry you."

"Shhh!" scolded Mrs. Potter, who was seated behind them. She rapped Paul's shoulder with her folded Spanish lace fan.

Paul turned around and said to the older woman, "I asked her to marry me, and she said yes!"

"Well, it's high time," Mrs. Potter whispered. "Now, face the front, young man, before I tan your hide like I used to when you were a naughty boy."

Paul's grin broadened. "Yes'm."

"Did you hear that?" Tricia asked her older brother. "Right in the middle of everything, Pa asked Miss Carter to marry him!"

Tyler grinned and rolled his eyes. "What're we s'posed to call her after *they* stand up there?"

Tricia hid her giggle behind a gloved hand.

Timmy tugged his big brother's sleeve. "What's all the whisperin' about?"

Tyler and Tricia exchanged amused glances. "Nothing," they said together. "Just a lot of grown-up wedding talk," Tricia explained quietly, patting her little brother's head.

At the sound of his daughter's voice, Paul met her eyes. *Why, she's positively beaming!* he thought. He glanced at Tyler and, finding the same expression on his son's face, felt his heart lurch with joy.

After the wedding, as Paul, Valerie, and the children waited their turn to congratulate the newlyweds in the receiving line, Timmy stood in the middle of the vestibule and proclaimed in a loud voice, "Miss Carter's gonna be my ma! Pa asked her to marry him, and she said yes!"

After a moment of stunned silence, much handshaking and cheek-kissing followed congratulatory wishes.

"Got a date set yet?" Josh Kent wanted to know.

"Planning to have more children right away?" asked Mrs. Potter.

And, from Doc, "We'll sure miss seein' your pretty face in town, Miss Valerie, when you move out to the farm."

"Vill you bring der young ones on der honeymoon?" Greta asked.

Paul blushed and Valerie giggled.

"What's a honeymoon?" Timmy asked, inspiring hearty laughter all around.

Valerie looked thrilled and overjoyed. But she said she did not want the attention that had been focused on their announcement to overshadow the happy couple. "This is Laura and Jonathan's day; there will be no more talk of any wedding but theirs!" she announced in her firmest schoolteacher's voice.

As part of the Fourth of July festivities every ear, Doc organized the Great Freeland Mule Race. For a dollar, anyone with a nag, pony, donkey, burro, or mule could register to run, and the winner received all the registration money. This year, a fancy Western saddle, donated by the new owner of the blacksmith shop, would be second prize. Third prize, as always, was a free supper for two at the Freelander Hotel.

Some of the men began betting on which entrant would come away with each prize. Josh's sturdy pony was the favorite, but Doc's keen eye chose Bertram Gardener's quarter horse to win.

Many proper and devout Christians clucked their tongues at the sinful practice of gambling. "*'Having food and raiment let us be therewith content,'*" they said, quoting the Good Book. "'...*For the love of money is the root of all evil: which while some coveted after, they have erred from the faith, and pierced themselves through with many sorrows.*'"

Valerie, however, was not as quick to pass judgment. She believed her parents to have been the most God-fearing, God-loving individuals she'd ever known. Their weekly tithes and donations to charities had been generous. They'd taught her to trust the Lord and to pray to Him. Yet they hadn't condemned gambling outright.

Soon after her father, Lee, had assumed management of Carter Hall, a storm had threatened to ruin his promising tobacco crop. So, to encourage his hired hands to harvest the crops before the storm blew through, Lee had allowed the men to bet on who would pick the most tobacco in the least amount of time. By sundown, Willis had filled ninety-nine and one-half bushels with the broad, green leaves, and he'd gone home to his wife and children in their white cottage nearly ten dollars richer. He'd used the money to buy a rugged little wagon and a nag named Beulah.

The hands had worked harder that day than they'd ever worked; the tobacco crop had come in long before the storm had torn through the river valley. And the work had been done by happy, satisfied men. Never before had Lee seen them smile as they worked; never before had he heard such laughter.

So, Lee had made it a regular event. He'd raised their incentive to work hard as each crop was harvested, whether it be corn or cotton or tobacco, by promising to match the number of quarters in the sack with an equal number of his own. Fun and profit, the astute businessman had learned, were excellent incentives.

Valerie often heard the good Christians of Freeland denounce betting and gambling. But if her good and decent father, who'd worked his fingers to the bone, side by side with his men, had thought it all right to place an occasional wager, then how could it possibly be wrong?

She'd overheard Paul, in the feed and grain, telling Greta that the long dry spell had all but destroyed his corn crop. "It'll take a hundred dollars to see us through the winter," he'd admitted to the elderly shopkeeper, "and to buy enough seed for next year's crop, too." His broad shoulders had slumped as he'd added, in a weaker voice, "But I don't expect it to happen."

The money Valerie had been squirreling away was burning a hole in her bread box. If she put the money on the Mule Race, and won, Paul would have the money he needed!

Doc was honest, straightforward, and smart; as such, he had been chosen to keep an accurate record of the wagers. Valerie slipped into his office and slapped ten dollars on his desk. "I think Bertram's horse will win the race," she announced.

Leaning back in his squeaking swivel chair, Doc smiled. "That's a lot of money to lose if you're wrong—"

"I know that. But it isn't money I earned. It's money I found in Mama's Bible. I saved it all this time for an emergency...."

His brow furrowed with concern. "There's nothing wrong, is there, Miss Valerie?"

She put him at ease with a grin and a wave of her hand. "No, of course not." She didn't feel right telling Doc about Paul's money troubles. "It's just that if I win, I can put the money to good use." She clapped her hands. "Maybe for a store-bought wedding gown!"

Nodding with approval, Doc opened his ledger book and added her name to the list of bettors, then wrote the amount of her bet beside it. "Good luck," he said, holding out his hand.

Valerie shook it. "I don't really believe in luck," she said, smiling, "but thanks just the same."

❀

The marching band had gathered on the hill overlooking Freeland Road and then marched down Oakland Road, right to the center of town, where the band members now surrounded the big, white gazebo in which Mayor Jenkins gave a long-winded "Why We're Thankful to Be Americans" speech. Then, Rev. Gemmill said grace, and the picnic began.

As the townsfolk ate, the gazebo became a stage where Jimmy Tucker did his juggling act, Tommy Morris showed his neighbors a few magic tricks, Billy Schuster played the banjo, and Marta Gemmill sang six country ballads, accompanying herself on the mandolin.

Just before one o'clock, the final preparations were underway for the big race. Horses and riders lined up in front of the blacksmith's shop as a crowd gathered on either side of Main Street. Rev. Gemmill said a prayer for the safety of all the participants, and then the riders settled into their saddles.

"On your mark," Doc called, his starter pistol aimed at the fluffy, white clouds overhead, "get set...go!"

With whoops and hollers, the riders were off, leaving nothing behind but the curious onlookers and a cloud of dust. The course wound through the town and its outskirts like a wrinkled ribbon. There were six steep hills, two shallow streams, one rocky gorge, and a deep valley to cross before the riders hit the trail that ran alongside Middletown Road. When they crossed the finish line in about an hour, they'd have traveled fifteen miles.

Paul and Valerie left the starting line and rejoined the children in the picnic area behind the church. Together, the soon-to-be-complete family enjoyed slices of Greta's famous apple pie. The cheers and applause of most of the bettors, still gathered up and down Main Street as they awaited the winner, could be heard from where they were sitting at a table beneath a huge silver maple tree.

"I truly don't understand why a man would take his hard-earned money and bet it on something as frivolous as a horse race," Paul said around a mouthful of pie.

His angry expression and tone of voice made Valerie stop chewing. Was Paul really among those who thought betting was wrong?

As if he'd heard her thoughts, Paul said, "I say any man who'd do such a thing isn't just a fool—he's a sinner, to boot."

Valerie swallowed the mouthful of pie and stared at what remained of the slice before her. She'd never heard such venom in his voice. Obviously, he felt very strongly about this issue. What would he say if she won? Surely, he wouldn't accept any money that came his way by what he believed to be wrongful means.

And when he learned about her bet, what would he think of her? Would he break off their engagement, unable to yoke himself to a fool...and a *sinner*?

Valerie's smile vanished, and she pushed her pie plate away. Suddenly, she had no stomach for sweets.

Chapter Twelve

Politely, but without explanation, Valerie excused herself from the table. She sought out Doc in the crowd and, when she found him, grasped his hand and pulled him gently away from the group with whom he had been standing.

"Say, missy, what's goin' on?" the confused man asked.

"Paul—he said—he's...."

Doc's grin became a frown. "Is everything all right?"

Valerie sighed and plopped onto a nearby bench. "No, it's *not* all right. I'm a—I'm a *sinner*!"

Doc sat down beside her and patted her hand. "Now, what on earth would make you say a silly thing like that? When it comes to bein' *good*, why, you could write a book!"

She glanced over at the finish line. Soon, one rider would cross it, and if that rider was Bertram....

She sighed. "Paul doesn't believe in gambling, Doc. And I put ten whole dollars on that race," she said, her voice trembling.

Doc snickered. "Is that all?"

She met his clear, blue eyes. "Is that *all*? Why, it's *everything*. He said anyone who would bet his hard-earned money is a fool and a sinner. He'll think I'm...." She paused, wringing her hands. "He'll *know* what I am when he finds out what I've done. It won't matter that I did it for him. To a good Christian like Paul, a sin is a sin. Oh, my, what am I going to do?"

Doc took a deep breath. "You placed a bet for a man who doesn't believe in gambling...." He shook his graying head. "Help me understand this, Valerie."

"Well, of course I didn't know he opposed gambling when I placed the bet," she explained. "You see, I did it only because I heard him telling Greta he was worried about making it through the winter. It's been so dry this year...and the corn crop is so poor...and this year's corn would pay for next season's seed.... I just thought if I could get the money, if I helped him...."

"You're rambling, Miss Valerie," Doc teased, gently chucking her under the chin.

Valerie blinked back the tears stinging her eyelids. "What am I going to do, Doc?"

He put a reassuring arm around her. "I brought Paul into this world, Valerie, so you could say I've known him all his life. He's a kind man. Patient. I'm sure that when he hears the whole story, he'll understand."

"But what if he thinks he made a mistake when he asked me to marry him? What if he doesn't want a sinner raising his children? What if he breaks our engagement?"

Doc laughed. "If he does that, then *he's* the fool." After a moment, he added, "And a sinner, too."

Valerie frowned. "Paul? A sinner? Hardly."

"Waste not, want not," Doc said. "I can't think of a greater waste than to let a woman like you go, now that he's got you."

But Valerie seemed not to have heard the doctor's reassuring words. "I can't wallow in fear and self-pity a moment longer. I have to *do* something before I lose my mind!" She sat up straight and lifted her chin. "It'll be best if I tell him myself. Before the riders get back, rather than after...."

"Probably," Doc agreed.

"I suppose I should go and find him now."

"I suppose."

"Maybe he won't be as angry as I think...."

"Maybe."

She stood up and nervously brushed imaginary crumbs from her skirt. "I guess there's no time like the present."

"I guess."

She met her older friend's eyes. "Thanks, Doc."

"Hey, what are friends for?" Then, winking, he added, "And, speaking of friends, maybe you ought to hunt down the reverend, get his view of things before you meet up with Paul."

She nodded. "Good advice. Thanks again."

Doc watched Valerie walk away, her tiny shoulders squared, her narrow back straight as an arrow. From what he'd heard, she'd survived a lot of misery in her short life, yet she acted now as if this thing with Paul was the biggest adversity she'd ever faced. Doc knew this much: If Paul Collins did reject Valerie over this difference of opinion, he wasn't the man he'd always thought him to be.

Rev. Gemmill was sitting alone on the glider swing behind the gazebo when Valerie found him. A mouthful of his wife's pie caused his cheek to protrude. "Valerie," he said, swallowing. "Please, won't you join me?"

She sat down next to him and smoothed her skirt.

"My, my, my. What's got that pretty face all twisted in sadness?"

Valerie sighed. It seemed she'd been doing a lot of that today. "I have a sin to confess—I think."

That inspired a quiet chuckle. "A sin...you *think*?"

Valerie nodded. "You see, I overheard Paul saying he needed money...." She leaned forward and whispered, "You'll keep that piece of information to yourself, of course...."

Smiling, Rev. Gemmill nodded. "Of course."

"Well, I had a little money saved up—not enough to see him through the winter, you understand—but enough. And I heard that some folks were betting on the Mule Race, and—"

The reverend held up his hand. "Let me guess: You placed a wager on...which, Bertram's horse?"

Valerie nodded.

"Well, first of all, let me say that if you're going to be a gambler, at least you're going to be a smart one. My daddy raised quarter horses, and I know something about 'em. And that filly of Bert's is a winner, for sure."

Valerie's heart fluttered. "Do you mean—"

"Now, don't misunderstand me. Just because I feel his horse will win doesn't mean I believe it's all right to place a bet on it."

Her heart sank.

"Gambling can be a dangerous thing. Like drink, it can tempt us into compulsions that are unhealthy—spiritually, emotionally, and bodily." He sat back and took a deep breath, then shook his head. "Now, I know there are those in town who don't believe there's a single thing wrong with placing an innocent little bet now and again. In fact, I happen to know that some of Freeland's most upstanding citizens do it regularly...though I'm sure they'd prefer to keep it secret from me," he added, smirking, "for fear I'd suggest the money would be better spent in the collection plate!"

Valerie explained her father's technique for gathering the tobacco harvest, hoping to justify why she'd done such an impetuous and foolish thing.

"Interesting. Very interesting. But here's the long and the short of it: In order for a gambler to win, everyone else must lose. Human nature dictates that somewhere deep inside, the gambler will actually begin to *hope* everyone else will lose so that he can collect the winnings, if you follow me.

"It's an issue of brotherly love, when you get right down to it. And what did Christ Jesus say about that? He said, *'Thou shalt love thy neighbour as thyself.'* Now, how can you love your neighbor at all if you're hoping against hope he'll lose his dollar so that you can win it?"

Valerie sighed again. The reverend was right, of course. Staring at her hands, folded primly in her lap, she shook her head, then looked up at him. "So, if a thing is wrong, then it's wrong always...and in all ways." She bit her lip to stop the tears that threatened. "Paul's right. I'm a fool and a sinner."

"Don't be so hard on yourself, child. Yours is more a sin of immaturity than a sin of evil. There's no question that you were misguided, just as there's no question that you did what you did to help the man you love."

The man you love, she repeated in her head.

Until today, Paul had loved her, too. She could only pray that, once she confessed everything to him, he'd love her enough to forgive her sin of covetousness.

"He's a good man," the reverend reminded her as she stood up to leave, "with a good and generous heart." He smiled gently. "Remember, in the truth, you'll find freedom."

Freedom in Freeland.

Ironic, she thought, that the first thing she saw when she looked away from his friendly face was the "Welcome to Freeland" sign that stood proudly in the town square.

Next, she saw Paul's tall silhouette headed straight toward her.

"Where on earth did you disappear to?" he wanted to know, wrapping her in a warm hug. "I've missed you!"

She found that she couldn't meet his eyes. Shame burned in her cheeks. "I've been...talking with friends," she answered.

"Is that so? Well, now it's time to talk to your future husband." He took her hand and led her to the courthouse steps. "I think it's high time we set a date. How would you feel about an autumn wedding?" he asked, sitting down on the top step and patting the space beside him.

She sat down. "Before I answer that, I've a confession to make."

Paul's quiet laughter soothed her—almost. "What could a sweet, young thing like you have to confess?"

She turned and faced him. "I think you should know, before we exchange lifetime vows, that you're linking yourself to a sinner. And a fool."

Confusion creased his brow.

"I'm afraid that—"

Just then, the hollering started. "They're coming!" someone shouted. "The riders are on their way!"

Paul jumped up and hurried down the brick courthouse steps. "Well, don't you want to see who'll win?"

She tucked in one corner of her mouth. "I'm not the least bit curious," she said sullenly.

"Well, come stand beside me, then, while I watch the winner cross the finish line." He held out his hand and waited until she put hers in it. "Go ahead," he said as they headed for the crowd. "Pick a winner, if you can."

"I'd really rather not."

"Don't be a spoilsport. Tell me who you think will win."

Valerie sighed. Again. "Bertram," she said dully. "I think Bert is going to win."

Paul nodded. "I agree. That filly of his is prime stock. Strong flanks. Good lines. Bert can surely use the prize money." He paused, then asked, "Since you're so astute at choosing winners, who'll come in second?"

"Josh's pony."

"Seriously?"

She nodded. "Almost as good as the quarter horse...."

"I think Josh will enjoy his new saddle." Then, almost as an afterthought, he said, "Know what I wish?"

Her heart swelled with love and admiration as she looked up at his handsome face. It hammered so loudly, in fact, that she barely heard the thundering hooves of the horses, just a mile or so from where they stood. "What do you wish?"

"I wish I had a fast horse."

"You would have entered the race?"

"Indeed, I would. But not for the money. Not for that saddle, either."

Valerie blinked, waiting for him to explain why he would have run the race.

"Third place would have been prize enough for me."

Third prize, she recalled, was dinner for two at the Freelander.

"I'd like nothing better than to treat you to a fancy evening out. You deserve only the best, you know."

The heart that had been pounding furiously skipped a beat. "No, that's where you're mistaken," she said.

"Does that nonsensical comment have anything to do with what you said back there at the courthouse about having a confession to make?"

Valerie nodded, and her heart went back to beating doubly fast.

He draped an arm over her shoulders. "Well, just for the record, no matter what you say, I'm gonna love you till the day I die."

She stood there, stiff and silent, praying it was true.

"Okay, spit it out. Tell me this awful thing that's been eating at you all afternoon."

Just then, Bertram blew by them on his prized horse, followed by Josh on his pony. One by one, the riders passed as the crowd applauded, cheered, and whistled through the thick cloud of street grit the horses had kicked up.

While everyone else ran over to congratulate the winners in front of the blacksmith's shop, Paul and Valerie hung back near the finish line.

"I love you, you know," he said quietly. "Nothing you say is going to change that."

Tears welled in her eyes, and a sob choked her words. How could she do this to him? How could she sentence him to a lifetime with a woman who knew so little about faith and spirituality and purity that she'd stupidly place a bet?

He deserved a woman with a good heart. A woman who knew the Bible as well as he did, so she could help instruct his children—and theirs, when they came along—in the ways of the Lord. He deserved a devout, pious, Christian woman, not some bumbling, fumbling fool who'd childishly gamble in the hopes of turning a profit at the expense of her friends and neighbors!

"Valerie, you're crying. Tell me what's wrong, sweetheart. You know, if we're to be married, we should be able to tell each other anything...."

If we're to be married....

She wanted to tell him to go and find the woman he deserved, for that woman surely wasn't she. But a sob stuck tight in her throat, allowing no sound to escape.

Even if she could swallow and make it go away, the tears that spilled down her cheeks would prevent her from telling him what he needed to hear.

Valerie took great pride in the fact that she'd never been one to run from trouble. Instead, she consistently faced it head-on. So, it confused her as much as it did Paul when she turned and ran toward the shelter of her little cottage behind the schoolhouse.

She sat alone at her tiny kitchen table and stared at the pile of money for nearly an hour. What would she do with it? She couldn't give her winnings to Paul; he'd made it crystal-clear how he felt about gambling. She couldn't donate it to the church; Rev. Gemmill had been equally emphatic about ill-gotten gains. And she certainly had no intentions of keeping it for herself....

Perhaps Doc could use it to buy some newfangled surgical tool. Or supplies. Or medical books.

Josh might take it—hadn't he said last week that the cots in the jailhouse were infested with lice?

The schoolhouse could use a new blackboard. New arithmetic books. New readers....

Valerie shunned that idea; it would be too much like keeping the money for herself.

Maybe I ought to stand up on the water tower and let the bills rain down on Main Street. Let folks think it's like manna from heaven, she mused.

Darkness had begun to settle over the town. Valerie got up to light a lantern, and as she did, she spied the lovely rocking chair Paul had made for her. He was such a good and thoughtful man. Life with him would be beautiful.

But enough of that!

She'd decided to give him the greatest gift of her love: freedom from the likes of her. And she'd started immediately after the race, when he'd followed her home and knocked on her door with the all-out persistence of a man in love. He'd hollered that he loved her. That no matter what awful thing she wanted to tell him, he'd keep on loving her. He'd seemed oblivious to the puzzled stares of fellow Freelanders who'd heard and seen his deliberate banging as they'd passed by on their way home from the race. He'd yelled that he'd scraped his knuckles on the wooden door and had promised to start conking his noggin against it if she didn't open it soon, then had asked how that would look to the gaggle of people who had gathered to witness his temporary insanity.

Valerie hadn't opened the door.

She hadn't answered his many questions.

Instead, she'd sat in the chair he'd made for her, hugging her knees to her chest and weeping for the love, now gone, that her own stupidity had cost her.

It's best this way, she told herself. *Best for Paul, anyway. He'll find a decent, God-fearing woman to share his life with, and with her, he'll know the happiness he deserves.*

Could she stay in this town and watch him spend his life with another woman?

She didn't think so.

Sally and her husband, according to her cousin's last letter, had decided to remain in England indefinitely. So, she had no real family here. Still, could she leave Freeland, her new home, and all the wonderful friends she'd made?

Absolutely not.

There was only one thing to do, as she saw it. She'd done it before—many times. Like a soldier, she'd march onward with eyes straight ahead, chin up, shoulders back. *Stop your bellyaching and take your medicine like a big girl,* she told herself. *You're getting what you deserve, after all....*

But what, exactly, *did* she deserve? The compassion and friendship of a man like Paul Collins? The love and acceptance of his adorable children?

No; all of that added up to too much happiness.

And that kind of happiness, Valerie decided, was simply not in God's greater plan for her life. At least, not yet. She'd prayed about it, long and hard. And what answer had the Lord given her? She believed He knew her immature heart well; knew He had much to teach her about patience, tolerance, and love before she could be a proper wife and mother to anyone, let alone a man and children who had been tossed about by life's cruel winds. Much as she wanted to be part of the Collins family, she felt unworthy of such an important task.

The pain of resignation, much to Valerie's amazement, didn't infuriate her. Rather, she accepted the matter with grace and dignity. She'd never retreat into her angry, spiteful attitude toward the Lord again. Instead, she'd devote herself to spreading His Word.

She'd turn her whole life over to Him and His church. If she couldn't have Paul, she didn't want marriage and all the comforting warmth that came with it, anyway. If she couldn't have Paul, she didn't want children, either. She'd continue to be satisfied with loving and teaching the children of her friends and neighbors.

She slept fitfully as one thought repeatedly flitted through her mind: She couldn't have Paul. She couldn't have Paul. She couldn't have Paul....

Scruffy's tongue against her cheek woke her just as the sun was peeking over the horizon. Oblivious to the troubles of his mistress, the dog was letting her know that his stomach commanded attention. "All right," she said, drying her cheek with the back of her hand, "I'm up, and you'll soon have your breakfast. I promise."

Standing at the kitchen sink, Valerie raised and lowered the pump handle and filled the enamel pan beneath it with cool, clear water. After splashing her face with some water, she patted it dry with a blue gingham tea towel. The morning world always looked better after she'd freshened her face.

Grinning at her pet, Valerie scooped several spoonfuls of leftover stew into Scruffy's dish. "There," she said, ruffling his sandy-colored fur, "are you happy now?"

The dog barked in approval, then buried his muzzle in the meal.

Since school had officially ended for the summer back in June, Valerie passed her days puttering in her flower gardens and tending her vegetable plot. She'd painted the entire interior of her house white and the trim cornflower blue. She'd painted the outside white, too, and slapped a coat of maroon on the shutters, doors, and porch floors.

Today, she decided, slipping into a well-worn pink cotton dress, she'd wash the windows. For a small house, there were a lot of them. Twelve in all, each with twelve separate panes.

But first, she'd take down the filmy curtains and give them a good cleaning. While they dried on the clothesline out back, she'd tackle the glass.

Perched on a stepladder so that she could reach the top row of kitchen window panes, Valerie didn't hear the footsteps. The sound of his voice startled her so much that she nearly dumped the tin bucket of vinegar water on his head.

Paul placed a hand on each of the ladder's support rails. "Now, I've got you where I want you," he said, "and you're not going anywhere until you talk to me."

Valerie wanted nothing more than to dive into his strong arms. To tell him what a silly little fool she'd been to place a bet. To beg his forgiveness and promise never to do such an un-Christian thing like gamble again.

But she knew herself too well. She'd always been impetuous. Quick to jump to conclusions. Too fast to make judgments. These were character traits that would, in all likelihood, be a part of her till the day she died. She couldn't subject Paul to spending the rest of his life with a human seesaw.

"I'm very busy, Paul."

"Yes," he said, his voice tinged with impatience, "I can see that. But the windows will wait. I will not."

"The almanac says it may rain tomorrow," she explained. "I want to get this job done today, so that—"

"I don't care what the almanac says." Anger rang in his voice and ebbed from his dark eyes. "Valerie Ann Carter, you will come down off that ladder right this minute, or I'll come up and *bring* you down."

Chapter Thirteen

But Pa misses you so," Tricia said.

Tears welling in the girl's pale eyes prompted Valerie to reach out and wrap her in a warm, protective embrace. "Your pa will be fine, in time," Valerie whispered, placing a kiss atop her blonde mop of curls. "You'll see."

"That's what folks said when Ma died. But he wasn't fine. Not fine at all. He was sad. So sad—all the time." Tricia pulled away from the hug to stare deep into Valerie's eyes. "It was *you* who made him happy again."

Valerie sighed. Paul had said as much during his last visit to her house. After much convincing, she'd come down off the ladder and gone into the kitchen with him. After much convincing, she'd listened quietly as he told her what he'd heard from Doc and Rev. Gemmill. After much convincing, she'd almost believed it didn't matter one whit to him that she'd placed a bet—something that by his standards was sinful and reprehensible.

She'd almost believed it....

And then it had been his turn to sit silently as she attempted to convince him what must be. "You deserve a good Christian woman," she'd said. "Someone who knows right from wrong, who knows without even thinking about it what the good Lord wants from her."

His left eyebrow had arched as one corner of his mouth had turned down. "Sometimes, for a woman who's so smart, you can say some very stupid things."

Valerie had gotten angry at that, and had stood so quickly that her chair had nearly tipped over. She'd refilled his glass with lemonade—not to be a good hostess, but to keep from slapping that look of righteous indignation off his face.

"Sit back down here and show me the courtesy, at least, of helping me understand what on God's green earth you're talking about," he'd insisted, pointing to her empty chair.

When she'd sat down, he'd added, "You say you were raised in a devout Christian household. You say you know the Bible inside and out." He'd grabbed her hands in his and peered deep into her eyes. "If you're so all-fired knowledgeable in the Word, why is it that you don't know the good Lord isn't judging you as a sinner for one minor transgression?"

On her feet again, Valerie had paced the space between the kitchen table and the back door. "It's not God's judgment I fear!" she'd snapped. "*You* taught me that His love forgives human error. What I did—that silly bet—it was a mistake. A misunderstanding, plain and simple." She'd stood still then, pointing her finger at him. "It's *you* I can't bear to face, Paul Collins. It's your perfect manner of living, your code of honor that scares the daylights out of me! I'm not as good as you, Paul. I'll never be able to live up to your standards. I'll be a constant source of disappointment to you."

Then, he'd gotten on his feet, too, fists resting on his hips as he faced her. His laughter, bitter and soft, had grated in her ears. "I'll say this for you, Valerie: you sure know how to hurt a man."

"But...." Valerie had blinked and looked from his wounded expression toward the door, outside of which was freedom from his pain. "But hurting you is exactly what I'm trying to *prevent*," she'd confessed. "I'm not good for you, Paul. I'm too...too flighty. Too unsettled.

Too immature to be the wife of any man, let alone a man with three needy children to raise. Too...."

"Too busy feeling sorry for herself," he'd interrupted her, "to see what's right under your nose."

He'd taken one step forward, closing the gap that separated them, and placed a hand on her shoulder. The fingertip of his free hand had lifted her chin, forcing her to meet his gaze. "I love you," he'd said, his voice raspy with emotion. "I love you because you have a heart the size of your head. Because you lived through terror and anguish, and you *survived.* You thrived and flourished in spite of it.

"I love you because you taught my children it was right and good to miss their mother, that laughing and loving again couldn't diminish her memory."

He'd held her close and whispered into her hair, "I love you because you taught *me* it was right and good to love again."

Then, Paul had held her at arm's length, his dark eyes boring intently into her green ones. "You're dead wrong when you say I'm perfect. I'm far from it. Just as you're wrong about that, you're right when you say you're not perfect. Believe it or not, I love *that* about you most of all. I can't imagine spending the rest of my days permanently bound to a woman who's insufferably perfect!"

Holding her close again, he'd added, "I won't lie to you, Valerie; I don't approve of gambling. But I certainly haven't judged you a sinner because you placed one bet. Don't you see?" he'd asked, tenderly taking her face in his hands. "Don't you *see,*" he'd repeated, "that I love you for the *reason* you placed that bet?"

Valerie hadn't been able to speak. Not in the presence of such pure, sweet love. Never before had a man looked at her with such complete trust. Such total admiration. Never before had a man put his heart in her hands for safekeeping. And never before had she felt more unworthy.

He was, by far, the best man she'd ever known. And, as such, he deserved only the best.

Everyone—including Doc, Rev. Gemmill, and God Himself—knew that the best was not Valerie Carter! Everyone, that is, but Paul. Somehow, she had to make him face that fact....

"Do you think I'd lie to you, Valerie?"

Blinking, she'd shaken her head. She'd known that he'd sooner cut off a limb than tell a deliberate falsehood.

"Do you think I'd ever do anything to harm you in any way?"

Again, she'd shaken her head.

"So, you trust me, then?"

"With my very life," she'd whispered. And she'd meant it, all the way down to the marrow of her bones.

"Then believe me when I say I love you. How much I owe to you!"

She'd walked a few steps away. "You owe me nothing. Nothing."

"Ah," he'd said, standing so close behind her that she'd felt his breath in her hair, "you're wrong. Dead wrong. I owe to you my children's happiness."

He'd turned her around and cupped her chin in his palm. "I owe to you my happiness."

How would she make him see that if she could so completely misunderstand God's Word regarding gambling, she might just as easily misunderstand some other important message in His Word? What if she transmitted that misunderstanding to the children? To those innocent, loving children, who looked to Paul—who would look to her, as their new mother—for guidance and instruction? And what if that misunderstanding led one of them astray? Valerie couldn't allow it to happen. *Wouldn't* allow it to happen.

She'd looked into Paul's wide, brown eyes—eyes so full of love for her that it had made her heart ache—and said what she felt had to be said: "Go home, Paul. Go home to your children. Go home and pray long and hard on this 'love' you declare you feel for me. I think you'll soon discover, with God's help, that it's not love at all but mere infatuation."

She'd patted his hand, much in the same way she'd comfort a student who couldn't figure out a difficult arithmetic problem. "In time, the Lord will introduce you to the woman He feels is worthy of you; the woman who'll be a dedicated and devoted wife to you; the woman He believes will be a good role model, a good influence, a good teacher of His Word...for your *children*."

"He's already shown me that woman."

He'd said it so quickly, so matter-of-factly, that it had stunned her into silence.

After a few moments, she'd taken a deep breath and walked purposefully to the door. Opening it, she'd stood with one hand on the knob and gestured toward the back porch. "Go home, Paul," she'd said again. "Get on with your life, and let me get on with mine. Please...."

He'd taken a few uncertain steps toward the opening but had stopped when they'd been side by side. "Give me a little credit, why don't you?" he'd said, anger brewing in his voice. "Don't you think I've already considered how a marriage between us would affect my children? Don't you think I've prayed long into the night whether or not you'd be a good mother? They've suffered enough, God knows. I certainly don't want to subject them to more.

"Don't you think I've asked for His guidance to show me whether or not you'd be a good wife? I'm not an idiot, Valerie. I made a good choice, for all the right reasons, and with God's blessing, I might add!"

Valerie had only been able to stare at the pointy toes of her black boots.

"All right," he'd said softly. "I'll go. But not in search of 'some other woman,' as you say I should." He'd pulled his cap over his head and walked out onto the porch. "I'll not find such a woman anywhere on this earth," he'd added, facing her, "because there *is* no woman for me but you." He'd started down the steps. "When you come to your senses," he'd said, his jaw set in determination, "you know where to find me."

He'd stopped at the end of her walk. "Be careful what you ask for, Valerie, or you might get it." With that, he'd been gone.

The same determined look that had been etched on Paul's face that morning was now evident on his daughter's lovely face. "You told me you loved him," Tricia said, bringing Valerie back into the present. "Wasn't it true? Have you changed your mind? Have you met someone else?"

"Of course not!" Valerie exclaimed. "There's no one like your father!"

Tricia sighed and shrugged. "Then, I don't understand."

How would Valerie explain to this eager-eyed young girl that, while she loved her father more than life itself, she couldn't yoke him to life with one who continually fell from the path of righteousness? How would she tell this innocent, budding young woman that, though she'd like nothing more than to spend the rest of her life with a man as good and decent as Paul Collins, she couldn't subject him to the ups and downs of a marriage to a backsliding Christian?

"Do you love him?"

It was a simple enough question, and Valerie searched for an equally simple answer.

"Well, do you?" Tricia pressed.

"Yes, I love him," Valerie admitted.

"How much do you love him?"

She met the girl's gaze. How much? *More than all the stars in the heavens. More than all the grains of sand on all the world's beaches. More than all the tea in China!* Valerie thought.

"Do you love him enough to make sacrifices?"

"Sacrifices?"

"Pa says when you love someone—*really* love someone—you sometimes have to put your own needs and feelings aside and do what's best for that person."

Valerie frowned. "I'm afraid I'm not following you, Tricia."

The girl sighed again. "You know that he loves you; you say you love him."

Valerie nodded. "Yes...."

"Well, he needs you, too. Maybe he needs you more than he'd ever admit to anybody. Even to you. You're what's best for Pa. Can't you see that?"

Valerie took the girl's hands in her own. She was touched that Tricia wanted her as a mother as much as she wanted to fill the role. "Don't you see, Tricia, that your pa deserves a good wife? And you and Tyler and Timmy deserve a good mother? I honestly don't know if I'm up to the task."

"Pa said God sent you to him. He said he prayed and prayed, and you were the answer to his prayers."

Valerie's heart fluttered. *He said that to his children?*

"Me an' the boys, we prayed the same prayer," Tricia added. "God didn't send us Miss Watson or Miss Hunter. God sent us *you*."

Later that evening, and long into the night, Valerie thought about everything Tricia had said. On the one hand, she felt honored to be called the answer to the heartfelt prayers of this fine man and his children. On the other hand, she cringed under the weighty responsibility of it. "Lord," she prayed aloud, "help me. Show me how to do what's best for them...."

❀

Valerie had been praying the same prayer nonstop, it seemed, for nearly a week, yet she hadn't heard God's answer. *The Lord must be trying to teach me a lesson in patience*, she told herself. *Isn't it amazing? The thing I do worst is the thing I'm expected to do most: wait.*

She was standing at the counter at Greta's feed and grain, waiting to pay for her purchases, when she looked through the window to see a black cloud roll in over the store, darkening the sky that had brightened its interior. "Dis could be one dangerous storm," Greta observed, stuffing Valerie's purchases into a box. "I hope no harm vill come to der farmers' fields."

Valerie nodded. She remembered that in Richmond, hard rains and high winds could cause more damage than just about anything to the tobacco crops. Throw in some lightning, and the threat of fire only made matters worse.

A loud clap of thunder caused Greta to squeal with fright. "Goodness!" she said. "Dat one vas too close for comfort! If der lightning follows soon behind, ve could be in trouble."

Valerie picked up her box and started toward the door. "Say a little prayer that I'll get home before trouble starts," she said over her shoulder, grinning as she left the store.

Greta followed her out onto the narrow porch. "You kin bet dat I vill," she said, nudging Valerie's shoulder playfully with her own.

Paul's wagon was parked outside the blacksmith's shop, loaded with sacks of flour, cornmeal, and sugar. His children were sitting in the wagon bed, and when they saw Valerie, all three shouted hello and waved.

Smiling, Valerie returned their friendly greeting. She hadn't seen Tricia since the week before, when the girl had demanded an explanation for the distance between her father and her teacher. As she neared the wagon, Valerie hoped that the subject of their separation wouldn't come up, for she still had no reasonable excuse for calling a halt to the engagement—at least, none that would appease the curious girl.

"Pa's inside," Timmy told her as she stepped alongside the wagon, "getting a new wheel made. He's gonna fix up the carriage."

Valerie remembered how he'd spent many a spare moment repairing the upholstery and fringe on the surrey he'd found in the barn upon his return to Freeland. "I have a lot of incentive to restore it now," he'd told her. "I want to whisk you away from the church in it on our wedding day...."

Suddenly, the children, who'd been lounging among the overstuffed, white cloth bags, bolted upright at another booming roll of thunder. "Look at that!" Timmy shouted, pointing at the horizon. "Smoke!"

Everyone's gaze followed his chubby forefinger. "Why, that's Bert's farm!" Greta exclaimed. "Lord above," she prayed, "let it be chust a tree dat's burning over dere...."

Thunder pealed a third time, louder than ever. Tricia's high-pitched scream echoed up and down Main Street.

In her fearful response to the scream, Sadie, Paul's big black mare, whinnied and reared up on her hind legs, loosing the reins, which were tethered to the hitching post. The wagon lurched forward precariously, then tipped up, up, until Tyler and Tricia were spilled out the back, along with the bags of feed and grain. Only Timmy remained on the wagon bed, clutching the rough-hewn sideboards.

"Pa!" Tyler shouted. "Pa, come quick! Sadie's gonna run off with Timmy!"

But Paul couldn't hear the boy's cries over the shrill sounds of the grinder's wheel deep in the bowels of the blacksmith's shop.

Valerie swiftly set down her box and moved quickly to the right side of the wagon, saying a silent prayer of thanks that the brake was still set. But Sadie's wild eyes and glistening flanks showed her fear. If she were allowed to continue bucking and pitching, she'd splinter the brake—and rush onward, taking Timmy with her. *No telling where she'll go in the state she's in*, Valerie realized.

She had to do something, and do it fast.

But what?

Valerie scrambled up into the wagon seat. As always, Paul had wound the leather leads around the brake handle. Quickly, Valerie unwound them and pulled back with all her might. "Whoa, Sadie!" she hollered. "Whoa, there!"

For a fraction of a second, it seemed like Sadie would respond. The horse, on all fours now, bobbed her head up and down and snorted. She'd just begun to quiet when another thunderbolt crashed.

Again, Sadie reared up, whinnying for all she was worth.

It seemed to Valerie that the next moments took half an hour to pass. First, she heard the sickening, cracking sounds that told her the brake handle was beginning to splinter. Next came the unmistakable groan of the wheels as the huge, heavy wagon began to move forward.

She'd wrapped the reins tightly around her hands, and the leather dug mercilessly into her flesh as the horse strained against the bit. "Whoa, Sadie!" Valerie shouted again. "Easy there, girl."

Sadie had had just about enough of the hustle and bustle of the storm. And she'd go home, lickety-split, if not for the tugging of one stubborn female in her master's seat.

This time, however, stubbornness couldn't win out over animal strength.

The suddenness of Sadie's forward motion flung Valerie from the driver's seat.

She clung for several frightening seconds to the underside of the wagon, her feet dragging and scraping along the gravelly grit of Main Street before she managed to pull herself back up into the wagon again.

The wagon hadn't been built for high speeds, even on smooth streets such as Freeland's. Soon, though, Valerie realized, they'd be on the road leading out of town... a road gouged with deep, rain-washed crevices and littered with large rocks that had been washed down from the hillside in the last big rain.

The last of Freeland's buildings whizzed by. Trees, distant farmhouses, barns, and pasturelands whirred past at a dizzying pace. A few minutes at this speed, and the wagon would fall apart completely.

A quick glance back told Valerie that Timmy's hold on the wagon wall was precarious, at best. A few more jolts, and his tiny hands would let go of the graying boards; a few more jolts, and he'd be sent sailing over those boards....

Valerie couldn't bear to think about where he'd land. She had to stop the wagon—or die trying. Timmy's life depended on it.

The steel bars on either side of Sadie kept her attached to her heavy burden. They looked strong. Stable. Secure. Could Valerie step out on one of them and manage to climb on Sadie's back? She'd been an able horsewoman in Richmond.... If she could climb aboard, would she be strong enough to force the terrified horse to stop?

Another glance back....

Where's Timmy?

She saw a lot in her next quick glance: a trickle of blood oozing from his forehead. Closed eyes. Limp limbs. *He's unconscious!* "Timmy!" Valerie screamed. "Timmy, can you hear me?"

The boy's eyes remained closed, and his little body flopped about with the movements of the wagon like a rag doll. Whether or not she could accomplish the feat was no longer a question. If she didn't succeed, Timmy would pay the price.

Valerie gathered up her flowing, blue gingham skirts and tucked them into the wide, matching cloth belt at her waist. Holding tightly to the driver's footrest, she placed one booted foot on the bar nearest her, then stepped out with the other foot, trying to remain steady on the vibrating metal.

Valerie's slight weight was still enough to tilt the harness and cause Sadie to turn off the road. The horse was running full throttle across the wide field alongside Freeland Road, and if she kept up at this pace, and in this direction, she'd run straight into Walker's Gorge. By Valerie's quick estimate, she had less than thirty seconds to jump onto Sadie's back and pull her to a halt, or Timmy, the wagon...all of them would plummet to their deaths at the bottom of the gorge.

"Lord," she prayed through clenched teeth, "grant me the strength to do what I must...."

To get from her tentative foothold on the harness to Sadie's back required a leap of nearly a yard—no small feat in a speeding, runaway wagon. If she missed....

Valerie couldn't think about that. It was a risk she had to take.

And so, she jumped, hands outstretched to grasp the straps cinched beneath Sadie's round belly. It seemed to take minutes, rather than seconds, to fly that short distance; it seemed her fingers would never close around the leather loops. But, finally, she was there, astride the big horse's broad back, grasping Sadie's mane like a lifeline.

"Whoa, Sadie!" she shouted. "Pull back, girl! Stop!"

With her hands full of the horse's soft hair, Valerie leaned back as far as the length of her arms would allow. "Let it be far enough, Lord.... Please, let it be enough...."

Sadie's thick neck tensed. Her head went high. Then, as suddenly as she'd started the journey on Main Street, she came to a dead halt.

Panting, Valerie hugged the horse's sweaty neck. Tears stung her eyes.

"What's goin' on?" called a panicked voice.

"Timmy!" Valerie shouted, turning around. "Praise the Lord, you're all right!"

He rubbed his head. "Guess I must'a cracked my skull some back there," he said, gesturing toward the town with a jerk of his tiny thumb. "Guess we oughtta get back before we're soaked to the skin," he added, blinking raindrops from his big, frightened eyes.

Valerie had been so busy trying to get from the wagon to Sadie's back that she hadn't even noticed that it had begun to rain. Huge, round drops plopped to the ground all around them, scattering dust, at first, and then matting it down in sodden puddles.

Slowly, so as not to spook Sadie again, Valerie slid to the ground, then climbed up into the wagon seat. "C'mon, Sadie," she said, gently urging the horse to turn around and head back to town. "Let's go home."

Chapter Fourteen

"You saved his life," Paul said, wrapping Timmy in a big, protective hug.

Blushing, Valerie grinned and brushed a wayward curl from her forehead.

Paul reached out and grasped her hand. "Look at you—you're bleeding!"

Only then did she notice that both her hands were swollen, raw, and bloody from straining against the reins. "I read that the folks who have settled out in the Wild West call newcomers 'tenderfeet' because they haven't developed calluses to protect them from the hot, sandy soil." Giggling nervously and winking at Timmy, Valerie added, "I guess you can just call me Tender Fingers from now on."

"Tender Fingers. That's funny," Timmy said, laughing around the red lollipop Doc had given him.

Paul still held her hand in his own. "You risked your life for him." His voice was hoarse with relief and gratitude. "You're a—well, a hero, that's what you are."

Blushing, Valerie protested, "I did what anyone would have."

Paul shook his head. "From what Greta says, the street was filled with people, some of 'em big, strappin' men. None of them climbed into that wagon…or onto Sadie's back." He looked at her for a silent moment. "But *you* did."

Paul stood up from where he'd been sitting with Timmy on the squeaky cot in Doc's office, pulling Valerie up next to him. "That was quite a gamble you took out there," he said, nodding toward the door.

"I suppose it was a risk, since I don't know much about driving a wagon."

His smile glimmered brightly in his eyes. "But I'll bet you know more now than you knew thirty minutes ago."

She squeezed his hand gently and winced at the discomfort the slight pressure caused her swollen, bruised fingers.

His brow furrowed with concern as he studied her hands. "To merely say thank you doesn't seem appropriate at all. Not after the chance you took...."

Gamble? Bet? Chance? Was he saying what she thought he was saying?

"I always believed gambling was a sin, cut and dry. No exceptions," he said, interrupting her thoughts. "Imagine my surprise—the son of a preacher learning such a lesson. And at my advanced age!"

Valerie giggled. "Listen to you! You make it sound as if you're as old as Father Time. Why, you're just a young whippersnapper!"

"Your sense of humor won't buy your way out of this one," Paul said, pulling her close. "You gambled with your own life to save my son's. There's nothing funny about that."

"Pa's right, Miss Carter," Timmy said. "You saved my life."

Paul laughed. "Tim, you're going to have to figure out something else to call her. It doesn't seem right calling your pa's wife 'Miss Carter,' now, does it?"

Timmy shook his head and gave the matter a moment's thought. His tiny brow wrinkled under the white bandage Doc had wrapped around his head. "D'you think Ma would mind if I called Miss Carter 'Ma'?"

Paul's smile seemed to warm the entire room as he looked from his son to Valerie and back again. "I'm sure she'd give her full approval." Then, he focused his attention on Valerie when he said, "What do you think, Miss Carter? Is it all right if my young'uns call you 'Ma'?"

Her heart was beating so furiously, Valerie thought it might leap right out of her chest. "It would be an honor," she said quietly. "But Paul, I need to explain.... I misinterpreted things so badly. I'd never read anything in the Bible that indicated gambling was a sin. Rev. Gemmill explained it all, so, now, I know better."

"That's because there's nothing specific in the Good Book that tells us whether it's right or wrong."

She slumped into Doc's wheeled armchair and sighed. "Still, I misunderstood the essence of God's Word. What if I do it again? And what if some stupid, silly, spur-of-the-moment thing I do leads the children away from God's path?"

Paul knelt before her and held her face in his hands, then silenced her with a soft, lingering kiss. "Nothing like that is going to happen. I know it like I know...like I know your name."

"Mrs. Paul Collins," Timmy said. "*That'll* be her name after the weddin', right, Pa?"

"Right, son."

"When's the weddin', Pa?"

Paul never took his eyes from Valerie's. "As soon as we can get Rev. Gemmill to agree to perform the ceremony."

"Tomorrow?" Timmy asked.

"Tonight, if I thought it was possible."

Valerie's eyes filled with tears. "Even though I—"

"The money will be mighty handy, come planting time," he said, interrupting her.

She looked at their hands.

"So, Valerie...what did you do with the money?"

It was all she could do to hide her grin. "Why, I put in the collection plate."

Paul's jaw dropped. "You did *what*?"

She met his gaze and smiled. "I knew you wouldn't want it—"

"But—"

"Gambling is for fools and sinners!"

He gathered her into his arms and pulled her to her feet. "Do you think the reverend can fit us in next Saturday?"

Nodding happily, Valerie sniffed.

"Can I tell Tyler and Tricia 'bout the weddin', Pa?"

In place of an answer, Paul pressed his lips to Valerie's and distractedly motioned his son out the door with a wave of his hand.

Moments later, all three Collins children were peering through the wide window in Doc's office. "I have a feeling we'll be playin' follow the leader down the center aisle in church real soon," Tyler said, grinning.

"Real soon," Tricia agreed, her hands folded over her chest.

"That's fine with me," Timmy said. "Follow the leader is my fav'rite game."

"Mine, too, Timmy," Valerie echoed. "Mine, too."

A Preview of

Beautiful Bandit

Book One in the Lone Star Legends Series

by Loree Lough

Coming in Summer 2010!

Chapter One

June 1888
San Antonio, Texas

The hot, sticky air in the banker's cluttered office made it hard to breathe. Josh ran a fingertip under his stiff collar as the image of cows dropping by the thousand reminded him why he'd come to San Antonio. Selling off the Rockin' N Ranch's uncontaminated acres would be the only way to protect the cows that remained—at least until they'd gotten the anthrax infection—under control.

He did his best not to glare at the decorous Bostonian sitting beside him. It wasn't the Swede's fault, after all, that anthrax had killed so many Neville cattle. In his shoes, Josh would have snapped up the land even more quickly. Trouble was, now this la-di-da Easterner would move to Eagle Pass, bringing his never-been-out-of-the-city wife and children with him. Worse yet, Josh had a sneaking suspicion that the former printing press operator would make a regular pest of himself by asking about Texas weather, irrigation, when to plant, and only the good Lord knew what else. If that didn't earn Josh a seat closer to the Throne, he didn't know what would.

Few things agitated him more than sitting in one spot. Especially indoors. How these fancy gents managed to look so calm and cool, all buttoned up in their dark suits, he didn't know. Wondering about it had only added to his restlessness, so he'd hung his Stetson on his left knee, mostly so he'd have something to do with his hands. Now, he moved it to his right knee as the banker explained the terms of the agreement.

He stared hard at the deep red Persian rug under his boots, searching his mind for something to else to focus on—anything other than the wretched document that would transfer ownership of Neville land to this foreigner. Moving his hat to his left knee again, he remembered the day he'd bought it, and how he'd picked up another just like it a year later, when Rockin' N business had put him in Garland, so he'd have one for riding the range and one for his wedding. He found it strange how Sadie's image could appear in his mind's eye from out of nowhere, even after two long, hard years without her....

Josh forced the thought of her from his mind. This get-together was more than painful enough without dwelling on the most agonizing episode of his life. He exhaled a harsh sigh, hoping the banker and the Swede hadn't heard the tremor in it. He blamed his pounding heat. His empty stomach. The ten-day ride from Eagle Pass that had left him too bone tired to sleep on the hotel's too-soft mattress. *A body would think that an establishment with Persian rugs and velvet curtains could afford to provide water for businessmen*, he thought, loosening his string tie as Griffin asked yet another inane question. *Father, give me the strength to keep from grabbing those papers and hotfooting it out of here!* he prayed silently.

Sadly, his woolgathering was doing little to distract him from the grim truth....

Josh had been the sole dissenting vote at the family meeting, and their loathsome decision had turned downright odious when he'd realized that, as the only Neville with a legal background, he would be the one responsible for transacting the sale. He groaned inwardly as grief engulfed him. *What a sorry state of affairs*, he thought, leaning forward to hide the tears that burned in his eyes. He loved every blessed acre that made up the Rockin' N, especially the acre where he'd built a small but solid home for Sadie and himself. He would hate letting it go, even if she *hadn't been* buried there!

Griffin, God bless him, had been the one to suggest that Josh hold on to that precious acre after Josh had asked permission to visit the graves of his wife and babies. "We'll build a fence around the land," Griffin had said, "to make sure your family is never disturbed." But Josh had known, even as he'd nodded in agreement, that crossing Griffin property to reach his little family would only heap one misery atop another.

With his elbows propped on his knees, Josh spun his hat round and round, watching through the window as three men dismounted sweaty horses outside. The lot of them looked as jumpy and agitated as he felt, and he wondered what ugly family business had brought *them* to the bank today. Maybe that explained the riderless horse....

"If you'll just sign here, Mr. Neville," Schaeffer said, redirecting Josh's attention to the transaction at hand.

Josh accepted the banker's fountain pen, and, as its freshly inked nib hovered over the document, a bead of sweat trickled down his spine. In that moment, he felt a disturbing kinship with the fat hen his mama had roasted for last Sunday's dinner.

Outside, the wind blew steadily, swirling street grit into tiny twisters that skittered up the parched road before bouncing under buggies and scurrying into alleyways. Even the burning breeze would feel better than the choking heat in Schaeffer's office. "Mind if I open the window? I'm sweatin' like a—"

Schaeffer peered over the rims of his gold spectacles. "I'd much rather you didn't. The wind is likely to scatter our paperwork hither and yon."

Hither and yon, indeed. Josh had read similar phrases in books, but what sort of person actually used words like that in—

Suddenly, shuffling footsteps and coarse whispers on the other side of the banker's door interrupted his thoughts. Inspired a stern frown on Schaeffer's heat-reddened face, too. "I declare," the man said through clenched teeth, "I can't take my eyes off that fool assistant of mine for fifteen minutes without some sort of mayhem erupting." Blotting his forehead with a starched, white hanky, he continued grumbling. "Looks like I'll have no choice but to replace him." Shoving his eyeglasses higher on his nose, he lifted his chin and arched one bushy gray eyebrow, a not-so-subtle prompt for Josh to sign the paper.

So, gritting his teeth, Josh inhaled a sharp breath and scratched his name on the thin, black line, then traded the pen for a banknote.

On his feet now, the Swede grabbed Josh's hand. "T'ank you," he said, shaking it. "Been a pleasure doing business wit' you, Neville."

Unable to make himself say "Likewise," Josh forced a stiff smile and pocketed the check. "You bet." God willing, perhaps the worst was behind for his family now.

The burnished, brass pendulum of the big clock behind the banker's desk swayed left with an audible *tick* as the men prepared to go their separate ways...and swung right as gunshots rang out in the lobby.

Schaeffer and Griffin ran for the door, but a flurry of activity drew Josh's attention back to the window.

Tick....

The three men he'd seen earlier were scrambling into their saddles. Only now, their faces were covered with bandannas, and a young woman had joined them. She climbed into the previously empty saddle as the biggest man hoisted a burlap sack over his horse's saddle horn, sunlight glinting off the pistol in his gloved hand.

Tick....

Josh grabbed his sidearm, pulling back the hammer with one hand, then pushed open the window with the other. He thought that maybe he could get off a shot or two before the robbers were swallowed up by the cyclone of dust kicked up by their horses' hooves.

Tick....

Perched on the sill, he took aim at the shoulder of the fattest bandit just as the woman's pony veered right, putting her square in the center of his gun sight.

Tick....

She looked back, and her green gaze fused to his. Josh released the pressure on the sweat-slicked trigger as fear traveled the invisible cord connecting her wide eyes to his.

Tick....

Josh didn't have time to make sense of the helpless expression on her pretty face, for, as quick as you please, she faced front again, her cornflower-blue skirt flapping like a tattered sail as she was swallowed up by a thick cloud of dust.

About the Author

Long before becoming a writer, best-selling author Loree Lough literally sang for her supper. She enjoyed receiving rave reviews and applause and touring the country, but sensed it wasn't what the Lord had in mind for her. She tried everything from shrink-wrapping torque wrenches to spinning pizza dough to working as a chef in a nursing home kitchen, to name just a few, without finding one job that fit her. Then, while visiting her parents in Baltimore, Loree worked for an insurance corporation, where she met the man she would marry.

Loree began writing when her husband, Larry, had a job change that moved the family to Richmond, Virginia. She started out writing a neighborhood column and soon began getting assignments from the publication's editor—as well as the editors of other publications. But it wasn't until she penned her first novel, the award-winning *Pocketful of Love*, that Loree finally understood what the Lord had in mind for her: Seventy-three books (and counting) later, she's still touching the hearts of readers worldwide.

In addition to her books, Loree has sixty-three short stories and 2,500 articles in print. Her stories have earned dozens of industry and Reader's Choice awards. Loree is a frequent guest speaker for writers' organizations, book clubs, private and government institutions, corporations, college and high school writing programs, and more, where she encourages aspiring writers with her comedic approach to learned-the-hard-way lessons about the craft and industry.

An avid wolf enthusiast, Loree is involved with the Wolf Sanctuary of Pennsylvania. She and Larry, along with a formerly abused, now-spoiled pointer named Cash, split their time between a remote cabin in the Allegheny Mountains and a humble house in the Baltimore suburbs.

Loree loves hearing from her readers, so feel free to write her at loree@loreelough.com. To learn more about Loree and her books, visit her Web site at www.loreelough.com.

Prevailing Love
Loree Lough

In *Sealed with a Kiss*, bachelor Ethan Burke suddenly becomes a father to Molly, the daughter of his best friends, after an auto accident claims their lives. When he takes Molly to see Christian counselor Hope Majors, he gains optimism about her healing—and about a future with the attractive counselor. In *The Wedding Wish*, Leah Jordan is dying of cancer, and she's scrambling to launch a matchmaking plot to make her two best friends, Jade Nelson and Riley Steele, marry and adopt her two-year-old daughter, Fiona, before it's too late. In *Montana Sky*, cattle rancher Chet Cozart and veterinarian Sky Allen are caught up in a wolf war in the wild Montana woods, where they flirt with danger—and with each other.

ISBN: 978-1-60374-166-8 • Trade • 496 pages

Love's Rescue
Tammy Barley

To escape the Civil War, Jessica Hale flees Kentucky with her family and heads to the Nevada Territory, only to lose them in a fire set by Unionists resentful of their Southern roots. The sole survivor, Jess is "kidnapped" by cattleman Jake Bennett and taken to his ranch in the Sierra Nevada wilderness. Angry at Jake for not saving her family, she makes numerous attempts to escape and return to Carson City, but she is apprehended each time. Why are Jake and his ranch hands determined to keep her there? She ponders this, wondering what God will bring out of her pain and loss.

ISBN: 978-1-60374-108-8 • Trade • 368 pages

Whitaker House